Sherlock Holmes: A Year of Mystery

1883

Sherlock Holmes: A Year of Mystery

1883

Edited by
Richard T. Ryan

Belanger Books
2022

Sherlock Holmes: A Year of Mystery 1883
© 2022 by Belanger Books, LLC

Print and Digital Edition © 2022 by Belanger Books, LLC All Rights Reserved. No part of this book may be used or reproduced in any manner whatsoever without written permission except in case of brief quotations embodied in critical articles or reviews.

This book is a work of fiction. Names, characters, businesses, organizations, places, events, and incidents either are the products of the author's imagination or are used fictitiously. Any resemblance to actual persons, living or dead, events, or locales is entirely coincidental.

For information contact:
Belanger Books, LLC
61 Theresa Ct.
Manchester, NH 03103

Cover and Design by Brian Belanger
www.belangerbooks.com and *www.redbubble.com/people/zhahadun*

Cover image ©2022 by Jeffrey McKeever All rights reserved.

Table of Contents

Timeline 1883 11
Introduction by Robert S. Katz, MD, BSI 13
Foreword 1883 by Richard T. Ryan 16
The Adventure of the Double Tomb by Katy Darby 18
The Problem of Lady Gravely by Will Murray 63
The Case of the Injured Orator by Dr. Martin Hill Ortiz 79
The Missing Detective by Paul Hiscock 103
The Body in the Box by Stephen Herczeg 129
The Victoria Hall Tragedy by Kevin P. Thornton 163
The Bishop's Curse by Greg Maughan 187
An Affair of State: Sir Charles Dilke by Frank Emerson 209
The Dunfermline Tarriance by David Marcum 227
The Adventure of the Wispy Widow by Derrick Belanger 254
The Spice of Life by Gustavo Bondoni 277
The Adventure of the Mummy's Menace by George Jacobs 302
Bonus Story: The Fairy Tale Mystery by Geri Schear 328

COPYRIGHT INFORMATION

All of the contributions in this collection are copyrighted by the authors listed below, except as noted. Grateful acknowledgement is given to the authors and/or their agents for the kind permission to use their work within these volumes.

"Introduction" ©2022 by Robert S. Katz, MD, BSI. All Rights Reserved. First publication, original to this collection. Printed by permission of the author.

"Foreword 1883" ©2022 by Richard T. Ryan. All Rights Reserved. First publication, original to this collection. Printed by permission of the author.

"The Adventure of the Double Tomb" ©2022 by Katy Darby. All Rights Reserved. First publication, original to this collection. Printed by permission of the author.

"The Problem of Lady Gravely" ©2022 by Will Murray. All Rights Reserved. First publication, original to this collection. Printed by permission of the author.

"The Case of the Injured Orator" ©2022 by Dr. Martin Hill Ortiz. All Rights Reserved. First publication, original to this collection. Printed by permission of the author.

"The Missing Detective" ©2022 by Paul Hiscock. All Rights Reserved. First publication, original to this collection. Printed by permission of the author.

"The Body in the Box" ©2022 by Stephen Herczeg. All Rights Reserved. First publication, original to this collection. Printed by permission of the author.

"The Victoria Hall Tragedy" ©2022 by Kevin P. Thornton. All Rights Reserved. First publication, original to this collection. Printed by permission of the author.

"The Bishop's Curse" ©2022 by Greg Maughan. All Rights Reserved. First publication, original to this collection. Printed by permission of the author.

"An Affair of State: Sir Charles Dilke" ©2022 by Frank Emerson. All Rights Reserved. First publication, original to this collection. Printed by permission of the author.

"The Dunfermline Tarriance" ©2022 by David Marcum. All Rights Reserved. First publication, original to this collection. Printed by permission of the author.

"The Adventure of the Wispy Widow" ©2022 by Derrick Belanger. All Rights Reserved. First publication, original to this collection. Printed by permission of the author.

"The Spice of Life" ©2022 by Gustavo Bondoni. All Rights Reserved. First publication, original to this collection. Printed by permission of the author.

"The Adventure of the Mummy's Menace" ©2022 by George Jacobs. All Rights Reserved. First publication, original to this collection. Printed by permission of the author.

"The Fairy Tale Mystery" ©2022 by Geri Schear. All Rights Reserved. First publication, original to this collection. Printed by permission of the author.

1883

Timeline 1883

Here are some of the key news-making events that occurred in 1883

January 1 – Augustus Pitt Rivers takes office as Britain's first Inspector of Ancient Monuments.
March 5 – Gloucester City A.F.C. is formed.
March 15 – Fenian dynamite campaign: An explosion at the Local Government Board, Charles Street, Mayfair (Westminster) causes more than £4,000 worth of damage and some minor injuries to people nearby. A second bomb at The Times newspaper offices in Queen Victoria Street, London does not explode.
March 29 – Edward Benson enthroned as Archbishop of Canterbury.
March 31 – Blackburn Olympic beat Old Etonians F.C. 2–1 in the FA Cup Final at The Oval, the Etonians being the last amateur team to reach the final and Olympic being the first northern working-class team to do so.
May 7 – Royal College of Music opens in London with George Grove as first Director.
May 11 – William Morris registers his Strawberry Thief printed textile design.
June 16 – Victoria Hall disaster: A rush for treats results in 183 children being asphyxiated in a concert hall in Sunderland.
July 3 – SS Daphne sinks on launch in Glasgow, leaving 124 dead.
August 1 – GPO introduces the Parcels Post service.
August 4 – first electric railway opens, the Volk's Railway at Brighton.
August 13 – Coventry City F.C. are formed as "Singers F.C."
August 29 – Dunfermline Carnegie Library, the first Carnegie library, is opened in Andrew Carnegie's hometown, Dunfermline.

September 11 – Major Evelyn Baring becomes Consul-General of Egypt under British rule.

September 12 – Bristol Rovers F.C. is founded as "Black Arabs F.C."

October – GPO officially replaces the title "letter carrier" with "postman."

October–November – Primrose League established in support of the Conservative Party.

October 4 – the Boys' Brigade is founded in Glasgow. It is the first uniformed youth organisation in existence.

October 24 – Cardiff University opens under the name of University College of South Wales and Monmouthshire.

October 30 – two Clan na Gael dynamite bombs explode in the London Underground, injuring several people. Next day Home Secretary William Vernon Harcourt drafts 300 policemen to guard the Underground and introduces the Explosives Bill.

November 3 –November 5 – Mahdist War: Anglo-Egyptian forces defeated at the Battle of El Obeid in Sudan.

Introduction

Filling in the Gaps

By Robert S. Katz, MD, BSI

For those of us fortunate enough to have read all sixty of the stories that comprise the Sherlockian Canon, and then to have reread and yet again reread them, a four-letter word comes to the forefront of our thoughts. The word is: MORE. The characters of Holmes and Watson, the Baker Street scene, the familiar supporting cast members, are all now part and parcel of our daily lives. We cherish those wonderful stories and return to them frequently. But....

Sixty is just not enough! We know that several of the adventures shared by Holmes and Watson were never told to us. At times they dealt with sensitive matters that were just "too hot to handle" and could not be published. From time to time, Holmes would forbid Watson from writing up certain cases as Holmes disapproved of the romanticization that Watson brought to his writing. While it may have enhanced the pleasure of reading the story, Holmes felt that it strayed from the exercises in logic and dedication that characterized his work. Since Watson did marry, at least once and perhaps more than that, we must assume that there were times when he was tending to practice and home and simply did not join Holmes on his journeys and investigations. It would not be surprising if the ever-secretive Sherlock just did not tell Watson about many of his cases. Perhaps he did not think them important enough to merit further discussion, even though we would have been overjoyed to have read them.

We also know that Holmes was out of sight and thought dead for three years. While he reappears and goes back into practice, we have but his word as to what he was doing during The Great Hiatus. Is it possible that he undertook assignments on behalf of his brother Mycroft while traveling abroad? Beyond his brief description of travels to Tibet, Mecca, and other venues, The Great Hiatus represents The Great Gap. And then there was the issue of the early retirement taken by Holmes. He does tell us that he dealt with two investigations during those years. Nonetheless, it is hard to believe that Holmes could resist the allure of a challenging crime and I, for one, suspect he undertook a lot more than bee-keeping while living on the Sussex Downs.

Somewhere along the way, he must have acquired the skills that made him such an efficient espionage agent and spy on the eve of The Great War. Was Mr. Altamont's mission the first he undertook on behalf of the Crown? I rather doubt it and suspect that, under some guise or other, Sherlock Holmes was periodically engaged in The Great Game of international politics and deception. Someday, I hope that one of the tellers of tales in this series will uncover evidence of a relation between Holmes, as teacher, and Sidney Reilly, as pupil. Mycroft could not have been unaware of The Ace of Spies and could have used Sherlock to serve as his "control," teacher, or even colleague.

This book takes us back to the earlier days of the Association. Holmes and Watson have been at Baker Street for about two years. We do have the benefit of Watson's recountings of some of the adventures that took place during that period in time. Yet, we all know that the young Holmes (he would have been just under thirty at this time) was hungry to establish himself as both the only and the finest of consulting detectives. He would have been loath to turn away clients and the eager Sherlockian harbors little doubt that more happened to Holmes and Watson than is recounted in the Canon.

The Editor and Publisher have assembled a skilled team of imaginative writers who provide manna to those of us continually repeating the mantra of "MORE." The original sixty stories provide an extraordinary foundation. This 1883 volume builds on that Baker Street bedrock and gives much to read, speculate over, and simply enjoy as yet additional visits with those remarkable friends who have become friends to all of us as well.

Foreword 1883

By Richard T. Ryan

For all that we know – or think we know – about the Great Detective and his Boswell, what we don't know might fill even more volumes than have already been written.

Despite all his success, which he was just beginning to enjoy in 1883, Holmes still depended upon the public to earn "his bread and cheese." However, for that calendar year, Watson apprises us of only one case – "The Adventure of the Speckled Band" – which we can safely place in April. Although a grateful Helen Stoner might have presented Holmes with a cheque of some substance for saving her life, solving the murder of her sister, and preserving her inheritance, would it have been enough to allow him to live for a year? Splitting the proceeds with Watson would have reduced the funds available for rent and staples even further.

Although Mrs. Hudson grew fond of Holmes as evidenced by her actions in "The Empty House," there was times when he must have tried her patience. At the beginning of "The Dying Detective," Watson enumerates some of the circumstances that attended the Great Detective's years at Baker Street and concludes that Holmes was "the very worst tenant in London."

In short, while Mrs. Hudson might have extended some credit with regard to the rent, one case in a year simply would not suffice. When you consider just a few of Holmes's myriad other expenses – disguises, food, brandy, tobacco in various forms, not to mention the rent on his "five small refuges" – it seems fairly safe to say that

Holmes must have had a fairly steady stream of income – even if we were not made privy to it

Given the fact that Watson tells us Holmes never varied his rates except when he chose to remit them altogether, we must conclude that even though Watson chose to inform us about only 60 of Holmes' cases, there must have been hundreds more – perhaps thousands of others.

The stories in the volumes in this series attempt to offer an explanation for how Holmes and Watson spent the at least some of the intervening weeks, months and years. After all, living costs money. Both Holmes and Watson had, what we call today, marketable skills – skills they would put to use to pay the rent and enjoy such creature comforts as they might.

Although you may not be familiar with the cases of the "Bishop's Curse." "The Body in the Box" or "The Injured Orator," they make up a very small part of the Holmesverse, and they do offer at least a partial explanation for how Holmes and Watson spent those periods between recorded cases. Perhaps more important, they also explain how our heroes dealt with the more mundane aspects of life such as keeping their pipes full and paying the rent.

All told here are 13 tales set in 1883 which was quite a busy year compared to 1884, but more about that in the next volume.

– Richard T. Ryan

The Adventure of the Double Tomb

By Katy Darby

I find in my notes for 1883 that it was upon the fifth of January, Twelfth Night itself, that Mr. Sherlock Holmes was first confronted with what he justly reckons was one of his most curious, and unquestionably most gruesome, cases to date. My own involvement in this problem was more than usually deep, drawing as it did as much on my medical experience as on my friend's detective skills; and if I recall the awful mystery of the double tomb with a shudder, I do so also with a modicum of pride.

The year had birthed grave-cold, and that evening was wild as any winter-spirit's wish, with plump, pale flakes of snow whirling before the windows like plucked goose-feathers, and the squally wind shrieking about the eaves like an unquiet soul. Yet despite the draught, my companion insisted on keeping the curtains open, claiming he found it "meditative" to watch the white flurries spin and flitter.

After a day of enforced laziness (for there was really almost nowhere to go, and nothing to do in the midst of such a snowfall as had all England in its grip) we had finished dinner, and Mrs. Hudson

The Adventure of the Double Tomb by Katy Darby

had stoked the hearth-fire to a cheerful, amber blaze which popped and snapped like a Christmas-cracker. Sherlock Holmes lounged beside the bow-window in his mouse-coloured dressing-gown, gazing dreamily into the deserted street as he smoked his pipe and sipped his wassail-punch.

"It is a very sly substance, you know, Watson," he mused aloud, breaking the silence of half-an-hour, which I had spent perusing a diverting account of the Zulu king Cetywayo by one Mr. Haggard.

"The punch?" I asked. (Having an evening engagement, I had confined myself to coffee). I rose and joined him at the window, shivering in the icy current which pried its tendrils through the casement-gaps.

He nodded at the white darkness.

"Snow, of course. It is the most interesting weather for a detective."

"How so?"

His thin lips quirked at my obtuseness. "Why, because it conceals and reveals, both at once. See there, on the street-corner, is a broken paving-stone. In ordinary weather all pedestrians avoid it. Yet now, beneath its deceptive coverlet of snow, it appears like all the others, making of itself an invisible trap."

As he spoke, a heavily bundled wassailing party turned the corner, one fellow stumbling as he stepped on the treacherous slab.

"A neat demonstration," smiled Holmes. "Conversely, no murderer or burglar can escape a crime-scene untraced when snow lies upon the ground, for his footprints will surely betray him – unless another fall erases them."

"I never considered snow a clue before," I replied.

"Naturally you did not," said he, a trifle condescendingly. "Detecting is not your trade. Still, I hardly envy you going to a party in this tonight."

The Adventure of the Double Tomb by Katy Darby

I started. Our mutual friend Stamford's invitation to a Twelfth-Night supper had arrived in the morning post, but I had not mentioned it, fearing Holmes might feel slighted at not having been asked.

"Before you ask how I know this," my companion drawled, "consider the following factors. Firstly, instead of consuming a hearty dinner and a convivial glass of punch, you merely picked at Mrs. Hudson's superb chop, drinking coffee after, as though 'saving room' for more refreshments later. Secondly, had you planned a serious evening of reading, you would have studied *The Lancet*, not browsed Rider Haggard. A note in Stamford's hand arrived for you this morning; but were you meeting at the club, you would not have shaved with Carter's Botanic Soap, the almond aroma of which is distinctive, and which you only use when anticipating female company. Finally, our friend Stamford is forever seeking suitors for his younger sister; hence, I am omitted from the party due to my unshakable bachelorhood and my tendency to monopolise you." He lifted a laconic eyebrow.

"You have made it sound amazingly obvious," I admitted.

"As indeed it is. I wish you joy of your evening. Raise a toast to 'absent friends'!"

He chuckled, turning back to the window. The supper-hour approaching, I bid him good evening, donned my thick overcoat, and hurried out into the storm.

* * *

As in the Scottish play, one might say of Stamford's small, awkward gathering that "nothing became me like the leaving of it," and it was with relief at an obligation discharged that I battled my way back to Baker Street, eagerly anticipating a nightcap with my anti-social friend.

What greeted me, however, was a cold and empty sitting-room, and a hasty note jotted across a four-day-old copy of *The Times*.

The Adventure of the Double Tomb by Katy Darby

Despairing at Holmes's disdain for ordinary notepaper, I squinted to decipher it:

> Watson,
>
> You have had the ill-fortune to miss a client, Miss Alice Lane Fox (a lady whose charms might eclipse even Sarah Stamford's) who begs our aid on behalf of her distinguished father, Lt. General Pitt Rivers.
>
> I am called away at once to Cranborne Chase & have promised you will follow: I anticipate a doctor will be vital. Catch the last train out of Waterloo for Tisbury. Pitt Rivers's man will collect you at the station.
>
> SH
>
> P.S. Bring your revolver.

This was how I found myself that night on a London & South Western train bound for Wiltshire, with no notion of what awaited me there. I had packed in haste, taking only essentials: clothes and shaving-kit, my *Bradshaw's Illustrated Guide*, and, as advised, my loaded service-revolver.

Despite the appalling weather, the robust machinery of the railway company delivered me with swift efficiency, and I used the journey profitably by reading about Cranborne Chase. According to *Bradshaw*, it was a vast, ancient estate of nearly 400 square miles, spanning the counties of Wiltshire and Dorset. Once the deer-hunting

The Adventure of the Double Tomb by Katy Darby

grounds of King John, it had belonged since the early 18th century to the Pitt family, of which the current head was Augustus Pitt Rivers.

By the time Tisbury's church spires showed blue shadows through the thick curtain of flakes, I felt well-apprised of the locale; yet still could not imagine what problem might oblige our illustrious client to call urgently upon the talents of my friend.

I dug out the *Times* with Holmes's note on it: This time, a brief announcement beneath his scrawled message caught my eye.

It reported that after his recent retirement from the Army, Her Majesty's Government was pleased to confirm the appointment of Lt. General Augustus Pitt Rivers, distinguished veteran of Crimea, musketry expert and renowned antiquarian, as Inspector of Ancient Monuments with effect from January 1, 1883. To the Inspector would attach the responsibility for examining, assessing and protecting such archaeological sites as he deemed to be of historical significance.

I read it over, but it did not dispel the fog of mystery surrounding Holmes's peremptory summons. It seemed improbable that anyone had conspired to abstract a stone circle.

At the station, a smart Clarence awaited me: a reassuringly impressive vehicle, boasting all comforts of the modern conveyance (including, thankfully, foot-warmers) married with the quaintness of another age. Its doors were freshly painted with our client's quartered coat-of-arms, and beneath were inscribed the words *Aequam Servare Mentem*: "to preserve a calm mind," if my Latin served.

The driver was a tall, massive, fierce-looking fellow, well over six feet and forty years, with a great grizzled beard and a general aura of reliable competence. I thought, too, I detected a military bearing; and was gratified to glimpse upon his many-caped driving-coat a badge enamelled with the insignia of the Royal Engineers.

He saluted, touching his snow-furred cap with the whip.

"Sapper, eh?" I remarked. "I was in the Fusiliers."

The Adventure of the Double Tomb by Katy Darby

His shaggy brows beetled in surprise, and I experienced the pleasing vindication Holmes might feel when one of his surmises hit the mark.

"Aye sir," the fellow grunted, his accent more Yorkshire than Wiltshire, "Sergeant Livens, as was: fifteen years the General's batman."

"I suppose we are going to Rushmore?" I ventured. The family seat was, judging by its illustration in *Bradshaw*, quite magnificent.

"Nay, to t' tomb," said he shortly.

A sinister thrill pulsed through me. "The tomb?" I repeated, envisioning family vaults and snowbound sepulchres.

A smile like the half-snarl of a lazy bear twitched the fellow's bushy beard. "Mr. Holmes said to say he'd explain everything when you arrived."

Intrigued, and now somewhat apprehensive, I climbed into the carriage. Beyond the frost-framed window the world galloped by, the snow-mounded fields and hedges glowing blue-white beneath a clear black sky thickly swept with stars.

Cranborne Chase was enormous indeed: It took Livens a full hour along narrow, drift-choked roads to reach the lonely location of the "tomb." Noting the high boundary-hedges, I guessed we had reached the edge of the General's lands as our horses toiled up a broad, shallow hill.

We stopped in a gated lane leading to a bleak, silent, snow-smothered field. At the top, a once-towering, immemorial oak lay like a slain giant, sheeted in snow as by a shroud, toppled, presumably, by one of the violent snowstorms scouring England since Christmas.

I descended into the crisp-frozen night air and looked about, perplexed, but saw no sign in the white waste of church nor graveyard, let alone any tomb. Livens jumped down, putting nosebags on the horses, and thick blankets over their sweat-sheened flanks. Lifting a side-lantern from the carriage, he motioned for me to follow, and began trudging through the field. Like a subdued schoolboy, I complied.

Near the crest of the moon-washed hill a great wall of black soil reared up, fringed with torn roots: this was the base of the fallen tree. Next to it a corresponding pit had been wrenched from the gently sloping hillside, exposing some deeper, darker structure within.

"Is it here?" I asked.

"Aye sir," said he. "That's the barrow."

"Oh!" Clarity descended as I recalled the prehistoric barrow-tombs upon which Pitt Rivers had built his archaeological reputation.

"General's found plenty on t' Chase before now," Livens said, "but this'n was hid till that tree blew ower and cracked it wide."

"Indeed?" I said, wondering why Holmes had insisted this case would need a doctor: Any occupant of so ancient a burial-mound would be far beyond my help.

Approaching, I saw that heavy snowfall had made of the barrow-entrance a shadowed cavern, overhung by frozen eaves, and carpeted in pristine white. Though its edges were heavily trampled, just three sets of fresh tracks led across this white carpet into the barrow.

"Livens!" came a hail from the darkness. "Have you brought him?" and a sturdy, bluff fellow of sixty-odd emerged from the tomb. General Pitt Rivers was a handsome, imposing fellow, with a square-jawed, manly face framed by dark side-whiskers, a broad mouth, and deeply hooded eyes, over which long, iron-grey hair fell. A lifetime of campaigning and, latterly, digging had left him robust and hale; only a slight stiffness in the limbs betrayed his seniority.

He was followed by a young lady of about twenty, swathed in a great fur pelisse, with a hood from beneath which golden, curling wisps of hair strayed. Her pale face, and lively, intelligent eyes, blue like her father's, shone out with fervid clarity: a captivating vision on a winter's night. I was momentarily surprised into silence – this must be the daughter, Alice, of whom Holmes's note had spoken. I wondered that she was here so late, in a place so desolate, and could only assume some profound secret, or calamity, or both, had touched the family.

"Doctor!" cried the General, shaking my hand with vigour. "I can hardly express my gratitude for your coming at such short notice. It is rather a ... confidential matter."

I bowed. "It is more a pleasure than a duty to oblige a man of your standing, sir."

Pitt Rivers looked suitably gratified. "Kind of you, Doctor. This is my daughter, Miss Alice Lane Fox. Your colleague's within, examining the evidence; the others are over there."

He gestured at the night-black shadow beneath the looming, uptorn base of the fallen oak ten yards distant. I realised that what I'd taken for large root-shapes were silhouettes of men sitting on a broken-off branch. As I neared, these resolved into two youngish gentlemen. One was fair-haired and slight beneath the muffling embrace of a huge beaver coat, with a handsome, clean-shaven face. The other, larger fellow was dark, bespectacled and bullish-looking, with a close-clipped moustache. The towheaded one lifted his silver hip-flask in the universal invitation to a tot of whisky – an offer I gratefully accepted.

His bright, amused brown eyes met mine: "If you've come for the show," murmured he laconically, lighting a cigarette, "you haven't missed a thing. That detective fellow's been crawling round in there for ages."

"I believe I am the show – or part of it," I said. "Dr. John Watson."

"Eustace St. Owens," he replied, gripping my proffered hand with frozen fingers. "Soon to be the late, lamented, if we stay out here much longer. I'm the neighbour: rode over this morning to help clear the tree, and got the shock of my life!" There was a pleasant air of loucheness about him, redolent of the masculine comforts of the billiard-table and the smoking-room.

I turned to the other man, whose nod was curt and indifferent.

The Adventure of the Double Tomb by Katy Darby

"Professor Clifford Chaplin," he said, snapping off the words like icicles.

"Oxford history fellow. General's blue-eyed boy." St. Owens lowered his voice to a conspiratorial whisper, "Chaplin found the body."

At last I understood my purpose here. "I suppose he doesn't mean bones?" I said to Chaplin.

"'Fraid not." he said tersely. "Poor devil. That's why the guv'nor called you in." His mouth twisted. "Thought it would be an ordinary dig, you understand. Didn't see him on the floor – too dark. Nearly tripped over him …" He clamped his hands together to still their sudden trembling.

"How awful," I said. Long-hardened to the spectacle of death in all its forms, Chaplin's horror reminded me how dreadful the sight of a corpse might be to more cloistered men. St. Owens seemed entirely unaffected, blowing smoke-rings into the frost-clear air, but then, he had not discovered the dead man.

At this juncture, Miss Lane Fox came up: "Dr Watson, Papa wonders if you would take another lamp in to Mr. Holmes?" She smiled an apology. "His oil must be almost gone, and we are forbidden to enter."

I jumped up. "Oh, certainly!"

I was wildly curious to see inside such a tomb (Neolithic? Palaeolithic? I ought to ask), and carried the shivering light toward the dark cavity in the hillside with mounting anticipation. This was what I found:

The Adventure of the Double Tomb by Katy Darby

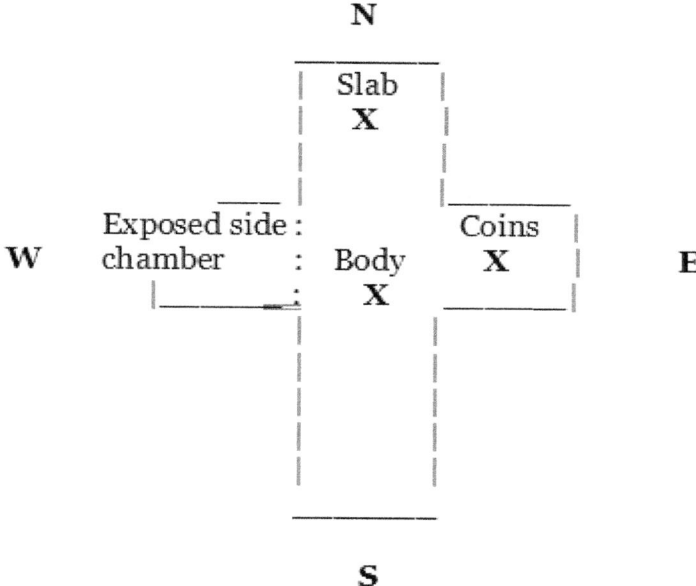

The western side of the tomb, which the tree's fall had exposed, was a small, low chamber, like a sort of vestibule. It seemed that it had, until this morning's dig, been sealed off from the large central chamber by a thick earthen wall, which had been partly demolished, creating a man-sized gap with a waist-high heap of rubble inside the main chamber to its right, where discarded earth had piled.

Suddenly my friend's keen face, its pallor smeared with dirt, emerged from the dark gap. Holmes wore his grey tweed Inverness cape against the weather, topped by an absurd-looking ear flapped hunting-cap. Nonetheless, his expression of profound solemnity spoke of some extraordinary riddle.

"Watson!" he said, "Thank Heaven you're here. You are my bellwether; I look to you for the common man's common-sense whenever my notions become too baroque."

He took my lantern, ushering me through into the long main chamber, and shining the light into every corner. The tomb was about twenty feet long and seven wide, vaguely cruciform, with two side-chambers or recesses to the west (whence I had come) and east. The body of a small man in a long dark coat lay in the middle of the floor, but otherwise, apart from a flat stone slab to my left and some coins scattered beyond the corpse, it seemed empty – though for all I knew it teemed with evidence both ancient and recent.

Its principal feature was the hole in the western wall behind me, and the pile of earth next to it, where the digging-party had broken through.

"One way in," said Holmes, hoisting his lamp toward the breached wall, "and one way out, and that way sealed until this morning. So, given that it was not through this gap, how did the dead man get in?"

I stared at him.

"It is a serious question," said Holmes. "I cannot answer it, nor can England's finest archaeologists outside. Can you?"

I took the light and inspected the chamber walls, which were of hard-packed earth buttressed by thick upright stones, something between menhirs and supporting pillars. I examined the floor and even the ceiling: I looked all around the stone slab, or grave-marker, and even knelt to confirm that it could not have been burrowed under.

"A mouse could not get in." I told him, rising and dusting my trouser-knees.

"My thoughts exactly." said Holmes. "Now, let us recapitulate this morning's discovery." He stuck his head through the wall-gap, calling the others inside. They gathered mute and wide-eyed.

"Professor Chaplin!" he said. "Though it was Mr. Livens who broke through the western wall, you entered first: correct?"

The academic's lips parted in an astonishment familiar to anyone who has spent time in Sherlock Holmes's company.

"How on earth –" Chaplin began.

"The footprints!" Holmes tutted. "Footprints are fundamental. The floor is dry earth, and your boots were damp with snow. Need I elaborate?"

"No," stammered Chaplin. "That is, yes, I was first in."

"And after you," Holmes observed, "judging by the state of the chamber-floor, came the deluge. A herd of elephants could not have done better at obscuring nearly all evidence of importance; fortunately, I am very minute in my examinations."

"I'll say," muttered St. Owens.

"So having hacked through this wall, Mr. Livens," said Holmes, turning to the sapper, "you laid down your mattock, and allowed the professor to precede you. Why?"

"I was afraid of damaging something," Livens replied.

Holmes cocked his head. "The General has praised your skill and delicacy assisting at excavations."

"Strong as an ox and careful as a cat," said Miss Lane Fox, with affection.

"Maybe so sir, but I'm no arch'ologist." muttered Livens.

"Your caution does you credit," conceded Holmes. "I understand, General, that antiquarians are as avid for evidence as we detectives, and that much valuable data may be destroyed or obscured by clumsy investigators?"

"Amateur bunglers," the General snorted, "do more harm than good."

"So I have found," said Holmes drily. "The Professor is no amateur, certainly. You stepped through the earth-wall into the main chamber, in which I now stand. There you discovered, in the northern recess," (he pointed to our left) "a stone slab, which you approached but did not disturb."

"Certainly not!" retorted Chaplin, stung.

"You examined it carefully – at one point kneeling to inspect some bone fragments on the floor, then rose. Something caught your eye, in the East-facing side-chamber behind me. You wheeled about abruptly, almost losing your footing."

Chaplin stared at my friend as if mesmerised, "Exactly."

"Your lamp," said Holmes, lifting his, "had caught a gleam from the ground –"

"Gold!" breathed St. Owens, all the pent-up drama of a first night at Drury Lane vibrating in his voice. Chaplin shot him a look like a poison dart.

"Gold, indeed," said Holmes. "Many large coins of considerable age and value."

"The coins' antiquity is nothing compared to that of the tomb," scoffed the General. "What this barrow may reveal about Neolithic burial customs is priceless!"

"Prehistoric barrows are often reused by later cultures," explained his daughter. "These coins are far more recent; they are of marginal interest."

"Pardon me for observing, Miss Lane Fox," said Holmes courteously, "that your special knowledge on this subject may blind you to a general fascination for buried gold of any vintage. Many would find such a treasure trove of great interest. The dead man, for one. Surely he was a looter who met a bad end?"

The General's face darkened, as if he yearned to deny the very existence of such baseness.

"The gold glittered," said Holmes, "but coins which have been interred centuries are dirty, not clean and bright. *This* coin," he produced a polished disc which dazzled like a miniature sun in the lamp-glow, "and its fellows, has been cleaned. Who did this but the deceased, intending to remove the hoard? The question is: How did this man come by his death?"

"The *question*," boomed the General, "is how he entered a sealed tomb in the first place?"

The Adventure of the Double Tomb by Katy Darby

"All in good time," said Holmes lightly. "Turning, Chaplin almost stumbled into the corpse. He staggered backward in surprise, dropping the lantern, recovered, then approached the body."

"I blamed a trick of the shadows," admitted Chaplin, "until I felt the poor fellow's hand."

"And shrieked like a cat with a trapped tail," said St. Owens, *sotto-voce*, to me.

"You knelt," said Holmes softly, "making sure he was dead."

Chaplin nodded. All colour had drained from his once-ruddy cheeks. "He was pale and pinched, but otherwise looked to be sleeping. The moment I touched him, though, I knew life was extinct."

"At your alarm, the others entered, as the footmark-record shows: first attempting to identify the body and subsequently, searching the chamber to find how he had got in; both efforts being fruitless."

"Y-yes, that's right." Chaplin shook himself, sketching a watery smile. "Forgive me: it was a horrid shock. You'll think that queer for one who's excavated so many graves, I suppose. Fact is, I don't mind bones in the least. It's flesh that bothers me."

"And how," said St. Owens in an undertone, passing me the flask again.

"I have made a thorough examination of the body," Holmes declared, "and there is no obvious cause of death – no cranial trauma, arterial wound, broken neck, crushed oesophagus, etc. Nor is it evident how the victim entered this central chamber, which had remained unbreached – how long?"

"More than twelve hundred years," volunteered Miss Lane Fox, glancing at her father for confirmation, "by my guess."

He gave her a look of paternal pride. "Certainly no less."

My head throbbed: How had this man broken in, left no sign of entry, then suddenly died? It was as if some ancient grave-robbers' curse had felled him.

The Adventure of the Double Tomb by Katy Darby

"His demise may have been accidental," Holmes said, "and I know, General, you wish to serve justice, while also preserving absolute discretion. But we must understand what killed him, whether natural or otherwise. And so," concluded my friend, turning to me, "Dr. Watson will now establish the cause of death."

* * *

Ten minutes later I knelt, sleeves rolled and lantern held over me by Miss Lane Fox, examining the dead man. A battlefield doctor soon learns to work in the most adverse and unconducive of conditions: in mud, in sand, amid screams, amid shells, with inadequate equipment and assistance, little, or none. But I had never before examined a corpse past midnight in an immemorial underground burial chamber, and I trust shall never be obliged to do so again.

Chaplin had excused himself, looking arsenic-green, but Holmes, Livens, St. Owens and Pitt Rivers all gathered solemnly to watch. The victim had been dead more than a day, and *rigor mortis* had passed. He was scrawny and stunted, looking forty but probably younger, undernourished with coarse dark hair, much-scarred hands and a week's black stubble bearding his thin, sunken cheeks.

A cursory examination confirmed no external fatal wound. A cardiac-seizure or poison might have killed him, yet neither seemed likely.

I examined his face, mouth and chest before moving down towards the stomach, which looked, despite the man's lean physique, oddly swollen. Palpating the otherwise shrunken sac, I found something hard and unyielding, or rather many small hard objects, like stones, which when I pressed down, made a strange metallic rustling.

"What is this?" I muttered. "What has he eaten?" I opened the jaw again, and felt around between his cheeks and gums. Something glinted within.

The Adventure of the Double Tomb by Katy Darby

"More light!" I urged. Miss Lane Fox advanced the lamp and in the wavering light, I gently plucked a small golden coin out of the dead man's mouth.

St. Owens flinched and gasped, while Livens crossed himself, turning quite grey; but Miss Lane Fox leaned closer to scrutinise the little object.

"May I?" Entranced, she took it, holding it under the light, and her blue eyes widened.

"A Saxon thrymsa!" cried she, showing it to Pitt Rivers. "See, the runic and Latin text together? Perhaps the coins are more interesting than we thought, Papa?"

"Extraordinary!" said he, with evident delight.

"I don't suppose, Doctor," she said curiously, "eating these killed him?"

"Lead's a poison," volunteered Livens. "Why not gold?"

"Gold is a noble metal," I explained. "Its cardinal property is that it is unreactive and does not rust; therefore, it is safe to eat, because it cannot be digested or absorbed. It was not his meal of gold that killed him."

Holmes's brows knit. "What then?" he demanded.

Like a snowflake melting on the tip of the tongue, I savoured the cool, evanescent pleasure of knowing something that Sherlock Holmes did not.

"Dehydration," I said. "He had not eaten or drunk for several days prior to death." I indicated the man's face: "See, his eyes and cheeks are sunken; and the cracked lips and dry tongue tell their own story."

Holmes sprang up, eyes alight. "I suspected it was slow, from the man's tracks on the floor: back and forth like a Swiss clock-figure upon his rails, first purposeful, then weaker; scratching and digging at the walls. Utterly trapped."

"But why swallow gold?" I said.

"Delirium?" suggested St. Owens.

The Adventure of the Double Tomb by Katy Darby

"Attempted suicide," the General opined.

"Some sort of message?" ventured Miss Lane Fox.

"None of these is impossible," Holmes conceded, "and yet none, I think, is correct. This is not a case of madness nor gluttony," he added enigmatically, "but of avarice."

Calling Chaplin back in, Holmes apprised him of our discovery. The professor's eyes sparkled in fascination, and he turned to his mentor.

"This is highly significant, General! It recalls certain pagan sacrificial customs: possibly ritual punishment. The Saxons were known to –"

"But who is he?" Rivers insisted, ignoring his protégé and addressing Holmes.

Holmes spread his hands. "I found nothing on the man's person to indicate his name. However," he continued, over the General's disappointed harrumph, "certain details may help identify him locally. The greater development of the left hand confirms he favoured that limb, and given the slight deformity of the palate, he would have spoken with a pronounced lisp. He was previously malnourished, yet his unpicked teeth show he has lately eaten meat and fresh fruit, and the burst vessels on his nose indicate he drank habitually and to excess."

Pitt Rivers stared at my friend as if he had claimed Bronze Age man wore a pocket-watch.

"Finally," Holmes concluded, "numerous healed shot-scars in his back, and of course his bespoke coat, prove he was a poacher." He flapped open the man's greatcoat with a flourish, displaying a long vertical pocket sewn into the lining.

"Oh!" Miss Lane Fox's hands flew to her throat, clutching a locket or pendant which had slipped beneath her blouse. The General was instantly at her side, St. Owens a close second.

The Adventure of the Double Tomb by Katy Darby

"A poacher!" she cried. "Oh Papa! I did not know him beneath the beard, before." She turned to Livens. "That is the man who was spying on me from the woods."

The General looked thunderous. "This is the first I've known of it!"

His daughter laid a soothing hand upon his arm. "It was nothing really, Papa: I only saw him a few times."

He glowered. "Well?"

"Some months ago," she said, "I noticed this impertinent fellow watching me on my morning ride. I thought he might be a poacher, and told Livens, but after a while I saw him no more."

"Foolish child!" scolded the General. "Any soldier would tell you all that meant was that he was better hidden, not that he'd gone away. Why did you say nothing?"

She met his eyes. "I did not wish to upset you, dear Papa, nor add to your … worries."

"So he was indeed local," said Holmes. He gestured at the body before us, looking sternly round the group. "Regard him again, please, gentlemen: Picture him clean-shaven, in life. Do any of you recognise him?"

Dutifully, they looked, variously with distaste, perplexity and horror, and shook their heads. I examined my friend's face as he watched theirs, but read nothing in it – not even disappointment.

"Well," said Holmes briskly. "We have made progress, and perhaps the morrow will shed more light."

As I followed the others out onto the moonlit hillside, I noticed the snow had commenced to fall again in earnest. Turning, I saw Holmes behind and above us, standing atop the barrow: he had walked up the gentle slope to the field's highest point, staring down at something below.

"Should we set a guard upon the tomb?" the General enquired, glancing up at Holmes.

"No need." Holmes pointed at the sky. "This weather will be guard enough; besides, I shall return at first light." He sprang down the incline like a mountain-goat.

"In that case," suggested St. Owens, "my house is nearby, Mr. Holmes: permit me to offer the party some refreshment?"

* * *

As we crammed into the ice-cold Clarence, it seemed the thickly plummeting snow would not soon ease. The General reluctantly allowing the imprudence of driving back to Rushmore in such weather, Livens turned the horses towards St. Owens's house.

We drew up before the portico of a fine old mansion. Still elegant notwithstanding some culpable neglect on its young master's part, it was a proud and stately edifice. Oddly, St. Owens did not ring at the front-door for the butler, instead leading us around the rear, through deep, virgin snow.

"We'll go in through the orangery," said he, opening a glass door into a large, light and lofty conservatory-cum-greenhouse, in the relative warmth of which various fruiting trees stood arrayed in enormous pots.

"Help yourselves," he said with a half-smile, turning; but Miss Lane Fox touched his arm.

"What happened to Burton?" she asked in a low voice.

St. Owens shrugged. "Dismissed."

"What! He was not stealing?"

"No," said he carelessly, "unless you count his astronomical wages; but economies were imperative. Don't worry, Alice," he added, with some *hauteur*, "I manage well enough alone."

Reaching a set of oaken double-doors, he flung them back with the drama of a stage-actor. Within was a vast, beautifully appointed drawing-room whose decayed grandeur spoke with eloquence of a

The Adventure of the Double Tomb by Katy Darby

once-great fortune. That this was all but extinct, the blank rectangles on the walls, where portraits had been sold, silently affirmed.

"Brandy-and-soda all round, I think," said St. Owens, and prepared six stiff glasses. "Livens, bring whatever's in the pantry, would you?" He raised his lead-crystal tumbler with an unsteady hand. "Your very good health." He tossed it off, immediately pouring another.

"Frightful business," said Chaplin at last. "Can't help imagining that fellow stumbling about in the dark." He flinched, and gulped his brandy. "Buried alive."

Miss Lane Fox winced, but her father glowered like an Old Testament patriarch, equally free of doubt and mercy. "Blasted grave-robbers get what they deserve!" he declared. "From Khartoum to Cairo, always the same. Either the curs murder each other, or the dead take their revenge."

Chaplin nodded. "The Saxons cursed their enemies and those who would rob them," he told us. "Victory runes and inscribed warnings, on Aedwen's brooch and the Chessell Down scabbard, for example."

"*'Increase to pain'*," muttered the General meaningly.

"Oh yes!" agreed Alice, her interest quickening, "Papa found a grave-curse inscribed on a pectoral cross last year." She coloured. "Of course, nobody on that dig died. I suppose it is a foolish superstition. Besides, we've found no such object here."

"Not yet," said Pitt Rivers, staring into the brown-gold depths of his drink.

"Come General!" scoffed St. Owens, halfway down his second brandy-and-soda already. "A treasure-trove of gold is no curse!" He laughed shortly. "Bellyfuls of coins and looters walking through walls, though, is a sight too Gothic. S'pose I've had a fortunate escape."

There came an awkward pause.

"Where is Livens?" I asked.

The Adventure of the Double Tomb by Katy Darby

"Got lost finding the kitchen, probably," said our host. "Should've sent him on a horse – would've found his way quick enough then. Damn' creatures will do anything for that man but win a race. Wouldn't like his luck. Ha!"

I glanced at Holmes; he was staring intently at the lap of Miss Lane Fox, in which lay nothing but her demurely-folded hands.

Fortunately, at that point Livens returned, carrying modest but welcome platters from St. Owens's larder, which revived us all considerably. Our host, his hysteric mood abated, recollected his manners, inviting us all to stay the night, given the circumstances. Holmes accepted graciously on our behalf; and I was surprised when Pitt Rivers refused.

"No need for that," said he stiffly. "Snow's stopped: we'll return to Rushmore. You could coax those beasts to drive across the North Pole, eh Livens? Come Chaplin, Alice."

I escorted them back to the carriage, offering Miss Lane Fox my arm. She took it with gratitude, and as we rounded the corner said abruptly, "You mustn't mind Eustace, you know. He may seem a little … wild sometimes, but he is a disappointed man."

I glanced at the august mansion beside us. "I should not be disappointed."

"It is mortgaged," she said sadly. "The money was long gone when he inherited, and despite his efforts to restore the family's wealth, nothing has yet prevailed. The barrow-field was his land, you know; he was compelled to sell it to Papa last year, to pay taxes. So, when he came by the excavation this morning, Papa felt honour-bound to let him watch. It is all rather difficult."

I was taken aback: perhaps this young man deserved compassion rather than the General's barely concealed hostility. I wondered what had sundered the neighbours so deeply that Pitt Rivers refused to spend a night under St. Owens's roof.

The Adventure of the Double Tomb by Katy Darby

Having arranged with the General that we would meet him at the nearest public-house tomorrow morning, I pressed Miss Lane Fox's slender fingers as I handed her into the coach.

"I shall remember," I murmured.

She smiled. "Sleep well."

When I returned, Holmes was listening attentively to our host's account of a recent neck-and-neck finish at Salisbury races.

"Livens was in the stands, looking awfully cut-up," concluded St. Owens: "Put his shirt on the lame nag, again! All that gold must've looked tempting when he first saw it in the barrow. Surprised he didn't take a souvenir!"

He chuckled bitterly, and Holmes frowned. "I imagine, no matter his debts, Mr. Livens has more respect than to abstract an artefact from a grave," he said severely.

Our host wheeled about; eyes brandy-bright. "Is that what you *imagine*, Mr. Holmes? Or what you *infer*?"

"I'd stake ten guineas on it," replied Holmes coolly.

"Ten!" grinned St. Owens, enticed despite himself by the wager. "Why, pray?"

Holmes enumerated his answer on his long thin fingers.

"Firstly, he has had extensive archaeological experience, and has evidently learned from this the contempt and disgust all antiquarians feel for plunderers. Secondly, even if tempted to filch a 'souvenir', discovery of any such theft by Pitt Rivers would result in disgraceful dismissal – hardly a risk a man with fifteen years' loyal service would run. Thirdly, had he wished to abstract artefacts unobserved he would have entered the tomb first, rather than ceding place to Chaplin. Fourthly –"

"Fourthly?" urged St. Owens, his grin gone, drink forgotten.

Holmes shrugged. "He is an honest man. My instinct and inference both, since you ask."

The Adventure of the Double Tomb by Katy Darby

"Come, Mr. Holmes!" chided St Owens. "You, if anyone, have peered into the black abyss of the human heart. Surely when need presses, there *is* no honest man?"

Holmes held his gaze. "I have had the honour to meet one or two." He inclined his head toward me. "Watson, for example."

I coloured with pleasure at the unlooked-for compliment.

"The good doctor," Holmes continued, "is incapable of deception: He has a 'speaking countenance,' as does friend Livens."

"Well," said our host, regarding me with pity, "that argues incompetence rather than incorruptibility, surely?" He glanced at the mantel-clock and yawned. "But the question is moot, and the hour is late. Gentlemen, I bid you good night."

He drained his glass, feeling in his pocket for something, then tossed a little glittering object casually to Holmes, who snatched it from the air with the speed of a viper.

"Return that to the General tomorrow, would you?" said St. Owens. "Can't have it thought George Livens is a better man than I!"

As the double-doors swung shut behind him, Holmes opened his palm to reveal a large gold coin: Plainly, our host himself had not resisted taking a "souvenir."

"What a ... surprising fellow," I said, recollecting Miss Lane Fox's words.

"Surprising that Pitt Rivers ever permitted his daughter to fall in love with him," mused Holmes, "though not remotely that the General broke off their engagement last year."

"What? They were ... Oh!" I sank into the settee, stunned. "That passed me by."

"Like so much, my dear innocent friend!" sighed Holmes, half-smiling. "Those who hide no lies, grudges, or secrets themselves rarely suspect them in others. Naturally, aristocratic young neighbours would be thrown much together, and perhaps Pitt Rivers once saw bright prospects for St. Owens. But by the faded ring-mark, the engagement-band Miss Lane Fox once wore was taken off months ago."

"She does not seem heartbroken," I said stoutly, fond hopes of deepening our acquaintance substantially crushed.

"No," mused Holmes, "she conceals it well. But there are women who, once they love a bad man, will not rest until they have made him good, or themselves miserable – the commoner result. As you surely observed, she still wears his ring covertly, on a chain beneath her blouse. Unlike poor squeamish Chaplin, there's hope for St. Owens yet!"

"Chaplin?" I echoed, bewildered: Holmes's revelations were coming too fast.

"Of course!" said Holmes, striding to the window to gaze up at the now-cloudless, star-stabbed sky. "What better way for the General's daughter to forget her old beau, than with a new? And what better candidate than his protégé and intellectual successor, Clifford Chaplin?"

"They're hardly a match!"

Holmes turned. "You, Watson, are a romantic. The prospective couple share an interest in archaeology. To Pitt Rivers, that alone should be enough."

"With such insights, I suppose you have solved the case already?"

"Alas," Holmes said drily, "I may have to dig deeper." His tone grew grim. "One of the people we met tonight, Watson, is a pitiless and unscrupulous killer. Someone sealed a man in that tomb and left him to die. Someone knew him, conspired with him, and then, when he threatened or opposed them, murdered him in ice-cold blood. And tomorrow, I hope to discover whom."

* * *

I slept ill that night, between the slightly damp sheets of St. Owens's guest-bed, awaking late yet little rested. At breakfast our host was nowhere visible; nor was Holmes. I ate alone, therefore, staring glumly out at a sky like tarnished pewter.

I had just risen to find my host, when Holmes strode in ruddy-cheeked, hat and coat almost white, and snow-soaked to the knee. Despite this, he looked remarkably satisfied.

"Been out?" I said.

"Nothing escapes you, Watson," replied Holmes, helping himself to kedgeree. He poured a generous cup of coffee from the sideboard pot, and drank it standing.

"I *have* been out this morning," he continued, "and a very bracing expedition it was too. Daylight has revealed further clues, and I was also able to make this."

He pulled a paper from his coat, and unfurled it. It was a likeness of the dead man, done in pencil with a precise eye and sure hand, skilfully capturing the poacher's feral, narrow features. The principal difference between portrait and corpse was that the eyelids were open. Dark eyes glared out from the page with all the sullen fire of life.

"I had to confirm their colour," explained Holmes, "and to show him dead would cause alarm."

"The resemblance is uncanny," I told him.

"Good! I am glad. A photograph being impossible, I thought this the next best thing. At the dawn of my career, Watson, I haunted the more notorious criminal trials at the Old Bailey, and amused myself by sketching the countenances of the criminals and barristers as I listened."

He regarded the drawing with satisfaction. "Art runs in my blood, you know: I trust Great-Uncle Vernet would not be utterly ashamed."

* * *

The Adventure of the Double Tomb by Katy Darby

As befitted an old soldier, Pitt Rivers was early meeting us at the Cranborne Arms, and had brought his troops. When we ascended to the upstairs room engaged by the General so we could converse privately, we found his daughter, Professor Chaplin, and Livens also present. Our client's furtive, hunted manner as we entered sat oddly with his natural air of patrician command: I could not fathom what made him nervous, unless it was the ever-nearing threat of scandal attaching itself to his name and position.

"Well, Mr. Holmes," said he brusquely, "what progress?"

Holmes's reply was interrupted by a knock, and a smartly aproned landlady entered with refreshments.

"Ah!" cried Holmes, "The very woman! Mrs. Claire Millington, is it not? Tell me, do you know all your regulars by sight?"

The landlady glanced at Livens with a broad, unaffected grin.

"I should say so, sir. Anyone in partic'lar?"

"This man." Holmes unrolled his pencil-portrait and held it before the woman's startled eyes.

"Why, that's Stephen Pye, to the life! Yes sir, he's a good customer when he's the money to be. Haven't seen him since New Year's Eve, mind: He was pretty merry then ..." She took in our sombre faces. "He's not in trouble again?"

"He was here six nights ago?" said Holmes eagerly. "Did he speak to anyone?"

"Too busy to say, sir: he might've. Spoke to me, of course, saucy devil."

"What time did he leave?"

The landlady pondered. "I was run off my feet: I can't say for sure, but it wasn't before midnight. George," she said, turning casually to Livens, "you was in on New Year's. Did you mark when Pye left?"

Livens's face went wax-white as all eyes turned upon him. Holmes alone seemed unperturbed by this accidental revelation.

"I – I don't recall ..." Livens stuttered. "I didn't see – I don't know him, sir," he added desperately, appealing to the General. "A man can drink in a pub and not know everyone, can't he?"

Not in a little place like Cranborne, thought I.

"Are you quite certain you didn't notice this fellow, Livens?" said Alice gently. It would help greatly, I'm sure, if you remembered anything?"

"Never seen him in my life," Livens insisted stoutly.

The landlady shrugged. "No matter: I'll ask the other regulars if it'll oblige you." And off she bustled, closing the door behind.

The General's face was bleak as a winter sky.

"Didn't *you* stop here on New Year's Eve, Chaplin?" he said.

The Professor peered about the room vaguely, eyes wide behind their lenses. "Perhaps ... All these country-taverns look the same to me, I'm afraid. I caught the last train and stopped in at *a* public-house; was it this one?"

"This is the only one for ten miles," said Alice, "Did you not see this Pye?"

"Possibly," said Chaplin, "I cannot be positive."

"Come," said Holmes impatiently: "you spent hours at an inn where a drunken man was making a merry show of himself. Did you remark him, or no?"

"There *was* a fellow being rather a nuisance," Chaplin acknowledged, "but I couldn't say whom. I mislaid my spectacles that night, and didn't find them until the next day. If you recall, Alice, when you came by next morning, I barely recognised even you?"

Holmes wore the look of intense internal calculation which manifested when new pieces of a puzzle emerged, and he was attempting to fit them into his mental pattern.

"I think," said he, "I must speak again to Mrs. Millington," and abruptly left. Silence fell soft and heavy as snow.

"From what the landlady said," I suggested tentatively, "this Pye fellow may have been known to the police. I wonder –"

The Adventure of the Double Tomb by Katy Darby

The General's thick fist descended upon the mahogany table with a startling crash.

"No, sir, no! I will not have it!" cried he, fear and fury simmering in his voice. "I told Alice, when I sent her to London; I told Mr. Holmes, and now, Dr Watson, I tell you: There are to be *no* police involved unless absolutely necessary! It was my land on which this trespasser was found, and I forbid it!"

His face was dangerously congested: I feared a strain on his heart. "But if it proves to be murder –" I began.

"Accident!" he barked. "Misadventure! Somehow this thief discovered the tomb, somehow he got in to rob it; somehow he trapped himself there. That is all! There's no murder nor mystery to it, and I'll thank you not to make any."

Even Chaplin looked discomfited. "But sir, surely –"

His mentor choked a laugh. "Good God, Clifford! You know as well as I that there's already enough poppycock and fairy-tales talked about excavations by the ignorant public! If it is not foolish yarns of buried treasure, it's scaremongering twaddle about desecrating graves."

He rounded on me, a fanatic light in his blue eyes: "Archaeology is a science, Doctor, not a sideshow, and I'll not have my life's work, the discipline I spent decades making respectable, mocked, traduced, or dragged through the mud! I have a sacred moral and legal duty, as Inspector of Ancient Monuments – appointed by Parliament, mark you! – to safeguard not only the material legacy of the past, but the respect and reverence our heritage is due. Who knows what invaluable archaeological evidence that idiot robber destroyed, stumbling around looking for gold? As I said yesternight, thieves get what they deserve!"

At this fraught moment, Holmes returned. "Preserve a calm mind, dear General," he advised smoothly. "As we brush away the dirt, the shape of the truth is revealed. An intelligent and observant woman, that landlady," he added, sitting and helping himself hungrily to beef-pudding.

"What did she say?" asked Alice. Chaplin appeared shaken, now, and Livens looked positively green.

"It seems Pye's partiality for Mrs. Millington made him loose-tongued in his cups: He said she'd been widowed long enough, and tonight was her last chance to marry him before he got rich. Subsequently, another regular glimpsed him leaving, around one a.m."

"He must have gone straight to the barrow," said I slowly. "Given how long he was in there, that was certainly the night he got trapped."

"Quite," said Holmes, "and perhaps most interestingly, he did not leave alone."

"What?" The General glanced at Chaplin, foreboding flooding his face.

"Or rather, whom?" said Holmes. "Alas, Mrs. Millington's sharp-eyed customer could not say who accompanied Pye; except that it was a tall, dark man."

* * *

After an understandably subdued luncheon, Holmes and I walked up to the barrow-site: It was no more than a mile, but took an hour through the snow.

"However did two drunken men manage this journey in the dark, after midnight?" I panted as we struggled up the hill, following Holmes's own footsteps from that morning.

"Only one was definitely drunk," said Holmes. "Besides which, the landlady informed me that New Year's Eve was the night the snow started. When they came this way, it would have been lighter on the ground, and the going far easier."

"Well," said I, as we stood before the shadowy tomb-mouth, "are we going in?"

The Adventure of the Double Tomb by Katy Darby

"No," he told me, "Today we go *on*, and you shall tell me what you see."

He led me up to where he had stood last night atop the barrow, surveying the snow-choked landscape. The shallow pit where the side-chamber had been wrenched open lay directly below us, and the toppled behemoth of the venerable oak stretched before us, slanting to the left, or southwest. The view from this elevation revealed not only its true size, but the violence of its fall: A white-heaped wreckage of shattered branches lay all around it where they had burst from the trunk.

"What do you see, Watson?"

I considered. "A snowy field; an uprooted tree, and its scattered limbs. I see a large crater in the ground, also snow-covered, and I know, though I do not see it, that there is a hole in the hillside below me."

"Good. Observe the broken branches," said Holmes. "Does anything strike you?"

Helplessly, I cast about for a detail. "One has fallen nearer than the others?" I indicated a long, misshapen white lump lying beside and slightly behind the tomb-entrance. It was perhaps a dozen feet long, and lay right up against the barrow-side.

Holmes's eyes glimmered. "Did it fall there?"

"What do you mean?"

"What I say. Look at the other limbs; the pattern they form around the parent trunk is natural. But yours is out of the pattern. It did not fall when the tree itself fell; it was probably rotten, and blew off days earlier, in the first storm. Now, examine the snow around it."

I strained my sight against snow-glare. "It has been churned up: there's a furrow, and a depression in the snow where the branch formerly lay, some yards further off."

"Conclusion?"

"It has been dragged."

"Avoid the passive voice, Watson! *Someone* dragged it!"

The Adventure of the Double Tomb by Katy Darby

"But the marks are barely visible. It must have been moved days ago."

"Indeed. And when did our looter enter the tomb?"

"Six nights ago – oh!"

"Now you see?" said he. "We could find no way into the tomb when we searched inside, so this morning I took the opposite approach and walked all around the barrow, looking carefully for where a passage might come out. There was nothing obvious, no dip or divot in the earth-walls; so I wondered if it had somehow been concealed."

"With the branch!" I cried.

"Precisely. I at once spotted this tree-limb pressed right up against the barrow, and reasoned that if this poacher had an accomplice, and that accomplice trapped him inside, he would want nobody else chancing along, hearing cries, and releasing his victim. The snow might conceal the blocked exit sufficiently; then again, it might not. So, as insurance, he covered it with a fallen branch. The murderer really was taking no risks."

"But why did we not spot the other end of this passage inside the chamber?" I wondered.

"Sheer chance. The hole happened to be near the western side-chamber torn open by the toppled tree. It was also small and low down; a slight man like Pye could have wriggled through quite a tight space. So when Livens and Chaplin broke through, and that interior wall crumbled, the rubble and earth fell in front of the tunnel entrance, concealing it entirely!"

"The rubble," I said, "the snow, the nearby branch: everything has gone in the murderer's favour."

"Everything until now," said Sherlock Holmes darkly, "and except me."

* * *

The Adventure of the Double Tomb by Katy Darby

The General had offered to host us at Rushmore that evening, arranging for Livens to collect us from St. Owens's before dinner. We trudged back to the mansion therefore, to gather our things, and discovered our host in the orangery. Snow lay thick over the glass roof, blocking half the weak winter light, and rendering the interior gloomy as an undersea cavern.

"Warmest place in the house," he insisted, though he looked chilled through even in his opulent beaver coat. "No point wasting coal in those great useless rooms. How'd you make out today? Solved the case yet?"

"Not quite," acknowledged Sherlock Holmes, "but it is becoming clearer."

"Unlike the weather!" St. Owens gestured outside where, with tedious predictability, it had again begun snowing. "How can you find anything in this?"

"I have my methods," said Holmes enigmatically.

"And what have they revealed?" asked St. Owens. His hand strayed towards his flask-pocket, though it was only mid-afternoon.

"That snow holds boot-marks, and boot-marks hold the key. I shall be sure tomorrow morning," he declared, with a confidence I could not share. He'd said nothing to me of boot-marks!

St. Owens looked almost interested. "So soon! You return there tonight, then?"

Holmes mirrored our host's gesture towards the whirling flakes beyond the glass. "Nobody is going there tonight. We are for Rushmore, a hot dinner, and a warm bed. We'll return tomorrow. And now I hear our carriage drawing up. We must not keep the good Livens waiting!"

At this, St. Owens stared so owlishly that I wondered whether he had not, after all, had recourse to his whisky flask already.

"The *good* Livens!" he snorted. "Livens, who was drinking with that poacher the night he vanished? Trained soldier and decorated killer George Livens? My dear sir, I hope you are a better judge of evidence than of character!"

"Sherlock Holmes has never been wrong yet, Mr. St. Owens." I said stalwartly; though things looked black for Livens in my private opinion.

"We shall see," said Holmes imperturbably. "Good-day, sir."

He bowed slightly, and we took our leave.

* * *

"Boot-marks?" echoed the General curiously over dinner at Rushmore, a delicious succession of warming leek-and-potato soup, tender roasted pork, and an array of fresh fruit after – from St. Owens's orangery, I guessed. It seemed that despite the broken engagement, the General, or perhaps Alice, was not too proud to accept neighbourly gifts.

"Boot-marks," Holmes confirmed, as Livens refilled our glasses with excellent Bordeaux, Alice and Chaplin declining. "Thanks to the shelter of a fallen branch, I've excellent hopes of finding the murderer's footmarks preserved in the snow, from the very night Pye was entombed. Did I not say footprints were fundamental? And have not you yourself written, in a certain learned journal, that 'nothing is too small to be noted, and its exact site duly marked'?"

Pitt Rivers's wine-glass stopped halfway to his lips and he gazed at my friend with a new respect. "I certainly have, Mr. Holmes. I'm glad to see your reading is not exclusively confined to the criminal pages."

"As am I, that we are of the same mind." said Holmes, looking around the circle of tense, candlelit faces. "I shall sleep better tonight in that knowledge."

* * *

The Adventure of the Double Tomb by Katy Darby

My room at Rushmore was immeasurably superior to St. Owens's accommodations, with a warm, soft bed; I had been blissfully asleep two hours when Holmes shook me from dreams at one a.m.

"Awake at last!" said he over his shoulder to a bundled figure lost in the darkness beyond my bedside candle. "Come Watson, you are an old campaigner! Did you really believe we were *not* guarding the tomb tonight, when I have laid the most tempting bait for the murderer there?"

He tossed me some clothes from my dressing-case. "Put these on, and don't forget your revolver."

When I emerged into the corridor, sleepy-eyed, I was astonished to see our co-conspirator was Miss Lane Fox, wrapped in her fur pelisse, her lovely face pale and resolute.

"I'll guide you," was all she said.

We took the Clarence; Holmes drove and she sat beside him to navigate: beneath their white quilt, all roads and fields looked identical; but she knew them intimately. The snow had ceased, and the new-hatched moon rode up the sky, golden as a coin, as we galloped through the silent, shrouded landscape. It seemed the whole world held its breath, awaiting the denouement of this outlandish and baffling mystery.

"He will come after moonrise, and on foot," was all Holmes would tell me: hence our driving, to ensure we reached the tomb first.

When we drew to a halt in the gated lane where Livens had brought me that first night, the stillness was palpable. Not a flake spiralled from the vast blackish-grey sky; not a dead leaf stirred; no creature scurried or rustled in distant woods.

We descended, Holmes and I stepping in our own tracks from this afternoon all the way up to the barrow, to conceal our recent presence from any other, wary visitor. Alice followed in my prints, her small light foot making barely a mark inside the deeper, wider outline of my own boots.

"And now," said Holmes, "we wait."

The Adventure of the Double Tomb by Katy Darby

"Where?" said Alice.

Holmes indicated the soil-wall formed by the uprooted base of the oak where Chaplin, St. Owens and I had huddled two nights ago.

"Watson and I will hide there, where we can see the branch beneath which, I suspect, the murderer will attempt to erase his damning footprints. Meanwhile, do you wait in the side-chamber's shelter, watching northwest down the hill. If anyone comes, wave like Robinson Crusoe!"

She gave a determined nod.

We waited. The moon sailed higher and shone brighter; the wind rose, wailed softly, and fell again. My fingers and toes grew numb, and I longed for a nip from St. Owens's flask.

And then we saw a figure.

Holmes's keen, kestrel vision spied him first; a black dot toiling and flailing across the huge field towards us. For many minutes the moon-shadows played tricks; I could not tell the size nor age of the person approaching.

And then I realised, with a leaden sensation in my gut, that it was George Livens.

Poor Livens, whom I had liked, yet who'd looked so ghastly and guilty in the Cranborne Arms; who Holmes himself had bet ten guineas was an honest man. St. Owens would indubitably demand full payment when he heard.

"Holmes –" I began, but he hissed me quiet. He wore an expression I had almost never seen before: equal parts surprise, incredulity, chagrin and defeat. So looks the face of Sherlock Holmes when he discovers himself to be utterly, undeniably, and catastrophically wrong.

"It *cannot* be he!" he muttered savagely.

I touched my friend's elbow. "Let's watch what he does."

"If he goes to the branch …" muttered Holmes. "But no. No!"

Together we watched, our breath steaming cold clouds, as Livens stumbled closer and closer. He must have waded across the fields all the way from Rushmore, several miles' journey: Royal Engineers were tough, but even the hulking Livens commenced to flounder and falter as he neared. He approached the white lump of the fallen branch, hesitated; then wearily plodded around it, down towards the barrow-entrance.

And then he did something entirely unexpected.

"Mr. Holmes!" he shouted in a raw, hoarse voice.

Holmes did not move.

Exhausted, the bearlike sapper sank to his knees.

"Dr. Watson! Miss Alice!" he bellowed. "I know you're there!" Then more quietly, his voice cracking like twigs: "Oh, let it be ended."

Unable to bear his plea, Alice emerged and ran to him.

"Livens?" she cried. "What are you doing here? Go back!"

He shook his shaggy head, pressing her dainty hands in his great ones.

"No, Miss. The law'll have me, and 'twill be a mercy."

Holmes walked from our shadow. "I had not pegged you for a murderer, Mr. Livens: well, well! Experience, I suppose, shall teach me; I am young yet."

The man looked up at Sherlock Holmes, his eyes black pits of despair. "I didn't mean murder, honest to God! I tried to find him; for days I tried. But I cou'n't, and now he's dead – and 'tis my fault!"

"You had better start from the beginning," I said, gently.

* * *

"I've always loved horses: to ride 'em, and watch 'em race, but after the General retired from the Army, and took me with him, the tedium of the deep countryside, as well as the nearness of Sandown meant I began to spend all my days off there, losing more than I won, and soon enough more than I could afford.

The Adventure of the Double Tomb by Katy Darby

"On New Year's Eve I was at the Cranborne Arms, drinking to forget a right heavy loss, when Stephen Pye, whose face I knew, sidled up, bought me a drink, and made me an offer. He'd found summat, he said: a gold coin, and maybe more in t' ground, and because I'd done excavations wi' Pitt Rivers on t' Chase, and knew a bit about 'ancient things' besides, he'd go halves wi' me if I'd help him dig the place up. He swore it was common land – we could be rich men, and no-one the poorer but the Crown, which could look after itself.

"I'd had a few jars by then, and the prospect looked fine through the bottom of a bottle, for I'd've had to borrow money to cover my debts soon, and eventually the General'd find out, and then ... I dared not think.

"He led me up hill and down dale, I believe to muddle me about where the place was. The snow'd started falling about midnight, and that confused the way yet more. But at last we came up this hill and he showed me a great stone half-sticking out of the earth. I recognised it at once as a barrow-stone, though I'd still no notion we were on the General's land, or I'd never ... A root of the oak had got under and lifted it up, for there was a half-foot hole beneath the snow where Pye had widened the gap.

"'Here's where I found this coin,' said he, showing me it. 'And there were two more, deeper down. But I can't get at the rest till we move the damned stone. That's your job.' He brought out a spade, and put it in my hands.

"I knew the coin was Saxon, for the General had found some like it near Rushmore, but never the grave they came from. I thought of the tomb that held such a hoard, of its history, and the still more marvellous treasures it might hide – and of the glory and wonder of being first to enter, to discover what had lain in darkness more 'n a thousand years. I cannot explain the feeling that came ower me: it was a fever, a frenzy! I'd seen men gripped by it on excavations across the

The Adventure of the Double Tomb by Katy Darby

years, but had never felt it myself, for I'd never broken ground on a new site. I was only ever a digger.

"So I dug. I dug till sweat soaked my brow and my shirt stuck, and at last I dug so far under that stone that with a mighty heave, Pye and I together just about managed to shift it a few feet so I could dig further into the hill and make a sort of tunnel to see what lay within. It was no wider than a foxhole, and I never thought even so skinny a fellow as Pye could get through, but the minute I broke the inner wall, quick as an eel he dived past me and slipped into the main chamber of the tomb, taking his lantern wi' him. I could not follow, being so much bigger – 'twould have taken hours to widen the gap enough to squeeze in.

"Lord, it was torture hearing his cries and giggles of greedy glee as he darted around inside, his ignorant gaze falling on treasures I'd gi' my eyes to see. At last he calmed, and in a high, queer voice, said we were rich men; we could share it all, a fortune! He started flinging coins up to me, saying there were more, many more, till I shouted him to stop.

"The frenzy had passed, the liquor had worn off, and the scales had fallen from my eyes. We were nowt more than looters, driven by gold-lust, and I was ashamed of myself. Pitt Rivers's faithful man, who'd had the best master and the best training, bringing disgrace on himself and destruction on a priceless piece of the past, for mere money's sake! I shouted down that I wanted no more to do wi' it. I'd report the site to the General in the morning, and we should get fair compensation, as first finders – enough to keep us both above water.

"'Are you mad?' he cried. 'We could be kings! Kings! And you would give it all away?' He cursed me roundly, trying to claw back from t' tunnel all the coins he'd flung up, and stuff 'em in his pockets. I saw what he was doing, but could not reach him, so I put my arm down far as I could and started collecting them too, to show the General.

The Adventure of the Double Tomb by Katy Darby

"'Come out of there,' I said, 'and make an honest man of yourself. 'Tis God'll judge you for robbing a tomb, not I!' I grabbed a nearby coin, and that's when he tried to stab me in t'arm. It was only a glancing blow, but I pulled back like a snake had bitten me as he struck wildly up the narrow shaft, again and again.

"'What?' I cried. 'Murder me, would you?' My mind span and my heart plummeted, for now I understood that he'd brought the knife with malice aforethought. All along, he'd meant to have me move the stone, get in himself, gather the treasure, then stab me from behind unawares. I leapt back and started heaving at the stone, to block t'tunnel so he couldn't get at me.

"Seeing this, he began to whimper, begging mercy, and at last my fury ebbed, and the awful thoughts I'd entertained withered. Still, I didn't trust that weasel an inch – if I went to tell the General what we'd found, Pye could loot the whole tomb and flee before I returned. I'd have to keep him there.

"'I'll spare you,' said I, 'on one condition. I'm putting this stone back,' (I ignored his wild pleas and cries) 'and I'll return tomorrow morning. If you'll come out then, and give up this gold like an honest fellow, we'll go together to t'General and he'll reward us handsomely, I'm sure. But,' I warned him, 'if I find a single coin on you, I'll turn you in for a grave-robber, and we'll see how well you're rewarded!"

A heaving sob escaped Livens.

"That was why he swallowed the coins," he said thickly, looking up to the black heavens as if to find forgiveness there. "So I would not find the gold in his pockets."

Holmes closed his eyes. "Of course."

"And then I stood," said Livens, "and braced myself against that great stone slab, and with a heave that near wrenched out my shoulders, I pushed it back whence it came with a doomcrack of a thud. I looked all around, but the snow had thickened greatly, and I could discern no landmarks through the flying flakes. So I noted the great oak that towered above me, the tallest for miles, to know the place again.

"When I woke wi' a start, late next evening, I knew at once something was awfully wrong. I'd meant to speak to the General that morning and now it was too late: but worse, the whole day I'd slept, it had snowed.

"I dragged myself, limbs stiff and eyes aching, to my window, and gazed with sick dread upon the transformed landscape. I knew Rushmore well, but not well enough to recognise it beneath its disguise of snow. Bushes were hills, frozen ponds flat fields ... if I didn't know the estate where I worked, how could I possibly find the barrow again? I was lost. Worse, Pye was trapped: without light, water or food he would surely starve, even if he didn't freeze.

"I stared out into the blizzard, praying for the snow to cease.

"It did not.

"Two more days that storm raged. Feet and feet of snowfall, fifty-knot winds, a storm such as the Chase had not seen in a century. And two days I gave out that I was ill in bed, instead stumbling miles in the white darkness, looking hopelessly for that tree atop that lonely hill, until all the world seemed a reeling flurry of snow. And when finally the storm stopped, I walked out into a world utterly changed. Trees and fences were blown flat, drifts piled feet high and sculpted by the wind into wild shapes, so a man would think himself in some Arctic hell.

"Nonetheless I set out again, with ice in my heart, to seek the great oak – that tree I should have seen for miles around, the only landmark to show where a buried man lay dying.

"As I walked I saw what the blizzard had wrought: torn-up saplings and flattened veterans, yet still I hoped that oak might have weathered the storm. Until I saw Rushmore's great elm; just as strong, just as mighty, and just as ancient, it'd been torn out of the pasture where for two hundred years it had stood.

"Then, I hoped no more.

The Adventure of the Double Tomb by Katy Darby

"Next day, the labourers near St. Owens's place found the fallen oak, the barrow's side-chamber laid open – and all the terrible rest you know."

Livens's eyes dulled as he finished his story. He stared emptily at his great work-worn hands as if he saw blood upon them, this accidental murderer whose guilt had compelled him, at last, to confess.

"That was why you would not enter the tomb first, of course," mused Holmes. "I thought it queer at the time."

"I knew what I should find within," said he, "and I feared to look upon that poor man's face as a sinner fears Judgment Day. I should have admitted everything then – but the General was there, and I couldn't abide him knowing what I'd done."

His hollow voice became abject: "All I beg, sirs, is that you take me away now, before I've to look him in the eye and know he knows my shame. The Sandown gaol will welcome me, I'm sure." He hung his great dark head. "'Tis only just."

I looked across at Alice, who had listened to all this in wordless dismay, and saw in her lovely eyes the shimmer of tears. She blinked, and they fell down her ashen cheeks.

"Oh George," she stammered, "I-I had no idea. I am so very sorry. For Pye, and for you. So sorry …"

He couldn't meet her eye. "Don't be, Miss Alice," he muttered. "Only, when I'm hanged, think of me as I was, and not of what I did."

Suddenly, Holmes straightened, silencing us with a violent slash of his hand. He looked around with the acute alertness of a hunting animal for prey, straining every nerve to listen.

"Hush!" he hissed. "Conceal yourselves. Someone is coming!"

Vehemently, he waved Alice toward the tomb-mouth, and we three retreated to the night-black shadow of the looming root-wall. We waited in wordless, motionless suspense as the low, creaking crunch of boots on snow grew louder and nearer, ascending the hill until I expected any moment to see the invisible walker's head crest the hedgerow.

The Adventure of the Double Tomb by Katy Darby

"At last, my proper prey!" whispered Holmes. His grey eyes kindled with ferocious triumph. "I knew I was not wrong!"

At that moment, Alice leapt up, waving wildly, just as Holmes had instructed. Her sightline was better; she must have seen the man first, and was signalling us to her aid. She began shouting: calling out like a woman drowning.

"Run!" she screamed with all the breath in her fragile body, "For God's sake, Eustace, run!"

I stood stock-still, confusion overwhelming volition, but the figure which had just appeared – a slight, lithe, blond-haired figure – dropped its thick beaver coat as a snake might shed its skin, turned, and fled down the hill with incredible speed.

Then Holmes was running too; but his legs were longer, his muscles harder, and he too shed his coat as his strides ate up the snowy ground. Steadily, he gained on his quarry, and as if gravity had briefly lightened, both men flew downhill until, at the gate, St. Owens made a mighty hurdler's leap to clear it, and Holmes launched himself forward in a still-mightier rugby-tackle to catch him. They wrestled together in the snow, struggling for dear life.

At last my fingers unfroze. I reached into my hip pocket, pulling out my revolver, and fired it once into the air. Both men stopped, shocked into momentary stillness: Alice shrieked and fell fainting to the ground, where Livens instantly ran to her aid.

I sprinted, keeping my gun raised and St. Owens marked, until I reached the pair and could clap it against his cold, sweating temple.

Holmes staggered up, panting, and regarded his enemy. "It *was* you," he said, relief battling triumph in his tone. "I knew it!"

St. Owens shook his head. "You doubted yourself, Mr. Holmes," he said, his *sangfroid* undented. "I gave you Livens: served him up on a silver platter, and just briefly, you believed me."

"No," said Holmes. "Livens only thought he had killed Pye, despite striving to save him. It was *you* who murdered him, without pity and without mercy. You were Pye's puppet-master all along. I don't know what hold you had over him; possibly you caught him poaching on your land and instead of prosecuting, you decided to use him. It was you who found the displaced barrow-stone, and the coins: enough gold to restore your fortune, to marry Alice, and in your own field, too! Or what had been, until you sold it to her father just before he called off the engagement.

"The treasure was so nearly yours – morally, you felt it *was* yours – but you could not legally get at it, and so you promised Pye half, if he would secretly help you plunder the grave: perhaps intending to murder him as he later planned to murder Livens, once the gold was safely in your hands.

"But when you and he together could not shift the stone, you sent Pye to enlist Livens. You knew of his losses on the horses; indeed, you drew my attention to them, to divert suspicion from yourself. And what a sweet, neat trick, to use your enemy's man against him! How delicious the savour of that revenge must have been, after the bitter humiliation of your broken engagement.

"For it was never Alice who wished to cast you off – it was the General all along. Your debts he might have forgiven; your gambling he would not. She took your ring from her finger, only to wear it on a chain near her heart. You exchanged secret messages through Pye for a time, but then, probably, some labourer saw him hanging about and she had to pretend he was a spying stranger. He ate your hothouse fruit and your good meat, he drank your brandy and did your bidding. But when he did not return the evening after he was meant to recruit Livens to burgle the barrow, you thought he'd either failed or betrayed you.

"First you enquired after Livens at Rushmore, to be told he was ill. So you returned to the barrow through the wild snowstorm, to see what had become of your creature. Oh, the relief he must have felt, the sheer joy at knowing he was found, when you swept the snow from the stone and knocked on it with a rock. He crawled up the tunnel and through the tiny gap, told you all that had passed, trusting you would rescue him. He would have been weak then, but not fatally so."

The Adventure of the Double Tomb by Katy Darby

Holmes looked down at the man, his eyes like grey ice. "You could have saved him, St. Owens. But instead you damned him.

"And oh, his agony, his sheer terror, when he had passed up enough coins, and you calmly told him that he had failed you, and that the price of his failure was death. Livens had not yet told Pitt Rivers of the hoard, or you would have heard it from Alice; only two other men knew your so-precious, dangerous secret. With Pye dead, Livens's silence was also assured, because he would believe himself the man's murderer. And with the coins Pye had surrendered to you, you could buy back the field from the General, and dig up what gold remained at your leisure.

"All you needed to do then, was ensure Livens could not find the barrow again; or if he found it, could not locate the entrance. So you blocked up the tiny tunnel-gap, even as the man within wept and implored you to spare him. Then you heaped snow back over the stone: it would only become better hidden the more the snowstorm raged. And then, the final, fatal touch! You took a dead branch – the tree still stood at this point, but old branches lay about – and dragged it before the stone, to further conceal your black deed.

"It was a thick branch, and made excellent camouflage. Fresh snow covered its tight-laced twigs like a blanket, but underneath it was quite sheltered from further snowfall. The temperature dropped like a stone, and the footprints you left that bloody night were frozen hard into the old snow, and protected as they were, no new fall obscured them.

"Meanwhile, Alice must know nothing. She loved you, poor child, and would have married you despite debt, dissipation and parental disapproval – but not despite murder. All you needed was the barrow to remain undisturbed. But you are not a lucky man, Mr. St. Owens, except in love. When that tree was uprooted, so too were your hopes of getting away with murder. It became a question of shifting the blame – and your scapegoat was ready-made. How could anyone prove he was *not* guilty?

The Adventure of the Double Tomb by Katy Darby

"An innocent man could have hanged for your crime, Mr. St. Owens," said Holmes, "But when Watson moves the revolver from your skull to your spine and we walk up that hill together, and Mr. Livens and Miss Lane Fox come with us as witnesses – then you will see where your guilt is written in the snow."

We walked up the hill, three of us, then five; a sombre party and a silent one. And when Sherlock Holmes found the branch and Livens and I heaved it up, underneath it was just as he had said: a perfectly preserved set of short, elegant boot-prints which told what Eustace St. Owens had done, and when, and how. It was even possible to see the marks of his naked hands in the frozen snow he had crammed against the base of the barrow-stone.

And lying forgotten beside the smothered stone, just where it had fallen all those days ago onto virgin white, lay a single golden coin.

February 1883

The Problem of Lady Gravely

By Will Murray

The last postal delivery on that cold Friday day in February of the year 1883 arrived at eight o'clock. It so happened that I approached my doorstep just as the letter carrier was about to insert the mail into the box.

I greeted him warmly, for the steadfast fellow had been making his rounds for as long as I had lived on Baker Street.

"Hello, Darcy."

"Good evening to you, Dr. Watson. Brisk night, is it not?"

"Quite bracing. But it does the blood good. Well, good night to you."

Accepting the packet of mail from Mr. Darcy, I carried it up the stairs to the first floor sitting-room, where Sherlock Holmes sat before a blazing hearth, smoking his customary briar pipe.

"Good evening, Holmes. I happened to catch the letter carrier as he made his last delivery."

Dressed in his silken dressing gown, Holmes was fussing with his pipe. That he had not taken up his black clay or cherrywood pipe

The Problem of Lady Gravely by Will Murray

told me that Holmes was not presently involved with a professional problem, for I had come to know the remarkable fellow's habits and moods quite well by this time.

"Very good," he murmured distractedly, as he applied a Lucifer to the bowl.

Going through the envelopes, I sorted them out into two lots. One I gave to Holmes. It was a collection of advertising circulars with a solitary letter from an address in Kent that I did not recognize.

Holmes accepted his portion, and began to go through it whilst I did the same once I had seated myself on the other side of the fireplace. My own mail was quickly disposed of and so I turned my attention to Holmes, who was so often the recipient of appeals for his assistance, some quite urgent.

One by one, Sherlock Holmes slipped the advertising circulars into the fire, but when he came to the letter, he sat staring at the envelope for some minutes. I noticed this and grew puzzled.

For reasons I cannot fathom, Holmes appeared reluctant to open the envelope. After taking a few puffs on his pipe, he tossed the envelope, still sealed, into the fire and watched it burn.

I was quite taken aback by this unfamiliar behavior and blurted out, "My word, Holmes! Did you just dispose of a letter without opening it?"

"I recognized the address, Watson. I am uninterested in the contents and so permanently exiled it from my sight in an appropriate fashion."

"You considered it unimportant, then?"

"I cannot say, Watson. I can only assert that opening the envelope would have led to more complications than burning it unexamined. And I dearly wished to evict the temptation to open it forevermore."

"That is so unlike you. Speaking strictly for myself, I could not contain my curiosity, and would at least have given the message a quick perusal."

The Problem of Lady Gravely by Will Murray

"It is better not to," said Holmes flatly.

I watched as the envelope curled up and blackened. It was soon consumed amid the cracking and snapping logs.

"Well," I remarked, "now you shall never know what the letter writer had to say."

"And she will never receive the courtesy of a reply. I am wholly satisfied with that outcome."

"I will not ask you for further explanation. Obviously, it is a private matter."

Sherlock Holmes shook his head slowly. "It's not what you imagine, Watson. The matter is not private so much as it is unpleasant. At least, it is not private to me, for I have no professional confidences to guard."

"Has it to do with a case?"

"Yes, one of the most confounding cases I had ever undertaken. This was before the time we first made each other's acquaintance, of course. I was new to the business of private consultations. I took my cases where I could. Word-of-mouth more than anything else brought me clients. And problems. No end of problems. But there was one problem that led to other problems that were unforeseen. I have always regretted taking on that particular client, and yet, my dear Doctor, there was lasting value in doing so."

"I should like to hear the story, if it is not inappropriate for you to tell it."

Holmes puffed his pipe thoughtfully, soon becoming wreathed in tobacco smoke. After some consideration, he took the stem from his mouth, released a fragrant cloud and stared at the dissipating haze for some while. I expected to hear a clipped answer in the negative, but my friend surprised me instead by saying, "I suppose it will do no harm to recount the tale. I will not name the client, but let us call her Lady Gravely."

"I will accept that. The story is what matters. Not the persons attached to it."

The Problem of Lady Gravely by Will Murray

"Lady Gravely came to me one afternoon and laid the following problem at my feet. The Dowager Countess of Gravely was a woman I knew by repute to be closer to the age of 50 than 20, widowed and living decently, if not comfortably. I was rather taken aback when she first entered my quarters, Watson. For she struck me as considerably youthful in appearance. She wore a veil of mourning, but her features were not heavily masked by the fine black lace. The woman was quite fair of hair and complexion, and her eyes were a rare striking shade of blue. I fancied that she pampered herself and possessed those recherché feminine wiles that permit a woman to retain her youth long after it has faded, provided that Mother Nature is of a disposition to cooperate.

"Her first words to me upon my reading her card were these, 'I fear that my daughter has run away with an untitled man.'

"'What can you tell me about the man?' I inquired.

"She looked at me with a rather disapproving expression. 'Do you not care to hear about my daughter first?'

"'If it suits you to begin there, by all means, Madame.'

"'My daughter, Corliss, is like her mother, fair of hair and rather beautiful. She has had many suitors, all of whom I considered to be acceptable. No, more than acceptable. Instead, however, she has fallen under the spell of a man I firmly hold to be beneath her station.'

"'That is unfortunate,' I told the woman. 'Now tell me about the man.'

"'He is rather tall, and I do not mean to suggest that he is without means. But it is his character that concerns me. I have been unable to discover much about his past. What I have been told, however, makes me suspicious about his truthfulness.'

"'Go on,' I invited.

"'His name is Aldace Alloway. He is an importer of some sort. Rum, tobacco, and assorted sundries. I know that he spends a great deal of time down at the London docks, gadding about here and there.'

"'Do you have any particulars?'

The Problem of Lady Gravely by Will Murray

"'I am afraid that I do not. I have heard the name of Saint Katherine Dock bandied about. But such mundane details never interested me very much.'

"'I see. When did you see your daughter last?'

"'Three days ago. She went into the City and never returned.'

"'Have you gone to the police?'

"'I did not think it necessary until today. For Corliss has friends in Mayfair. I have just come from visiting them. They inform me that she never called upon them. Naturally, I became concerned, and thought of you, and the unique and confidential service for which you are becoming known.'

"'I am flattered, Lady Gravely. But once again I must ask, why seek out my services and not those of Scotland Yard? After three days' absence, I would think their assistance is mandatory.'

"'I do not disagree, Mr. Holmes. Nevertheless, I have come to you, and only you.'

"'Very well, then. I must have a place to start, beginning with a full and complete description of this fellow Alloway. Then I must commence scouring Saint Katherine Dock."

"'Thank you, Mr. Holmes. I will be happy to pay your fee upon completion of your duty. Now as to the man, Alloway. As I told you, he is tall, dark of hair and dark of complexion, but not excessively so. I imagine the docks have darkened him. The color of his eyes is, I would say, hazel in hue.'

"Has he any distinguishing features?'

"'I would say that he is handsome, but in a rough and ready manner. His features are, frankly, Hibernian, and he possesses rather long fingers. They are the longest fingers I have ever seen on a man. He wears no ring.'

"As Lady Gravely continued her recitation, Watson, I pressed her on certain points. The appearance of the man's feet, so that I could judge his shoe size. The cut of his coat and his habitual style of clothes. The types of hats he wore. To every question I put to Lady Gravely, she responded forthrightly. I would not call her an especially keen observer, but her fund of knowledge on this man's appearance was more than satisfactory. At the end of my questioning, I had a rather complete picture of him."

"And what did you think, Holmes?" I inquired.

"That Aldace Alloway was a bit of an eccentric. The clothes that were described to me told of one type of fellow, but his hat, a John Bull topper, and other particulars, suggested quite another. It was as if his clothes did not quite match, as they should.

"After agreeing upon my fee, I put on appropriate clothing and went out to comb the docks of London. As you could imagine, Watson, this took considerable time and effort. Wherever I went, no one seemed to know of this importer, Alloway."

"Why did you not look for the woman?"

"By looking for the man, I naturally sought the woman as well. Lady Gravely had provided me with a careful description of her daughter, adding that the resemblance to herself when she was younger was quite marked, right down to her fair complexion and penetrating blue eyes. This, I believe, was more than sufficient to identify the missing woman should I run across her.

"Two weeks passed and I accomplished precisely nothing. This was early in my career, you will remember, and I was not as polished as I am now.

"At the end of two weeks, I dispatched a letter to Lady Gravely, reporting my failure to make progress and requesting an audience with her.

"By return mail, I was invited to visit her country estate. This was in Kent. I arrived the following day and was greeted by a rather awkward butler.

"While waiting for Lady Gravely to receive me, I observed all that I could. It appeared that the household was a rather modest one. There were a few servants. And, of course, there was no man of the house. Otherwise, I detected nothing out of sorts.

"Upon entering, Lady Gravely said without preamble, 'I am disappointed in you, Mr. Holmes. You have a reputation for accomplishing what you set out to do.'

"I did not take umbrage at this remark, Watson. Instead, I returned, 'I have not yet admitted defeat. I am here to gather more data.'

"'I will tell you what I am able.'

"'Are you certain that Alloway is the fellow's correct name?'

"'It is the name he gave. I did not see any reason to question it. Do you doubt that it is the truth?'

"'If Alloway is an importer, he is unknown to the London docks. That by itself is suspicious. I suspect he may not be what he purported to be.'

"'My daughter is now missing for these two weeks, Mr. Holmes. Do you think they could have sailed away together, for that is my fear?'

"'If she has not returned home, it is one of the likely possibilities. But if Aldace Alloway is not who he claims to be, the possibility ceases to be persuasive.'

"'I see.'

"'You do not seem excessively worried.'

"'I long ago resigned myself to my daughter's waywardness, Mr. Holmes. She is both incorrigible and uncontrollable. I fear that Corliss has secretly married this man and is only awaiting the proper time to return home and confess all.'

"'That is perhaps the best outcome that could be hoped for at this late date,' I told Lady Gravely. 'I think we are past the time of informing Scotland Yard.'

"'I do not feel in my heart that my daughter is in any danger. Can you not accept a mother's feelings as proof?'

"'I will consider them to be relevant, but proof they are not. Are you adamant on this point?'

"'I do not believe my daughter has come to physical harm. I wish only that she be found, and my strong feelings vindicated.'

The Problem of Lady Gravely by Will Murray

"I could see that Lady Gravely was supremely stubborn, Watson, so I pressed her on further details, and she was just as forthcoming as she had been previously.

"Whereupon, I left, fortified with what I felt was sufficient information to renew my quest. That it was doomed to failure, I did not yet suspect. Had the same circumstances come to me at a year or so later, I would not have been satisfied with the trend of Lady Gravely's cooperation."

"Why did you not consult with Scotland Yard on your own?" I asked Holmes.

"Lady Gravely enjoined me not to. I had no choice but to accede to her wishes. My reputation was merely sprouting in those days, and I could not afford to acquire the repute of being insensitive to a client's reasonable requests."

"So what did you do?"

"I expanded the compass of my search, going to the railway stations and the cab ranks, inquiring everywhere about both parties. I received certain helpful pointers, but alas, all soon petered out and proved fruitless.

"Once more, Watson, I was forced to report to Lady Gravely.

"'I think, Madam,' I told her, 'you must reconsider your reluctance to secure the help of Scotland Yard. I am not sure what more I can do for you. I have exhausted my resources without positive result.'

"'I am willing to give you another week, Mr. Holmes, if you were willing to put in the time.'

"Here, Watson, I hesitated. Although I could not anticipate results in advance—for who could?—I could not imagine achieving any positive outcome without a greater measure of luck than skill, and I much prefer to exercise the latter than be the beneficiary of the former."

"'I fear that it would do no good, Lady Gravely,' I informed her. 'If you are not willing to appeal to Scotland Yard, especially at this late date, I regret that I do not feel that I can pursue the matter any further.'

"'I had higher hopes for you, Mr. Holmes,' she said in a tone of voice I found to be vaguely insulting. I think she meant for me to take that offense, but I did not at the time comprehend why she would take that tone with me.

"Right then and there we settled the matter of my fee. And I will give Lady Gravely credit for neither wilting nor welching.

"Four days later, I received a letter from the woman. In the envelope was enclosed a note she had received from her daughter, and I read it. It ran as follows, she had gone to Scotland with this man, Alloway. A marriage had taken place. Lady Gravely objected to this development, of course, and wished me to fetch her daughter back to Kent, but with the proviso that Aldace Alloway not be permitted to accompany us.

"I read this letter carefully twice and something about it I found perturbing. I could not put my finger on it, Watson.

"I wrote the woman directly that I was pleased that she had heard from her daughter at last, but I did not feel it was my duty to go to Scotland and bring her back to London. She was a married woman now and had made a choice. There was nothing in the letter that struck me as suspicious. But arrogating to separate a newly married woman from her husband seemed to me a fool's errand.

"Lady Gravely wrote back and asked me to reconsider. But I declined her handsome offer to go to Scotland and at the very least determine that her daughter was in a safe position. I did remind her that the authorities in Aberdeen could do that for her.

"I did not hear from Lady Gravely for nearly a month after that. When I did, the news was shocking. Lady Gravely solemnly informed me that her daughter had died in Aberdeen. The circumstances were at that time yet unknown. Her body had been discovered, and it was in wretched condition.

"Good Lord!" I cried out.

The Problem of Lady Gravely by Will Murray

"As you can imagine, Watson, this came as a distinct shock to me. I was quite unsettled by it. And so did not answer Lady Gravely's letter for three days. But when I did, I conveyed my sincere condolences, for what else was there for me to do?

"The next communication was to beseech me to investigate what Lady Gravely believed to be her daughter's murder. My dear Watson, I felt I had no choice in the matter. So I once more took up Lady Gravely's now-fallen standard, as it were. I agreed to go to Aberdeen."

"What did you discover there?"

"Stark murder, Watson. Nothing less. The facts were sordid, and undeniable. A woman's body had been found floating in the River Dee, yet her body had been burned most frightfully. Unquestionably, here was a murder. The deceased was identified only by certain jewelry on her person. Of Alloway, there was no sign. I was obliged to accompany the shrouded body back to London. The burial was private, for the scandal was too much for Lady Gravely to bear.

"And so the matter rested for a considerable number of months."

"I take it that the authorities in Aberdeen made no progress in their investigation?"

"None at all, Watson. My impression of the Aberdeenshire constabulary was that of a cohort of purblind gropers stumbling over obvious facts and entertaining theories that advanced nothing except their shared illusion of an investigation. Since I had no standing in Scotland, for I was little known even in London in those days, I could not pursue the matter, not even out of curiosity. The Aberdeen authorities wanted nothing to do with me, whom they considered to be not much more than a meddler."

"Pity."

"Then came the day when I read in the morning *Times* of Lady Gravely's marriage. This was in the month of September. Naturally, I read the notice and I was quite surprised to discover that Lady Gravely herself had married a man some 25 years younger than herself."

"Such a union is not unheard of," I pointed out.

"Not unheard of, Watson, but certainly peculiar. And the man she married was an untitled commoner."

"Such things happen from time to time."

"It was that simple yet arresting fact that caused me to review in my mind the entire body of the affair. Only then, Watson, did I begin to notice that the things I thought were simply odd were, in fact, out of place. Alarmingly out of place."

"Kindly enumerate them."

"Lady Gravely's remarkably youthful appearance was the first thing. Her emotional coolness all through the case, starting with her daughter's disappearance, which stretched and stretched out in time, only to conclude in a murder. She took it all in admirable stride."

"I cannot think of another mother who would behave in such a reserved manner."

"I am sure," replied Holmes. "It was at that point, simply to satisfy a growing suspicion, that I decided to investigate the Gravely household. I began by speaking to local cab men, carriage drivers, and other tradesmen in the neighborhood, and I learned several things of a concerning nature.

"The first was that the household staff had been dismissed the week before Lady Gravely first paid me a call. They were replaced by two persons, a butler and a maid. The other situations were not filled.

"Secondly, there was some confusion about when the daughter was last seen. Of course, this was several months later and memories could not be relied upon. But some were certain that the daughter had been seen in Kent *after* Lady Gravely had reported her missing to me. I also came to understand that Lady Gravely herself had become something of a recluse over the period following the death of Lord Gravely, and was herself rarely seen in public.

"This caused me to reconsider and review the entirety of the affair. Take the manner in which Lady Gravely described her daughter's paramour. From the apparel described to me, I imagined an eccentric fellow. But upon reflection, it occurred to me that I was merely handed a random collection of articles of clothing unrelated to any living personality."

"That places an entirely different complexion on the question," I agreed.

"Indeed. Bear in mind that at no time had I ever heard a whisper of a man named Aldace Alloway. He might have been a phantom. He might not have ever existed. And if he never existed, then Lady Gravely's daughter could not have run off with him."

"I will admit that is logical. But I do not see where you are going, friend Holmes."

"Be patient, Watson, for I will soon arrive at my destination. To continue, I made inquiries by letter to the authorities in Aberdeen and learned that it was their belief that the body found burned in their city encountered its doom several weeks *before* Lady Gravely assured me that she had last seen her daughter."

"Astonishing!"

"Do you now see where I am bound, Watson?"

"I perceive that the circumstances are exceedingly suspicious. Are you saying that Lady Gravely somehow contrived to have her own daughter murdered?"

"Oh, Watson, sometimes you are impossible. No, that is not where the facts led me."

"Well, then I do not see where you are going with your narrative. Unless you mean to suggest that Lady Gravely murdered her own daughter."

"Not at all. That is not even remotely possible."

"Well, surely you admit that it is not *impossible!*" I ejaculated.

The Problem of Lady Gravely by Will Murray

"It is quite impossible, Watson, and for this reason: Lady Gravely's daughter was not murdered. The burnt body belonged to Lady Gravely herself."

"Then who was the woman who came to you pretending to be Lady Gravely?"

Sherlock Holmes fixed me with an eye that was close to scornful. Then it dawned on me. Or perhaps I should say instead that the awful truth struck like a silent thunderbolt.

"Lady Gravely's daughter murdered her mother and then took her place!"

Holmes paused to relight his pipe. "Not exactly, Watson. I suspect the man whom the daughter subsequently married was the killer. But that is only supposition. There is no question that Lady Gravely's daughter, Corliss, arranged the entire diabolical scheme. The mother had relatives in Aberdeen. She had gone to visit them. During that sojourn, she was murdered by an agent of her daughter so that said daughter, as the sole surviving heir, could take over the household and marry the man she desired, for the portion of the story asserting that Lady Gravely objected to the marriage was all too true. The foundation of the case is as simple and as cold-blooded as that. The body was first burned and, after a suitable interval during which decomposition barred easy recognition, set adrift in the Dee to obliterate all possibility of a correct identification, but at a point that assured its eventual discovery, which was an important element of the overall scheme. For without a body, inheritance became difficult, if not impossible. The Dowager Countess of Gravely no longer lived, yet her social existence continued in the body of her conscienceless daughter, unsuspected by the good people of Kent, who had long ago learned that Lady Gravely preferred her own company to that of others."

"Astounding! It beggars belief to accept that such an audacious crime could be executed with no one the wiser."

"With the household staff replaced, and the new Lady Gravely observing a strict period of private mourning, there was no one in a social position of noticing what had happened. No other relatives lived in the vicinity of Kent. What few friends Lady Gravely had, they seemed unable to pierce the wall of solitude erected during her widowhood. Seemingly, the woman had no circle of friends sufficiently intimate to take note of her absence."

"So what did you do about this?"

"What could I do? I had no standing in Scotland and very little in London. Who would believe me? What proof had I? The body had been buried, and to disinter it would require a court order from the police, or a formal request from the family. The new Lady Gravely would hardly consent to that. No, Watson, it was a dead end. I could accomplish nothing."

"Quite regrettable," I observed. "Did you attempt to dig any further?"

"I had no solid ground in which to insert my spade. Reluctantly, I came to the conclusion that there was no way forward. Even today, I have maintained a judicious silence about the matter, even with Scotland Yard. And I enjoin you to preserve that silence."

"If that is your wish. So that was the end of it until this letter arrived?"

"No, for there have been other letters of appeal from time to time. I have ignored all of them. My suspicion is that Lady Gravely's conscience is bothering her."

"And well it should!"

"But it is also possible that she suspects that I have over time come to see through her charade. And she fears that I will expose her, especially now that I enjoy such good standing with Scotland Yard."

"Surely, she would know that you would never accept a bribe to preserve her secret."

"I do not know what the present Lady Gravely contemplates, Watson. But among the possibilities that have crossed my mind is to lure me to my destruction through some artful subterfuge, and thus ensure my complete and utter silence. I cannot have that."

"I take your point, Holmes. Under the circumstances, burning her letters of entreaty is most assuredly the best course of action."

"I wish it were otherwise. But the frequency with which these letters sometimes come, along with reports in the newspapers of troubles in her household, owing to terrible domestic quarrels fueled by liquor, suggest to me that her cunning mind may be crumbling under the weight of her terrible crime."

"If so, she has earned her own undoing. And I imagine you learnt a valuable lesson so early in your career."

Sherlock Holmes nodded sagely. "My chief error, Watson—and I will admit to many lesser errors such as failing to question why the woman first came to me with her features veiled by black lace, as if in mourning—was in accepting my client at face value and not being skeptical of her story from the beginning. I had early on fallen into the distressing habit of seeing my clients as the protagonists, as it were, in their personal dramas, and only questioning them in so far as needed in getting to the particulars of the problem they presented to me.

"I may also have been gulled by the sympathetic appeal of a woman, particularly a mother in distress. A cold appraisal of Lady Gravely would have caused me to question her lack of deep emotion, as well as her failure to see the matter as urgent. Even after the body had been found, her emotions were tempered, restrained and methodical. Too much so."

"Why did you think the treacherous woman hired you in the first place?"

"Initially, because she did not want to involve the police, but wished to create a chain of circumstances that would absolve her of any suspicion once the Metropolitan Police were brought into the case, as they must be. But I imagine that the false Lady Gravely had a secondary reason to keep appealing to me. Although my reputation in those days was rather modest, it was growing. I believe she took the risks that she did to keep me from becoming interested in the case from a point of view that was other than sympathetic to her own."

"I see," said I. "Lady Gravely was misusing you right from the start, believing that a private person such as yourself might eventually take an interest in the matter, whereas the police would hesitate to pry into affairs where suspicions had not gathered too darkly."

"Perhaps guilt and the fear of discovery both combined to impel her to continually lure me back into the game. Underneath it all, I believe she was not of sound mind. What daughter, capable of murdering her own mother in such a dispassionate and contrived way, could be?"

I cast my glance at the hearth fire, which now showed no traces of the burnt letter.

"I remain curious as to what the wicked woman wants from you at this late date."

"I know not, and I do not care," stated Holmes. "The matter is beyond remedy. I could bring the issue to the attention of Inspector Lestrade, but he would yet be in possession of no justifiable evidence to investigate a murder which took place in Scotland. The dead are dead and buried. The perpetrator has managed to perpetuate her imposture, and if she is liable to face justice, it will not be in this world."

"If what you say about the crumbling of her mind is true," I pointed out, "perhaps justice is exerting its proper due day by day."

"I should like to believe so, Watson," murmured Sherlock Holmes, knocking the dottle out of his briar. "I should like to believe so...."

March 1883

The Case of the Injured Orator

By Dr. Martin Hill Ortiz

It was at the dawn of spring in 1883 and Holmes and I had just completed an adventure that had drawn us off to Brighton. Resolving that case tested Holmes's athletic skills as much as it did his mental prowess, culminating in a battle that allowed my friend to demonstrate his mastery of cudgels, defeating the former Spanish champion of singlesticks, Desiderio Acha.

I was partaking of a plate of eggs and ham at 221B Baker Street. Holmes, often erratic in his eating habits, ignored his breakfast, instead pacing about the floor and glancing out the window.

My attention, meanwhile, was engaged by a different Holmes: the American physician, Oliver Wendell Holmes, also renowned as a polymath, poet, and scholar. He had written several lively collections of essays, and I was entranced by one appropriately titled, *The Autocrat at the Breakfast-Table.*

Glancing up, I saw my friend halt in his tracks. A smile overtook his lean face. "Watson?" he said.

The Case of the Injured Orator by Dr. Martin Hill Ortiz

I grunted to let him know he had my ear.

"A curious item appeared in yesterday's *Evening Tribune*," he said. I perked up. Perhaps he had come across a quandary worthy of scrutiny. "Did you by chance read about the young man at Speaker's Corner?" For those readers residing far outside London, the Speaker's Corner is an area in Hyde Park where all manner of public debate and free speech are sanctioned.

"I cannot always match your stamina, Holmes. After returning at one in the morning, I made a quick rendezvous with my mattress."

Holmes seized the paper from the bureau top and opened it to page three. I set aside my book.

"A short piece," he announced and then read. "This afternoon, a young man in Hyde Park took to the soap-box proclaiming that his father was a murderer. Some nearby Irish radicals, the recent death of Karl Marx, their messiah, undoubtedly stirring their emotions, attacked the speaker, thrusting him to the ground and stomping on his leg."

"That is, indeed, a singular story," I admitted, "even though it is scarce on details."

"And from it, I derived several inferences," Holmes said. "A bit less rigorous than my usual standards, but no matter of immediate consequence rested upon their shoulders.

"First, the young victim was well-dressed. The followers of Marx are not so aggrieved by an orator shouting murder who is sloven in jacket and trousers. Second, in most instances, the *Tribune* has no reticence regarding naming names when the names add to the sensation and sales. Therefore, the identity of that well-dressed man must have been so prominent as to stifle their indelicate leanings."

"Or they were unable to learn who it was," I offered.

"That is unlikely. A man willing to publicly accuse his father of murder would covet the coverage of such news."

"A reasonable conclusion," I conceded, gracious in part because this was purely a conjectural argument.

The Case of the Injured Orator by Dr. Martin Hill Ortiz

"Third, the police have rejected his case. No man of privilege would resort to Speaker's Corner if there were authorities who would listen to him. Fourth, I determined he would come visit me. Those with privilege often believe they have a special license to my services, and this man is a desperate sidewalk shouter who has exhausted all other recourse."

"All that follows to reason," I said, nodding.

My friend squared off to face me. He had that smile of the devil's fiddler which told me there was more. "After his injury, he was fixed with a starch bandage around his right foot and a plaster of Paris splint over his right shin."

"Holmes!" I cried. "I was perfectly fine with your previous speculations, but how could you determine his wounds and their dressings?"

"Ah, my dear Watson. The reason I presented this story to you at this moment is because I saw outside the window a finely dressed young man step out of a hansom in front of our residence. I could make out a rigid bulge beneath his right trouser leg and flexion at his right ankle. He wore no shoe on that foot, undoubtedly, his shoe would not fit. Furthermore, while I was recounting the above, Mrs. Hudson, being of a soft heart, allowed the injured gentleman to pass. Now, I hear the thump of a cane, the softer tap of a swaddled foot, and the sturdy footfall of a healthy leg ascending our stairs."

In all fairness, I might have also heard, if I had not focused my listening on Holmes's discourse.

Mrs. Hudson spoke from the top of the steps, saying, "Let me announce you." Her shuffling feet came to our door, followed by a rap. "Mr. Holmes? Doctor? Are you decent?"

"I am in my best dressing gown," my friend said. "Please, show the gentleman inside."

The door parted and a young man on the shy side of twenty years hobbled in. Immaculately dressed, he was somewhat wan. Deep worry etched his face and he trembled with agitation. I stood and presented the tray with the scant remains of my breakfast to Mrs. Hudson, saying, "Mrs. Hudson, if you would please. . ."

Holmes took a seat.

"I'm sorry, I didn't first ask you if it was a suitable time for a visitor," she said, accepting my tray, "but this gentleman went straight to the stairs, and I couldn't intervene with his progress on account of his game leg and all."

"It is of no concern," Holmes said, waving a dismissive hand. "I would have invited him up, regardless of his forwardness. Mrs. Hudson, could you kindly remove my plate? I fear digestion might interfere with my cerebrations."

"A good meal wasted," she said, sniffing. She placed his full tray over mine and backed out of the door. She closed it with an assertive thud.

The visitor set his cane forward for balance, then leaned toward me and extended his hand.

"Wilton Trevelyan," he said, "of the Berkshire Trevelyans." We shook.

"John Watson," I said. "And this is Sherlock Holmes." My friend tipped his head. "Please, take a seat."

"Thank you." He dropped into our wickerwork chair with a pained sigh. "My injury is fresh, and yet already I find my good leg twinging with cramps."

"Employ the cane on the side opposite to your wound," I advised.

He raised his brows, then nodded. "Oh, yes, you are a doctor."

Holmes studied the young man, undoubtedly cataloguing that assortment of details that often fails to register on less-trained eyes. He said, "The Berkshire Trevelyans. Your family name once came up during an unrelated case. As I recall, you are the masters of Lessington Manor and are renowned for wealth, power, and statesmanship. Your home possesses a cellar with a greater assemblage of French wines than any other outside the Continent, some selections going back to

Napoleon's day. Your grandfather, Charles Trevelyan, bred four winners at the Royal Ascot."

"And three more winners at the Derby in Epsom Downs," Wilton said. A blush of pride spread over his cheeks.

That ruddiness bloomed into a fiery red when Holmes said, "I know why you are here."

"Then you've heard of my father's foul deed!"

"I know you claim he is a murderer."

"And I would shout it to the heavens!" the young man said excitedly, clutching the chair's arms and leaning as though to leap from his seat. "But who is there to heed my cries? The papers have feared printing his name lest they be sued for liable. All the world fears my father's reach, but not I."

"Pray tell, who was your father's victim?"

"My older brother, Charles the Third. Everyone called him Charlie. In January of last year, on the day before his eighteenth birthday, my father shot him dead."

I shuddered. I don't know why his declaration shook me; murder is oft *une affaire du famille.*

"Certainly, an inquest was performed," my friend said.

"A sham! As was the police investigation. My father has the power to control the authorities!"

"All the proofs swept away in a conspiracy? That is not a convincing argument for fact."

I described the young man as wan. Yes, he needed sun, but flames roiled inside him.

"Facts? You wish for facts? How do these suit you? The official inquest verdict said that the killing was a robbery gone amiss. My brother's bedroom rests on the upper floor of our manor. His window was shattered, the police say, to gain entrance. Yes, there is an ivy-covered trellis that can be climbed to the site. But why would a robber seek entrance on the upper floor? How is it this intruder happened upon one of the few rooms occupied? Why would he kill my brother and then steal nothing?"

"If *why's* pervade an argument, you have questions, not evidence," Holmes stated. "The thief may have been seeking a less-likely-to-be-guarded entrance and found himself surprised by his encounter."

"Mr. Holmes, save your dismissals until I have fully finished."

"And you, young man, should moderate your zeal until after you have more completely convinced me that you have a case." A moment of silence passed. "Proceed."

"Charlie's execution happened in the hours before dawn on a Friday. The whole of the investigation took place that day, and he was interred in the church graveyard shortly before midnight. Indeed, although my father is a faithful member of the Church of England, in the rush, no funeral service was provided. My father, my mother, and one of Charlie's classmates were the only attendants at the burial."

"That is telling," Sherlock said. "The classmate's name?"

"Arthur Reynolds."

"He may be worth contacting. Where were you at the time of the incident?"

"Incident? You call it a mere incident? Even the inquest declared it to be murder!"

Holmes did not respond to this provocation, instead allowing the young man to collect himself.

"I was away at school. After being notified of Charlie's murder, I managed an early Saturday train. I had already planned to be there that weekend for his birthday."

"You were absent for the police investigation and the burial," Holmes said. Before the young man could respond, he added, "That was a statement, not a question. Who discovered the body?"

"According to his testimony at the inquest, my father. He and, indeed, the whole house were awakened by the report of a gun firing. My father arrived first and allowed no others to enter Charlie's bedroom, he claimed, because of the horrific scene. He ordered Mr. Tate, our butler, to go to town and return with the constable. Not even my mother was allowed into the bed chamber."

Holmes tented his fingers and leaned his chin over their peak. He said, "If a robber were ever seen escaping down the halls, there would be no question of the guilty party. So, the robber was said to have escaped from the same window that he entered?"

"Yes. If he had entered the hall after the gunshot, he would have been seen by several before making the passage to the stairs."

"Fascinating. Your brother was Charles the Third. Charlie. So, your father is Charles, the Second."

"Yes."

"It is your contention that Charles, the Second, merely claimed he was the first to respond, when the whole time he was in the room?"

"That is my conclusion. No one saw him in the hall answering the gunshot."

"And yet the others responded with near immediacy to the sound?"

"Correct. And, Mr. Holmes, I know this is the sort of detail you covet. According to the inquest, a glass pane was broken in my brother's window allowing the intruder to reach in and unlatch the lock."

"So you have told me."

"However, the constable testified that he found shards of glass in the dirt below."

"Yes," Holmes said, "I suspected that there would be."

"If some scofflaw broke the window from the outside, wouldn't the glass fall into the room? And if my father staged the break-in, wouldn't the glass fall outwards?"

"I have already concluded that the robbery was staged," Holmes said.

I was beginning to be won over by the youth's arguments. Holmes had a self-satisfied turn to his lips. Had he also concluded that the father must be the murderer?

"What motive did your father have for killing your brother, his son?" Holmes inquired.

"In that lies my strongest piece of evidence," Wilton said, slapping his plaster cast. "Let me draw you the picture. My brother Charlie and I were close to our grandfather, the first Charles Trevelyan. He was an illustrious man, perhaps you have heard of him."

"I have," Sherlock said.

"You need to understand, my grandfather and my father had a falling out, one so severe that my grandfather virtually disinherited him, his only child."

"This is becoming more and more intriguing," Holmes said.

"I agree," I blurted.

"My grandfather left all his considerable fortune to be divided between Charlie and myself. My father, and by extension my mother, receive fifteen thousand pounds a year stipend to support us and the manor until we turned eighteen at which time we were to each receive one-half of the wealth and estate."

"And you said your brother died one day before he turned eighteen," I remarked. "One day before coming into his inheritance."

"One-half of a vast fortune. And now all shall come to me."

Holmes clucked his tongue. "I hazard the reason for your recent and most elevated engrossment by your brother's death, an event which had occurred over one year past, is that you, yourself, are about to turn eighteen," he said.

"Tomorrow – if I survive until my birthday. My grandfather's will did not expressly forbid my father's future claims. I fear my father intends to murder me and ply the courts to lay claim to the whole of the inheritance."

"Ah! Now I understand the quickening of your nerves," Sherlock said.

The Case of the Injured Orator by Dr. Martin Hill Ortiz

"Certainly, the simplest of solutions is to go into a safe hiding," I recommended.

"That was my plan, but then I received a note." Wilton took a half-sheet of paper from his pocket. He read it out loud. "'If you want to learn all, meet me at your brother's grave at 9 p.m. on Friday.' That's tonight."

"Was there a signature or initials?" I asked.

"None. But what aroused my wonderment even more than the bizarre summons is that the note includes these three figures: YØ8. Five years ago, Charlie and I were there at my grandfather's deathbed. He spoke to us. His last words were: 'Why not eight?'"

"Why not eight?" I echoed.

"I believe he meant to say more and not leave his words to mystery, but at that moment he seized up, never to speak again."

"Ha!" Holmes cried. "You saved the most fascinating detail for the last! Do not go into journalism, or your editor will surely have you by your throat."

"Why not eight?" I repeated. "Whatever does that mean?"

"My brother and I had speculated about that very thing. My grandfather bred seven winning horses. Perhaps he was encouraging us to follow in his field?"

"Pooh," Holmes cried. "It was hardly so mundane a matter."

"How did the writer of the note know to include such a message? I have never told another of my grandfather's words. I believed them to be Charlie's and my own personal puzzle. He must have shared the secret. Perhaps with my father. Perhaps my father set down this summons and included those characters to lure me to the cemetery in a plan to finish me off."

"May I see the note?" Sherlock said. The young man handed it over.

The great detective studied it for several moments, front and back. He took a brief sniff. "Fine stationery, suitable for an invitation.

A billet page, creased and torn in half. No particular odour. Is this your father's writing?"

"No," Wilton said, "not unless it is disguised."

"Which it may well be. Your brother could have conveyed 'YØ8' to your parents, his friends, or a dozen others. The extent of his communications is something we can no longer ascertain."

"This case presents so many curious mysteries, it makes my head spin," I confessed.

"So many? I count a mere two," Holmes said, rising to his feet. "Mr. Trevelyan, I recommend that you reside at St. George's Hotel for safekeeping for the next two days. I know and trust the hotelier, and he will be certain to keep your stay a secret. A most lonely birthday, but perhaps we can persuade Mrs. Hudson to deliver you her fine chocolate loaf cake. In the meantime, come with me, Watson – that is, if you are up for another adventure so soon."

"But, of course."

"Excellent. Mr. Trevelyan, Watson and I shall visit your family estate and, if need be, we will make the rendezvous at your brother's grave."

"Mr. Holmes, do you truly believe you can find justice for Charlie?"

"I already know who killed your brother."

"Is that possible?" the young man cried. "Do you recognize the evidence as proof against my father?"

Holmes raised a finger to his lips. "Tut-tut, I cannot yet point out the perpetrator, not without a proper confirmation. Beyond that, there are two other vexing questions that I hope to clear up."

"Mr. Holmes. You are a god-send."

"Am I? I fear my findings will bring you much anguish."

"It is an anguish I already feel."

Holmes said to me, "Start packing for a weekend's outing." Then he addressed young Trevelyan. "I will require two items. First, the directions to Charlie's grave. Cemetery location and the pathways;

we will be searching for it well past sundown. Second, does your family or household know of your crusade against your father?"

"No. I have kept it quiet to continue my investigations. It is not until now and in London that I have solicited publicity."

"Excellent," said Holmes. "You will write a letter that introduces Dr. Watson and I as wine connoisseurs. I will present that to your father, or if he is not there, to Tate, your butler. Contrive for us some aliases, I certainly don't want our identities to be readily revealed."

"Any sort of pseudonym?"

"Something with the odour of aristocrats. I could invent one, but I wouldn't want to select a last name with which your family is too familiar. I trust your name and signature will be enough to allow us access to your family manor?"

"It should," Wilton said. "The butler, Tate, is an agreeable fellow and giving tours of the cellar is a passion of my father. But that will not provide you with free-run of the estate or entry into my brother's room."

"Let me be concerned with those matters," Holmes said.

And with that, we placed a few clothing items and miscellany into a carpet bag, along with the ever-important tobacco pouch and pipe.

We took the one o'clock train to Reading, where we hired out a brougham, paying the driver for the trip and to wait at our call while we visited the Lessington Manor. All along the passage, Holmes resisted my efforts to be forthcoming and share his conclusions.

"Trust me, Watson. To air my thoughts would be premature. Besides I want you to be considering the evidence with an open mind, recognizing clues that I by some small chance might otherwise overlook, my mind already being so much convinced."

"So, there still exists a prospect that you are wrong?"

"Distant and near to fading."

I pored over Wilton's narrative in my mind, desperate to wring out some certainties from a thick fog of mystery. If Holmes had already had enough evidence to come to a conclusion, then the only possibility was that Charles Trevelyan, the father, must be the murderer. Then I happened upon a notion. "Holmes!"

"What is it?"

"I have a thought! The butler's name is Tate. Perhaps the grandfather's last words were 'Why not *Tate?*"

"Admirable, my dear Watson," Holmes said. "You are truly applying a sense of imagination to the facts! Such reasoning will serve you well in many of our future cases. However, in this instance you are completely wrong. Why not Tate? I am already aware of what the last words mean and how, years later, they initiated Charlie's demise."

I was flabbergasted – he knew the meaning of 'Why not eight?' I was also a bit humbled by my failed attempt at thinking like Holmes. I kept quiet for the last several minutes of our journey.

It was mid-afternoon when we arrived at Lessington Manor. The great house formed a dominating presence on the hilltop where it was set: It could well have been a palace. Three floors tall, it had towers at both corners. A full fifteen sets of windows crossed each floor. The upper floors were set high above the ground floor and, even with a trellis for a thief to climb, to access such an entrance represented an alpine feat.

The gardens were freshly tilled, prepared for spring planting.

After a tug of a rope and a ring of its bell, a solid-looking man in his middle forties answered the door.

"Hello," Holmes said. "From young Wilton's description, you must be Tate, the butler."

"Indeed, sir. How may I be of service?" Tate asked. Holmes proffered the letter of introduction and Tate eyed it over. "Mr. Buford Alden?" he said.

"That is I," I responded.

The Case of the Injured Orator by Dr. Martin Hill Ortiz

"And I am Sir Jeremy Roonce," Holmes said with a nod.

"Gentlemen. Although Master Trevelyan does very much enjoy giving tours of his cellar, he is indisposed as of this moment, having spent hours labouring in the greenhouse."

"Are you advising us to return another time?" I queried.

"By no means," the butler said. "Mr. Trevelyan always enjoys the visits of fellow wine enthusiasts. I was merely offering the reason why you must wait. Follow me." As we entered the foyer, Tate spoke to another, possibly a footman, "Tell Mr. Trevelyan he has wine guests, and present him this letter from his son." The footman took the note.

Tate then led us to a parlour and bade us to sit in a pair of plush velvet chairs with a small round table set between. The ceilings must have been fifteen feet in height. An ornate tapestry covered the wall behind us: a scene of a fox hunt. Across from us was a dour painting of the venerable baronet, Charles Trevelyan I, 1806 - 1878. I could see some of Wilton in his features.

"Near how long do you suppose it to be?" Holmes asked the butler.

"I cannot foretell my master's schedule, but typically fifteen minutes. He knows you are here, and your wait will be pleasant. We should have a savoury vintage for sampling on its way."

After a few moments passed, a bell beside a dumbwaiter tinkled and the butler attended its call. When he drew up the cover, it revealed a bottle of burgundy, already breathing, and a pair of wine glasses.

"Mr. Trevelyan has sent this from the stock in his room."

Tate brought it to our table, set down the glasses and presented to us the label, a Château Lynch-Bages, '75. I know little of wines, and yet I have heard of the superiority of their vineyards.

My friend took one look and exclaimed, "This will not do!"

"Mr. . . . Roonce!" I cried, taking a moment to remember his name.

The Case of the Injured Orator by Dr. Martin Hill Ortiz

"Sir!" Tate said, bridling. "My master's offering does not deserve such an offense."

"You have the finest cellar in England," Holmes said. "I demand a Bourgogne '68."

"Sir!" The manservant was clearly ruffled.

"I will pay double its cost," Holmes said with an aristocratic sniff, "and a sovereign for your inconvenience."

"Your demand is highly irregular."

"Go! Make haste. Do not offend your guests!" Holmes whisked the man away.

The moment the butler exited the room, I cried, "Holmes. I have never known you to show such rudeness to a host."

He leaned toward me to confide, "With any luck, my gesture will circumvent the need for a long and tedious hunt."

"You sent the butler out to allow us a time to explore while alone?" I queried.

"No." Holmes sampled his burgundy. "Quite flavourful. I wish I had the time to properly enjoy it." He proceeded to a writing desk where he scribbled out a note.

"You cannot inform me of your plan?" I asked.

"Soon, Watson, soon."

I sipped my wine, relishing its fine flavour. We spent several minutes in silence until Tate returned.

"I do not know the price, sir," the butler said, passing over a bottle. "I shall take that up with my master. You are free to open it and fill the glass yourself." He set down a cork-screw. "I will be speaking with my employer about your brazen demands." He strode out of the room.

"Let's hope that Charles Trevelyan, Jr. is still idling in his chambers," Holmes said. He took the corkscrew and briefly scratched its tip against the wine bottle label. With this done, he took the full bottle and the note he had written setting it in the dumbwaiter. He hauled the freight up and tinkled the bell.

The Case of the Injured Orator by Dr. Martin Hill Ortiz

"There!" Holmes said with a bit of triumph. "If I am correct, and if this shaft is a decent conduit for sound, we shall soon hear a reaction." After a moment, a cry rang out.

"I achieved the result I had hoped for," Holmes said. "Come, Watson, we haven't much time. I do not desire an unpleasant confrontation. We must leave." He was rushing to the door before I had time to get to my feet.

Once we were ensconced within the brougham, Holmes called to the driver, "To the telegraph office! Quickly!" With a snap of the reins, the horses commenced speeding to a lively trot.

I turned to my friend and said, "Have you lost your mind?"

"My dear Watson. By now my unorthodox methods should have earned a parcel of your trust." He clapped his hands as though in triumph. "Have Tate and his master hurried out on the grounds to gain a glimpse of us?"

I looked out the back window of the brougham to witness a pair of men rushing down the front steps. "The gentleman with Tate seems rather frantic."

A smile of self-satisfaction grew over Holmes. "Let me explain to you my reasoning and actions in this matter."

"It is past time that you do."

Holmes's face tightened. Only now did I realize that he was holding inside such agitation. "Oh, Watson. We have before us a terrible bit of tragedy. If, as Wilton claimed, his father was the murderer that would be horrific in its own right. Inasmuch as he was covering up for someone else, it is still awful."

So many questions crowded my head. Even before he could go into pointing out the murderer, one puzzlement was bothering me foremost and I had to ask, "Why did you demand that bottle of wine, scratch it, and then send it up to Mr. Trevelyan?"

"A provocation. I had to know whether he recognized its significance. I altered the bottle so that it bore the cipher YØ8. I took the bottle of '68 Bourgogne and hollowed out the number six so that it could look like a zero. It was to let him know that his guest was aware of the cypher and its meaning.

"When I first heard Wilton speak his grandfather's last words, the solution formed instantly in my mind, out of association with the mansion's cellars. He told his grandsons, 'Wine ought-eight.' With a wine-cellar going back to Napoleon, Trevelyan intended to instruct his grandchildren to seek out a bottle of wine from the year 1808. Even with his magnificent collection, such an item would probably be unique."

"What great consequence could there be in a wine?"

"The bottle was emptied, I am certain. Something else was set inside. The baronet had intended to say more, to direct his grandchildren straightaway to the bottle and its secrets, but he seized up and soon perished. Charlie, Charles the Third, only realized the true meaning and sought out the bottle near the time of his eighteenth birthday."

"Wine ought-eight. What did he find inside that bottle? And what was in the note you sent to his father?"

"In my note I advised him to meet us at his son's grave at 9 p.m."

"He was not the one who wrote the first note?"

"I suspected not and now I am certain."

"Holmes, what was in the bottle?"

"Some items that led to Charlie's death," my friend said. "I recognized who killed Charlie from the moment Wilton told me about the burial." A weariness settled over his face. *"Felo de se,"* the words came out as a hoarse whisper.

Although I am a physician and I have studied Latin, the immediate import of that phrase escaped me. Perhaps my mind was too firmly set elsewhere: They struck my ears as nonsense syllables. And then, recognizing their meaning I slumped in my cab seat and tilted my head back. "Suicide."

The Case of the Injured Orator by Dr. Martin Hill Ortiz

"Until July this past year," Holmes said, "the Church of England refused to provide burial services to those who committed 'the crime' of suicide. All interments for such perpetrators had to take place between nine p.m. and midnight. The strange funeral arrangements pointed to the hand behind Charlie's death."

"Parliament changed those restrictions," I said. "I remember reading about the new law in the papers."

"Perhaps Charles the Second, with his great influence, had a hand in that change."

"It being suicide," I said, "and with all that took place after, I suppose the father was in the room at the time. He saw his son shoot himself."

Holmes nodded. "That would explain why no one saw him in the hall. He was probably there at the moment trying to sway his son's determination and to stay his hand. After Charlie discharged the fatal shot, his father covered it up. Out of fear of a scandal? Maybe. Or else he sought to spare the feelings of his wife and Wilton. I believe the constable was complicit in the pretense. The faking of the robbery was clumsy, but the father required all the testimony he could in favor of the invented story.

"Out of a need to unburden his soul, or because he believed he could confide in a man of the cloth, he went on to tell the local parish clergyman. I suspect Charles regretted his honesty. His words resulted in the invocation of the rules regarding burying those who took their own lives."

"Who wrote the note to Wilton regarding the meeting at the graveyard?"

"That is the one remaining mystery," Holmes said. "I have several suspects in mind. Perhaps the mother, perhaps Tate, but I lean to another."

"Could it not have been the father?"

"If it were the father, he would have had a different reaction to my note. Besides, the selection of the cemetery tells me the person is an outsider. Otherwise, why not tell Wilton in his home? No, I most suspect the one outsider who attended the funeral, the classmate, Arthur Reynolds. But it could also be anyone who knew the code and the contents of the bottle, the secret that drove the young Charles to suicide."

"Which leaves the question: what was in the bottle that provoked Charlie to take his own life?"

"Ah, my dear Watson, that harkens back to my very first conjecture in this case. I was wrong: Wilton wasn't beaten up because his assailants were Marxists who didn't like his clothes. He was assaulted because they were Irish."

"What the deuce?" I said incredulously. I can usually form more practicable questions, but I was taken aback. Holmes was not one for casually disparaging the Irish.

"But no further about that for now. I believe the stranger at our rendezvous knows the story more fully than I and owns the right to tell it. Let us send a telegram to Wilton. I am now certain the graveyard meeting will be safe. With some luck he will be able to still catch the evening train to join us at our graveyard engagement."

Sundown came at 6:30. A nearby church bell rang the half-hour. At twilight, we sent the wire in the hopes that it would make it into young Wilton's hands in time.

Upon the brougham driver's recommendation, we were whisked off to The Hind's Head, a pub and rooming house going back a-half-a-thousand years. Holmes paid for our cabbie's service and added a generous gratuity.

Holmes, who had not eaten all day, declared that he had rediscovered his appetite. Although dinnertime, he ordered ham and eggs. I satisfied myself with a beef and Guinness stew. We shared a bottle of wine. When we were done with it, Holmes peered down its opening. "You could fit a whole sheaf of papers inside. That is, if you were to cut them short, roll them up, and insert them one by one."

The Case of the Injured Orator by Dr. Martin Hill Ortiz

We booked a room where we freshened up, and Holmes packed and smoked a full pipe. Puffing away, he stared out the window. Typically, when he did that, he was waiting for someone. In this instance, I sensed a melancholia.

"Let us meet the eight-thirty train," my friend said. "Either Wilton will be there or else he will miss the rendezvous."

The evening train from London arrived at Reading on time. A porter aided Wilton in descending the step from the coach and carried his bag. The young man appeared rested and less fiery. He caught sight of us. A pinched look of anticipation dominated his face as though he were squinting to see the future.

"Mr. Holmes? Did you find the proofs you sought?" he asked, limping toward us. I took the bag from the porter and spared him a shilling.

"I have uncovered the truth behind your brother's demise," Holmes said.

"My father?"

"It was not your father."

"Can you be certain?" Wilton seemed almost disappointed. I suppose he had invested a great deal of fury in his beliefs.

"Yes. The one who summoned you to your brother's grave did so to inform you of what happened to your brother. He knows that you will be facing the same challenges and does not wish to see you come to the same end."

I hailed a cab, again a brougham, this one with a cabin large enough to seat three. "St. Birinus," I told the driver.

As we crossed town, Holmes related the basics of the story. Wilton fought back at each point, but Holmes set forth a convincing logic behind each of his conclusions ending with, "The people we meet at the cemetery will confirm the account of what happened." The young man wept bitter tears; as a doctor I would declare it was a catharsis long in waiting.

The Case of the Injured Orator by Dr. Martin Hill Ortiz

"But what was in the bottle that could have driven him to such an awful end?" Wilton asked. At this moment we arrived at our destination.

St. Birinus is a stone church on the outskirts of Reading. It has a tented roof and a prominent belltower at its fore. In contrast to some of the local centuries-old places of worship, it appears recently built. The graveyard, dimly lit by the half moon, is filled with recent markers, sepulchres, and crosses white and tall and none of those grey slabs of other churchyards with their weatherworn years and names.

I saw Wilton's father standing near a tomb. His hat covered his heart.

"Father!" Wilton cried out. He limped toward the man.

"Wilton, are you hurt?" They met in an embrace.

"I'll be fine." He started weeping.

The elder Trevelyan looked to us with a rage in his eyes. "And you? Sir Roonce and Mr. Alden!"

"Sherlock Holmes," my friend said, "and this is Dr. John Watson."

"The *detective* Sherlock Holmes?" the man asked as though there might be another with that name occupying a different profession.

"Your son hired us to answer some questions regarding his brother's death."

"Charlie!" his father cried in anguish. "My dear Lord."

"He now knows it was suicide," my friend said.

"I'm sorry," the father wailed. "I'm sorry I never told you. I wanted to spare you." He swallowed his son in his arms.

Holmes said, "And I apologize for the brutish means I employed to provoke you to come to this meeting. I believed that you should be part of this conciliation."

"But why, father?" Wilton said. "Why did Charlie do it?"

The Case of the Injured Orator by Dr. Martin Hill Ortiz

A young man stepped free of the shadows. He was thin and dapperly dressed in a dark suit and trousers. His tie had a perfect Windsor knot. He had the aspect of a juvenile scholar from one of the finer schools. Given another setting, I suspect he would be wearing a gown and mortarboard.

"Arthur!" Wilton shouted out.

"Wilton, Mr. Trevelyan," Arthur Reynolds said, and then nodding to us, added, "Mr. Holmes and Dr. Watson. No, I don't know your faces; I overheard your introductions."

"Arthur Reynolds," Holmes said. "You were my most likely pick for being the stranger behind the mysterious note. You were friends with Charlie Trevelyan and present for the burial. You knew of his last hours."

Arthur nodded gravely. "It feels as though it happened just last night. Wilton – I wrote you the note telling you to come here because you are turning eighteen. Along with your inheritance, you deserve the truth behind what had happened. Surely, someday you would have learnt of the papers hidden in that bottle, and I don't want you to fall into the same sort of despair. So I decided to present the matter to you here and now."

"I would never kill myself." Then Wilton conjured up one more moment of denial: "Charlie would never!"

"He hid from you his melancholia," Arthur said. "I knew it well. He had worshipped his grandfather and imagined his father was against him."

"That was not the reason he killed himself," Charles the Second said. "I am not speaking defensively or apologetically. It's just that when I learned the secret, I had a falling out with my father. When Charlie learned it. . ."

Arthur said, "Allow me. I came here to tell Wilton the full account. Since Charlie's death I have become somewhat of a scholar regarding the matter that drove him to his suicide.

The Case of the Injured Orator by Dr. Martin Hill Ortiz

"First, the deep history. It began in the seventeenth century. When the Protestants took control of Ireland, they forbade Catholics from owning land. This didn't change until less than a century ago. Although Catholics began to possess the ground where they lived and toiled, the change was slow. They were still poor and kept poor by having to send a tithe of their earnings to the Protestant church. The Protestant landowners, surrounded by those who resented them, fled to England and Scotland. In the 1840s when the potato blight struck, the landlords weren't on hand to witness the devastation. They continued to demand the profits from their tenants. Although the blight did wipe out the potato crop, it didn't hurt the wheat or barley or oats. Ireland had enough food to feed itself."

Charles the Second raised a staying hand. "My family, my turn," he said. "The British Parliament set my father in place to deal with the famine. He insisted that the grains be exported, and the money go to the landlords. He considered the Irish and those who tried to reserve food for themselves and their families to be no more than thieves. He considered them less than human and was outspoken regarding his beliefs.

"Years ago, when I learned of the hatred for the Irish expressed in his letters, and the annihilation of so many lives in his deeds, I confronted my father, and we had a falling out. I was cut from his will.

"My father remained proud of his vile malice. He directed my sons to the documents he had hidden inside a wine bottle. To him, they were lessons in what it took to be a man. Those documents spelled out his role in the obliteration of half-a-million lives."

"I saw the documents from the bottle," Arthur said. "It wasn't merely negligence. It wasn't merely turning a blind eye. It was murder. He declared the extermination to be a good thing. The Baronet Charles wrote that the famine was 'a direct stroke of an all-wise and all-merciful Providence.' He saw himself as the Angel of Death. I would count the toll at a million.

The Case of the Injured Orator by Dr. Martin Hill Ortiz

"When Charlie learned of this, and his grandfather's evil glee, he felt the shame of bearing the same name. He dropped into a profound despondency, not wanting to inherit the family fortune. I never realized the depths of his despair. Not until it was too late."

The father said, "I was there when he took his life. I wanted no one to know of my son's deed, not wanting him to be remembered that way. So, I plotted to make it appear as though there had been an intruder, a lie I maintained to all others, including your mother. I took the gun from his hand. I broke the window and, when Constable Anderson arrived, we arranged the story. I made one error: confiding in Reverend Griffin."

Wilton was weeping again.

"It is a lot to bear on your shoulders," the father said. "I know, I carry the same burden, the same name. He was my father."

Wilton wiped his face. "Father, you can have Charlie's half of the inheritance," he said. "Perhaps I can use some of my wealth to make reparations."

Holmes and I sipped some late evening ale at the Hind's Head, where we were booked to spend the night. Both of us were gloomy.

Holmes said, "Remember when I told you that young Wilton was assaulted because the attackers were Irish?"

"Yes, and that seemed a petty aspersion."

"The moment Wilton mentioned his brother, the victim, by name, those of Irish blood were inflamed. They knew their history and there are not many who bear such a distinct appellation as that of Charles Trevelyan. Insulated by living in a great home in the shire, the young Trevelyans grew up never learning what many others knew."

"I hadn't known," I admitted.

"To kill a single man," Holmes said, "you are a murderer. To kill a multitude, you are a statesman. The same sort of forced starvation played out in '76 upon hundreds of thousands in Madras, India."

The Case of the Injured Orator by Dr. Martin Hill Ortiz

I asked Holmes, "What good are our adventures in finding justice for single individuals when such large-scale atrocities pass unaddressed?"

"Ah, my dear Watson, our work and your accounts act toward the greatest purpose: To care about the fortunes of one life is the first step toward caring about them all."

* * *

Author's note: This story centers around the actions of Charles Trevelyan, first Baronet, of Wallington, who was the genocidal racist in charge of the British response to the Great Irish Famine. He made pronouncements that the extinguishment of Irish lives was for the good. May his name be remembered and reviled. The other family members and their story are fictional, as is Lessington Manor in Berkshire.

April 1883

The Missing Detective

By Paul Hiscock

When Sherlock Holmes left our rooms in Baker Street on the morning of Wednesday, 11 April, 1883, he gave me no reason to suppose that he would not return later that day. He did not mention where he was going, and I did not think to ask. When he did not come home that evening, I thought nothing of it. Despite the friendship that had developed between us, we each had interests and work that did not involve the other. Long hours at the surgery meant that I barely marked his absence over the next couple of days, and so it was not until the weekend that I started to wonder where he might be.

My first port of call was Mrs. Hudson, as there was very little which took place in the building that escaped her notice. However, I found that she knew no more than I did.

"I am worried," I told her. "It is unlike Holmes to disappear like this, without telling us."

She looked at me, slightly askance. "Do you think so? If you would pardon me, but you young gentlemen rush in and out of here all the time, without a word of explanation. Not that it bothers me. It is none of my business where you go. Only it would be nice to know if you will be eating here, just so as I know to prepare something for you."

With embarrassment, I thought back to all the times we had dashed out to track down clues in Holmes's latest case, without saying anything to her.

"I am sorry. I will try to be more considerate in the future. However, this feels different. I have not seen nor heard from Holmes for days now. Are you sure that he did not say anything?"

"No, but I really would not worry. Just wait until tomorrow. I'm sure he will be back for his Sunday dinner. I have a lovely joint of beef in the pantry."

I assured her that the meal sounded delicious, but I remained unconvinced. When Sunday came and went, without any news, I resolved to start searching for Holmes in earnest.

* * *

I had seen them at hospitals in the past, desperate relatives searching for news of missing loved ones, hoping that they might have been injured because the alternative was just too painful to contemplate. I had never spoken to them, always too busy attending to my own work to take the time. Now, I wished that I had taken a moment for them. I had not realised how agonising it was just waiting for news.

"I am looking for a patient," I told the nurse on duty, when she finally had a moment to speak to me.

"Name?"

"Mr. Sherlock Holmes."

"When was he admitted?"

"I am not sure. He might not even be here."

The Missing Detective by Paul Hiscock

I could see that she was about to dismiss me as a time waster, but I was luckier than most. Even though I did not work at the London Hospital, my status as a doctor lent me a certain authority.

"My name is Dr. Watson. This man is one of my patients. He has been missing since last Wednesday, and has a history of placing himself in harmful situations."

I saw her attitude change as soon as I introduced myself. "Of course, Doctor. Just let me fetch the records."

She scurried off and returned a few minutes holding a folder thick with paper.

"These are the admission lists. You are welcome to look through them."

"Which ones are for the last week?" I asked.

"Why, all of them. We are very busy here."

"Is there somewhere I could sit?

"I suppose you can use my desk. I don't have time to sit at it anyway."

I started to thank her, but she was already rushing away, so I settled down to look through the stack of paper.

I had feared that the notes would be almost unintelligible. Doctors are always in a hurry, and we are not known for our clear penmanship. However, the admissions records were all neatly completed, and I suspected they were the work of the diligent ward sisters.

Unfortunately, there was no sign of Holmes's name on the lists, although I was not entirely surprised. If he had been capable of sharing such information, he would surely have sent word of his predicament to Mrs. Hudson and myself. The more interesting entries on the list were the individuals who remained unidentified for some reason. Four people had been admitted during the period with injuries severe enough that they remained unconscious. I quickly ruled out the young woman found beaten in a gutter and an elderly gentleman who had collapsed in the street.

"Can you show me where this patient is?" I asked the nurse when she next came past.

She glanced at the record I indicated then pointed in the direction of the stairs.

"He's in ward fourteen. It's on the first floor, but I don't have time to take you up there. You'll have to find it yourself."

I thanked her and handed back the list.

"He must be an important person," she said as I turned to leave.

"I think so," I replied.

* * *

The eight beds on ward fourteen were all occupied. However, it was immediately obvious which was the man I sought. While all his fellow patients were sitting up, reading or playing cards, he lay still in his bed in the far right-hand corner of the room. His head was swaddled in bandages, covering the almost fatal head wound that had brought him to this place.

"What happened to you, Holmes?" I said as I approached the bed.

To my surprise, the man in the bed opened his eyes and responded.

"I'm sorry, do I know you?"

His voice was not what I expected. It was high and reedy. Also, now that I was close I could see that his nose was a little too round, his chin not quite pointed enough, and his arms slightly too short. Whoever this man was, it was not Holmes.

"Pardon me, I thought you were someone else," I said.

"Oh," replied the man, obviously disappointed. "I had hoped you might know me. I don't remember much of anything."

"I am sorry, but I am sure it will come back to you in time."

The Missing Detective by Paul Hiscock

"I hope it will. Mainly I want to remember who did this to me." He reached up and touched his head, only to wince in pain. "I have a score to settle with them."

I realised the ward had gone quiet, and looking around, I realised that the other men were all staring at us.

"Sorry to disturb you gentlemen," I said as I backed out of the room, feeling dejected.

* * *

I had been hoping that the mystery man in ward fourteen was Holmes. For while another mystery man of approximately the correct age had been admitted in the past few days, he had not fared so well. His stab wound had been deep, and he had bled out before regaining consciousness. If it were Holmes, all I could do for him was claim his body and give him a decent burial.

The man's body had been removed to the mortuary to await burial, but luckily had not been interred yet. It took the attendant some time to find the correct corpse. When he showed me to it, I found myself holding my breath waiting for him to pull back the sheet, only to release it in an explosion of relief. The unfortunate dead man looked nothing like Holmes. For a moment I felt euphoric, before remembering that this resolved nothing. Holmes was still missing and could still be dead.

"Are you done?" asked the mortuary attendant.

"Yes, thank you," I said, and he dropped the sheet. "Do you have any other unclaimed bodies here?"

"You're not going to find anything fresher than that one."

"Pardon me?"

"To slice up, or whatever it is you do with them."

"Slice up?" I replied in horror.

"I'm sorry, I know you doctors prefer to call it dissecting. Look, it makes no difference to me, just so long as you pay me."

Belatedly, I realised he was trying to sell me a cadaver for medical experimentation.

"No. No, I am not here to buy a body. I am looking for my friend."

"Oh well." The attendant did not seem the slightest bit ashamed of having tried to make money out of these poor dead people. "You'll just be after the young men like this one." He looked down a list. "Sorry, I don't think I have anything to interest you. Nearest is in his forties. Are you sure you aren't interested in buying? I could let you have that one at a discount. He's been here a few days now, and is getting a little ripe, if you know what I mean?"

"No, absolutely not," I replied, and left as quickly as possible before he could make any more distasteful offers.

* * *

"I'm sure he'll turn up. He always does, eventually."

Lestrade's dismissiveness surprised me. I knew that he was not close to Holmes, their relationship based on mutual assistance rather than friendship. Nevertheless, I had expected him to care slightly more about Holmes's disappearance.

"He has been gone almost a week now," I said.

"Longest I can remember was a month. Could have used his help a couple of times, not that he cared. Look, we both know he's brilliant. Not a finer mind for criminal problems in London. But he's not like the police. We might be a bit slower, but we're the professionals. For him it's just a hobby, and I'm sorry to say, I've learnt that you can't rely on him to always be there to help. Mark my words, he'll turn up in a few days just like nothing has happened, and accuse you of being foolish for making a fuss."

I wanted to defend Holmes and explain that he was not like that. However, I knew that, so far, the evidence was against me.

The Missing Detective by Paul Hiscock

* * *

"Have you found him?" asked Mrs. Hudson, as soon as I stepped into the house.

"Not yet, but I am sure he has a very important reason for staying away."

"Of course he does. But it will just be supper for one tonight, yes?"

"Yes, thank you, Mrs. Hudson."

I climbed the stairs slowly, unable to muster much enthusiasm for the evening ahead. I realised that I had grown used to returning from work only to find a desperate client waiting for our help, or for Holmes to rush me straight back out the door on a new adventure. When I stepped through the door, it was disconcerting to see that all his belongings were still there — papers and books strewn all over the place as though Holmes had been reading them moments before and only just stepped out.

I decided that, with little else to do, I might as well tidy up, only to stop myself just in time. If Holmes were a missing person, then this was a crime scene. Amidst all of the confusion, there might be some evidence to suggest why he left and where he was going. With a renewed sense of purpose, I sat down at his desk and tried to imagine how Holmes would spot the clues hidden there.

* * *

For hours I pored over the piles of paper. The articles he had selected to clip from the newspapers on the morning he disappeared were the most interesting, providing a fascinating insight into what Holmes considered important. There was a report on the outcome of the Neville trial, marking the successful conclusion of a case that Holmes had solved in the previous year. Major Neville was safely locked up, but could Holmes's disappearance be the work of another criminal he had thwarted in the past? Even in the couple of years I had known him, Holmes had solved dozens of cases, and I knew there had been many more before we met.

It was harder to figure out why he had kept the announcement of Lord Havering's engagement, the article notifying passengers about changes to the Folkestone train schedule the next week, or the advertisement for a magic show. The show was not scheduled to begin for another month, so I could not see how that was relevant, but I could call upon Lord Havering, or travel to Folkestone to make enquiries there.

However, the questions raised by the newspaper clippings were as nothing compared to those presented in the cryptic collection of notes that had also been left on the desk. Most contained just one or two words, or even just initials or a string of numbers. I quickly decided that trying to decipher them was a waste of time. I had no doubt that Holmes would have been able to piece together a comprehensive picture of criminal activities in London with these messages from his informants, but they meant nothing to me.

The final item of interest on the desk was a map of London. Holmes had left it open, folded so that the area around Southwark was visible. I examined it closely, but it did not seem as though he had marked any specific points of interest. However, looking at the place names sparked a memory. I rifled through the pile of notes, until I found the one I had recalled. It was just a small scrap of paper, which read, "George L. Br." It had not meant anything to me when I first saw it, but now I wondered if it might refer to London Bridge Station. Maybe he had been meeting this "George" there. It was a slim thread, and maybe it was just the sense of satisfaction at decoding one of Holmes's notes, but this lead somehow seemed more promising than any of the others I had found.

I stood up, and was preparing to head over to the station immediately, when I realised that it was already dark outside. I had been so engrossed that I had not noticed night fall, or that Mrs. Hudson had left my, now cold, supper on the table. I was frustrated, but it was too late to start asking questions that day. I tried to reassure myself that Holmes had been missing for days and a few more hours would not hurt.

* * *

I awoke the next morning determined to press on with my investigation, only to remember that I was committed to serve as a locum at a local surgery for the morning. As a result, I did not reach London Bridge until the middle of the afternoon.

Narrowing my search down to a single station had seemed like an achievement the night before. However, stepping onto the crowded concourse, I realised how difficult my search would be. People rushed past me with their heads down, focussed on catching their trains. Even if one of them had happened to brush past Holmes on a previous journey, they probably would not have even noticed him. The only possibility that held any hope was to enquire at the ticket office.

"Where to?" asked the clerk, without even looking up.

"I am looking for my friend. I think he might have been here last Wednesday, or maybe Thursday. Within the last week at least."

Now the clerk looked at me, an expression of incredulity on his face, as I proceeded to give a brief description of Holmes's appearance.

"You're asking about one passenger, who bought a ticket a week ago?"

"He might have done, or he might just have been meeting someone."

"Can you see that queue of people behind you? They're all waiting to buy tickets and to catch trains this afternoon, and unless one of them turns out to be Queen Victoria herself, I doubt I will remember any of them by the time I get home today. Apart from you. I will definitely remember you wasting my time. Now are you going to buy a ticket, or are you going to get out of the way of these paying customers."

"I am sorry," I said. I started to turn away, then remembered the other question that I had needed to ask him. "Does the name George mean anything to you? Maybe someone who works here?"

This time the clerk completely ignored me. He shouted, "Next!" and I had to step aside quickly as the man behind me in the queue stepped up to the window.

I moved out of the way, and then stopped to consider my options. It looked like the note was not going to help me after all, but I did have other leads to follow. Since I was at the station, I could get on a train to Folkestone, but I had no idea what I would do once I was there.

"Any luggage, mister?"

I turned to see who had spoken, and realised that a young porter was standing behind me.

"No, thank you," I replied. "I am not travelling. I am just looking for a friend. He was meant to be meeting someone called George here."

"If you were meant to be meeting him at the George, you're in the wrong place. It's just down the road."

"No, I was asking if you knew someone called...." I stopped mid-sentence, as I reassessed what he had said. "There is a place called the George near here?"

"That's right. The public house on Borough High Street."

I thanked him, and gave him a coin for his assistance, before heading out of the station.

* * *

The George was an old coaching inn in a courtyard, with open galleries along the length of the first and second floors. It was still early in the afternoon, and so quiet inside, but I imagined it would get busier when the market closed for the day. Wary of repeating my mistake at the ticket office, I made a point of ordering a drink and checking that nobody else was waiting before asking the landlord about Holmes.

He pondered my description for a moment, then to my delight he nodded.

"I do recall him. Came in middle of last week. Spent the whole afternoon sitting in that corner over there. Didn't say much, and drank less."

"Did he say why he was here?"

"No, but I think he must have been looking for someone. He seemed to study everyone who came in."

"Do you know where he went after he left?"

"No, I didn't even see him leave. He must have slipped out during the evening rush."

I thanked the landlord for his time, and took my drink over to the table where Holmes had sat before me. I was not sure that I had made much progress. Most of the week was still unaccounted for, but still it was a relief to know that somebody had seen Holmes after he had left Baker Street that Wednesday.

I was wondering what I should do next when a man's shadow fell over my table.

"Don't mind if I join you?" he said in a wheezy voice, then sat down before I could reply. He was a scruffy-looking man, dressed in grease-stained clothes. He had a patchy beard, and his nose was oddly shaped, as though it had been broken at some point and reset badly.

"I don't suppose you'd take pity on a poor man and buy him a drink?"

As he finished speaking, he started coughing violently and I drew back in disgust.

"I am sorry. I would prefer to be left alone please," I said, shaking my head.

"Are you sure? Only I was here last week. It might be that I know something about this friend you are looking for."

"Did you speak to him? Do you know where he went?"

The man coughed again, sending a globule of phlegm flying across the table to land next to my glass.

"I'm sorry. My lungs are bad. It makes it hard to speak. Maybe if I had a brandy to warm my throat?"

"Very well."

He turned to the landlord and shouted, his voice suddenly much clearer. "A double brandy, Pete. This fine gentleman is buying."

The landlord looked at me for confirmation, and I nodded reluctantly. He shrugged, then poured a glass and brought it over. The man took it from him, and knocked it all back in one large gulp, before handing back the empty glass.

"Another?" he asked, but I shook my head.

"Tell me what you know first."

"Well, your friend was in here last Wednesday. Watching the room like a hawk, he was. That's a man looking for information, I said to myself, and I know everything that happens around here. Work the railyards and the markets. Anything you need to get hold of, I'm your man. Ask anyone. They all know Hartley."

This Hartley was obviously a petty criminal, and I was loath to trust him. However, I knew he was the type of informant Holmes often used, and so I let him continue.

"So, your friend says he's a detective, and that makes me have second thoughts. I mean, I don't want no trouble with the police, but he says he's not with them, and I can trust him to keep anything between us."

"What did he want to know?"

"Said he was looking for this thief by the name of Napier. Nasty violent cove what has been burgling high-end houses across London. Hurts anyone unlucky enough to interrupt him. Well, I say, I don't have dealings with his type. My hands aren't milky white, but there's no blood on them."

Hartley held up his grubby hands, as though to somehow prove his point.

"Anyway, your friend thinks Napier has a hideout around here, and like I said, I avoid people like him, so I know what he's talking about. Napier had a place down in Mermaid Court, only he ain't there anymore. It was getting too well-known. He disappeared a month or so back, and rumour has it he moved up Euston way."

"What then?"

"Well, that was it. Your friend thanks me and buys me a drink, seeing as I've been so helpful, and then heads off. If I were a gambling man, I'd be betting that he headed across the river to keep looking."

"And you haven't seen him since?"

"No, he's not been back."

"Very well. Thank you for your help."

I stood up to leave, but Hartley put his grubby hand on my arm.

"Maybe you might buy me another drink before you go, like your friend. I do find that talking so much makes my throat hurt something terrible." He finished with another hacking cough to emphasise his point.

I sighed and nodded. At the bar I ordered another drink and settled my bill, then made a swift exit before Hartley could make any further requests.

* * *

It was a relief to have a solid lead to follow at last. I considered heading straight to Euston to look for Napier, but I decided it would be better to speak to Lestrade first. It seemed likely that Holmes had fallen afoul of this thief, and I did not want to repeat the same mistake. It would be better to have the police with me when I tracked him down.

I was about to hail a hansom to take me to Scotland Yard when I realised that I was not wearing my hat. I cursed in annoyance and headed back to the George Inn.

When I went inside, Hartley was nowhere to be seen. I worried for a moment that he might have taken my hat, but it turned out to be on the seat where I had left it. Relieved, I waved farewell to the landlord again and went outside.

I was about to cross the courtyard and head back out on to the street, when I heard voices coming from the gallery above.

"Are you sure he's not going to cause any problems?" a man asked. "He was asking a lot of questions."

There was a familiar, hacking cough, and then a familiar voice replied.

"There's nothing to worry about," said Hartley. "That busybody is halfway to Euston by now. We won't be seeing him again."

Realising that he was talking about me, I stepped back as far as possible beneath the overhanging gallery, so that I could listen without being seen.

"And the friend he was looking for? You said he wouldn't be a problem."

"He won't be. My employer has made sure he won't be snooping around anymore. I keep telling you, Mr. Morton's taken care of everything. All you need to do is follow his plan and you'll be rich men by this time tomorrow."

"We'll see. I want to meet this Morton fellow first. See if he's the 'criminal mastermind' that you claim he is, because I'm not doing anything on the say so of a thieving little weasel like you."

"You won't have to. Just be at the old tobacco warehouse at the end of Hays Lane in one hour, like we agreed. I promise you'll be impressed."

I could not believe I had fallen for that disgusting man's lies. Holmes would never have believed Hartley, although I was afraid that his perspicacity had led him to suffer a far worse fate than a wasted trip to Euston.

There was the sound of movement from the gallery above, then the man who had been speaking before asked, "Where are you going?"

"I've got work to do," replied Hartley. "Did you think my only job was to look after you? Mr. Morton relies on me, you know. I'm sure you can get to the meeting without me to show you the way, yes?"

"Just get out of here," growled the other man.

I did not wait to hear if Hartley replied. I knew that I needed to have left before he emerged. Keeping close to the wall below the gallery for as long as possible, I hurried out of the courtyard and into the street beyond.

Once I was a few streets away, I paused to assess my options. The safest course of action was to stick to my earlier plan and speak to Lestrade. Yet what did I have to tell him? A man whom I had not seen might be intending to commit an unknown crime, planned by another man I had not met, and they might have done something to Holmes, or just sent him on a fool's errand as they had tried to with me. The only solid intelligence I had was that a meeting was taking place shortly, and there was not time to travel to Scotland Yard and back before it started.

It seemed to me that the only logical plan was to eavesdrop on the meeting and then report to Lestrade once I had all the facts. I decided to head to the warehouse immediately to try to find a hiding place before anyone else arrived.

* * *

The warehouses by the river were still busy, even late in the afternoon, making the one I was looking for easy to find. While people and goods moved in and out of the other buildings, the tobacco warehouse that Hartley had mentioned was dark and empty. For a moment, I wondered how I was going to get in, but then I spotted that the padlock on one of the doors had been broken and was hanging loose. Obviously someone, probably Hartley, had been here already to prepare the site for the meeting.

I crept inside as quietly as I could, in case anyone was already there, but the place seemed deserted. The warehouse still contained a few crates that had been left behind by the previous occupants. I found a place, not too far from the door, where I could hide behind some of them, and sat down on the ground to wait.

Despite the danger, I must have fallen asleep, as the sound of people talking in the warehouse jolted me awake.

"It seems deserted, boss."

"So where is he?"

"Maybe he's late."

"Or maybe this was all a waste of my time. I knew I shouldn't have trusted that greasy little trickster Hartley. Why would some criminal genius have anything to do with the likes of him?"

I peeked through a gap between the crates and was able to make out three men standing there. One was smartly dressed in a suit, while his two accomplices simply wore shirts with rolled up sleeves. However, more striking than their attire were the guns that they carried, and I found myself regretting the fact that I had not picked up my service revolver before embarking on this adventure.

"You don't suppose this is some kind of trap, boss?" asked one of the men in shirt sleeves. "What if the police are coming?"

"What if they do?" said the man in the suit, and I recognised his voice as that of the man I had overheard speaking to Hartley at the George Inn. "All we've done is walk into an old warehouse. The door was unlocked and we're just good citizens checking that nothing is wrong."

"I can assure you there are no police near here."

The three men turned towards the door, towards a fourth man who had just entered the room. I also tried to get a look at him, but I could not find a way to see him from behind the crates without revealing myself.

"You must be Morton," said the man in the suit.

"I am Mr. Morton, and you are Mr. Pryce, the notorious bank robber and safe-cracker."

"Very well then, Mr. Morton. Now that the pleasantries are over, your man, Hartley, reckons you can help us with a job we have planned. Where is that little worm, by the way? I thought he would be with you."

"Mr. Hartley is out procuring essential supplies to ensure the success of your robbery tomorrow. Rest assured, if you agree to work with me, you will see him again soon enough. "

"Why should we work with you?" asked one of Pryce's associates. "The boss has always led us right in the past."

"This is a bigger job than anything you have attempted in the past, and I am afraid that Mr. Pryce's plan, while audacious, is fatally flawed. If you would gather round?"

Mr. Morton moved over to a crate near the centre of the warehouse, and spread out a map on top of it. Now that he had moved, I could see him through the gap in the crates. He was quite tall, with slightly hunched shoulders, and wore a black frock coat and top hat. I thought I caught a glimpse of a beard before he turned away from me and bent over the map.

"The bullion train will leave London Bridge Station at 10:35 tomorrow morning, heading to Folkestone and then on to France. You plan to block the tracks and stop it here." Mr. Morton pointed at the map.

Pryce opened his mouth to speak, but Mr. Morton cut him off. "It does not matter how I know the details of your plan. Suffice to say, this is my city. I know about every crime that is committed here, down to the lowliest pick-pocket. As I was saying, you plan to stop the train here, where the police will surround you and have you in custody before you even breach the door."

"What would you do then?" asked Pryce.

"I would be patient, and wait until the train is further from London before I strike. The level crossing here at Aylesford is the ideal spot. You can make the blockage look like an accident, maintaining the element of surprise, and the rural police will be far slower to respond. Especially if someone were to arrange a distraction to lead them in the opposite direction at the crucial time."

Pryce studied the map intently for a minute, and then nodded in approval. "I still maintain my plan would have worked, but this has advantages. How do you intend to distract the police?"

"You need not worry about that. I have associates already taking care of it."

"You are that sure I will say yes?"

"I am certain you cannot do this without me."

"And what do you get for this assistance?"

"I would say a fifteen percent cut of the bullion sounds reasonable."

"Fifteen percent? Have you forgotten we are the ones taking all the risks, unless you are planning to join us tomorrow."

"I prefer not to get involved at the scene of the crime. That is why I use people like you. However, my associate Mr. Hartley will be joining you."

"We don't need him," said one of Pryce's men, and his colleague nodded in agreement.

"I am afraid that I must insist on his involvement. He will be there to safeguard my interests, but he will also be bringing the explosives you will need."

"We already have explosives," said Pryce.

"Pitiful little things that will be of no use against the reinforced gold car. No, you will require the explosives that Mr. Hartley is currently acquiring if you wish to make it through the doors."

"Very well," said Pryce. "He can meet us here at six, and we will travel there together."

The Missing Detective by Paul Hiscock

Mr. Morton leaned over and rolled up the map. "Excellent. It has been a pleasure doing business with you. I look forward to the news of your successful heist."

Then he turned, and for the first time I was able to see his face clearly. He had a dark moustache and beard, which formed a small circle around his mouth. However, it was Mr. Morton's nose that held my attention, for it was strikingly familiar. Surely another man could not have the same hawk-like nose as Sherlock Holmes? Yet what was he doing here, helping a gang of criminals?

Convinced that it must be my friend, I almost shouted out to him, before stifling myself. Even if Mr. Morton were actually Holmes, alerting Mr. Pryce and his armed thugs to my presence would probably still get me killed.

I hoped that Pryce and his men would leave first, giving me an opportunity to speak to Holmes, if it really were he. However, the chance did not present itself, and so, after waiting for a good ten minutes to be certain the coast was clear, I left the warehouse and caught the first hansom I could find to Scotland Yard.

* * *

"You are a very foolish man, Dr. Watson," said Lestrade. "I have grown used to such antics from Mr. Holmes, but I thought you had more sense."

"If I had not been there, you would not know anything about the heist."

"And if they had spotted you, you would have been killed."

"I told you, I am certain the man they were meeting with was Holmes. He would not have let them shoot me."

"But you didn't know that before you went, and besides, I'm not so certain that he would have saved you."

"How can you say that?" I asked, shocked by the suggestion. "He is my friend, and yours too, I thought."

"I know he has assisted the police on a few occasions in the past, but what if that was just a cover? You hear rumours when you work in the detective branch, whispers about a master criminal, a shadowy figure behind the biggest crimes in the city. I never believed the stories myself. The man would have to be a genius with informants all over the city. However, now that you have raised the possibility, I realise there is one man who could pull it off."

"You are not suggesting that Holmes is really a criminal mastermind? Surely what I saw today was just an act?"

"Can you be certain, Dr. Watson? If it was really an act, wouldn't he have told us about the planned train robbery, rather than telling the thieves how to evade us?"

"But look at how many crimes he has solved."

"A clever ruse to gain our trust, no doubt about it. He has played the long game well, but not well enough to fool me."

"What do you plan to do then?"

"Mr. Holmes will turn up eventually, and I'll arrest him then. However, in the meantime, we need to stop this train robbery he has planned. They'll get a shock when it is a full complement of metropolitan officers they face tomorrow, rather than a couple of rural constables."

"I would like to go with you and your men," I said. Lestrade hesitated, but I continued, "I was the one who discovered the plan."

Lestrade sighed. "Very well, as long as you stay out of the way. However, if Mr. Holmes is there after all, you must not assist him. He must be treated as though he is just another criminal from here on out."

* * *

I slept poorly that night, wondering if it were possible that Lestrade might be correct. I had hoped that he might have had a change of heart overnight, but when I arrived at Scotland Yard, just before dawn, I found that he was more convinced than ever that he had unmasked London's criminal mastermind.

Just before we set off, he asked, "Are you still sure you want to come, Dr. Watson? It could be dangerous."

I patted the pocket of my overcoat and felt the reassuring weight of my service revolver. "I am ready," I replied.

* * *

The local police station we arrived at was little more than a small office, and the officer on duty was dumbfounded when three police wagons drew up outside.

"Did you not warn them we were coming?" I asked Lestrade, as we waited in the street.

"You told me that Mr. Holmes was making arrangements to keep the local officers out of the way. I couldn't take the risk that he might have bribed them."

"It was Mr. Morton. We still do not know for sure that he is actually Holmes."

"Regardless, I couldn't risk the details of our operation being passed to the enemy. However, I suppose now that we are here, I should brief them."

However, before we could move an officer came running out of the station.

"Excuse me, inspector. We've just received word. There's a robbery in progress over in East Malling. They are calling for all officers. Did you know about it? Is this why you are here?"

"No, it isn't," said Lestrade.

"I think this is the distraction Mr Morton planned to keep the police away from the train heist," I said.

"Then we mustn't fall for it. Don't go anywhere, constable."

"I think he should go," I replied. "Even if it is intended as a distraction, it could still be a real robbery. Besides, it will look suspicious if he does not go. You have plenty of men without him."

"Very well," said Lestrade. "You can go, constable, but do not breathe a word about us being here to anyone. You hear me?"

"Yes, sir."

* * *

We waited outside the police station for another half an hour before Lestrade gave the order for us to move. When we had examined the map it had been obvious why Mr. Morton, or Holmes, had chosen that spot. It would have been impossible to conceal the officers we had brought near the level crossing. Instead we would have to wait until the very last minute, just as the train arrived, to swoop in and catch the villains in the act.

At last Lestrade gave the signal to stand-by. He counted down the last minute on his pocket watch and then gave the order to go.

The police wagons raced down the narrow country lanes. I heard the insistent blast of a train whistle, as the driver tried to get the vehicle obstructing the track to move. Then we rounded a corner, and I could see the level crossing at last.

However, things were not as they should have been. The train was still a little way down the track and had yet to draw to a halt. Consequently, the robbers had not yet moved. Most of them were still sitting in their cart, pretending that they had become stuck there.

Only one man was on the ground, and as we approached, I recognised that it was Hartley. However, the robbers had also seen us, and they obviously had no intention of waiting to be arrested. The man in the driver's seat picked up the reins and shouted for the horses to move.

Hartley must have been afraid of being left behind, because he jumped out in front of the horses and tried to stop them. I watched in horror, fearing that he would be trampled, but they reared up in front of him toppling the cart instead. Pryce and his men tumbled out of the cart, cursing Hartley for spoiling their escape. They tried to run, but by then it was too late. Lestrade's men quickly apprehended them and bundled them into the waiting police wagons.

Only Hartley had not tried to run. He was sitting on the ground where he had fallen after stopping the horses.

I walked over to arrest him with Lestrade, but when we reached him, he surprised me by reaching out his hand to me.

"Could you help me out of the mud, Watson?" he asked. Yet the request was not accompanied by any of Hartley's characteristic coughing and wheezing. Instead, it was made in a very familiar voice.

"Holmes, is that you?" I asked.

He reached up to his face and pulled off the fake nose and whiskers, revealing his true features. Delighted, I reached down and helped him to his feet.

Lestrade looked confused. "I thought you said Mr. Holmes wasn't going to be here," he said to me.

"I said Mr. Morton would not be here, but it turns out Holmes was Hartley."

"So if he wasn't Mr. Morton, should I still be arresting him, or is there another criminal mastermind out there?"

"Ah, Inspector Lestrade," said Holmes. "What would Scotland Yard do without your razor-sharp intellect? Please do not worry. I promise to explain everything. However, right now our priority is clearing the line. We must get this bullion train moving again."

* * *

It took the combined efforts of all Lestrade's men to shift the overturned cart. The train guards looked on anxiously, worried at how exposed the bullion was while the train was stopped. It might have gone faster if they had been willing to help, but their orders were not to leave their posts under any circumstances, and they followed them rigidly.

Once the train was finally under way, we boarded the police wagons and started the journey back to Scotland Yard.

"I started hearing rumours that someone was planning to rob the bullion train early last week," said Holmes as we travelled.

"These transfers are meant to be a secret," complained Lestrade. "How did they know when it was happening?"

"It is easy enough to work out," replied Holmes. "The railway has to alter the timetable to let the bullion train through. They create a gap just long enough for a train to pass through. It is easy enough to spot, if you know what you are looking for."

"Why did you disappear?" I asked. "Surely you could have just told Lestrade about the threat."

"I did not have enough information. One of my informants pointed me towards a gang that was using the George Inn. It was easy enough to spot them, but they were never going to reveal their plans to me. Therefore, I created the persona of Hartley and set about trying to ingratiate myself with them."

"But why did you not come home?" I asked. "Were you really playing the part of Hartley day and night?"

"I set off for Baker Street at the end of the first day, but I quickly spotted that I was being followed. Pryce was very suspicious of anyone taking an interest in his operation. I could have lost the man tailing me easily enough, but I would never have got close to Pryce again. So instead I headed for a nearby doss house where I have been staying ever since. It was all going well, until you came looking for me, Watson. That was unexpected. I tried to divert you, for your own safety, but I should have realised you would not be so easily dissuaded, once I knew you were searching for me. However, it all turned out for the best."

I was about to ask what Holmes meant by that, when Lestrade asked, "So what about this Morton fellow? We should arrest him quickly, before he hears what has happened. Do you know where we might find him, Holmes?"

"Holmes was Morton," I said. "We worked that out last night."

"But he turned out to be Hartley?"

"I was both of them," said Holmes. I needed to create a reason why Pryce would discuss his plans with me. It became clear he was never going to trust Hartley, so I needed to use a second identity, one whose assistance Pryce could ill afford to dismiss."

"So are you, or are you not, this infamous criminal mastermind, Holmes?"

"Of course I am not, Lestrade. However, Pryce had heard the rumours, just like you. It was easy enough, with my knowledge of the criminal underworld, to convince him that I was this shadowy figure."

Lestrade seemed relieved, but something was still bothering me.

"What would you have done if I had not uncovered Pryce's plan? If we had not been there today, he would have got away with it."

"I was concerned about how I would get a message to Lestrade. It was hard enough playing both Hartley and Mr. Morton without Pryce suspecting something. However, as soon as I saw you return to the inn, I realised that you could be my messenger, and you played your role perfectly."

"You knew I was there the whole time?"

"Of course. Why else would I have made a point of repeating the details of the meeting with Mr. Morton? Pryce already knew where he was going. Luckily he just attributed the unnecessary reminder to Hartley's unpleasant personality."

"And you knew I was at the warehouse too?"

"Naturally. You were meant to realise I was putting on a show for you. I would never have adopted such a feeble disguise if I had not intended for you to see through it. I knew I could rely on you."

I knew he thought that he was paying me a compliment, but I had felt a sense of satisfaction at having solved the mystery of his disappearance, and hearing how he had used me seemed to tarnish that victory.

"Maybe next time you could just tell me what you are doing?" I said crossly.

For once, Holmes actually looked chastened.

"I did not realise you would be worried," he admitted, and my anger faded slightly.

"It is only natural that I should have wondered where you were," I said, "but it was not fair to keep Mrs. Hudson in the dark. You know how she worries."

"Mrs. Hudson. Yes, of course. I will try to be more considerate of her feelings in the future."

I smiled. I was certain that this would not be the last time that Holmes disappeared on a case, but at least I now knew what to expect.

Holmes leaned out the window, and shouted to the driver, "Please drop us off at Baker Street. I have a sudden craving for a good home cooked meal."

May 1888

The Body in the Box

By Stephen Herczeg

"And who are you then?" asked Mrs. Hudson, staring down at the two filthy street urchins standing before her on the threshold of 221B Baker Street.

The taller one slid his flat cap from his head and held it close to his chest. "Tommy Bones, Ma'am. Wiggins sent me to speak wiv Mr. 'Olmes. 'E said we 'ad to use the bell, not charge in unannounced like."

"Good. I'll not have your like sullying up my house," Mrs. Hudson retorted.

Sitting in the parlour of the rooms that I shared with my friend Sherlock Holmes, I had just finished the day's papers and was a little lost for further diversion. When the bell rang downstairs, I felt the urge to investigate, but found Mrs. Hudson, our landlady, already addressing the visitors.

"What have we here, Mrs. Hudson?"

She glanced in my direction, barely hiding the slight look of disgust at the state of the two urchins on the doorstep. "These two are after Mr. Holmes. They are supposedly part of the riff-raff he pays to spy on half of London."

Looking through the doorway, I recognised Tommy Bones from a previous encounter, but the younger boy was a mystery to me. "What is it you want with Holmes, Tommy?"

"Good morning, Mr. Watson, it's little Nicky 'ere. I found 'im wandering around down near the river. 'E was senseless and kept muttering about a body in a box."

"That's Doctor Watson," Mrs. Hudson reminded the boy.

Dismissing the slight, I asked him to elaborate. "A body? In a box? Near the Thames?" The smaller boy's eyes drew slowly up into mine. He nodded but remained silent. I posed my next question to Tommy. "Is he one of the Irregulars?"

Shaking his head, Tommy said, "No, but I've seen 'im around. Pickpocket, 'e is. Runs with Solomon's gang."

"Oh," I said, "Marvelous, I'm sure Holmes will be delighted."

* * *

Quelling Mrs. Hudson's protestations, I brought our two guests up to the rooms that I had shared, for almost two and a half two years now, with Sherlock Holmes consulting detective. Tommy Bones was part of a group that Holmes called *The Baker Street Irregulars*, a rough and tumble crew of street urchins, that he paid to keep an eye and an ear to the cobbles and provide him with all manner of information.

Ushering Tommy and Nicky into our parlour, I was startled to see Holmes standing in his doorway. The dark shadows beneath his eyes indicated that he'd had another late night, probably prowling the back alleys of London in search of his next big adventure.

"What do we have here, Watson?"

"Tommy Bones has brought you something of interest, I hope. Little Nicky here says he found a body or some such." I bade the two boys sit on the settee, part of me hoping I could clean off any mess left behind.

Holmes strolled out, lighting a cigarette as he did so, and sat in the armchair facing the boys. I sat in the chair to his right. Addressing the small, frightened boy, he said, "Now, hello Nicky, I'm Sherlock Holmes. You've met my associate Doctor Watson, and it seems you know Tommy Bones, a long-time member of the Baker Street Irregulars. If Tommy has brought you to me, then you must have a tale of some intrigue."

Nicky's eyes flicked between me and Holmes several times while he seemed to build up his confidence. "I found a body. In a box."

"That must have been frightening."

"Yes, it was. I thoughts there'd be booty or somefin', but there was a body. I got scared and runs away, like. I don't knows what to do. Tommy founds me and says 'e knows a geezer."

Holmes smiled. "Yes, I would be that geezer." Pausing for a moment, he added, "Can you start at the beginning of your story, I don't think you simply happened on a body."

Nicky shook his head. "No. I didn't want nuffin' to do with no body. Just wanted the man's wallet."

"Ah, go on then."

His eyes grew wide. I could tell that he felt that little nugget of information might get him into trouble. It was Tommy that calmed him down. "Now, don't worry Nicky, Mr. 'Olmes knows what it's like on the streets, 'e don't care none about that stuff. You tell 'im what you told me."

His eyes flicking between Holmes's and mine once more, Nicky began. "I was down the docks like always. Lots of marks down there. Mr. Solomon makes us work the area. 'E says we blend in, like."

"Yes, there are many of your ilk down at the docks. I'm sure Solomon has a great many young urchins working in those areas. Shame really, most of them grow up to be adult criminals, and that's where I come in at times."

Nicky's eyes grew wide. "I don't want you coming after me, Mr. 'Olmes. I've 'eard o' you. You done put away loads o' geezers."

I had to smile at the fact this young delinquent was afeared of Holmes's reputation.

"Yes, well let's hear your story, then consider your future later."

"Right," said the boy, taking a deep breath. "It was only late yesterday. I was working down Smithfield way when I sees this geezer and made a move. 'E was all dressed up nice, expensive shoes an' all, and not paying much attention. Perfect mark, as Mr. Solomon tells us."

"Indeed, go on."

"Well, I sidles up to 'im. Does the bump and run, and ducks down an alley before 'e even notices. Finking I'd got some nice loot, I finds that I've only got a key and a scrap o' paper."

Pulling his hand from the pocket of his cardigan, Nicky held out the items. Holmes took each in turn and examined them.

"Hmmm. Looks like a Milner strongbox key. Tarnished and old, some scratches on the end, indicating it has been used recently." Placing the key on the table before him, he looked at the slightly crumpled paper, turning it which way and that, before carefully unfolding it and reading the writing inside. "Standard parchment, no watermarks. Hmm. An address in Limehouse, on Narrow Street."

"Yeah, I went straight there. Thought it must be important, could be some good stuff for Mr. Solomon." Nicky shook his head. "Nah, building was burnt out. Nothing left, 'cept the box."

"Box?"

"Yeah. Metal box. All black with soot from a fire. I almost left it but got curious. I wish I'd left it now."

"That's where the body was?"

Nicky's mouth quivered, and his eyes grew wide and distant. The hollow look of abject horror. He slowly nodded. "Yeah. That's where I found 'er."

"A woman?"

The Body in the Box by Stephen Herczeg

"No. A girl. About Tommy's age, from what I saw. I can still see 'er poor face lookin' up at me. All covered in blood. 'Orrible it was."

"My word," I said, "You poor little fellow."

It was at that point that Mrs. Hudson arrived at the doorway, with a tray of tea and biscuits. "Thought you and your, ahem, guests, might need some refreshments." We remained silent while Mrs. Hudson placed the tray down, and I doled out the tea. The two boys hoed into the biscuits like there was no tomorrow. Nicky had apparently recovered from the fear of his remembrance.

When all was quiet once more, Holmes pressed the young boy further. "What did you do next, Nicky?"

Shaking his head, he answered, "I don't rightly know, Sir. I must 'ave left. The next thing I knows is that Tommy 'ere took me aside, talked wiv me a while, then we ends up 'ere."

"Kept 'im wiv me all night, like," added Tommy.

"You didn't touch the body?" Holmes asked.

"No, Sir. I don't remember doing that."

"But you had the key and note?"

"I found them in my pocket. Must 'ave put them away when I unlocked the box."

"I don't suppose you thought about going to the police?" I asked.

Nicky drew back in terror. He shook his head, his eyes staring at me. "Not the bobbies. No. Never."

Holmes let out a slight chuckle. "I would be very surprised if a young urchin, in Nicky's trade, would seek out the constabulary." He grew silent for a moment, picking up the key and note in turn, before speaking. "I think you should continue to stay with Tommy, here. I doubt if the fellow you took these from would be able to tell you apart from any other child of the street, but it would be safer if he didn't have the chance. The man we are looking for is obviously involved in something nefarious, but I'd like to confirm everything

The Body in the Box by Stephen Herczeg

myself before proceeding." Turning to the young Irregular, he added, "Tommy, can you inform Wiggins that he has a new member, temporary for now, but who knows what the future holds." Glancing at the younger boy, he asked, "Is that all right with you Nicky?"

"I don't know if Mr. Solomon will be 'appy."

"Leave Mr. Solomon to me. I know his story, and I'm sure he wouldn't appreciate the interest of my acquaintances at the Yard."

* * *

The journey to Limehouse took much longer than I imagined. There were a lot of carts and wagons on the roads past the tower, and the docks area around St. Katherine's that held us up for what seemed like ages.

By the time we were dropped off at the address on Narrow Street, I was bathed in sweat. The warm spring weather on that day in late May sapped the strength from my bones and brought out blossoms of moisture in my armpits.

Stepping down from the hansom, I studied the burnt-out hulk before me.

"This is recent," said Holmes standing to my left.

"How so?" I asked, examining the carcass of the two-story building, with its scorched brickwork and missing door.

Holmes pointed to the adjoining houses, each was attached to the burnt place, but seemed to be relatively unaffected by the conflagration that had besieged their neighbour. "The curtains on each of the upper floors of the adjacent properties are drawn back with the windows wide open. That suggests that they may have been affected by smoke and are airing out their rooms, but the occupants are not at home."

"What gives you that idea?"

"The windows and doors are shut fast on the ground floor. If the occupants were home, they too would be open. It would be a brave or desperate soul that would shimmy up to the first floor to gain entry." He peered closer at both houses for a moment, before smiling. "And the presence of broken bottles and glass lining the windowsills of both properties indicate a primitive, but a quite effective form of protection from would-be burglars."

"Devilishly clever."

Holmes turned his attention to the property before us. "Now, what have we here?"

The front of the property had been scorched and marked from the flames and smoke escaping from the conflagration inside but appeared structurally sound. A multitude of sooty footprints led through the doorway; I could sense Holmes's annoyance at the obliteration of any evidence that may have existed.

The door itself had been broken open when the Metropolitan Fire Brigade or some of the locals had attended to the fire. The windows however had survived but were blackened and restricted any view into the interior of the building.

Holmes stood on the threshold for a moment and stared inside. The light spilling in from outside was diffused due to the smoke-blackened windows, but there was enough to allow us to make out several details.

The front door opened into a small entryway with a sitting room off to one side through another doorway. Even from where we stood, I could tell that the fire had started in the parlour and raced through into the entryway. A line of black boot marks led to and from that room. The damage inside looked far less extensive than I had expected but was enough to make me concerned about the safety of the rafters and upper floor area.

"I assume you've noticed the origin of the fire."

I pointed to the side room. "In there. The scorching of the flames runs out towards the entrance but didn't advance down the hallway towards the back of the house."

The Body in the Box by Stephen Herczeg

"Yes. The floor is relatively unscathed the further one advances. These footmarks and water damage are from the firemen themselves. So, most of the damage is limited to this room." He carefully stepped into the entrance, and moved to the doorway of the parlour, stopping for a moment before entering the room.

I followed and surveyed the scene of devastation. Even though it was limited to that one room, the fire must have burnt the majority of the furniture. The only piece left was a blackened steel box sitting in the far corner, its lid swung open revealing an empty, but almost pristine interior. The floor was a mess of black ash, mushed into a soggy pulp from feet and water. Some of the more intact pieces still glistened with moisture. "That's very strange. All the furniture has been burnt away, but that box remains relatively intact."

"And that is the box in question. It's a fireproof safe box, supplied by Thomas Milner. They are reportedly able to withstand the most intense of fires. As to the furniture, it's there." Holmes pointed to a pile of ashes and coals that surrounded the box. "Whatever furniture was in this room, was broken apart and piled around the box, before being set alight." Craning to look around the box, and then inspecting the insides, he added, "The miscreant attempted to burn the box, and its contents, which we believe to be a young girl's body, though we only have young Nicky's word on that."

"It would seem strange to attempt to burn a fireproof safe box."

"Yes, which leads me to believe that the perpetrator either didn't realise that fact or could not stomach the burning of the body itself out in the open." Stopping, he scanned the area once more, stepping towards the small fireplace. It was blackened from soot acquired from both its operation and the fire in the room. He bent down for a while, before pulling out his glass and inspecting the area around the base of the fireplace. He shuffled away, before pointing at a dark patch on one of the hearthstones. "What do you make of this?"

I hunkered down next to him and stared at the blackened area. It appeared more solid than the smoke and soot stains affecting the other parts of the fireplace. "Something resting there melted, or something was spilt and dried, then burnt in place?"

"Or could it be dried and burnt blood?"

Squinting, I peered closer, before reaching out and prodding the patch. It had dried to a hard crust, but pushing at it, broke the hardened skin, causing flakes to break away. Holding my finger up into a beam of light, Holmes studied the flecks on my fingertip through his glass. "Hmm." He pursed his lips. "Inconclusive, but I wouldn't rule it out at this point. Could be that the poor missing girl was felled at this spot, bundled up into that box and set alight in the hopes of covering up the crime. Unsubstantiated at this point, but still probable."

Standing again, Holmes moved back to the box and pulling Nicky's key from his pocket, inserted it into the lock. It turned easily, triggering the locking mechanism. "Well, it is the owner of this key then." Replacing the key in his pocket, Holmes peered once more inside the box, murmuring as he studied the lining. "There's certainly blood or other similar stains in here. Dried now due to the heat from the fire, but not obscured. The rest of the box is dry, which indicates it served its purpose and kept the contents safe from the water used to douse the fire." Pushing his hand into the box, he exclaimed, "Aha, what have we here?"

Rising to his full height, he held articles in both hands. His left held two small strands of hair, the other a small swatch of fabric between his thumb and index finger. Rubbing the material between his fingers, he said, "Wool. Slightly poor quality. Grey."

"Not a fashionable colour. Very workmanlike I would think."

"If young Nicky found a body completely contained in this box, then I do not think the person was fully grown, more likely a child or teenager, as he said." Holding the swatch of fabric up into the light, Holmes pulled out his glass and studied it carefully. "Hmm," he murmured, "It is a very coarse weave. The type of material used in uniforms."

"Military? Nurse?"

"Unsure, could even be from a school. Only someone who would be very reticent about speaking up would allow themselves to wear such a fabric. Even those in the military or medical services would baulk at this. But, as we know, the strict regimes of some educational facilities can dampen any type of protest."

"That would fit if the victim were a child. As you said, the box is too small for a fully grown adult. But, where?"

"I can only imagine that the school would be in a more impoverished area, such as this one. There are several in the area. I would also think that it may be a residential school where the uniforms are supplied, rather than procured by the parents. These establishments tend to ensure that the costs are kept to a minimum. I think it would take too long to visit them all, I will first undertake some research before pursuing more information." Looking at the tiny strands of hair, he added, "And this will need a closer inspection. It's too dark in here, and I will need my scope."

"Should we bring in Lestrade? He may be able to provide constables to take some of the load off your shoulders."

"There's no reason as yet. We have no body and very scant evidence. The testimony of a small street urchin, one who dabbles in unseemly activities, would not be much to base a full police investigation on."

"Hmm. Point taken."

* * *

"Ah, Watson, be a good chap and put that down before someone gets hurt."

I glanced down at the hand holding my service revolver, then over at the reason I had brought it with me.

The previous night had been a late one. No sooner had Holmes and I returned to 221B Baker Street than a message arrived for me.

The Body in the Box by Stephen Herczeg

One of my newly acquired patients had taken ill and I was forced to bid a hasty retreat to my room, before embarking on a call to the older lady and providing whatever ministrations she required. That little trip finished well into the darkness of night and found me back in bed long past midnight.

It was after only two or three hours' sleep, still in the early hours before sunrise, that I awoke and heard a noise from outside. Donning my dressing gown, I listened at my door, hoping that it was simply the fog of sleep that had dulled my senses. The sound continued. A slight creaking of floorboards and a rustling of papers.

Glancing at the crack beneath my door, I saw the flickering of candlelight beyond.

Creeping across to my footlocker, I drew my service revolver out, ensuring it was loaded and returned to the door. Breathing a sigh of relief when it opened with nary a creak or groan, I found a figure rooting around Holmes's desk and bookcase. The person was dressed in the shabbiest of clothing. From my viewpoint, I spied a torn and dirty overcoat that smacked of one from the slums or streets, possibly from the area we had visited only the previous day.

As I stepped forward, the figure stopped momentarily, and then spoke.

"Ah, Watson, be a good chap and put that down before someone gets hurt."

"Holmes?"

The man turned. I expected my colleague, but spied instead a bent-backed figure, with a messy scruff of hair upon his head, a large bulbous nose, and the red-flushed cheeks of a heavy drinker.

"Who in the blazes are you?" I repeated, bringing my revolver back to bare on the figure, "And why do you sound like Holmes?"

A smile split the man's ruddy face, and he stood up to his full height, sloughing off the dirty coat, and suddenly taking on the form of Sherlock Holmes. "It's me, Watson. I would have thought you had become used to my disguises." He brought a hand to his face and quickly pulled away the face putty, and cheek fillers used to change his visage so remarkably.

My mouth dropped open as the dirty street dweller dissolved into my erstwhile companion. "Good Lord Holmes, I could have shot you."

"On that subject," he said, nodding at the revolver.

I gasped at the realisation that I still held the gun, cocked and ready to fire. Moving it away, I disarmed it and flicked on the safety, before popping it into the pocket of my gown. "Why are you dressed like that? And at this time of the morning?"

"Well, Watson, sometimes the best way to elicit information is to join in with the brethren of the street. I find that I can blend in much better in such a form, than if I were to appear as you would expect."

Shaking my head I added, "I still can't get used to this part of you."

A slight chuckle came from my friend. "Again, I have my ways, and sometimes they do pay off."

My interest piqued, I asked, "And?"

Turning back to the table, he pointed at a map of the Limehouse area. "As luck would have it, for us it seems, not for the poor unfortunate object of our hunt, a body was pulled from the Thames late yesterday afternoon. Down here." He pointed to a spot on the Thames, not far from the burnt-out house."

"Oh, no. Is it the missing lass?"

"That I don't know. All I could find out, from the street denizens of the area, was that the body was taken to the East London Hospital, they have a morgue there devoted to children."

"That's a tad sad if you think about it."

"Sign of the times, really. I didn't believe my disguise would be appropriate for a visit to the hospital, so I returned here to investigate other matters further."

"Such as?"

"Schools. I found that there are three residential schools for girls in the Limehouse area, with several more scattered further afield." Pointing at a list before him, he added, "I've listed them here, for visitation later in the day."

Consulting our mantel clock, I said, "It's four in the morning, I do hope you will at least sleep before setting out once more."

A broad smile came to his face. "Well, I may not sleep much, but I can see no benefit in setting out before a hearty breakfast, and possibly a bath. Let us set a time of ten o'clock, shall we?"

Nodding, I turned sluggishly away and ventured back to my bed, hoping that Holmes would at least attempt to attain a higher level of silence during the remainder of the night.

* * *

The East London Hospital for Children was slightly more than five years old and still looked virtually new. It was set apart from the buildings around it and towered three storeys above Glamis Road. My understanding was that the benefactor previously ran the hospital from a nearby warehouse and bequeathed a large sum on his death, in 1871, for a new hospital to be built on the site.

As Holmes had stated, it was a sad reality that a hospital devoted to the health of children and their mothers would require a mortuary for when the outcome is not altogether positive.

A brief inquiry at the reception area found us led to the bowels of the hospital and let into a surprisingly bright room with gaslighting. Several beds lay along the far wall, each holding a small lump covered with a white sheet.

"So many children," I said under my breath.

"Yes, mostly from those areas that have less access to health care," said a voice from behind us.

Turning I saw a young man, whom I would place in his mid-twenties, dressed in a white coat over a neatly pressed white shirt and

The Body in the Box by Stephen Herczeg

dark slacks. Even with his young age, he had the lines and shadowed eyes of one much older. I presumed it was from the stress of his work environment.

Looking us both up and down, the doctor continued. "I'm Doctor Robson, is there something I can help you with, or are you lost?"

Holmes replied first. "Pleased to meet you, Doctor, I am hoping we are not lost. I am Sherlock Holmes, and this is my associate, Doctor John Watson." I noticed Holmes put particular emphasis on my title. I assumed it was to secure a professional bond with Robson.

He nodded towards me and smiled. "Ah, a fellow physician?" When I nodded, he asked, "And what can I help you gentlemen with? It is quite unusual for members of the public to be brought down here. Are you relatives of one of these unfortunates?"

"No. I am a professional consulting detective and have taken on a case involving a missing person, possibly a young schoolgirl from the Limehouse area. I believe that you have taken delivery of someone who may fit the description. I have scant information, but," reaching into his coat, he brought out a small envelope and removed the two clues discovered so far. "She is young, possibly early to mid-teens. With brown hair, possibly shoulder length, and wearing a grey woollen tunic or dress."

Robson's eyes grew narrow. "That's a remarkably precise description, on scant information."

"Why would you say that?" I asked.

Instead of answering, he crossed the room to one of the beds and drew the sheet back from its resident, stopping just below the neck. Immediately, I saw why. Lying on the bed, was the blue-tinged body of a young girl with dark hair, which clung to her head in knotted clumps, some sporting the detritus of the river.

"She was pulled from the Thames only yesterday. Down near the Limehouse docks. I put her age as about fourteen. Her hair is dark brown, hard to tell, but the length falls just below her shoulders. Her eyes are cloudy from the water but have a distinctive green tinge to them."

"Was she clothed?"

Nodding, Robson pointed to a small set of shelves. "Only just put the dress and shirt back there. They were soddened, so we dried them out." I noticed his nose wrinkle at a memory. "Still stink, though."

All three of us moved across to the shelves. Holmes at once found the tunic and compared the swatch of fabric to it. "Hmmm. The dress is a little stained, but the colour matches to a high enough degree. Any identification found?"

Robson shook his head. "No. She is as she was found. I performed a quick examination and found a wound on the back of her head. Serious enough to be the cause of her demise, or at least to have disabled her enough so that a quick swim was the end of her. I'd like to do a full autopsy, but we just don't have the funds, time or," he shrugged, "need. A young child such as this, found in the river, could be foul play, could have been a childish lark. The police won't be interested, so the administrators take the easy path."

"No autopsy?"

"No, and the strangest thing is, I'm sure she has been dead for a good week or more, but the presentation of her skin and flesh tells me that she was only in the water for a day."

Holmes nodded, a studious look on his face as he processed these new facts. "That is very telling, thank you, Doctor." Slipping his hand into his coat once more, he presented his card to Robson and said, "If anyone comes asking about the poor girl, could you please contact me?"

"Do you know what happened?"

"Not yet. Admittedly, an autopsy would tell us a little more, such as whether she inhaled water or not, but I'll have to do without it seems."

Robson placed a gentle hand on my forearm. "Please keep me informed. I see so many poor young souls come through here. It would be nice to see one find peace in the resolution of their demise."

Patting the hand, I added, "Of course. Again, thank you for your help."

* * *

Our immediate concern was to visit the schools that Holmes had identified from his research earlier that morning. I was immediately astounded by Holmes's knowledge of the Limehouse area. This was a situation I would find myself in, on numerous occasions over the course of our future association. Many schools are not listed on regular street maps of London, but Holmes appeared to have an almost encyclopaedic knowledge of their names and locations, even some of the uniforms they issued.

"There are three residential schools within a short distance from the burnt-out premises. In fact, all are within walking distance, which gives me pause for thought on the matter before us."

"How so?"

"Even though my career as a consulting detective is relatively short, I have already borne witness to the worst depravities of the human condition. We were fortunate enough to have not shared poor young Nicky's view of the body in the box. Though from the scant evidence we have seen and been told about, this affair involves the probable death of a young girl, of school age, possibly a resident of a nearby school, whose remains were deposited within a fireproof strongbox, only to have a fire set in a probable attempt to erase that fact."

"Yes, when you put it that way, very horrid. What of the house? Why was she there?"

"Ah, now there's a question. There are several possible answers, the two most likely are that she was brought there of her own free will, or even against it; or that she was visiting someone. I'm leaning to the former, as the perpetrator had no real attachment to the property, given the fact they set a fire before fleeing."

"Hmmm. It hinges mostly on the identity of the girl. Would the perpetrator have returned to remove her corpse?"

"Now there's a question. Either he did or another was co-opted into doing so. Nicky mentioned a tall well-dressed man. That piques my interest, it may mean nothing, or it may mean everything."

"Why?"

"Well, I must admit that to Nicky, well-dressed could mean anyone that isn't living on the streets, but if the man were not of the same class as others from this area, what was he doing here?"

Our first stop was at the Northey Street School for Girls, a mere half-mile walk from the derelict house. Even before entering, we realised there was no need to go further. The students were enjoying their morning break and were milling and playing in the small, grassed area between buildings. Every girl wore the same uniform, a dark blue tunic, with a white blouse beneath. None, that we could see, sported a woollen garment bearing the same colour as the little grey swatch that Holmes held.

"Hmm. I know of two others, one of which will be of no use as well, for much the same reason. The Stepney girls' school to our North, is also known as the Greencoat School. Their uniforms are similar to these, but the tunics are a dark, bottle green. That leaves us with one more obvious candidate."

The Thomas Street Boarding School for Girls straddled the area between Thomas Street and the Limehouse Cut, a purpose-built canal built to connect the Limehouse docks with the River Lea.

In direct opposition to our previous destination, the favourability of this one was immediate. A group of girls, possibly as young as thirteen, exited from the main doors as we approached. All wore the same strict uniform, a grey tunic, with a white blouse beneath. Even from a distance, the tunic appeared to be made from a loosely spun woollen fabric, much like the piece that Holmes found.

"Hmmm," he said, "I think we have a strong candidate."

Stepping in through the front doors, we found a studious looking woman working alone at a desk behind a small partition. Within a few minutes of approaching her, we were ushered into the office of the headmistress, a stern and matronly looking woman in her fifties. The nameplate on her desk said, "Cordelia Smeekins," and her disapproving look told me that interruptions were not welcome.

"We are dreadfully sorry to impose on your time, Mrs. Smeekins," started Holmes.

"Miss," came a terse reply.

"So sorry, Miss Smeekins. I am Sherlock Holmes, and this is my associate, Doctor John Watson."

"Yes? And?"

"I am a consulting detective and am investigating the apparent disappearance of a young girl from a nearby Limehouse residence. We only have a few strands of hair, and this small swatch of material." He held up the piece of fabric. "A witness stated that the young girl was of school age, and this fabric appears to be similar to the tunics that form part of your uniform. These facts have led us to your premises. So, my question is, are any of your students missing?"

I'm sure Holmes saw it too, but a faint hint of trepidation crossed that proud, uncompromising façade before it flashed away once more.

Silence hung in the air for a good few seconds, before Holmes spoke again. "I do apologise, I'm sure if there are, you would have quickly advised the authorities and their parents, so silly of me to even presume." He started to rise, almost gaining his full height before Miss Smeekins bade him sit again.

"No. No, I should apologise for being harsh. Please sit down. I think you might be of some help."

Holmes sat down once more, remaining silent to allow Miss Smeekins time to regain her composure and continue. "As alarming, and indeed embarrassing, as it is, yes, one of our girls has gone missing. Now, this does happen quite often, but either their money runs out, or they find the streets of London a much more harrowing experience than they presumed and will generally saunter back after a day or two with their tails between their legs."

"But not this time?"

Miss Smeekins shook her head slowly. "No. The young lass left over a week ago. Slipped out in the early morning, well before breakfast time. None of the other girls saw her leave, and she only took the clothes on her back."

"Her school uniform?"

"Why, yes, as you've seen it is of the same colour as that piece of fabric, but that could be from anything, really." Holmes produced the small swatch of material, placing it on the headmistress's desk and sliding it across to her. Miss Smeekins picked up the piece of fabric and studied it, intently before nodding. "Hmm, yes, on second thoughts, this could definitely be from one of our uniforms." Sliding it back to Holmes, she added, "Forgive us, but the girls are only meant to wear these on the school premises or surrounds, so we aim for a hardwearing, but inexpensive material. I'm very disappointed, but not surprised by our Penelope."

"Penelope?" I asked.

"Yes." Miss Smeekins looked confused for a moment, "Penelope Burdett. Didn't I mention her name?" Dropping her gaze and shaking her head slowly, she added, "I'm sorry. This last week has been very upsetting. I do not enjoy having our students wandering about, so."

"Would she have, perhaps, returned to her parents?" I asked.

"Oh, no, poor Penelope is an orphan. Her dear mother passed just late last year. The young girl has been beside herself. Changing from fits of grief to anger and back again. The awkward years are tough enough on young girls, but put this in the mix and it's a harrowing experience. The girls reside here for much of the year, returning home during the holidays, but poor Penelope had to spend Christmas and Easter with us here. She was so distraught."

Holmes brought the headmistress back to our inquiry. "Could you describe this Penelope?"

"Oh, yes. Fourteen years old, just this past February. Five-foot two in height. Brown shoulder-length hair. Slim build. Pretty much average, really. Her most striking feature was her eyes. Bright green."

"Hmmm," murmured Holmes. "The height and weight fit. The hair and eyes fit. And then there is that." He nodded at the small piece of cloth. "It seems that we may be interested in finding the same young girl. Do you happen to have an address for her mother? Maybe there are other witnesses that may have seen her."

"Oh, yes." She reached for a thick ledger from within one of her desk drawers. After flipping several pages, Miss Smeekins said, "11 Narrow Street, Limehouse. But, as I said, the poor woman died almost six months ago."

I gasped at the address, looking sideways at Holmes, he held his composure.

"Hmmm. That address tells us more than you are aware."

"How do you mean?" the headmistress asked.

"I am sorry to inform you that we believe your student to be dead." It was Miss Smeekins's turn to gasp. "The hair, I mentioned, and that swatch of cloth were found inside a steel strongbox in a burnt-out house, 11 Narrow Street, Limehouse, to be exact. It matches the uniform worn by a young girl, whose body was pulled out of the Thames yesterday afternoon."

"My word, that poor girl."

"We haven't informed the police as yet, but they will need to be involved soon. They will also need a positive identification, so if there is any way to find a relative or someone who knew the girl, then we need to pursue that avenue of inquiry."

"Or it will be I who must identify her, the poor thing."

"Yes, sadly."

"Sorry to be direct, but there was no father then?" I asked.

"No," she said, shaking her head and dabbing at the edges of her eyes with a kerchief. I was surprised to see such a matronly woman taken to emotion, but I could only imagine that Miss Smeekins looked upon her students as faux children.

"No other guardian?" I asked. Another shake.

Holmes thought for a moment. "I assume then that with no funds coming in to pay for Penelope's tuition, you would have had to terminate her residency here."

"No, not at all. Penelope's fees are paid through an intermediary. The funds appear in our accounts every year without fail."

"Intriguing, the mother set up a trust or some such?"

Miss Smeekins thought for a moment. "It never occurred to me before how she could afford it. Miss Lyra Burdett was a simple seamstress. As far as I know, she barely had two pennies to rub together, but that was never my business. As long as the fee was paid, I was more than happy to accommodate the young lass."

"Could I be so bold as to ask for the details of this intermediary? They may be able to shed light on a close relative."

"Ah for that, I will need to consult with my assistant." The headmistress rose and moved across to her office door, pulling it open so swiftly that her assistant spilt to the office floor. "So, Agnes, I presume you heard the request."

I stifled a slight chuckle as I watched the poor woman stand up and compose herself, before nodding. "Yes, Miss Smeekins, I have it right here." She hurried off, returning quickly, with another ledger. Ignoring both Holmes and me, she moved to the desk and opened it. Turning several pages, she pointed to an entry.

"Ah, that's right," said Miss Smeekins before writing the contact details onto a card and handing it to Holmes.

As he read, a small smile grew on his face.

"Pardon me, Miss Smeekins, but are the students able to contact people outside of the school during term time?"

The headmistress nodded. "Oh, yes, we're not some sort of prison. If a student wishes to send a message to a relative or someone else, then they can approach Agnes here, and she will arrange it."

Turning towards the assistance, Holmes asked, "Did Penelope Burdett attempt to contact someone recently?"

Agnes withdrew to her desk and shuffled through a pile of papers impaled on a bill spike. Eventually, she tore one off and held it up. "Yes, she did, I forgot all about it, but she sent a note to Mr. Cumbage," she said, nodding towards the card in Holmes's hand.

"I don't suppose you know what the message said, do you?"

"Oh, yes, Sir, it's right here." Her eyes dropped to the page. "Mr. Cumbage. I need to meet him. Tomorrow. Before school starts. Home."

"Do you know what date that was sent?"

Reading the message further, Agnes answered. "The twelfth."

"That was the day before she disappeared," said Miss Smeekins, "How could you have failed to tell me this, Agnes?"

"I do apologise, Miss."

* * *

"Who is Hyram Cumbage? You seem to know him, or at least know of him?" I asked Holmes, as I read the name on the card once more.

"I've not met the man, but I have come across his name in various dealings. He is a solicitor, but let us say that he specialises in practices that only stay on the right side of the law through plain good luck, rather than design. If he is involved, then I am forming more of a complete picture than I had previously."

Handing back the card, I nestled back in the seat of the cab and watched the streets of London pass by as we bumped our way through them. Within a few minutes we headed into Gossett Street near Shoreditch and the cab stopped before a small Georgian terrace with a sign outside that proclaimed it to be the offices of one, *Hyram Cumbage, Solicitor at law.*"

The sole occupant of the office was a short, bald little man, with a strangely lined face that gave him the appearance of an apple that had been left in the sun for far too long. He sat behind a large, dark wooden desk and looked up from a pile of paperwork through extremely thick eyeglasses. "Can I help you, gentlemen?"

"Ah, Mr. Cumbage? Mr. Hyram Cumbage?" asked Holmes with an air of innocence that I could tell was drawn from his acting days.

"Yes? I'm at a loss, Sir. You know me, presumably from the name on the board outside, but I do not know you."

Removing his hat, Holmes said, "I am Sherlock Holmes, and this is my colleague, Doctor John Watson."

The scrunch-faced man's expression remained impassive for a moment until a look of confusion crossed it. "Sherlock Holmes? That name seems familiar, but I cannot place it or you." Placing his pen back into its holder, he waved a hand and said, "Never mind. Please state your business. I am a busy man as you can see. If you are a new client, then have a seat. If you are selling something, then the door is behind you."

"Neither I'm afraid. But, we have come about a client of yours."

"Client? Whatever business you have with one of my clients is between you and them. So, in that case, please leave."

"The client is Penelope Burdett." A twinkle of recognition crossed Cumbage's face. "Of 11 Narrow Street, Limehouse." The solicitor remained silent. "You arrange the payments for her schooling at the Thomas Street Boarding School for Girls." Holmes went silent and waited.

After a moment, Cumbage finally replied. "So? What of it?"

"Well, she contacted you only a week ago, asking to meet with, as she said, *him*." Holmes held up the note that he had retrieved from Agnes. "Now, she's dead." Holmes dropped the bombshell and let its effect hang in the air for a few moments.

A stunned look dawned on the solicitor's face. "Dead?" Cumbage said, his voice more of a whisper, his eyes staring into Holmes's "When? How?"

"That is what I am trying to determine."

"Sherlock Holmes. Now it's come to me. You're the private detective that has been circulating through Soho and Whitechapel for the last couple of years."

"And many other parts of London, to be honest, but yes, that is I."

"And Penelope's dead?"

"Yes. Sadly, she was drawn from the Thames only yesterday morning. The police have not been informed as yet, but they will need someone to identify the body. For my part, I wish to identify the reason for the poor girl's demise. To do that I will need your help."

"Well, I don't really know the girl, only by name. I simply manage her affairs."

"On, whose request?"

"I can't tell you that, I need to protect my client's identity and interests."

Holmes placed two hands on the solicitor's desk and leaned in, staring directly into the oversized lenses and through into Cumbage's eyes. "Would that be Lyra Burdett?" He remained still, the older man squirming but shaking his head.

"I don't know who that is?"

"That would be Penelope's mother. So, if you do not know her mother, then you must be working for her father?" I was intrigued.

The Body in the Box by Stephen Herczeg

The solicitor showed no outward signs, but Holmes began to smile. "Ah, yes, her father. Now, it would be very helpful if you could tell me his name."

"I can't."

"Hmmm." Holmes continued to stare into the man's eyes. There was no hint of malice in my colleague's actions, but the proximity of their faces was more than unnerving to the solicitor. "I understand your concern, Mr. Cumbage, so, it will need to be you that identifies the body of poor Miss Penelope Burdett."

"But, I've never seen her. I only act on behalf of ..."

"Her father. Yes. What is his name then? We can inform the police and he can identify the body."

"I...I..."

"I'm sure that the police would be very interested in your other cases. Especially, young Malcolm Dalgleish." Cumbage's eyes darted down to the open folder to his right. "Doesn't he run with the Lambeth Lads? I hear he is under scrutiny over an assault and robbery that ended with the victim's unfortunate death. Only last Saturday night, wasn't it? That would be of interest to my friend Inspector Lestrade, I'm sure." Holmes lifted one hand and pointed to another file. "Or that one, Percy Renton. I know of him personally. A burglar working the Hamstead Heath area. Nothing of note, or at least nothing that has drawn any of his victims to me, but he has a reputation that has been growing down the East End of late. Inspector Bradstreet would find that information interesting."

Cumbage's face grew red, and I could see him visibly shaking. I started to worry that the man might have a turn and burst a blood vessel.

"Driesbach. Millard Driesbach. That's all I'm going to tell you. Now please, leave me be." He fell back into his chair, drawing deep breaths and fetching a kerchief from his breast pocket, which he used to wipe the beads of sweat that had burst from his forehead.

"Millard Driesbach? Hmmm." Turning away from the solicitor, Holmes added, "Come, Watson, a quick trip to Islington is required."

* * *

After a short side trip, the hansom took us north through the great metropolis.

"I've had my eye on Mr. Driesbach for quite some time," said Holmes as we approached the entrance to Liverpool Street in Islington. "He runs an importation business that sources furniture and artefacts from the sub-continent. Two years ago, I was requested to investigate a matter of several items that were brought into the country. Investigating Driesbach and two other businesses like his revealed nothing but led me to several dock workers who were intercepting the items and removing them before they reached the importation companies."

"But, you weren't convinced; otherwise, why would you still have Mr. Driesbach in your sights?"

"Quite so, even though I stopped the operation, I never found out who had been organising the smuggling from the sub-continent end?"

"Does this Driesbach know you, or anything about this surveillance?"

"No. No, I don't think he does. We've never met, but that may become useful."

For a man on the rise in business, Mr. Driesbach's premises were very quiet. The outer door opened into a small reception area, with a desk, which was currently unoccupied, sitting in the centre of the room. A coat rack stood near the main door holding several items, one particular coat attracting Holmes's attention. He moved across and studied the sleeves, before leaning in and sniffing the material. I was a little perturbed at his actions, but that was something I was becoming used to.

At opposite ends of the room, were two doors. Each sported a plaque with the name of the occupier of the room beyond. Holmes nodded towards the right-hand room, and we fronted the door, whose plaque said, "M Driesbach."

Holmes grasped the doorknob, before turning it and knocking at the same time. As he opened the door, he said, "Sorry to bother you Mr. Driesbach, but your reception area was unattended." Thrusting the door wide open, we spied a slightly startled man sitting behind a large mahogany desk. A virtual mountain of paperwork sat in baskets on either side of his desk, some of which he had been feverishly working through at the time of our intrusion.

"Who the devil are you? Where is Clarence?"

Rather than answer, Holmes strolled into the room, assuming an air of innocence. "I do apologise again, Mr. Driesbach, but the outer office was empty, I wasn't sure of any protocols in place to see you, so I sort of barged right in."

Confusion reigned on the man's face, but eventually, after looking the two of us up and down for a moment, he regained his composure. "Well, you're here now, what is it you want?"

"Ah, let me introduce myself, I am Sherlock Holmes, and this is my associate, Doctor John Watson. We have just come from a visit with Mr. Hyram Cumbage, whom you know."

With the mention of my name, I noticed his eyes flick from Holmes to myself, then return and linger on Holmes when he said Cumbage's name. It was those eyes that caught my complete attention. When they opened completely and caught the light, I realised they were a startling green colour. His hair was non-descript but did hold a deep brown tinge to it. His expression didn't change though, suggesting he was hiding his knowledge of the solicitor and feigning ignorance. Instead, he took a different tack.

"Holmes? I know that name, don't I? Though, I don't think we've met." Staring at my colleague for a moment, Driesbach seemed to search his memories before continuing. "Yes. You investigated those smuggling shenanigans down at the docks some years back. It seems I have to thank you for that; your intervention caused me to avoid a lot of unwanted attention and damage to my reputation."

He stood, reaching his hand across the desk. Holmes stepped forward and took it, shaking firmly. "No need to thank me, it was all part of the service I provided to my client at the time."

Releasing Holmes's hand, Driesbach sat down, a slightly relieved look on his face. "Well, again, I thank you. There was no need to visit, all that business is water under the bridge, as they say."

"Oh, that has nothing to do with why we are here. As I said, we have just come from the offices of Mr. Hyram Cumbage, a solicitor of slightly dubious reputation."

"Yes. So?"

"Mr. Cumbage was kind enough to help with our inquiries regarding a young schoolgirl by the name of Penelope Burdett." Only a slight movement in those green eyes, the lids opening somewhat, before relaxing once more.

"Who?"

Holmes paused, a sly grin lifting his mouth at the side. "Penelope Burdett. Fourteen years old. Slight frame. Brown shoulder-length hair, a similar shade to yours I think. Startling green eyes, almost identical to yours."

"What are you saying, Sir?"

He pulled something from his pocket, placed it on the desk and slid it across, pushing aside several sheets of parchment. "Penelope Burdett. Killed, then squeezed into a steel strongbox, which can be opened with this key." Driesbach's eyes went wide as he stared at the key. Probably something he never thought he'd see again. "A strongbox that sits in the parlour of 11 Narrow Street, Limehouse." Holmes's hand darted into his pocket again, withdrawing the piece of paper with the address written on it. "The same address that is written on this paper. In a script very reminiscent to that which appears on the papers sitting before you on this desk."

"A key? Something scrawled on a piece of paper? What are you implying?"

"These items. Your striking resemblance to the young girl. Add to that, scorch marks and the smell of smoke on your coat. One last thing. How often does your man clean your shoes?"

"Well, I don't have a man. I do it myself, once every two weeks, why?"

"You have burn marks on the leather as well. Plus, some scuffing that may have come from leaving the scene of a fire in much haste."

"What fire?"

"Don't play the fool, Mr. Driesbach. Let me put it to you, that young Miss Penelope Burdett, is your daughter from a liaison many years ago with Lyra Burdett of Limehouse." Nodding towards a framed photograph sitting on a bookcase shelf behind Driesbach, Holmes added, "I assume that your current wife does not know about your previous dalliance and the issue that resulted."

The man turned and spied the photograph. With that, his entire reluctance to cooperate seemed to evaporate. He slumped back in the chair, staring at his desk while Holmes spoke further.

"To hide the fact of Penelope's existence, you employed Mr. Hyram Cumbage to facilitate the child's schooling, and deal with the money, keeping it all secret, as he is very good at doing."

Eyeing Holmes for a few moments, Driesbach's composure reasserted itself. "All right then, I admit it. It was before I was married, a stupid liaison with a woman of lower class down near the docks. I was stevedoring, working my way towards my own business. It was just another encumbrance that I didn't need at the time. I had no love for Lyra and no wish for a child at that time. So, I set them both up in that house."

"But Lyra died last year."

"Yes. I had hoped that would be the end of it, until Penelope left school, but…"

"She contacted you last week."

"Yes. With her mother gone, she wanted me to become her full-time family." He thumped the desk, shocking me, but bringing a smile to Holmes's face. "I couldn't have it. I've worked so hard on both this business and my marriage, to have this urchin bring down my reputation."

"But you did meet her."

"Yes. Last week, Wednesday I think, at the Limehouse place. She's fourteen. Old enough to start life. Without me. I offered her money. In exchange for her disappearing from my life."

"But she became angry. Went into a rage. A candle fell. The curtains caught fire. The place went up in a matter of seconds. I fled. I can only assume that she fled as well. When I turned back the place was engulfed. The brigade was already on its way. Their bells ringing through the streets. So, I returned home and thought no more of it. If I heard more from Penelope, I would deal with it at that time. With the money I gave her, I presumed she'd disappear from my life, and until you turned up, I've heard nothing."

"What a load of codswallop!" I cried out, incensed at the blatant lies of the man.

Holmes held up a hand to quiet me. "Patience Watson. Mr. Driesbach has told us his tale. We will get to the truth."

"That is the truth."

"Hmm. Perhaps, but it doesn't explain many things."

"Like what?"

"The blood, hair, and swatch of Penelope's uniform inside the strongbox, for a start. The strongbox that a witness said he found your daughter's body in."

"What witness?"

The Body in the Box by Stephen Herczeg

Holmes held a hand up towards Driesbach. "In time. The other inconsistency is the dark, dried pool of blood on the hearthstones of the fireplace." Driesbach went silent for a moment but kept his eyes on Holmes as he continued. "It is my conjecture, that during your, so-called, argument with Penelope, she fell, or was pushed, striking her head against the hearthstone, where she died or passed out. In your fear, you placed her body inside of the strongbox, locking it and taking the key."

I noticed Driesbach remain passive, but with his jaw clenched in anger. "Fanciful, but go on."

"You then set the fire, by breaking up the small sticks of furniture, but made one small mistake. The strongbox was extremely fireproof, a good old Thomas Milner. Penelope's corpse was preserved, only to be found days later by our witness, who procured the key and address note from your pocket or whoever you hired to retrieve the body."

"You keep mentioning a body." Driesbach's disposition moved from anger to assured. I sensed his appreciation of the situation was strangely calm, given the facts laid out by Holmes. "Where is this body? You've only mentioned finding a strong box with hair and blood, but no body, so I assume it was empty. Again, fanciful. Penelope took the money I gave her and escaped."

Holding up a finger, Holmes said, "Not so fast. True, Penelope wasn't in the strongbox, but she was found in the Thames yesterday. She is lying in the East London Hospital morgue, a sad figure left bereft of any chance to achieve adulthood through no fault of her own."

Driesbach muttered a curse under his breath.

"I can only assume that the person hired by your solicitor failed in your eyes. The police will no doubt see it differently."

Anger welled behind Driesbach's eyes. He stood slowly, pushing himself up with his balled fists pressed against the desk. "None of this should ever have happened. I was young. Stupid. Lyra

The Body in the Box by Stephen Herczeg

was a single dalliance. A bit of fun on a Saturday night. How was I to know what would happen? Then nine months later, she found me. Showed me the babe. I only had to look into her eyes and knew she was mine." He moved from behind the desk and approached a nearby window that looked out onto the street. "I did what I could. There was no way I would have married the woman, I had already met my future bride, and nothing was going to threaten that."

"Yes, your bride is the daughter of another businessman, isn't she? I assume he has invested heavily in your company."

Driesbach turned to face Holmes. His eyes stared deep into my colleague's own. "Yes, but I have built this business. It is mine until I pay back the old man."

"What happened in Limehouse? Please tell us again. The truth this time."

As the memories filled his mind, Driesbach's haughty demeanour failed him. His shoulders slumped, and his eyes dropped to the floor. Slowly shaking his head, he confessed all. "A week ago, Cumbage sent me a telegram. Penelope wished to speak with me, in her mother's house. Well, my house really, but that's just semantics. She complained that she was lonely. She wanted away from the school. She wanted a family." He looked up. "I couldn't give her that." Indicating the photograph. "I have my own family. I promised her money, to help set her up, away from London where she could start afresh. She became enraged, knocked the money from my hand. Pushed at me. I…I…" He struggled back to his chair and flopped down. "I pushed back. She stumbled. Fell. Hit her head on the fireplace step. I was stunned. When she no longer moved. I panicked. I was worried that the neighbours had heard us, and would come and find me. I spied the old strongbox, something Lyra's father left her." Shaking his head, he added, "I know it was horrible, but I picked up the poor little thing and stuffed her in that box. I needed to cover my tracks and get rid of the body, so I broke some furniture and set the fire. It was only when I returned home that I remembered the damn box. For some reason, I'd kept the key in my pocket, and I recalled how proud Lyra was of that box. Strong and fireproof, she had said. Fireproof. The words rang through my head. I stupidly waited to hear any news that she had been found, but when nothing but a small account of the fire appeared in the papers, I set out for Cumbage's office, with the key and a note with the address. I wanted him to arrange for someone to retrieve Penelope's body and dispose of it. On arrival, the key and note were gone. Damn pickpockets. Cumbage said he would organise someone, but obviously, the old fool failed at that properly."

I studied the man, as he deflated in his chair. He was defeated. All the pent-up emotion and anger at the situation of his own making had taken its toll.

"Fourteen years. This whole fiasco has lasted fourteen years. I've hidden Penelope's existence from my wife for fourteen years. And now it's over, but not the conclusion I wanted." He looked up into Holmes's face, his eyes red-rimmed, with tears threatening to pour from them. "What happens now?"

Before my colleague could speak, the front door opened, and a familiar voice shouted out. "Holmes?"

"Well, that is for my invited guest to decide."

The office door opened and in walked Lestrade, a little flushed from his trip.

"I received your telegram. What in the blazes did you mean about a body in a box?"

* * *

That evening, ensconced in our parlour, with a small fire in the hearth to warm the still chilly nights, Holmes and I sat back ruminating about the adventure.

"What will become of Driesbach now?" I asked, sipping at my brandy.

"According to Lestrade, he is convinced that the girl's death was accidental, but it was the treatment of her poor body post mortem that will be the focus of his investigation. The father will definitely end up in Wandsworth; he made mistakes after all."

"I'm probably happy about that. It is one thing to sire an unwanted child, but it is another to simply wish that child out of your life, and then to turn your back completely on her such as he did. Shocking really."

"Yes, granted Mr. Driesbach had his reasons, they were fully selfish and the situation could have been handled in a much gentler and more moderate way. We all make mistakes, but it speaks to the character of the person on how they handle those mistakes. I'm afraid Driesbach failed and will pay the penalty, not just in a penitentiary, but in his private life as well."

"Hmm. Yes, I think prison will be nothing compared to what happens on the home front."

"Quite so."

June 1883

The Victoria Hall Tragedy

By Kevin P. Thornton

Towards the end of the nineteenth century the speed at which information moved around the world seemed to be epoch-changing. News that had taken weeks and even months to reach London now flowed to the capital of the greatest empire the world had ever known daily, and sometimes even by the hour. From its far-flung outposts – and with an alarming alacrity that seemed to us mere mortals to be more likely dragged from the annals of Jules Verne than the scientific advances of Cambridge or Oxford – Her Majesty's realm was linked with such rapidity that one could scarcely imagine the world could get any faster. And yet, inexorably, day upon day, it did.

Ships scythed through the oceans powered by mighty engines that halved the Atlantic crossing; trains travelled in excess of sixty miles per hour on the Great Western Railway; hot air balloons flew higher and farther than ever before and there was even talk of the possibility of directed, controllable flight by lighter-than-air machines with wings attached. In addition, mail was delivered up to twelve times a day in the city, so much so that it was possible to have a conversation with one's neighbour by letter – a facile yet intriguing possibility. Furthermore, a delay of as little as thirty minutes for an appointment could be ameliorated by an immediate telegram to one's anxious host.

There had even been reports of a talking telegraph – a telephone I believe the press were calling it – where people would be able to converse with other people across the city and even further. I mentioned the instrument in question to my friend Sherlock Holmes as we sat in languid comfort in our rooms in Baker Street. Not to my surprise he was all for it. Although a Luddite in many ways – I was reasonably sure he had no idea of the mechanics behind a steam engine, nor did he care – in other fields, those pertinent to his life's work, he was remarkably astute. By way of example, while he seemed mystified how holes developed in socks, his knowledge of poisons was both exacting and a trifle worrisome. Mrs. Hudson had banished him from her cooking range on more than one occasion. "He'll put the wrong leaves in my game pie and then we'll all be done for," she once muttered to me, and while I was sure her fears were groundless, I was happy that her control of her domain remained absolute. The smell of his experiments in our rooms was a small price to pay for culinary peace of mind.

However, I could see why he was so interested in speedier communications. It would be a boon to a man who viewed information as the lifeblood of his work. I continued with the topic. "Don't you find some of the suggestions somewhat fanciful, Holmes? The telephone for starters, and then there is this fanciful idea they won't even need wires to communicate, doing it instead through the air. Radiating telegraphy or some such. It's all just a bit much isn't it?"

"Mark my words, Watson. The day will come within our lifetimes where we will look back on this period as the smallest part of the new renaissance, the renaissance of technology and science. Imagine having a machine in this room whereby we could connect to the outside world, maybe even have information transmitted to us along the same path. That is what a telephone will do, and the technology is available. If sounds can be transmitted, as has already been proven with the telegraph, then the rest is all mere tinkering waiting to happen. I see no reason to prevent documents being transferable by wire, even pictures. Did you know that there are developments of pictures in motion, such as to show the galloping of a horse? Why Watson, you may yet live to see the races at Cheltenham within the comfort of your own home." I laughed at the very thought, and even Holmes seemed to find it a tad fanciful. Moving pictures indeed. He might have well said Jules Verne was right, and we would one day travel through space to the moon.

"But dash it all, Holmes, it seems as if it's all happening too quickly. There is only so much information a man can absorb. Why, today *The Times* reported the baseball score from a game in New York. I was halfway through reading it before I realized it wasn't the scorecard on the Gentlemen vs Players match in Brighton. I have never cared for rounders and do not understand the way the Americans present their scores – it is a far more confusing sport of bat and ball than our own cricket, which is orderly and logical. Yet there I was reading all about the New York Gothams and the Boston Beaneaters simply because the information was in front of me."

"As I have said before, Watson, one needs to filter the facts until the salient details emerge. There are advantages to the wide and sometimes over-looming dispersal of news. I did read the cricket report so I can tell you the game was tied, a first in the history of the fixture and one that will no doubt have cricket scorers all atwitter as they try to find a way to describe such an anomaly.(1)

"More importantly," he continued, "I am expecting a visitor who has some concerns about the recent catastrophe in the Northeast. Without the news reporters' ability to tell us stories from afar I would not be anywhere near as prepared for his enquiry. As it is, I have a leaping start on the facts, insofar as I trust any journalist, but it would

The Victoria Hall Tragedy by Kevin P. Thornton

be much more useful if the entire contents of the investigation were transmittable to my door. Consequently, I expect to spend some time in the north for I believe my client will wish to get to the bottom of this with some alacrity.

"Do you mean the disaster that occurred in the Victoria Hall?" I asked. "What a monstrous calamity that was."

"Indeed," said Holmes. "I have kept cuttings from all the major newspapers in that folder on the corner of the table if you wish to refresh your memory."

I thanked him and began to read although in truth the story had been occupying the front pages for some days now, and I had read all the reports. The Victoria Hall tragedy had captured the heartstrings of the nation and tugged mercilessly at them.

Saturday, the 18th of June, 1883, will be remembered as one of the saddest in our nation. The death by asphyxia and crushing of 183 children in the Victoria Hall tore at the hearts of all of us. As I re-read, I noted that even the journalists had seemed to struggle for words. It could have been no worse had some madman taken a machine gun to them, as unlikely as that would be in a civilized society.

After the initial reports and mourning, the tone turned to one of investigative anger as the newspapers scrabbled for someone to blame. The worst was that it had initially been an event of such innocence. A husband-and-wife team of itinerant magicians with some small reputation for wholesome entertainment leased the hall and advertised a children's magic show, something they had done many times before at venues up and down the east coast. The hall itself had been built by a family of renowned Quaker businessmen and was of a grand design aimed at the betterment of the people, in accordance with Quaker philosophy. It was a relatively new building in good repair and the audience was within the seating limitations.

The magician show promised a number of prizes at the end of the entertainment, drawn against the attendees' entrance tickets. The show was a great success; the children by all accounts had a wonderful

The Victoria Hall Tragedy by Kevin P. Thornton

time, and when at the end of the show they began to leave, no one could have foreseen the imminent disaster. As they were departing, the audience was reminded of the draw for prizes. The children in the upstairs gallery, alerted to the excitement by the sounds below, rushed down the stairs. The door at the bottom, which opened inward, was locked into such a position that there was only a twenty-inch gap. This had been ideal to control the flow of children entering before the show started but as more and more children came down, the ones at the front found themselves jammed against a door that was locked in such a manner that easy egress was soon blocked by bodies being crushed to their deaths. As the catastrophe evidenced itself, various adults ran around the outside to help. The children nearest the door, already dying or dead and jam-packed by the weight of numbers behind, blocked the efforts of the rescuers for some minutes.

There were estimated to be as many as three thousand of the poor mites in attendance. By the time the door was ripped from its hinges by the adults, nearly 200 were dead.

I kept reading. I thought I was a strong man, toughened by war, steeled by the trials and tribulations of a life spent in medicine. Every now and then, though I forced myself to re-read the reports, I had to pause and take a moment as my eyes lost their focus. One reporter had chanced to see the firefighters on the scene, helpless to help. "Even men as hardened as these brave souls," he wrote, "were unable to face the unfolding cataclysmic calamity. Eventually they began to lay the bodies out in a gathering area so designated by the constabulary, and the wailing and mourning was biblical in its proportions when the parents came to search for their children and found instead the corpses of the poor wee mites laid out as if at rest."

Several families had lost all of their children. The oldest victims were fourteen years of age, the youngest barely three. An entire Bible study class from a local church died in the chaos, thirty souls taken from the warmth of their families and fellow worshippers. As I read on, tragedy was piled upon tribulation. The story had affected the entire nation. Her Majesty sent letters of condolence twice and started the fundraising effort with a sizeable donation. But to what avail? What could Her Majesty say to all the mothers who had lost children?

At length, I finished the cuttings, and for once Holmes, who had been pacing up and down, let his busyness rest. He settled into his chair and looked at me.

"It is a calamity the like of which I hope we will never see again," he said. "I wish I need not ask you to be with me during this investigation, but please say you will be at my side, Watson. I will need your strength of purpose."

Holmes had never been this charged before in all the cases I had seen with him. "Of course," I said. "You know I will stand beside you."

"Splendid," he said. "And I hear from the stairwell that it sounds as if Mrs. Hudson brings my client to meet us."

Sir Hopewell Cadwallader by his name alone appeared to be a co-religionist of the builders of Victoria Hall, a fact he affirmed immediately. "Just as an O'Rourke is most often Irish," he said, "and there are many Evans from Wales, if you bump up against a Cadwallader he is likely a member of the Society of Friends. Quakers as you might know us, although we are so peaceful we hardly make anyone quake, and if you did bump into us we'd likely be the ones apologising." Cadwallader may have rambled further had Holmes's impatience not gained the better of him.

"Sir," he said, "I am a busy man. I assume you are too. Please come to the point."

Sir Hopewell's face fell. He had the look of a jovial man bereft of all jollity. However, Holmes's abruptness seemed to jolt him into some sensibility.

"Of course," he said. "I apologize. The last two weeks have been horrendous. Let me be succinct in my storytelling. I am a banker here in London, but due to a merger five years ago I spend time in the

The Victoria Hall Tragedy by Kevin P. Thornton

Northeast, attending to our branches and investments in Sunderland and Newcastle. I have been fortunate in life and have been able to support several charities in the community. One such is a home for wayward mothers. In addition to helping them through the birth of their children, we attempt to reconcile them with the fathers of their children and try to help the families get back together." As I looked at Holmes, Sir Hopewell must have seen me for he addressed me in a mild yet firm rebuke.

"We are not naïve, Doctor, nor unduly idealistic, and if we lead some of these fallen women to our own faith, well I would hope they come to us by way of example, not coercion. The sins of the flesh do not need to be a final damnation. The fruits of such labour," and at this he permitted himself a tiny smile, "can also lead to the happiest of families."

"How many children did your charity lose?" said Holmes, and he was as gentle as I had ever heard him.

"Nine," said Sir Hopewell. "Five of our mothers lost a child each, ranging in age from four to seven, and Henrietta Kanneh and her husband, Gladstone, lost four children. The youngest was four, and the oldest nine."

Holmes appeared startled. "Your mathematics is troubling, Sir. If the Gladstone Kanneh to whom you refer is the boxing champion, why, he can only be twenty-three years of age himself. How is it possible he has lost a child so old?"

"Gladstone Kanneh is indeed the same man, the former bare-knuckle champion of the Northeast of England. He retired so as to be a father to his children, and I had him in my employ as one of the bank's liverymen. I say had because since the day of this horrible cataclysm of events until now, Gladstone has been missing from the family home. He came back once, for the funeral, and stood next to Henrietta, his grieving wife, with a visage set as if in granite. Not a muscle moved on his stony face all the way through the funeral and when it was over he walked out of the church alone. I rushed after him to try to talk to him. He said not a word, indeed he seemed to look through me as if he saw nothing."

Cadwallader had paused as if in need of a prompt, so I obliged before Holmes's charm was tested once more. "Do carry on please, Sir Hopewell," I said.

"Gladstone Kanneh was indeed still a young man, scarcely twenty-three. He had lived on the streets as an urchin and took shelter with Henrietta on the docks. Although she is two years older, he was big for his age. He protected her, became a father for the first time at thirteen, learned how to fight and did so for money for some years." The pacifist part of Sir Hopewell shuddered at the thought, but he continued. "It has taken a while for him to find happiness with the mother of his children but I had thought him one of our success stories. Now he has gone missing."

"And you want him found?" said Holmes.

"More than that, Mister Holmes. I want him found before he acts without thought. There is something seething within him now. I wish for you to find him before he causes harm to himself or to others."

"Is his wife safe?" I asked.

"Yes," said Sir Hopewell, "I have taken the liberty of bringing Henrietta home to my own wife to help with our youngest child. In truth we have enough nannies, but we feared for Henrietta alone in a house of empty memories."

"Very well," said Holmes. "Watson and I will head for the north by the next available train and find your young old man for you." Cadwallader left and I said to Holmes, "Babies having babies, Holmes. How did Gladstone ever have a chance to be a father himself? And now they're all dead. Dear Lord, life is cruel."

"He still has a chance, Watson," said my friend. "As long as we find him before he does anything bad, he still has a chance."

Less than two hours later we were ensconced in a carriage at King's Cross station en route to the north. A younger man of military

The Victoria Hall Tragedy by Kevin P. Thornton

bearing and a high and tight hairstyle joined us in the carriage. He seemed quite cheerful and dapper, and he carried an attaché case that was locked to his wrist.

"I have been ordered to turn over the documents within this case to Mister Sherlock Holmes. If the blasted contraption weren't attached to me with this manacle I would happily leave it with you and be off to eye the pretty maids in the dining carriage. As it is, oh I say that is dashed clever of you." This last was uttered as Holmes, as if a master prestidigitator, passed his hand over the manacle, unlocked it and waved our messenger on his way. "Thank you so much, Sir," he said as he dashed away," I shall return for the documents at the end of the journey."

I nearly hadn't seen Holmes sleight of hand as he pocketed one of his lock-picks then used another to unlock the case itself. It had a foolscap sized envelope within, bulging with papers.

Holmes briefly showed me one of his collections of lockpicks."I am not without influence in the halls of government," Holmes said. "These are transcripts of the official investigation so far. Its scope and size have momentarily transformed the various departments into a cohesive whole, spurred on by their express purposing for this task by Her Majesty, who has commanded a speedy conclusion to the matter."

"If you have such friends," I said, "surely they could have provided a key?"

"He knew I wouldn't need one." Holmes opened the box and split the documents into two even piles. "Amidst all this sadness, this gives me some small hope, Watson. The investigation into the charge of the Light Brigade at Balaclava was rumoured to have taken sixteen years and arrived at an inconclusive summary of the facts. At least this investigation has been pursued with both alacrity and brevity, in part due no doubt to the Queen's show of interest. It is barely two weeks since the events in question, and it appears that conclusions might soon be possible." He picked up his pile and placed it on his lap. "There is a succinctness here that was also missing in the official investigation into the Balaclava carnage, which ran to several rooms full of documents. Read quickly, Watson. Our Royal Guard will return in about four hours."

"What are we looking for?" I asked. "Royal Guard?" Holmes ignored the second part of my query, choosing only to answer the first.

"Someone to blame for all this," said Holmes. "Gladstone Kanneh may say he has given up the life of a warrior, but he will be looking to assuage his rage. The man that I knew could have been the greatest fighter in the world were it not for his temper. Pugilism is an art and a science at its purest. Gladstone did not understand that, which is why my nose is only slightly bent out of shape."

"Slightly bent? Holmes, whatever do you mean?"

"I met and bested him in a bare-knuckle fist fight shortly before I met you. That is why we need to find him, Watson. Gladstone Kanneh is a soul in torment and a formidable fighter with fists like horseshoes. If he believes he has found who is guilty of this monstrous calamity, well, I'd as soon he doesn't."

We spent the entire trip reading. Even though the reports were written in the boring language of all government reports everywhere, the conclusions were the same. The Victoria Hall Tragedy was exactly that – a tragedy. It could have been prevented, but likely only by lessons learned from this event. The Hall design could have been better, again something heretofore unknown. The doors would no doubt be rehung in all future venues. The reports on the magician, his wife and their troupe were similarly benign. They had presented a hundred similar shows in thirty similar places, all incident free.

If we were looking for who was to blame it would be difficult. One look at my friend as we slowed to enter Sunderland and I knew he had drawn the same conclusions.

"The doors were badly designed," I said, for want of something to say.

"They were the same as all others in the land. They will be changed, but there is no hint of shoddy workmanship. The building is well-constructed and less than twenty years old."

"Part of the building was unfinished," I said, "but it was only the outer décor. The structure itself is sound." I shrugged and Holmes agreed with the slightest of nods.

"The investigation has been very thorough. Unless there is something as yet unreported it would appear that while no one is ever entirely blameless, there really is in this instance, no one to hold accountable. Even the crackpot theories hold no water."

He pointed at the report outlining the two most repeated. I glanced over it. "Anarchists?" I said. "How would that even be possible? Are the warmongers now coming for us through the murder of our children? Ludicrous. Civilization is surely doomed if children become the targets of rage."

The other was no better and again I said as much to Holmes.

"The Quakers? Oh, Holmes that is too much. They may be an annoyingly twee religion but for heaven's sake they're pacifists and bankers mostly. The only reason anyone could disagree with them is the interest rates at Barclays."

"I agree, Watson. It appears there is nothing to investigate save the whereabouts of Gladstone Kanneh. As his disappearance is linked to the tragedy, I will arrange for the continued deliveries of these reports to our hotel, where I must burden you with the troublesome task of continued reading and notetaking. As we have already been doing, I must charge you with looking for something untoward."

"I will do what you need Holmes, you know that. In the meantime, what will you be up to?

"I shall be about the highways and byways of Sunderland, Watson, looking for Gladstone." There was a knock on the cabin door and the young man in charge of the papers came back to retrieve them.

"You are not a soldier, are you?" said Holmes. "There is something in your walk that allows me to infer you are used to a rocking motion in your work. Not a cavalryman, though you can ride, and do so often." He continued to look the young man up and down. "Watson, I do believe that our young acquaintance is a midshipman, seconded temporarily to the service of the Crown."

"I had heard of your skills, Mister Holmes," said the young man," but that is truly amazing. You can tell all that by the way I walk?"

"I can, and I deduce things from my abilities more often than not. But you have forgotten that we met once before at your family home. I was wondering how your grandmother would ensure she'd be kept up to date on the investigation. Inserting someone she trusts is clever even for her, and you may assure her that all our work and conclusions in this calamity will be made available."

The young man stretched taller, as if his pride made his backbone lengthen. "I shall do so, Mister Holmes. Thank you."

He left our compartment. I turned to my friend. "Holmes, what the devil is going on? Who is that young man, and is there a spy in our midst?"

"In a way, there is, Watson. Cadwallader is reporting to a higher authority. The midshipman's name is George Frederick Ernest Albert of Wales, a young naval officer destined for great things. He is a scion of the realm, son of the Prince of Wales, and grandson to Queen Victoria herself."

"But-but-but-but . . ?" I'm sure Holmes found it amusing that I was at a loss for words. Eventually I found my voice. "But Holmes," I said, "You dislike interference."

"In Her case and in these circumstances, I'm prepared to make an exception."

The hotel was the newest and best in the downtown, and we had several rooms at our disposal, one of which I set up as a command post of sorts. Cadwallader was not skimping,

The Victoria Hall Tragedy by Kevin P. Thornton

"I remember you mentioned McMurdo the prizefighter," I said, as Holmes prepared to leave. He had dressed down for his excursion and if I didn't know better I would have taken him for a fighter. He had changed his walk and the way his body hung in the air, gone from gentleman to thug in the blink of an eye. "It appears you also fought Kanneh," I continued. "Did you once make a habit of trying to get yourself killed?"

"Ah Watson, I arranged to be taught by them so there was less chance of my death. Once I chose my career, I knew it would be dangerous on occasion. I sought out the best fighters to learn from them, and they taught me so much more than mere fisticuffs. There is a strange honour among men of the bare-knuckle trade. Five minutes after knocking seven bells out of each other they will be tending to their wounds and having a beer and a laugh. Because it is such a pointless yet manly sport, it has its own code of honour that is both fascinating and dignified. If Gladstone Kanneh is anywhere in Sunderland he will be among those friends he trusts most: prizefighters, gamblers and other honourable scoundrels. While you continue with the laborious task of reading all the reports the young prince brings to you, I will make my way into the darker denizens of the port and docklands hunting for Gladstone."

"So you will go adventuring while I read reports."

Holmes looked at me through those steely eyes, so clear yet so daunting. "Please understand when I say we must divide the work to find him. These reports are the transcriptions of public hearings. If anything is said pointing a finger of guilt, the word will spread quickly. We must hear the accusation first so that guilty or innocent, we may stop Gladstone from doing something he may hang for."

"You are right, Holmes. I will not let you down. How will I contact you?"

"Why Watson, you finally understand the need for speedy information. Absent the invention of any of the gadgets we spoke about earlier today, there is a telegraph office in the heart of the docks.

You may message me there and I shall check on a regular basis. Best not use my name. There was an old prizefighter whom I admired when he was young, before McMurdo rang his bell for good in his last fight. He's a punch-drunk old soak now, and harmless. We'll use his name. Message me as Roger Thomas Esquire." I made a note.

For the next three days I barely left the room. Prince George arrived soon after Holmes left the first time with another valise, this one unchained and unlocked. He started to leave. Then he stopped. "Let me help, please." He said, "I'm smarter than they say, and I want to help."

He was. The gutter press had called him the dullard in the family but only, I fancy, because there was nothing to report about him. He was far more intelligent than he let on to anyone, and I enjoyed his company and his insights. I still didn't know what to call him, and after about an hour of my minding my Ps and Qs so as not to offend a member of the Royal Family, he said to me, "If I call you Doctor, would you honour me by using my family name. I have found that not much gets done when people worry too much about titles." He stuck out his hand. "Bertie," he said, "in honour of my grandfather."

"And I am John," I replied. "Delighted, I'm sure, and honoured."

We paused after a couple of hours and he asked me somewhat hesitantly, "What if our conclusions clash?"

"What do you mean?"

"Your job differs from mine in that you wish to rescue this fighter from himself, while my Grandmother wishes to know the truth."

"Not quite. Holmes always wants to know the truth. In this case he has deputised us to find anything that has any bearing on what happened. He wants to use the information available to head Kanneh off before he does anything he can't back out of."

"We'd better get back to it then," he said.

The Victoria Hall Tragedy by Kevin P. Thornton

We spent the next two days poring over reports, sending whatever updates we could to Holmes – mostly nothing – and receiving even less in return. At some point Bertie left the room for a while. Thereafter the reports were brought by another young midshipman, food and ale appeared, enough to charge us fully and more, and the room was serviced more often than I expected, receiving obsequious attention from the hotel management. When a telegram arrived at our door from an admiral, I asked him what he had done.

"It is most important," he said, "that we find what the great detective needs to prevent any further tragedy. My Uncle, the Duke of Edinburgh, is the vice-admiral in charge of the fleet based at Malta. I asked him by telegram to persuade the nearest naval station to provide assistance to us." He grinned a little shamefacedly as he said so.

"But you're a midshipman, "I said.

"Well, I am merely a midshipman," he said, "and almost everyone in the navy outranks me, but . . ." and as he said this there was a naughty little spark in his eyes, "I am also third in line to the throne and will only become irrelevant when my brother, the future Prince of Wales inherits the throne from my father, the current Prince of Wales. Until then, I say if you have connections, one might as well use them."(2)

Holmes returned and said nothing about the new research arrangements in the hotel room. He reported what little he had. "He has been around, in the places I would expect him to go," he said. "I think he knows I am looking for him, or at least he's guessed, and he seems as if he is ahead of me all the time. What of the public investigation?"

"More of the same as when we came up on the train," I said "The conclusions so far will be that this was a tragedy that could not be prevented but might well be avoided in the future."

"Just like a caveman," said Bertie. He saw the puzzlement on my face. "My father has a story that was told to him by his father. The first caveman, having discovered fire, didn't know it was hot until he was burnt. If the second caveman, knowing what the first caveman knows, makes the same mistake, well, he's at fault."

"If another building causes another tragedy?" I asked.

"We're all to blame," said Holmes.

He watched us working, going through everything again, then he left us and we continued our reading. I had asked Bertie to look at everything anew, including what we had read on the way up, and it was this, and an experience he'd had during training, that gave us a breakthrough.

The varied editions of the local newspaper, The Sunderland Daily Echo and Shipping Gazette arrived through the day along with the Newcastle Daily Chronicle. I had the latest copy of the Echo open when I noticed a new report.

"Look at this," I said. The Prince read it over my shoulder.

"All the owners of the Victoria Hall are going to meet there this afternoon," he said as he read.

"Fourth name down is our client," I said. "Some of the other names have also been in our reports. They're all Quakers."

"As a group, the have a reputation for peace and piety."

"And making money. They own half the banks in the Northeast. Kanneh should have no grudge against Cadwallader. He has helped Gladstone's family through all this, taking in his wife even as Kanneh deserted her."

Bertie reached across, pointing at the spread of papers on the table. "Here's another mention of the Quakers, and another, and another. We have also seen mention of their religion often in the reports of the investigation."

"Kanneh won't have heard those," I said. "And they were mostly anecdotal, used to clarify points of investigation."

"What if he's being more logical than we think?" said Bertie. "He might not risk going to the enquiry but he could be talking to people who are. It's open to the public"

"That's unusual," I said.

"He flushed a little as he said, "Grandmama felt it would be cathartic.""

"And no one denies Her Majesty?"

"Not that I know of. My aunts and uncles couldn't wait to get married and away from Buckingham Palace, my father is scared of her and even my mother, a formidable woman in her own way, is cautiously coy."

"I would love to hear more," I said, "but where does this all this mention of the Quakers leave us. It doesn't add anything. There was no conspiracy. It's impossible to even think of such a thing."

"To men such as you and I maybe, John. What if we're wrong?" He paused, as if planning his next words. "During midshipman training two years ago, we had a cadet who was dragging us all down. We were being penalized as a group for his laziness, his unfitness, his tardiness his slovenliness. We even had a nickname for him."

"Ness?" I asked. He looked surprised until I said, "I was in the army."

"I persuaded the others to try to help. We'd all get through together, working with each other. Only, Ness got the wrong end of the stick and thought, when we were trying to help, that we were actually teasing and hindering him. He was so wound up he could see nothing except the conclusion that fit his own story."

"And?"

"And what if Kanneh gets the wrong end of the stick and sees his helpers as the enemy? They're rich, they're looking into the building where his children died. Maybe he thinks they're hiding evidence. He knows they have his wife, Henrietta. There has been some talk of anarchists, talk that would be exaggerated in the saloons where he travels now."

"Cadwallader is trying to help him," I said.

"What if he doesn't see that? If he wants to blame someone, they're ideal for his purposes."

I looked at the time. "They meet in half-an-hour. If Holmes is by the docks, he cannot make it in time."

"But we can," said Bertie.

We made it to the hall in twenty-seven minutes. "What if we're wrong?" asked Bertie.

"Then we do nothing," I said, momentarily surprised. He had been so magnificent a companion over the last few days it was hard to remember he was still only eighteen. A bit of doubt was in keeping with his age and experience, until we reached the hall. There was still a police presence, two of them manning a line to keep the gawkers away, another on the door. Judging by the resting horses with their expensive carriages by the side of the hall I assumed the delegation was already inside, and we had no way to join them until I saw the other side of His Royal Highness. As he stepped from the carriage and set his cap on his head, it was if his walk and demeanour had transformed into a man of bearing. He moved with a casual snap to his gait, a purposeful movement with his arms behind his back as if he listened to all and missed nothing. The policeman in charge took one look at him and snapped to attention as the Prince murmured something. Then he moved the barricade aside and saluted us through.

"What did you say?"

"I may have mentioned I was here at Her Majesty's behest. As I said before, if you have connections, one might as well use them."

"But, one minute you were . . . and then . . ."

His Royal Highness was now Bertie again. "I have been taught since birth to be Royal. What you saw there is the way my father expects me to do things, and my grandmother, and all the other Royals. I choose not to be Royal as much as I can, but it is useful on occasion."

The hall, imposing from the outside, was ethereally charming within. I now wonder how much was my imagination but at the time it felt more cathedral-like than a public auditorium. I shuddered as we walked through the hall to the bottom of the stairs, lately the scene of the deaths of so many innocents. We could hear talk above us so we ran up the stairs as fast as we could. As we turned the corner onto the upper gallery, we stopped. Gladstone Kanneh had the entire attention of five well-dressed portly men. In his one hand he had a cricket bat that looked as if it had delivered many a sturdy knock, and was capable of many more. In the other he had a fiendishly curved, bladed-edge knife nearly half a yard long. It was a khukuri, a popular souvenir for sailors of the Far East and easy enough to find in a harbour town. It was an evil weapon, heavy, a combination of an axe and a knife. I had seen one wielded in India and it took a goat's head clean off the body. It looked as if Gladstone Kanneh were going to put it to the test. He had the blade aimed at Cadwallader, and he sounded quite mad, shouting incoherently and gesturing as he herded them closer to the balcony. If he attacked Cadwallader, it was likely some of the others would fall to their deaths with him. I didn't know what to do. Any rash move on our part would rouse Kanneh to use either of his weapons. Next to me I could feel Bertie tense as if to spring. I wasn't sure if I could stop him but as I reached across to try, I was rescued by the most amazing sight. From high above the stage in the rafters, and with all the grace and elegance of a circus performer, Sherlock Holmes swung down on a rope, gaining momentum as the arc increased. At the last second Kanneh heard the swish of the swinging rope and turned just in time to feel the two feet of the detective hit him right in the midriff. With a whoosh the air was expelled from within and Kanneh collapsed to the ground.

"Watson, Midshipman, tie up Kanneh. He mustn't get away. There is only one cure for all this now. We must act quickly before the authorities arrive."

We did as he asked, then Holmes took Bertie to one side and spoke to him. Bertie ran down the stairs, and Holmes addressed the bankers. "You have been through a terrible time of it, and normally I wouldn't hesitate to hand over your assailant to the police. But I ask for your mercy. If I can demonstrate to you that your lives will not be in any more danger, I will then ask you to consider clemency. This man lost all four of his children in this very building. Even though the justice he sought was wrong, I believe I can promise that this ends here today." He looked over at where Gladstone Kanneh sat tied to one of the chairs. "When we first met in the ring, Gladstone, you were a man of honour. What you have tried to do here was madness."

"But they are responsible," he said. "They need to pay."

"On my word," said Bertie, coming back up the stairs, "They were not. Doctor Watson and I have gone over all the reports. This was a tragedy we can prevent from happening again, and we will, but this event could not have been prevented."

"No," shouted Kanneh, "it's not fair! Why did they all have to die? My babies, my babies!" He screamed in agony as if under Afghani torture, and there was not a man there whose heart was not affected. Gladstone Kanneh screamed and cried and howled, and the world closed in on us all, a sadder, more tragic place.

Eventually his agony subsided briefly. Bertie looked at him with sadness, and said to him, in a voice loud enough for all to hear, "Mister Kanneh, my name is George Frederick Ernest Albert, and I am the son of the Prince of Wales." Left unsaid was who else he was related to; the collective gasp from the bankers was enough, but it also registered with Gladstone Kanneh. "I promise you there will be building reform. The findings of this enquiry will have weight. You have suffered too much, you and your wife. This must not happen again." As he said this, a young woman dressed as if in service came round the corner and ran across to Gladstone, bending down to hug him. She held his face in her hands, and Holmes said, "He's no danger anymore. Untie him please, Watson."

I was hesitant for a brief moment until I heard the wisp of the couple's conversation, then I did so. Kanneh remained seated hugging his wife. They were both crying. I walked over to the bankers and Holmes.

"Thank you, Mister Holmes," said Cadwallader. "You're every bit as excellent as we thought, but there is still no guarantee Kanneh won't attack us again."

"Yes there is," said Holmes. "When I fetched his wife earlier, she gave me one valuable piece of information that will ensure his behaviour, even more valid than the promise of a Prince of the Realm.to do right by the victims."

"And what was that?" said Cadwallader.

"She is with child."

We went back to the hotel, the three of us. Cadwallader had no heart to fetch the police in, so the Kannehs were left to pick up the pieces of their old life and start anew if they could. I had hope for them.

Holmes and I would depart in the morning, Bertie had to leave soonest to report to Buckingham Palace before returning to his ship.

"Whatever happened to Ness?" I asked Bertie.

"He shot himself in the foot and was discharged from service," said Bertie.

"And?" I asked.

"You seem sure I know more."

"The man I have been working with these last days would have followed up."

"I did," said Bertie. "We all felt guilty at how events turned out, but it may have been for the best. He now works in the city as a trader of some sort, has a polished ebony and ivory cane to aid his limp and in the last six months has made enough money to buy my Grandmama at least twice." He shook my hand and turned to leave. "Thank you, John. It has been a pleasure to work with you."

"Likewise, Your Highness," I said and he smiled as he left us in the foyer.

"How did you get there in time?" I asked Holmes. "We had only just worked it out, and I knew a telegram wouldn't reach you which was why we rushed to the hall. But you were already there?"

"Ah, that is quite simple, Watson. For all the technological advances and proliferation of information, there is still the matter of what one does with it all of it, and am I not the greatest detective in the world? I deduced what would happen hours before it did, went to fetch Kanneh's wife and even had time to set up in such a spot that I could react quickly no matter where they gathered. The information that Henrietta was with child was merely the icing on the cake, so to speak."

"I did wonder how you'd arranged that."

There was one more matter that needed answering. "Holmes," I said, "when we started down this path you asked me in a most particular way to be with you while you investigated this distressful occurrence, yet I feel I have never been less use to you. All the investigating was done by you alone, you could find no one to blame and even when you had to save your client from his own sad madness, I was no help at all. So why did you feel you needed me?"

"Watson, in the time I have known you, you have proved yourself to be a redoubtable friend and a strong moral ally. We see some dark deeds as a result of my profession, but none, I hope most fervently, more dire than this. I needed you to centre me on the human importance of all that had to be done, to take away the numbers and remind myself of all the feelings of so many families. Every time I looked at you Watson, I was reminded of the goodness still in the world." He smiled ever so slightly. "It is true that your involvement in most of my investigations is peripheral, in that you joyfully stumble to the wrong conclusions and are of no practical use." The wryness in his eyes took away any possible sting as he concluded with, "Perhaps that is your biggest gift to me. You are the epitome of the English gentleman and a reminder of all the good we stand for."

The Victoria Hall Tragedy by Kevin P. Thornton

Such sentiment from Holmes was most unusual, but it had been an unusual adventure. I harrumphed myself back behind my newspaper. It wasn't long before I found something to be outraged about so as to clear away the emotions in danger of being laid bare.

"There are now reports out of Germany," I said, "that they are close to inventing horseless carriages, driven by combusting motors of some sort. Really Holmes, it's simply too much."

"That may be an advance too far," said Holmes, and there was the slight wry smile I had learned was the most mirth he could normally manage. "If horses are replaced, how will Mrs. Hudson be able to gather fertilizer for her flower boxes?" He saw the astonished look on my face and for once I saw the slightest scintilla of confusion before he realized. "My word Watson, do you mean to tell me that you didn't know that Mrs. Hudson's roses are grown in the finest horse manure deposited on Baker Street?"

"I did wonder why the emanating odour was so strong, but I attributed it to the streets below and what I considered to be my keen sense of smell."

Now the astonishment was on his face. Years later he told me he thought I was joking. At the time, words for once failed him and he was only able to express his incredulity in one way, as the rarest of sounds erupted from his lips.
Sherlock Holmes laughed.

* * *

(1) In this instance Holmes was, if not wrong, then not entirely right. A tied match occurs only when everything is equal on the last ball of the match. These include wickets lost (up to 40) and runs

scored, (a limitless total). Given the statistical unlikelihood of a tie, the advent of better reporting has not increased their known number. Unlike a drawn game, which is common to the sport and consists merely of neither side having won nor lost, a tied game remains a rarity in cricket, occurring with a similar frequency to a perfect game of baseball.

(2) Prince George's life as the spare to the heir took a turn away from this path when his older brother, Prince Albert Victor, Duke of Clarence and Avondale, died in the influenza pandemic of 1892. As King George V he led his country through societal changes few had ever seen, including the Great War. He was a good man and a steady king, and if he had fond memories of his time in Sunderland, he kept them to himself.

July 1883

The Bishop's Curse

By Greg Maughan

The summer of 1883 was proving to be unseasonably hot. Those long, cloudless days fed into a lethargy that had taken hold of Sherlock Holmes since the conclusion of our most recent case. I busied myself with the recording of our adventures and worked long into those close, light evenings drafting and redrafting tales that I was sure would capture the imagination of the reading public if only I could find a home for them. But my companion seemed more likely than ever to reach in boredom for his "seven-percent solution" and let the summer nights wash over him. Try as I might to engage him in conversation, nothing seemed to shake him from his ennui. I would ask him to clarify this point of an investigation or ask how that turn of events might best be expressed in prose, only to be brusquely rebuffed as he reached for his neat morocco case.

"My dear Watson, the facts were there to see. Surely it is enough that I explained them to you at the time. I cannot be expected to constantly turn over old ground to satisfy the curiosity of your imagined readership."

The Bishop's Curse by Greg Maughan

It had only been a matter of weeks since the conclusion of our most recent adventure and yet – I feared for Sherlock Holmes – it felt much longer. He kept increasingly odd hours; inevitably, I would rise before him and though always nothing less than presentable when he did turn out, he would remain in his silk dressing gown throughout the day. He appeared as a wraith in his own home, hollowed out by lack of stimulation.

As the calendar turned to July, I could see no end in sight and eventually found his mood rubbing off onto me. It became harder each day to plough on through my duties. Watching Sherlock Holmes disappear further within himself I found I was wishing for a caller with a case to stimulate that brilliant brain. A challenge to once again bring out the man I knew existed within the depth of my current listless companion. Thus, it was with great enthusiasm that I greeted our caller that fateful morning. Had I known in advance the horrors we were to confront, I would have satisfied myself to let Sherlock Holmes remain in his torpor a little longer.

* * *

Holmes sat in his silk dressing gown, staring into the hearth. The fact that no fire was needed at this time of year did not seem to put him off, and he focused intently on empty air with the look of a boy mesmerised by dancing flames. A rap at the door failed to induce even a flinch, and a second, louder rap was wholeheartedly ignored.

For my part, I had been sitting at the breakfast table trying to idly peruse the morning's *Times*. Though, even this most simple of pleasures seemed forced within the atmosphere that now enveloped 221B Baker Street. At the first rap, I was up like a shot and heading straight for the entranceway, keen of any distraction and hopeful the caller might offer up mystery enough to rouse Sherlock Holmes once again to action.

The Bishop's Curse by Greg Maughan

On the doorstep, I was greeted by a sorrowful sight. The man before me, even to my untrained eyes, had let himself go. His clothes were clearly well-tailored, but dishevelled and worn loosely. And while the caller's fair hair went some way to disguising the number of days' beard he wore, it was still noticeable that he was in dire need of a close shave.

"I have come to seek an audience with the great detective, Sherlock Holmes," he declared with practiced gravitas. "Are you he?" he added, more meekly.

Explaining that I was a mere acquaintance of Sherlock Holmes, I ushered our caller through the doorway, up the stairs and into the parlour with some haste, keen as I was to hear what he had to say. And, more to the point, to see what effect it had on the mood of that "great detective."

Back in the parlour, Holmes had not moved from the spot where I had left him. Nor had his eyes deviated from their fixed point in the hearth. Our caller hesitated in the doorway, such was the oppressiveness of the atmosphere within.

Finally, Holmes spoke to usher him in. "My dear sir, you have travelled a long way for this audience – overnight, I can see. And you are clearly anxious for your story to be heard. Do not wait a moment longer, be seated and speak." At this, Holmes finally broke his statuesque repose and turned to our visitor, indicating open-palmed the Chesterfield which sat opposite him about the hearth. "If nothing else, it should give us a distraction for at least the time of the telling," offered Holmes as an aside to me.

"It's hardly just a distraction I have come here with," the man declared as he stepped forward at Holmes's instruction and took his seat, "but a tale of sorrow and tragedy. And, more so, a mystery with even more lives to pay should it remain so this next fortnight!"

"What is mysterious to the layman is often clear as day to the trained mind once the facts of the matter are laid out." Holmes's voice

The Bishop's Curse by Greg Maughan

was dismissive, but I detected a glint in his eye which gave me hope. He leaned in slightly towards our caller and bade him continue.

"My name is Charles Winterton," our caller began, as he settled himself into the scarlet Chesterfield, "most recent in that famous dynasty of philanthropists, heir to the Winterton estate and possessor of everything a man could want for a long, settled happy life. Or at least I was until a few short years ago." At this, his face darkened and his back straightened, taking a few controlled breaths to ready himself for the tale he had to tell.

"In the spring of 1878, I knew happiness I had never before thought possible. I had spent much of the previous year completing the Grand Tour, rounding off my education and getting a taste of the world before my planned return home to take on the responsibility of the day-to-day running of father's estate. Necessary preparation for a day we all hoped would be many years ahead of us. Truly, it was an eye-opening journey. I saw beauty I could never have dreamt of in both art and nature across the Continent. But the greatest beauty of all fell into my lap on the final leg of the tour.

"Stopping off a few nights in Paris, readying ourselves to finally cross over the Channel again, a chance encounter in a café changed the course of my heart. She was only a waitress, worlds apart. But there was a connection there neither of us could ignore, and from the moment we met I knew I always had to be with her, my beautiful belle, Delphine." Winterton fought to control his emotions as he told his tale, red-eyed at the thought of his love.

"Take your time, sir. And when you are ready continue," Holmes instructed. "Whatever events occurred following your meeting have greatly shaken you. If a puzzle has presented itself, I can solve it. But detail is the key, so compose yourself and, when ready, give us that detail." This was as close to compassion as I had seen Holmes display in our time together. Though I could not tell if he were touched by the emotion our visitor had displayed or concerned that it

The Bishop's Curse by Greg Maughan

would interfere in the picture he got of the mystery to come. In any case, after a few moments, Winterton continued his tale.

"From that moment on, we were inseparable. I delayed my return to England for as long as possible, remaining in Paris for a few more blissful days. Then, when my responsibilities could be delayed no longer, I took the only action I could – I asked Delphine to be my bride. It goes without saying, this caused quite a stir when we arrived home. The village of Carcroft had never seen such an exotic beauty as Delphine. Of course, the fact that she did not come from money was brought up too. But our happiness together was undeniable. Whatever misgivings my father might have had ebbed away as he saw a lightness in his son and heir that, truly, had not been there before.

"The month that followed felt like a rehearsal for a long, settled life together. I was learning the ropes, as it were, managing the estate and spending every moment not at work in the arms of my beloved, falling deeper and deeper in love with her. Between my work and our relationship, I saw my future laid out before me. And it filled me with a sense of ease, as though I had finally reached a moment that the rest of my life would comfortably pivot on. Then, disaster struck.

"Delphine and I had taken to indulging in long constitutionals around the grounds of the estate. We could spend hours slowly wandering, lost in each other's company. On that particular day, we walked under a baking sun in the direction towards the stables. As she held a parasol over herself to shade her delicate skin, I explained the story of St. Swithin, the ancient Bishop of Winchester, whose day it was. Delphine seemed bemused by our strange English folklore and giggled playfully at me while I swore we were guaranteed forty more days of blazing sun.

"My story was interrupted at that point by our coachman, who trotted towards us on his way to collect visiting family members from the train station. Delphine was such a gentle soul and reached out to pet the beasts. None of this was unusual and she had petted the creatures many times without incident. But then, something happened that will haunt me until my dying breath.

"Out of nowhere, the horses reared up above her. I was frozen in terror and could do nothing but watch as their wretched hooves rained down on my beloved. After the first shattering blow, it was clear nothing could be done. The blows that followed simply added to the horror of the scene." Tears ran down Winterton's cheeks now; he no longer made any effort to hold them back. He stared into the empty hearth, just as Holmes had done earlier. Though this time I dared not imagine what it was he saw in front of him.

"At that point, I was overwhelmed and, I'm sorry to say, I blacked out altogether. I have come to accept that there was nothing I could have done to save my Delphine, but it is to my eternal shame that when confronted with such tragedy I could not even bring myself to try. You must understand, when I say I was frozen, I mean I was truly paralysed, unable to act, only to watch until even that became too much.

"I was told afterwards that the coachman suffered a heart attack and that his sudden tensing of the reins startled the horses and caused them to rear up. An unlikely accident, but an accident nonetheless. But in the years since, I have come to believe that there's more to it. You see, just as St. Swithin's day decides the weather for the month following so that day has set the tone for the years since. Truly, I fear that Bishop has cursed me! My Delphine, though hers is the death that truly haunts me the most, was only the first to lose their life on July 15th.

"Each year since, death has struck another." Winterton had composed himself somewhat and delivered the final lines of his tale with measured solemnity. "I have come to believe that I am cursed and for the next forty years from that fateful day I am destined to experience another death amongst those closest to me. Mr. Holmes, we are in July now and the day approaches. I beg you, prove me wrong."

The Bishop's Curse by Greg Maughan

"What of these deaths that followed?" Holmes kept a neutral tone. "Tell us more of how this 'curse' struck."

"In the year that followed, I had done my best to recover from the tragedy that had befallen my beloved. I had thrown myself into my work, mastering the management of my father's grand estate and taking on more and more responsibility for the family's wide business interests. I took no joy in anything I did, life had lost its taste, but I kept going nonetheless. As the anniversary of Delphine's death approached, I felt a dread build up in my soul in the preceding weeks. On the day itself, I could not see nor speak with anyone. I took myself out of the house early on and traced the routes round the grounds we used to walk together.

"Losing track of time, tied up in reminiscence as I was, it was getting on for three before I came back to myself and realised I should make my way back home for afternoon tea. On my approach to the house, I saw a group amassed on the front drive. They were bustling around a large carriage with some commotion. As I got closer it became clear it was a doctor's carriage. A man with a medical bag stood behind it while a gurney was manoeuvred into its rear.

"Panic overcame me and I broke into a run. As I approached, my eldest cousin, Edward, broke off from comforting my younger sister, Nancy, to hold me back from the scene. It was my father. Another freak accident, apparently. A wretched gargoyle of all things had fallen from the cornice and knocked my poor father cold.

"Head of the household now, but lost to myself, I regret to say I neglected my daily duties and much of the family business fell to my cousin. Edward has been a great help to me in these years since, though I dare say I haven't shown him the appreciation I should. My mind has been taken up with the sorrows that beset me. You see, St. Swithin's curse struck twice more, and twice more I felt the blows of such loss as no man should have to endure.

"In 1880 I saw my younger brother, Lawrence, fall from his horse while in 1881 my poor sister fell victim to the curse on our boating lake." Winterton was understandably choking up and ran through these deaths with the perfunctoriness of one who could no longer contemplate what it was he said.

But Sherlock Holmes pressed him nonetheless. "The boating lake, you say? Was Nancy rowing?"

Winterton looked off in the middle-distance, lost to us for a moment, before he continued. "N-no, she lost her footing on the bank as best we could tell. I was not far from her when it happened and was torn from my memories by her cries. I ran to the lakeside and dived in, but was too late."

"Well, you tried, dear chap. That's as much as any man could do." I did my best to comfort the fellow. His tale was hard to contemplate. Bad luck seemed too weak a term for the terrifying run of things he had faced. And what, I felt myself asking, if it were a curse? What if he were doomed to repeat this horror year after year. Why, he'd have no family left for the curse to strike soon enough!

"In the years since Delphine's death," he took up again, "I have spent a long time contemplating my inaction. As tragedy has visited since, yes, I have done all a man could do. But it has never been enough. Now, I again count down the days and await that fateful visit once more."

"Holmes sat back and raised his hands to his chin, fingers interlaced steeple-like. I knew better than to interrupt while he contemplated what had just been shared with us, but the silence that filled the room was thick. Eventually, he spoke. "There is no mystery here, merely tragedy upon tragedy. My advice to you is simple. Lock yourself away on this fearful anniversary, sleep, meditate, do all you can to think nothing of this curse and soon a year shall pass where nothing of note occurs. Then you shall see you have made a pattern where one was not."

I was aghast at the thought of it and had to interject. "But Holmes, surely we cannot take that risk! If anything can be done to avert another tragedy then it must! Has this man not endured enough?"

"H-he is right, Mr Holmes," Winterton chimed in, "I am convinced that the curse will strike again whatever action I take. But could a mind such as yours not identify who it will strike in advance? Could we not act to avert their death and thus set a new tradition for the day?"

Holmes tutted and looked sharply at us both, but after much persuading he acquiesced. Winterton returned home that day and it was agreed that we would follow by train the next.

"How could you tell Winterton had travelled overnight to see us?" I asked casually as we were making our preparations for travel.

"Simple observation, Watson. Nothing more. No doubt you took in our caller's dishevelled appearance. His once well-tailored clothes that now hang loosely on him following years of nervous weight-loss. Should you have taken the time to notice his shoes, you too would have seen the mud that still clung to them. The mineral content of earth varies greatly across this isle, so it was simplicity itself to identify that he had recently walked a field of the West Riding. Add to that the hour of his call and it was clear that he must have taken the overnight train and come to us directly from it on arrival."

I smiled with great warmth, wondering at the way the mind of my companion worked. It was good to have him back!

* * *

For all he had insisted there was no mystery to the events, once he had agreed to take on the case, there was a marked change in the mood of my companion. He packed his travel case with a vigour I had not seen in him for some weeks and rose before me the next morn, already sitting at a hearty breakfast of links and eggs when I joined him.

"Nothing gives one an appetite like fresh purpose, Watson. We have a death to avert and a ticking clock, I feel the game is about to commence." I could not help but question the turnaround in my companion's opinion of the case, to which he was sharp in answer. "I made my opinions on the matter clear enough. When that course was rejected, another had to be sought. And the course we now take means we must act swiftly to avoid further unnecessary death."

We left directly after breakfast. Heading north from St Pancras, I confess I could not share my companion's enthusiasm for our trip. The tale that Winterton had shared with us had shaken me somewhat. I tried to put into practice the analytical approach that Holmes had shared with me over the course of our adventures together. But there was nothing I could see that pointed to a solution to the problem. Gathering my thoughts, I attempted to share my apprehension with him.

"I dare say, Holmes, if everything that Winterton has told us is true then what can we hope to achieve attending to this case? An act of God is unavoidable by its very nature. Would this curse not fall into the same damned category?"

"You really have learnt nothing from our time together, Watson," he chided. "None has put it better than Sir Isaac Newton when he said 'A man may imagine things that are false, but he can only understand things that are true.' We must not be led by the imaginings of Winterton, no matter how sincere his belief in them is, when the facts point us to a very different truth."

"I hope for all our sakes you are right," I replied. But I could not see the "truth" that Holmes referred to and instead was filled with dread of the thought that the Bishop's curse would strike again. Shuddering at the notion, I turned my sights to the vistas that rolled past us while Holmes sat in silence seemingly oblivious to all for the rest of our long journey.

* * *

On our arrival in Carcroft, we were collected by the Winterton family coach and a short while later reached the grand estate of which

The Bishop's Curse by Greg Maughan

Charles Winterton now sat at the head. It was a splendid old English house, the sort with a history seemingly as long and storied as our isle itself. Years from now, I thought, the curse that consumed Winterton's every waking moment would simply be another footnote in a winding family history taking in triumphs and tragedy along the way. That is, as long as the curse could be moved on from and there were heirs to talk about these dark days.

As we made our way up the long driveway, I was stuck by a vision of the house fallen to ruin, empty and dark. It was only at this point that I was able to put my misgivings to one side and finally felt committed to doing all we could to solve this particular conundrum. It just would not do to let such a dark shadow be cast over so grand a site!

For Holmes's part, he had said little since our arrival. He was quick to jump from the carriage when it pulled to a stop and perfunctory in his greeting to Winterton who stood in attendance to meet us on our arrival. The poor chap, I thought. Just as dishevelled as he had been when last we saw him; it was clearly some effort to greet us as he did. Yet Holmes brushed him off as if he were a footman. Thank heaven for the small mercy that Holmes didn't simply hand him his bag!

While I felt obliged to stay and make what small talk I could with our host, Holmes stalked off instantly to inspect the grounds. My conversation contained nothing of note. But Holmes recounted to me his initial investigations later that evening and I will do my best to replicate them here in his own telling.

"It was clear to me that the key to the mystery was a knowledge of the space in which it took place. And so, on our arrival I was keen to explore as soon as possible. I recalled from Winterton's original telling that the grounds of the estate offered much space to meander, as he did with the dearly departed Delphine. Years after each event, it was unlikely that I would find much physical evidence at this juncture. But the lie of the land offered a key to understanding what had occurred. I traced the outline of the grand lawn adjacent to the driveway until I could see in the distance the stables from which the cursed beast had emerged on that fateful day.

"Cutting over to the path that led to the stables, the spot where Delphine fell was clear as day, marked out as it is by a metal urn for flowers to be left in tribute. I took in the dried stalks that presently sat in the urn then checked the line of sight in each direction. To the east could be seen a row of juniper bushes marking off the edge of the boating lake where poor Nancy had met her end the previous summer. While westward was the edge of the stables and the tradesman's entrance at the back of the house.

"Next to the tradesman's way I could just make out a figure propping himself against the door. My course set, I ventured towards the figure to further my enquiries.

"'You there!' I called, 'have you a moment?'

"On hearing me, the figure straightened up and disposed of what I later identified as a Wild Woodbine. As any gentleman knows, a good pipe can be conducive to thought and help work one's way through a problem. But the cigarette burns too quickly to be of use and offers little more than a means to idle away a moment that could be better employed elsewhere.

"Of course, I did not share this observation with my new companion. Instead, I reassured him that his indolence would not be shared with his master and asked where the entrance way led to.

"'Round to the left there sits the pantry, sir. And beyond that is the kitchen. 'Tis a grand house but it h'aint no different to any other of its kinds, I dare say. Save for the tragedy it's seen, bless their souls.' At this the footman bowed his head as a display of respect. Though he kept his eyes fixed on my feet for longer than he ought have, clear in his hope that this was the end of our exchange.

"'Can you get further up into the house from here? To the roof, even?' I pressed.

"'Yes sir, that you can. The whole back-end of the house has stairs and passages so we can go about our work unseen. The young master's father was generous to a fault, but he still preferred us not to clutter the place up if we could avoid it.'

"'You might be unseen, but I'm sure you see well yourself. Tell me, do you remember the day of the accident, three years since, when the senior Winterton passed?'

"'Oh no, sir. You see, since the business with young Winterton's fiancée none of the staff works on St. Swithin's Day. It's only family on the grounds that day; still need the time to mourn, I suppose. Though with what the years since have seen, I'm glad to be out of it, to be honest. That is, if you don't mind me saying so, sir.'

"'Not at all,' I reassured him. Then, seeing as his eyes were still fixed on the ground and his discomfort in our conversation was palpable, I bid him good day. I had found out all I wished from him, anyway.

"From there, I continued pacing the grounds, climbing the odd tree and checking lines of sight until the first flecks of a sunset bled into the sky. At which point, I returned to find you at supper, Watson, and shared my observations of the day."

We were sitting in the drawing room of the grand house. Winterton had given his apologies early and retired for the night. Tomorrow was likely to take a toll on him even if further tragedy could be avoided. I had spent some time conversing with his cousin, Edward, who seemed to be a semi-permanent resident now, what with his prominent role in the Winterton family business. He had told me that a few more cousins were traveling through the next day to try to raise Winterton's spirits, though he was as doubtful of their chances of success as I. Then, after he had gone back about his business, I had waited ruefully for Holmes to return, when we eventually shared notes from the afternoon.

"I dare say your afternoon has been more eventful than mine! I have done little more than settle into my room for the night, freshen up and change from the clothes that I travelled in." As I contemplated all I had heard so far, I could not help but feel a knot building up in my stomach. The tension I felt on that eve could be only a fraction of what Winterton must have felt. I had to pluck up the courage for my next question, chided as I had been for enquiring along similar lines previously, but I felt it had to be asked. "Now that we are here and you have seen where this horrific story unfolded, is there any part of you that believes it could be a curse?"

Thankfully, this time Holmes replied more gently than he had before. "You have as much information as I, Watson. Apply logic and reason and tell me what conclusions you draw from it."

I thought for some time and tried to put my previous experiences with Holmes into practice. Often, we had been faced by the most baffling of problems that, when my companion outlined the steps that had taken him to a solution, seemed almost banal in their simplicity. With some hesitancy, I began to try to articulate the same process.

"Well, if we rule out the curse, which I pray we can, then there are only two solutions open to us. One is bad luck, pure and simple. But, the chances of, so far, four deadly accidents striking the same family on the same day each year are infinitesimally small." My blood ran cold as I knew what I was about to say. "So, we must conclude that these deaths were not accidents. Some hidden hand is at work."

"Very good," Holmes encouraged me. "At least you have dismissed the superstitious distraction of the curse! Why, we'll make a detective of you yet. Now, go on. Tell me more of this 'hidden hand.'"

"Murder is a serious affair and something one does not undertake lightly," I pontificated, my confidence growing through Holmes's praise. "We know from your conversation with the footman that only members of the Winterton clan have been present on the estate on St. Swithin's Day these last few years. A third party could sneak onto the grounds, it is true, but the most likely conclusion to draw is that our killer lies within the family. Then, we must determine what can be gained from such heinous acts. Truly, this is the grandest estate I have ever been welcomed into, and it is well known that 'the love of money is the root of all evil.' Winterton has gained a world but lost everything in the process."

My mind raced to what seemed the obvious conclusion. "But his cousin! Why, that blackguard has been present each year and now only Winterton himself stands in the way of him stepping in and taking the lot. It must be! There is our killer, and tomorrow our host, Charles Winterton, must be his final target."

I worked back through my reasoning and became increasingly confident in my conclusions. Though awful in the extreme, I confess I was distracted from this fact by my pride in my deduction. There were one or two parts that did not quite fit, but I was sure these could be explained away.

"Of course, the heart attack that ailed the coachman was induced by poison. Winterton himself was the true target that day, but too many variables presented themselves. In the years since, the empty house has allowed that fiend to take a more direct hand in his treacherous acts."

"Ha!" cried Holmes. "Dear Watson, you never seek to astonish."

"Then I have it?" I replied, a grin creeping over my face despite the circumstances.

"I fear not. Rather, what is astonishing is how a seemingly intelligent man can conclude such hokum when the truth lies in plain sight." The wind taken from my sails, my grin disappeared completely and I began to bluster in protest. But Holmes cut me off sharply and continued. "If Nancy, an unmarried young girl, were to be the last of the Wintertons, is it likely that she would take full inheritance? Of course not! What world do you think we live in, Watson? The estate would have gone into trust, with Edward as the remaining senior male in the extended family at its head. Or, if he wished to take more direct control it would have been a simple enough matter to arrange a marriage, would it not?" I sheepishly nodded in agreement. "And using a horse as a murder weapon? As you say yourself, there are clearly too many variables. That act, at least, was clearly nothing more than a tragic accident. But the years since are another matter altogether. Only, why would a killer strike on the same day each year? If, as you contest, the inheritance is the motivation, doesn't the unusual pattern risk drawing attention? And why wait year upon year before the deck is finally cleared and he can reap his reward? No, a much more frightful motivation underlines this all. And tomorrow will confirm it for us."

At that, Sherlock Holmes retired to bed with a spring in his step. I, however, was more sluggish on my ascent of the grand staircase and faced a sleepless night, filled with worry of what the morning would bring.

* * *

The next morning, Winterton breakfasted with us in near total silence. Then, he made his apologies and explained that, as had become his tradition, he would spend the day alone, walking the grounds in remembrance of his lost love. He thanked us for our presence that day and begged forgiveness that he would not be able to remain with us to help in our investigations. But, alas, it was all still too much for him.

"And what of you?" I asked his cousin. "Do you plan much for today?"

"I'm afraid not. Duty obliges me to be here for Charles, but there is little I can do for him still. I am likely to spend the day at work, looking over the books of the household. If Charles will not let me help in his mourning, then the least I can do is try to ensure that his business affairs remain in order."

The Bishop's Curse by Greg Maughan

"And do you not fear for this so-called curse?" I asked in hushed tones.

"Pshaw!" his cousin replied. "I admit that this house has seen near-limitless tragedy these last few years. But I cannot allow myself to believe it to be anything more than luck. Charles says this curse could last forty years, I counter that by asserting that bad luck runs in threes. When this day is through, I pray we can finally move on from that which has struck us."

True to his word, Winterton's cousin retired to the library, and there he remained for most of the day.

In previous years, a good number of the wider family had visited on this day, keen as they were to check on Winterton and offer him what comfort they could on this woeful anniversary. As each year passed, the number diminished, whittled away by Winterton's refusal to engage with the comfort they offered and also the growing dread of fresh tragedy.

This year, his cousin, Edward, had spent the night and breakfasted with us while a few younger cousins arrived by coach at about mid-day. Sherlock Holmes greeted them and ushered them into the drawing room, instructing them to remain there until he directed otherwise.

"I say!" piped up one of the young visitors, "We didn't travel all this way to be cooped up in here. Where's Charles? We came with plans of games and gaiety to distract him from his troubles."

I felt somewhat tense by this point and snapped at the young man. "How can you talk of gaiety on a day like this? Do you not realise the threat that looms over you all?"

"What nonsense," he replied.

"Nonsense or not," Holmes butted in, "for our game to develop the way I wish, it is of vital importance that the moving parts are limited and that I have total control of my pieces on the board. So, in this room you shall remain, whether you like it or not!"

To this, there was little argument given, and at that point Holmes faded into the shadows of the house, darting unseen from alcove to archway observing the movements of its occupants.

For my part, I spent the next few hours in the company of the younger cousins and was even convinced to take part in a hand of Gin Rummy. By about half past two I have to admit I was actually beginning to enjoy myself. There is something about the upper classes, whether it is courage in the face of adversity or a confidence in their position in the world regardless of what threat may present itself that makes them most amiable company in a crisis. I was drawn from my reverie, however, by a terrible commotion taking place outside.

Up like a shot, I indicated to the young cousins to remain where they were and darted out of the room towards the entrance way. The scene I was greeted by shocked and confused me. But Holmes had a better perspective on it all, and later that day did his best to enlighten me.

"I had spent the last few hours carefully observing movements about the house from the shadows. I was aware that Winterton was away, walking the grounds and did not concern myself too much with his movements. I was confident that anyone likely to be targeted by the 'curse' was within these walls."

"Were you not concerned that poor Charles Winterton could be a victim?" I asked.

"Unfortunately not, Watson. Of that I had been confident from the outset! And at half two this afternoon, my theory was proved correct. His cousin had risen once from his paperwork to prepare a simple sandwich about half an hour earlier. Then, after consuming this, he proceeded to exit the building and take in some fresh air to help with digestion. I continued my observations, unseen from behind the exterior of a window bay. Across the field, I saw Winterton approaching. As he drew nearer, I saw his cousin spot him too and offer a friendly wave in greeting. Winterton did not wave in response, but his pace quickened. There was a determination to his walk – direct and purposeful. I knew I had to ready myself for action.

"Not far off now, Edward walked casually towards him and called out a greeting, with still no response forthcoming.

"'I say Charles, are you all right?' he asked. In reply, Winterton raised his right hand, revealing a rock he had been carrying, and made to rain down a blow on his cousin.

"Shocked, Edward stepped backwards. Catching his heel, he tripped and fell leaving an easy target for the demented Winterton. But I was quick to respond. I threw myself forward and speared Winterton with a rugby tackle with enough force that it knocked the wind from me. The impact hurled Winterton back, felling him to the ground and causing him to drop the rock.

"While I struggled to my knees, Winterton was up like a flash, pushing me to one side and proceeding with determination back towards his cousin.

"Edward had regained his footing as well and held his arms aloft in supplication crying with great confusion, begging for mercy.

"'Have you lost your mind, Charles? Please, I've done nothing to call for this.'

"I grabbed Winterton's arm from behind and pulled him to face me. Although by this point I was confident of the facts, I must admit that his eyes chilled me to the bone. The focus did not seem right, as though he were looking straight through me.

"But of course, I had no time to dwell on this in the moment. It was clear that Winterton would have to be incapacitated somehow, such was the singular determination with which he pursued his current course of action.

"As you well know, Watson, I'm not unfamiliar with the noble art and so I took up a fighting stance. I delivered two short jabs to the face followed by a mighty right hook, each finding its mark with ease. Winterton did not seem to even attempt to block or defend himself. But he also did not seem to waiver from the impact. A trickle of blood drew a line from nose to chin, yet he made no move to wipe it away. And the look in his eyes had not changed at all.

"He responded in kind, throwing blow after blow at me. His punches were wild and undisciplined, easily blocked, and yet the power behind them was unbelievable. It felt as though nothing were held back and though none made its mark, each punch which I blocked rattled the bones throughout my body."

That was the scene which had greeted me when I ran outside to see what had caused such a commotion – Holmes and Charles Winterton engaged in a vicious bareknuckle contest the likes of which I had never seen.

I rushed to check on Edward, who was deathly pale and unsteady on his feet. Once I had ascertained his health, I turned to the scuffle and looked for an opening to jump to my companion's aid. But Sherlock Holmes was considering a different tact.

He moved to create distance between Winterton and himself, then reached inside the pocket of his Ulster to withdraw a quartz pendulum. I watched with some interest as Holmes danced backwards, staying just out of Winterton's reach, while he rocked the pendulum from side to side while in sonorous voice he commanded that Winterton be still.

Gradually, the blows Winterton threw slowed and his steps became heavier until, eventually, he was still. For the life of me, I could not say what I had witnessed, but at least I knew at that point it was over.

"It was a simple act of neurophrenology," Holmes explained to me later that day. "More commonly known as hypnotism. You see, Winterton could not be subdued by physical means as he was not present within himself to recognise and react to physical stimuli."

It was not unusual for Holmes's explanation of events to initially leave me even more confused, and I shared this observation with him.

The Bishop's Curse by Greg Maughan

"Charles Winterton had entered into what would be called a blackout state. Overwhelmed by the mental strain of the memories invoked by this awful anniversary, he was literally in flight from himself. His habit of tracing the route of the walks he had shared with the departed Delphine and reliving memories that he clung so tightly to had the effect of working him into a heightened state of mental agitation and distance from the present. Until, as he reached the point when she met her death, these memories became overwhelming and Winterton snapped, attempting to flee his own identity.

Holmes continued, "I must admit I feared as much when he first told us his story at Baker Street. That empty look when I pushed him on his recollections of the days his family members met their fate. It was not a look of evasion; even the most experienced of card players has a tell that the expert can identify, but if a man does not know what he holds in his hand there is nothing he can give away.

"Yet that lack of knowledge was the key for me, and I offered what I thought would be a perfectly acceptable solution in Winterton locking himself away for the anniversary. But he would not have it and so we find ourselves here."

As unbelievable as it seemed, Holmes's reasoning combined with the events I had witnessed convinced me. Yet I could not understand his casual attitude towards such horrific killings.
"So, poor Delphine's death truly was a tragic accident, but the memory of this was enough to push Winterton into some sort of frenzy each year?"

"Crudely put. But close enough to the mark, yes."

"Then how could locking oneself away each year be an adequate solution for Winterton? If he has killed, surely he should be punished!"

"For 364 days of the year, Winterton was no threat to anyone. True, he had let himself go these last few years and was clearly still in mourning, but his freedom presented no risk. Yes, on the one day of the year that he was a threat, and a deadly one at that, he was completely unaware of his actions. But what would be gained by detaining him for those remaining 364 days?"

I was flabbergasted! For a man who had dedicated his life to the pursuit of truth, Sherlock Holmes's moral compass seemed askew. I'm not afraid to admit, I got on my high horse somewhat and told him as much in no uncertain terms! "It's not enough to simply prevent more deaths. Surely, justice must be seen to be done!"

As we argued, that poor wretch Winterton was being bundled away in a carriage, bound for the East Riding Lunatic Asylum, a northern Bedlam. I shuddered to think of the nights and weeks ahead of him. His next St. Swithin's Day would be a very different affair for him indeed.

"I find myself to be quite pragmatic at heart, Watson. But if it is punishment you want, know now that Winterton will be haunted by his actions not just on their anniversary but every day on the calendar for the rest of his cursed existence."

Oftentimes I found myself enraptured by Holmes's brilliant insights and enlivened by the spirit which he brought to a mystery. But, on occasion I felt somewhat grubby in the face of the truths he uncovered. This was one of those occasions. A mystery had been solved, but it felt as though no one had benefited from it.

On the return journey to London, we were both quiet. I could already feel the atmosphere around Holmes changing as boredom set back in. I vowed to myself on that train that this time I would happily endure his temperament for as long as necessary to avoid another tragic encounter like that we had faced with the ill-fated Charles Winterton.

August 1883

An Affair of State: Sir Charles Dilke

By Frank Emerson

When I glanced over my notes and records of the Sherlock Holmes cases between the years '82 and '90, I was faced by so many which presented strange and interesting features that it is no easy matter to know which to choose to edit and which to leave for another time. Finally, one set of notes nearly leapt out of my files and fairly presented itself to me to be revealed now in this momentous year of 1912.

The story I am about to relate is unique in that it is the only example in the Holmes annals in which neither he nor I played what could be referred to as active parts as it unfolded. We were more or less relegated to roles of observers and perhaps enablers of the drama. Nonetheless, the case that presented itself in that year was easily one of the most convoluted and of such national importance as any we embarked upon since that it is easy to understand why I have secreted it for so long. It is only now, after the passage of more than three decades and after the death of the principal, that I feel comfortable in recalling the details of the scandalous episode. Here they are, as I have reconstructed them from my notes.

The year 1883 was my third as partner, friend and by his own admission, "Boswell" to the world's first consulting detective, Mr. Sherlock Holmes. It was a surprisingly pleasant twilight following a rather humid day in August. Holmes and I had enjoyed the usual pleasant repast courtesy of Mrs. Hudson. Now we sat at the window of our sitting room, I with a briar bowl of Arcadia Mixture and Holmes with one of his fine Cuban cigars, looking out over the comings and goings of Baker Street. "Holmes," I remarked, "do you mind that bearded fellow coming toward us who appears to be searching for a specific address?"

"I do indeed, Watson, and if I am not mistaken, which I am not, the address he seeks is 221B."

Shortly thereafter, we heard the ringing of the bell and then came the ensuing knock on our door from Mrs. Hudson, who announced our visitor.

"Thank you, Mrs. Hudson. Please, Sir," Holmes continued, "You are most welcome. Come in and take a seat. I must confess that the newspapers have done an excellent job in rendering your likeness. However, by your expression and your somewhat agitated manner, I fear that your reason for calling on us is less than pleasurable."

"Holmes," I interjected, "how can you possibly know that?"

"I am surprised at you, Watson, for having let your customary awareness of national matters slip in this instance. This is none other than Sir Charles Dilke, Liberal Member of Parliament for Chelsea and the Undersecretary of State for Foreign Affairs who, as I gather from the intimations of certain journalists, is in danger of becoming embroiled in a scandal that may jeopardize his position and future prospects. Dr. Watson and I will be most anxious to learn more of your plight and honoured to offer our assistance."

Sir Charles seemed visibly relieved that he would not have to go through any uncomfortable preliminaries. "Dr. Watson, Mr.

Holmes, I am indeed in need of your assistance. I must confess, that although my behavior regarding this matter has been less than exemplary or even admirable, it is not out of the ordinary, but the matters of which I have been accused – and will not doubt be coming to light in the near future – are scurrilous and not worthy of consideration."

"Well then," said Holmes, "we must not waste any time. However, Watson, if you would do the honours, I think a single malt all round might be called for. Now then, Sir Charles. Please illuminate us and I implore you to spare no details."

"Very well then," said Sir Charles. "A week ago, I received a letter from a friend of mine, Mrs. Christina Rogerson, stating that she had some grave information to impart to me."

Holmes gave a small start. "I believe I recognize that name. That is but one of the surnames and titles adopted by a woman of some notoriety, if I am not mistaken and again, I am certain that I am not. You are not, by any chance, a resident of Knightsbridge or the Sloane Street area of Chelsea? But pray tell, what did this Mrs. Rogerson have to impart?"

"Why yes, Mr. Holmes, I do maintain a flat in Sloane Street. I am a bachelor, and the nearby Knightsbridge area affords houses of diversion which can be appealing to unattached or discreetly attached individuals of a certain status. In fact, Mrs. Rogerson acts as proprietress at one of these establishments. Through this, we have become close friends, dare I say, confidants."

"Ah yes," said Holmes in a somewhat accusatory manner, "I believe I understand. Please continue."

"Coming to my flat the following morning, Mrs. Rogerson informed me that her brother is a solicitor who is acting in a divorce case being brought by Mr. Donald Crawford, a fellow Liberal Member of Parliament, against his young wife, Virginia, whose sister, Maye, is the widow of my dead brother. My concern in the case is that I am being named as co-respondent. What complicates the matter is that I have never had intimate relations with Mrs. Crawford."

"So, the young lady is lying," I interjected. Sir Charles nodded in response.

"I suspect," said Holmes turning to me, "that this is just the leading edge of the predicament in which Sir Charles is enmeshed. Am I right, Sir Charles?"

"Indeed you are," said Sir Charles. "Mrs. Crawford also contends that our relationship was not exclusive and that we had engaged in what the French refer to as a *menage à trois* at my residence with a maid in my employ named Miss Fanny Grey."

"I take it that you also deny this accusation," Holmes said.

"Most emphatically," Sir Charles asserted, "as does the maligned Miss Grey. Although I know Mrs. Crawford and have met her under various circumstances, I can honestly tell you that she has never been to my flat."

"Ah," said Holmes as he stood and crossed to the fireplace. "If we consider that what you tell us is the truth and that Mrs. Crawford is lying, there must be another reason she holds such animus toward you. Do you have any idea as to what this might be?"

"In order to clear the water and to more fully apprise you of the convoluted nature of this affair, I must confess that although I had no dalliance with Mrs. Crawford, her mother, Mrs. Ellen Smith, and I did enjoy a brief, congenial episode some time ago."

Holmes and I exchanged startled looks. "You're late brother's mother-in law?"

"Yes, that is so. I can understand how that might appear unseemly. However," he continued, "I terminated the arrangement when I became aware that her daughter sought my attention in a manner that caused me great discomfort."

"Was Ellen Smith married at the time?" I asked.

"Oh yes, to Thomas Smith, the noted shipbuilder. She still is, in fact, though I believe she is still somewhat partial to me and would like to rekindle our relationship."

"I take it then," said Holmes, "that her marriage is somewhat less than ideal."

"Quite so. In fact, she allowed that her daughter's marriage to Mr. Crawford was considerably less than pleasant, what with the fact that he is twice her age. He is my contemporary."

"I see," said Holmes. "It would not be out of the question, then, that Mrs. Crawford's actions in naming you as co-respondent might be predicated on feelings of revenge for you having treated her mother in what she perceived to be a cavalier fashion. This could be compounded by the fact that she may still harbour amorous feelings for you herself, which you had also rejected."

"Yes, but ..."

"Furthermore, this ungainly set of circumstances could adequately serve as the impetus for young Virginia to seek an exit from her unhappy marriage. Your self-admitted actions, effectively branding you as ungentlemanly at best, would certainly be enough to make you a likely candidate for the title of co-respondent."

"But, Mr. Holmes, I am innocent!"

Holmes shared a look with me and was about to speak when I took the opportunity to speak for both of us. "Really, Sir Charles, I hardly think that 'innocent' is an appropriate description of your satyr-like behavior."

"Are you saying" asked Sir Charles, "that you will not investigate the case?"

"On the contrary," said Holmes. "I think Dr. Watson will concur that, considering the singular nature of the circumstances and the effect that they will undoubtedly have on your political future, it presents an intriguing opportunity for investigation."

"Thank you, Mr. Holmes. I am indeed relieved."

"You may or may not be relieved, Sir Charles, depending on where our investigation takes us, for we play no favourites and only seek truth and justice. If that is not acceptable to you, you may wish to seek assistance elsewhere."

"No, no, Mr. Holmes. I am at your service."

"Very well, then," said Holmes. "I presume you have spoken with Mrs. Crawford regarding this, to understate it, this contretemps?"

"I have indeed, Mr. Holmes. I confronted her several days ago at the home of her sister, my former sister-in-law, Maye. I demanded that she withdraw the farrago of lies. She refused, saying that she was unforgivably insulted that I should make such an unreasonable appeal, and left the room in a huff. Her statement and reaction stunned me. It is my understanding that there were other gentlemen with whom she was, shall we say, acquainted, any of whom would have been much more likely candidates for the dubious title of co-respondent. I can only conclude that she was most anxious to extricate herself from her brief marriage and would go to any lengths to accomplish this aim."

Holmes could barely conceal his disgust, but his interest was piqued. "As a first step in the investigation, Sir Charles, I believe that this calls for an interview with Mr. Crawford," said Holmes. "Mrs. Hudson will see you out and we shall be in touch as our investigation progresses."

After Sir Charles departed, Holmes turned to me. "Considering the outrageous nature of this case, I don't feel that we should be slaves to propriety, Watson. Come, we'll hail a cab and make straightaway for the home of Mr. Donald Crawford, MP to learn more of this scurrilous intrigue."

One hour later, we arrived at the lodgings of Mr. Donald Crawford, the address of which had been provided with some hesitancy by Sir Charles. Admitted by a liveried footman, we identified ourselves, were announced, and summarily shown to a sitting room where Mr. Crawford stood to greet us.

An Affair of State: Sir Charles Dilke by Frank Emerson

"Mr. Crawford," said Holmes, "thank you for agreeing to see us, and I apologize for not having contacted you in advance, but I fear that under the circumstances, time is of the essence."

"Think nothing of it, Mr. Holmes, Dr. Watson. I can only surmise that you are here to question me on my divorce petition. That being the case, I further surmise that you have been in contact with Sir Charles Dilke. Has he retained you?"

"We have been in contact," answered Holmes, "but we have not been retained. The nature of the problem so provoked our interest that we decided to conduct an independent investigation in the hope of uncovering whatever truths there are to be uncovered in this scandal-prone jumble."

"I see," said Mr. Crawford. "You have been apprised of Dilke's explanations and now you wish to hear me out. I am more than happy to present my evidence, as it were. Almost from the beginning, I realized that my marriage to Virginia was perhaps not fated to be a congenial one. I must confess that I, encouraged by Virginia, virtually ignored the disparity between our ages. I should have paid more attention to it, and I should have taken into consideration the difference in our characters.

"While devoted to her and providing for her every comfort, I was also quite dutiful to my responsibilities in government, which occupied a good deal of my time. Virginia, on the other hand, sought out the enthusiastic, frivolous lifestyle of other young women of her age and station. Her actions along these lines progressed to the point where she took to absenting herself from our home much more than what I would consider a proper or acceptable amount. That is to say: often. Much too often, in my opinion.

"Unfortunately, my suspicions proved to be well-founded. I had retained the services of private investigators to report on Virginia's movements and activities. They informed me that Virginia, often with her older, unhappily married sister, Helen, was seen to enter a Knightsbridge establishment called The Professor's Divan, which has a somewhat notorious reputation. After some time, the sisters exited in high spirits, often in the company of one Captain Henry Forster of the Royal Horse Artillery.

"The inference proved to be too much for me and I confronted Virginia and accused her of infidelities. Rather than make any outright denials, she qualified her answer by stating that though she was unfaithful, it was only with her one true love, Sir Charles Dilke. They had had assignations in various locations including Dilke's residence in Sloane Street. Not only that, Mr. Holmes, she said that sometimes Sir Charles insisted upon the active participation of a servant girl in his employ. The entire shocking admission proved more than sufficient for me to institute divorce proceedings.

"To be made a cuckold is bad enough under any circumstances, but to have it done by a fellow MP, and one of my own party to boot, is more than any honourable man should be asked to tolerate. If this were an earlier age, I would be hard put not to cast down the gauntlet."

"Thank you for your candor, Mr. Crawford," said Holmes. "You have been most helpful and enlightening. Dr. Watson and I extend you our sympathies for this undoubtedly painful situation you are being forced to endure. We shall take our leave of you now so that we might continue our investigation."

We left Mr. Crawford's residence and hailed another cab. "I believe, Watson, that our next stop should be the aforementioned Professor's Divan in Knightsbridge, where I feel certain we shall be fortunate enough to encounter Mrs. Christina Rogerson."

With an arched eyebrow barely stifling a small accusatory smile, I said, "Holmes, by way of some of your comments and actions, it would seem that you are already familiar with Mrs. Rogerson, to say nothing of the Professor's Divan."

"Watson, my good fellow, I believe you have it in you to become a detective yet! However, to save you from an incorrect deduction, allow me to explain. As you know, I try to keep myself well-prepared in any and all aspects that might pertain to the successful performance of my duties as a consulting detective. In addition to being a devotee of physical culture and a constant student of the world of chemical science, I am an ardent observer of the comings-and-goings of the untoward segments of society, that is to say, the underworld. In this, I am an avid reader of the *Police Gazette* or as you may know it, *The Hue and Cry*. I consider it my almanac, my indispensable cyclopaedia in my continuing education of sensational and nefarious activities. It is through this organ I became introduced to the denizens of the, dare I say 'fancy houses' of the Knightsbridge-Sloane Street district and came to be familiar with none other than Mrs. Christina Rogerson through her involvement with the Professor's Divan. I became further acquainted with Mrs. Rogerson and her uncle – the professor referred to in the 'Professor's Divan' – by way of her occasional appearances at The Old Bailey and once or twice, I believe, at the quarterly Assizes. This professor, James Moriarty by name, is an odd case. He holds the mathematical chair at one of the most prestigious small universities in England and is the author of numerous highly respected treatises, yet his interests seem to tend more toward the more opprobrious sectors of society – hence his proprietorship of the Professor's Divan. But that is of no consequence at the moment, yet it bears some awareness."

Thus gently chastised for my presumption, we straight away arrived at the Professor's Divan, the hack driver seeming to be familiar with the route and destination. We took note of this.

Welcomed into the front parlour by a well-appointed individual of imposing stature, we were shown to a divan in a comfortable side room, where we were instructed to wait for "Madam," as he termed her.

Shortly, amid a display of taffeta and surrounded by what seemed a living vapor of not unpleasant but perhaps heavy-handed floral scent, Mrs. Christina Rogerson wafted into the room; whereupon seeing and recognizing Mr. Sherlock Holmes, she came to an abrupt halt. "Why Mr. Holmes, I certainly hope you have graced us with your presence in pursuit of pleasure and not business – at least not your business."

"Mrs. Rogerson," Holmes responded, "I assume that is your preferred surname these days, is it not?"

She gave a condescending nod of her elegantly coiffed head. She was a not unattractive woman of a certain age, as it is sometimes referred in the society pages, yet with the unmistakable aura of experience tinged with no small amount of corruption to complete the picture.

"Mrs. Rogerson it is then," said Holmes. "So sorry to disappoint you, but Dr. Watson and I are indeed here on business and it is business of a most serious nature, so I must implore you not to waste your considerable wiles on us. Yet with good humour, we would be most appreciative if you would cooperate with our investigation and not force me to resort to actions which might prove to be a hindrance to your continued semi-legal operations."

"Why of course, Mr. Holmes. I only wish to be of any and all help to your investigation. I am at your service in any way you wish."

I could not help but harrumph at the inference, but Holmes, with a cold smile, said, "Capital then. Now, what can you tell us about Sir Charles Dilke?"

"Dilke," she said, "is a Member of Parliament, very close to Gladstone and a dishonourable cad of the first order."

"Please explain."

"This paragon of public service, this champion of liberal politics, played false with my attentions, with which I was most generous, and after having assured me that I would become the wife of a baronet, consequently abruptly shunned me and left me a woman scorned. I do not wish him well."

"I see," said Holmes. "Can you tell me, Mrs. Rogerson, what do you know of Mrs, Virginia Crawford?"

"My dear friend, young Virginia, has availed herself of my advice and hospitality on numerous occasions, as has her sister, Helen.

Both have found themselves involved in less than satisfactory marriages, situations which I tried to mitigate in my humble way and through certain methods at my disposal. I was only more determined to do so after learning of Virginia's treatment, so similar to that of my own, at the hands of the rotter, Sir Charles Dilke."

"I take it then," said Holmes, "that by certain methods, you generally intend the use of these premises for assignations of sorts?"

"Why certainly, Mr. Holmes. What better way to assuage the suffering of a woman twice wronged in the arena of affection than to offer acceptance and comfort and assurances of a comparable nature to that woman? What better way to do this than through the attentions of upstanding honourable gentlemen?"

"Your customers, I presume?" asked Holmes.

"Categorize them as you will, Sir, but I am very selective as to my clientele. In fact, if I am not mistaken, I believe that Virginia may have met a more suitable life companion here."

"That person wouldn't be Captain Henry Forster of the Royal Horse Artillery, would it?"

"Why, Mr. Holmes, your deductive powers are indeed impressive. Captain Forster is the gentleman who has captured the heart of young Virginia. But there is no need to mention him in the context of these events, since he had nothing to do with the boorish and underhanded behavior of Sir Charles. His relationship with Virginia did not come to bloom until well after the events."

"I understand your desire for discretion, Mrs. Rogerson. So, was it your advice to Virginia that she confess to her husband the affair with Sir Charles?"

"Yes, of course it was, Mr. Holmes. It would serve not only to spur Mr. Crawford into suing for divorce, which would extricate Virginia from her unfortunate marriage, but it would expose Sir Charles Dilke for the unscrupulous scoundrel that he is, as evidenced by his treatment of Virginia, his affair with Virginia's mother, and his breech of promise in my own case."

An Affair of State: Sir Charles Dilke by Frank Emerson

"You do realize of course, Mrs. Rogerson, that such a lawsuit, whether justified or not, whether successful or not, could readily hamper the political future of a respected MP and member of the cabinet."

"My dear Mr. Holmes, you have just hit on it. I want the man's career in ruins! You have heard, I am certain, as I have heard from my uncle, who keeps abreast of such things, the rumblings that Sir Charles is considered to be a strong candidate to become the next Prime Minister. That a man of such reprehensible behavior should be elevated to the highest office in the land cannot be allowed to happen. Besides that, my uncle, who is very intelligent and an astute judge of human character, is against it. Therefore, I am prepared do anything I can to prevent that from coming to fruition."

With Mrs. Rogerson's explanation, all our questions as to motivation and intent were answered with finality. On our way back to Sir Charles' residence, Holmes commented on the influence this somewhat obscure academician, Moriarty, might have on the future of the government. I opined that perhaps Holmes was overstating his case and his involvement was a side issue at best and that we should not make too much out of it. Holmes responded with a barely audible, "Hmm, I wonder, though. Ah well, perhaps you're right, Watson."

On the ride to Sir Charles' lodgings, we were consumed by our own thoughts about the matter. I am certain that Holmes felt as I did in that though we were somewhat reluctant to report to Sir Charles, we realized it was our duty to do so since he had requested our services to begin with.

"Sir Charles," Holmes began, as we seated ourselves in Dilke's front parlour, "I am sorely afraid and fairly confident that there is considerable viable evidence against you, and that your chances in the upcoming hearing do not appear to be favourable in the least."

"But Mr. Holmes," Dilke exclaimed, "I am innocent!"

Holmes shook his head and with a knowing dry cough said, "So you say. However, I can report only what our investigation has led us to conclude. To wit: It doesn't matter if you are innocent or not. And certainly, considering your, what shall we call them – varied activities – 'innocent' is hardly the appropriate word in this situation."

"But Mr. Holmes …"

"Believe me, Sir Charles, I am just making an *a priori* observation. The mere fact that these proceedings will undoubtedly smack of salaciousness can do nothing to advance your political career."

"So you are telling me that I have no hope? No recourse?"

"What I am telling you, Sir Charles, is that if you truly believe that you have been wronged in this matter, you should retain an accomplished barrister who can plead you not guilty and can see to it that the arguments put forth strictly pertain to the singular accusation and that the opposition is confined only to Mrs. Crawford's germane evidence."

Dilke nodded grimly in understanding, stood, turned and walked to a side table whereupon he poured himself a generous portion of what I presumed to be Scotch, which he summarily drank and proffered the decanter in our direction.

"Thank you, no," said Holmes. "Watson?"

"I think not," I said, "but thank you."

Dilke poured himself another portion and said, "Dr. Watson, Mr. Holmes, though I am disappointed with your findings, I do appreciate your honesty. I must tell you that I intend to mount a firm defence. I have already retained Sir Charles Russell, the newly appointed attorney general to represent me. I shall also rely on the help and advice of a fellow MP and cabinet member, my close friend, Mr. Joseph Chamberlain."

"Well then," Holmes said as we both stood to take our leave, "we trust that you are in capable hands."

"I truly hope," said Sir Charles, "that you will attend the proceedings, as they are scheduled to convene one week hence in the

Probate, Divorce and Admiralty Division of the High Court before Mr. Justice Sir Charles Butt."

"Well, well," Holmes said, "your chances seem to be enhanced somewhat with another Liberal MP residing on the bench. It should be interesting. Don't you agree, Watson?"

"I most assuredly do agree, Holmes. Sir Charles, we wouldn't dream of missing the event." So saying, we returned to Baker Street.

The following week brought nothing untoward into our lives, as we idly speculated as to the possible outcomes of the hearing. On the appointed morning we made our way to the Law Courts on the Strand in Westminster, entered and took seats in the appropriate gallery.

As the proceedings got underway, we could not help but note the absence of Mrs. Crawford and Mrs. Rogerson, nor were they in attendance for the entirety of the hearing. Mr. Crawford testified as to the confession of his wife to him of having committed adultery with Sir Charles Dilke on numerous occasions. Dilke, his attorney and Joseph Chamberlain sat listening in rapt attention to the accusations. After a short conference, Sir Charles Russell, Dilke's attorney, declined to question Mr. Crawford. Furthermore, he announced that Dilke would not take the stand in his defence. I questioned the wisdom of this tactic. Holmes enlightened me.

"It is one of many quirks of the English justice system that though a wife's confession of guilt to her husband is evidence of her guilt, it does not carry the corollary that her co-respondent is likewise guilty. Therefore, the defence opted not to have Dilke testify. *Ipso facto*, the adultery charge is unproven. However, Watson, I am not at all certain of the wisdom of the move nor that this spells victory for the libidinous Sir Charles Dilke. We shall see how this plays."

In a paradox of British law, the judge could do nothing other than dismiss the charges against Dilke. In effect, the court found that while Mrs. Crawford had indeed committed adultery with Dilke, he had not done so with her. Mr. Crawford was granted his divorce *in nisi*, which meant that the decree would not become final for six months, during which hiatus, evidence pro or con might be gathered to be presented at a final hearing to determine mitigation. In what would seem to be an odd turn, the court also ordered Crawford, the aggrieved party, to pay court costs.

At the conclusion of the proceedings, Dilke sought us out. "Mr. Holmes! Dr. Watson! There you are, I see! I must introduce you to my good friend, Mr. Joseph Chamberlain."

Chamberlain stepped forward to shake hands and announced, "Mr. Holmes, Dr. Watson. I am so glad to meet you both, particularly you, Dr. Watson. My son, Neville, will be jealous for he has expressed to me a desire not to follow in my political footsteps, but to cultivate his creative talents in the field of literature."

"I am flattered," I said, "but success in literature, even on so lowly a level as my own, is difficult to achieve. Perhaps his energies might better be applied to your world of national service and diplomacy."

Chamberlain expressed his thanks and retreated as Dilke stepped forward. "So, Mr. Holmes, what do you think?"

Holmes glanced in my direction and then turned toward Dilke, "Congratulations are due, I suppose, since the charges against you were indeed dismissed," he said in a matter-of-fact manner.

"Yes, thank you," said Dilke, oblivious to the sarcasm. "But my fight is not over yet. My reputation has been sullied by irresponsible innuendo and scurrilous insinuations and false reportage in the press. It is within my rights to petition the Queen's Proctor to re-open the case to prove that the verdict had been rendered on adultery which had not taken place so that I might clear my name."

"I see," said Sherlock Holmes. "Certainly, you are perfectly entitled to pursue that course of action; but might it not be a more prudent decision to accept the verdict as given and then proceed to minister to your smeared character, perhaps by utilizing the same instruments of mass communication that you claim to have been brought to bear against you?"

"With all due respect, Mr. Holmes," said Dilke bringing himself up to his full height, "you are but a consulting detective, while as you are aware, my counsel consists of my more-than-able attorney, Sir Charles Russell, as well as Mr. Chamberlain, a member of the Crown's Privy Council. They have advised me not to be satisfied with this lukewarm decision, but to proceed forward toward full vindication and to expose Mrs. Virginia Crawford for the liar and adventuress that she is."

"Yes, I fully understand," said Holmes. Turning to me, he continued, "Watson, I believe this might be a fine time for a whisky and soda at the Red Lion, don't you agree?"

"I do indeed, Holmes, I do indeed." With that, we bade farewell to Sir Charles Dilke, repaired straightaway to the Red Lion, where we enjoyed a pleasant conclave discussing the merits and demerits of the Dilke case.

Over the following two months, we thought little of Sir Charles except when prodded by the numerous articles in the press – notably those of W.T. Stead in *The Pall Mall Gazette* – as to his character, his career, the trial itself, its participants, Dilke's future and his efforts to secure a second hearing. Finally, it was announced that his case would be heard again. Just before the trial, Dilke received the devastating news that he had been rejected by the voters of Chelsea, thereby losing his seat in Parliament. Holmes and I could not help but think that this might prove to be an ill omen in the case of Sir Charles Dilke. With this in mind, we once again journeyed to the Law Courts.

Public interest had built to the point that we feared that we would be unable to gain access to the court room, but we finally managed to secure seats. Much to Dilke's chagrin, he realized too late that he should have taken Holmes's advice suggesting that he forego a second trial.

An Affair of State: Sir Charles Dilke by Frank Emerson

"Look there," said Holmes to me, "note how there is a heated discussion going on between Dilke's attorney, the Queen's Counsel, and the presiding judge. What I was certain would come to fruition has done just that.

"Because our Mr. Dilke was in effect cleared and the charges dismissed in the first trial, the court has ruled, and quite rightly according to British law, that he has no standing as a participant in this trial. He has received terrible legal advice all around. Consequently, because Dilke is not a defendant, his lawyers cannot present his argument since the case legally concerns only the divorce decree. Dilke can only appear as a witness, as which I fear he will be called. Considering that the Queen's Counsel is the noted barrister, Henry Matthews, a Conservative, this may spell doom for the Liberal Sir Charles."

Sir Charles was the first to be called to the witness box. Under Mr. Matthews' incisive and deadly accurate questioning, Dilke was compelled to confess his affair with Virginia's mother.
Christina Rogerson; Virginia Crawford; and Virginia's sister, Maye – Dilke's former sister-in-law – were in attendance. Having the advantage of hearing Sir Charles' pleas of innocence and admission of indiscretion, the women presented devastating testimony that cast further doubts as to the nature of Dilke's character and reinforced the validity of the initial verdict. The jury took but fifteen minutes to uphold the decree of the first trial and seemingly put an end to Sir Charles' public life.

As I sit here now in the autumn of 1912, Holmes and I long retired from our respective professions, I feel compelled to report on the ensuing lives of some of the characters in the drama. Mr. Donald Crawford, Virginia's husband, served as an MP until 1895 at which point he was named Sheriff of Aberdeen, an office he holds to this day. Following her divorce, Mrs. Virginia Crawford continued her relationship with Captain Henry Forster until she tired of him. She subsequently underwent a reformation of sorts, forswearing her rather libertine ways, becoming a Roman Catholic, an author and an activist for women's suffrage, a role in which she continues to receive public notoriety. Sir Charles never stopped trying to clear his name and in some ways was successful. Though he never realized his desire to become a member of the cabinet, he nonetheless was elected MP for the Forest of Dean in 1892, which position he held until he passed away last year at the age of 67. Ironically, as an MP, Sir Charles campaigned vehemently for women's suffrage.

As to Mrs. Christina Rogerson, whose letters sparked the affair, she simply faded into the bowels of the London underworld, wherein her uncle, Professor James Moriarty, held sway as the Napoleon of crime, as Holmes referred to him, until that fateful confrontation between the two of them in 1891 at the Reichenbach Falls in Switzerland, but you know all about that from *The Adventure of the Final Problem.*

September 1888

The Dunfermline Tarriance

By David Marcum

If truth be told, I have never cared for Dunfermline. Such feelings initially derive from when I was a boy of six, and my parents chose to make the long and tedious journey there from Stranraer to attend a cousin's wedding. I have some memory that my father hoped to gain favor by our presence, as that branch of the family was enjoying a period of extended prosperity.

In the days of my youth, the word "unpleasant" was possibly the most polite way to describe extended travel. The railway system was not yet nearly as established or extensive, and most journeys across those distances were accomplished by way of massive horse-drawn coaches, with frequent stops to change animals or obtain victuals at notable coaching inns. At that young age, when time spent in unpleasant situations stretches to painful infinities, the trip was simply terrible – hour upon hour crammed into an overcrowded and odiferous box, squeezed between irritated adults in stifling heat and constricted within uncomfortably hot clothing, being rocked from side to side without any helpful view of the outside world which might provide the smallest bit of spatial awareness.

I remember that one fat man insisted on smoking within the coach's confines, while I was queasy in varying degrees all along the western coast up to Glasgow, and then on to Stirling before turning east beside the Firth of Forth and into Dunfermline. What followed were several days of confusion as we navigated through a few people that we knew amongst scores of strangers – all of whom were much taller than I.

In particular, I seemed to have been singled out by one middle-aged woman, a great-aunt I was told, who took it upon herself to terrorize me, illuminating every real or imagined fault of character that might manifest itself in a shy six-year-old boy over the course of a two-day encounter. Ironically, her name was Grace, and from what little I could observe at that diminished and intimidated age, I was the only one who received such attentions, and also the only one who found her to be unpleasant. Was it possible that no one else saw her true nature? By the end of the trip, I came to understand that it was she whom my parents had hoped to impress, gaining some sort of unspecified favor.

Eventually, we made the reverse journey toward home – with my parents in even worse moods than they had been on the outward-bound segment of our sojourn, as whatever they'd hoped to accomplish or gain at the wedding had most definitely not materialized. I had to wonder if it were due to Great-aunt Grace's unfavorable opinion of me – a question that I wisely chose not to explore with my parents, as they didn't seem to realize it on their own.

Now, a quarter-century later, I was back in Dunfermline, a grown man recently turned thirty-one, and even though my older perspective revealed a town that was charming in a way that I could never have appreciated as a child, I had also just learned that it held horrors.

The Dunfermline Tarriance by David Marcum

A day earlier, my friend Sherlock Holmes and I had made our way north with important new facts related to the sinking of the *Daphne* in Linthouse, just west of Glasgow. The tragedy had occurred just two months earlier, upon the ship's deep-water launch from the shipyard where she was being constructed. Nearly two-hundred workmen and boys were on board, prepared to continue their labors as soon as she was afloat – the typical procedure, as was later reported in the newspapers. However, the two anchored cables on either side of the ship failed, allowing the current to unexpectedly take the overloaded ship and heel her hard over onto her port side. She rolled and sank almost immediately, and one-hundred-twenty-four lives were lost.

The subsequent inquiry found the tragedy to be an unforeseen accident, apparently caused by instability of the failed cables combined with too many workers overcrowding the upper deck. Some alleged that there were other more deliberate causes for the sinking which were being hidden to protect the company, but that talk quickly faded away.

Then, while investigating a completely separate matter in London, Holmes came across sickening evidence that the sinking had been deliberate after all – over ten-dozen lives lost so that one man could be removed in order to accommodate another's insatiable greed. In Dunfermline, we – along with a representative of The Crown – had cornered the titled beast who had arranged such a terrible crime. It was not without cost – Holmes had taken a minor bullet wound across the shoulder, messy but fortunately superficial.

In spite of that, he had handily disarmed the man who we sought. His guilt revealed, the nobleman was unrepentant and arrogant. Knowing as he did how deeply rooted he was in the fabric of the Kingdom, he bragged that his exposure would do far greater damage than what he'd caused by taking the lives of those lost on the ship – "insignificants," he called them. He declared that his position was invulnerable, and that he was protected by a hundred other men of similar rank and title who had also benefited from his actions. "If I wasn't already knighted, Mr. Holmes . . ." he had sneered.

Hearing these vile pronouncements left me speechless, and I could see that Holmes was affected the same way. As I watched the exposed criminal – madman, really – smugly look from one of us to the other, I felt a rage growing inside that had only rarely known itself in the past. Yet before we could gather our wits, the Crown's man who had accompanied us from London spoke quietly, his tones level and his words measured. The nobleman's expression changed – he still projected arrogant confidence, but there was one flicker of doubt now weighing on his expression. He seemed as if he'd been listening to the perfect symphony before perceiving in the distance a sole dissonant note – an out-of-tune horn that was getting closer and louder with each heartbeat.

The agent from London then excused us both from the brightly lit room, so pleasant a place that it seemed as if nothing bad could ever occur there. It was more of an order than a suggestion or request, and knowing the man's authority, we did as he said, making no argument, confident that justice was about to be enacted while we silently made our way outside, and then back through the darkened and deserted streets to the inn where we had left our bags. The last we heard from the previously confident killer was a timid request for us to stay, his tone now tremulous and uncertain. We ignored him, pulled the door to his study shut, and departed.

It was no surprise the following morning to read in the early newspapers that the man we had exposed had been found in his study where we had left him. It seemed that he had, while carelessly cleaning his shotgun the night before, blown off his own head. His actions were inexplicable, as he had servants for such tedious work. As he had no heirs, the article tastelessly speculated as to the disposition of his sizable estate.

Holmes and I were at the small table in the sitting room adjoining our bedrooms, confronting a perfectly acceptable breakfast that we had no desire to eat, and with neither of us feeling the need for additional conversation or speculation. It was still some time before our London train would depart, and we had nothing better to do than wait. There was certainly nowhere that I wished to visit before we left, and any of those distant relatives that I met when I was a boy would have no memory of me, should they even still live there or be alive.

With a sigh, I glanced at the window and noticed it had begun to rain.

I have never cared for Dunfermline.

I was considering that it was time to check Holmes's wound when a strong knock sounded on the hallway door – surprising both of us, as we hadn't heard the approach of any footsteps.

I rose and crossed the short distance, opening it to find a staid, middle-aged fellow, hat in hand, and another younger man, tall and well-dressed, his agitation obvious and immediate.

The older man nodded, his lips pursed in distaste, saying, "Dr. Watson? I'm Inspector McCrae. Might we speak with you and Mr. Holmes on a matter of some urgency?"

Considering that Holmes and I wished to shake the dust of this town from our feet as soon as possible, and worrying that we might be asked questions about the night before, I was tempted to tell him no and shut the door without explanation. And if it were already another case, Holmes was wounded, however slight, and he had no business overtaxing his recovery.

"Come in," said my friend from behind me, which was no surprise at all. I stepped aside and allowed the two men to enter. In the meantime, Holmes was moving from the table, his breakfast mostly untouched, to one of the two chairs facing a small sofa.

"Inspector McRae," repeated the older man, shaking Holmes's hand, and then turning to do the same with me. "This is Albert McCreevy. He's – "

The younger man stepped forward, offering his hand to me. "I'm Mr. Andrew Carnegie's personal assistant," he said in a curiously flat American accent. He pronounced his employer's name in the American fashion, with the syllables having equal emphasis, in contrast to the Scottish Car-*nay*-gie, with the weight on the middle syllable.

He was quite tall and thin, and there was something curiously reptilian about him, from the greenish tint of his foreign-looking and expensive suit to the way his forehead sloped back a little too steeply from his thin brows to his high thin hairline. What hair to be found there was combed straight back, and his skull was wide at the top, narrowing around his eyes, and then widening again where the mandible joined behind the zygomatic bones. He wore *pince-nez* over a flat nose, turned up so that one could see slightly into his pinkish nostrils. His mouth was a thin line over a minor bump of a chin; in fact, his Adam's apple peeking above his collar was more pronounced than the front of his jaw.

It was no surprise that his grip was cold and damp and limp.

McCrae was made of sterner stuff. He was at least fifty, solid and weathered, with short gray hair and matching military-trimmed mustache. His wool suit looked very much like one of my own favorites, and his handshake had been warm, dry, and firm.

"We're sorry to bother you," he began, his Scottish burr indicating that he was from further north, and not a native of Dunfermline. When my superiors learned that you were here, Mr. Holmes, I was – "

"Mr. Carnegie has been kidnapped!" interrupted McCreevy, his voice on the edge of being shrill. Whereas McCrae had settled back into the sofa, the younger man remained perched on the edge, his feet pulled in, as if he intended to rise and flee at any moment, or perhaps punctuate a statement by jumping to his feet for dramatic effect.

"Andrew Carnegie the millionaire?" asked Holmes, his tone neutral, and giving no indication whether he was intrigued enough to commit his time or energies.

McCreevy nodded. "The same. We're here because of his new library – it opened last month. Mr. Carnegie has been making a quiet tour of Europe – meeting with investors, visiting his holdings – and he didn't want to miss the chance to revisit the town of his birth and see the library."

I knew that at times such as these, Holmes missed having access to his commonplace books, where he recorded any number of wide-ranging facts which might be of some use. Still, he appeared to recall more than I would have expected.

"A quiet tour, you say? Surely such a visit would have been reported in the newspapers."

McCreevy shook his head. "That's exactly what Mr. Carnegie didn't want. In spite of his wealth, he tries to live without seeking attention. I'm sure you're aware of his philanthropic endeavors?"

I nodded, saying, "Indeed. His charitable contributions over the last couple of years have been noteworthy."

"That's only the beginning. He intended to begin distributing his fortune much earlier, but life has a way of revising plans. However, now that he's started, he intends to spend the rest of his life giving away most of his wealth."

"But you're talking about millions of dollars," I said, trying to picture a rich man who would freely distribute his accumulated hoard. I would have bet that such a notion was impossible. Having already met a number of rich men by way of my association with Holmes, I couldn't imagine it. Even the best of them, when peeled down to their essential core, were greedy and felt that they deserved what they had.

"Mr. Carnegie is made of different stuff. He was born here in Dunfermline. His father was a weaver, and his family shared a main room with another family in a small house – he and I saw it just yesterday, not long after our arrival. After the family emigrated to Pennsylvania, he found employment as a messenger boy while only fourteen. Through canniness and hard work, he advanced to supervisory positions, making friends and investments where he could. By the time the Civil War started, he had founded his fortune and was appointed as the superintendent of the Northern military's railways and telegraph lines. In the meantime, he invested in oil and bridges and steel, so that after the War – "

Holmes had heard enough. He raised a hand. "Are you here to convince us to buy shares in one of Carnegie's companies, or to seek assistance in the matter of his kidnapping?"

The reptilian man was caught up short, his enthusiastic spiel nipped just as it was gaining momentum. He looked at Holmes and me, and then to the inspector, as if seeking the help of an older adult to redress his perceived grievance.

McCrae cleared his throat. "Two days ago, we – the police – received a wire from London that Mr. Carnegie would be arriving to see his new library. You may have read of it. It's apparently his intention – as part of giving away his entire fortune – to build libraries all over the world. The first is here in Dunfermline. He and his mother visited here a couple of years ago, attracting a great deal more attention then. He's provided money right along, and last month, it finally opened."

McCreevy nodded and started to speak, but McCrae continued first. "As stated, he wanted a quiet visit this time – no dinners or parades. He would just slip in and slip out for a couple of days – visiting the library, and a few other places that meant something to him when he was young, before leaving for America."

"This was to be his last European stop," interrupted McCreevy. "When we'd seen the library and the old house on Moodie Street, we planned to travel on and sail for home."

"Mr. Carnegie and Mr. McCreevy presented themselves at the police station," continued McCrae, "and I was assigned to accompany them – more as a courtesy than due to any concerns. Yesterday we visited the library and the old house – without making announcements who he was – and also a few other spots which meant something to him."

"Who knew that he would be here?"

"No one," said McCreevy. "No one except the police, whom we notified before departing London." He looked at the inspector with an accusing expression.

McCrae shook his head. "Respecting Mr. Carnegie's wishes, we kept the information close. My superintendent knew, and a discreet sergeant that I'd trust with my life. In fact, we discussed the matter ahead of time upon receiving the notification that he was coming, and the three of us agreed to refer to our famed visitor as 'Mr. Smith.'" He looked at the younger man. "We saw no need to call Mr. McCreevy by any other name."

"A pity," said Holmes, his eyes narrowing in something of a smile. "I believe that 'Mr. Jones' would suit him rather well."

McCreevy looked from Holmes to the policeman with confusion in his face, sensing that he was being ridiculed in some subtle way, but not quite understanding how.

"And the kidnapping?" asked Holmes. "How was that accomplished?"

McCrae nodded to the secretary. "We returned to our small hotel last night about seven and ordered dinner sent to our rooms. Mr. Carnegie ate alone, and at eight, I rejoined him as planned to go over some wires about ongoing business deals and to discuss our travel arrangements. Then, an hour or so later, I said good night and returned to my own room, with the understanding that I'd be joining him for breakfast at six this morning."

"That's quite early," I commented.

McCreevy nodded. "Mr. Carnegie sleeps very little and is an early riser. At the appointed time, I knocked on the door and entered. It was still a few minutes before breakfast was to be served, and I expected to find him waiting for me in his sitting room. He wasn't there. The door to his bedroom was open, and his bed hadn't been slept in. I thought that he'd gone out for some reason, although I couldn't imagine why he hadn't slept there. Then I saw the note on the table."

He looked to McCrae, who reached into his coat, pulling out a folded document. "No envelope." He handed it to Holmes, who studied it for a moment before passing it my way. It was a typical sheet of stationery, approximately twenty-four bond, with no markings or decorations. A message was centered on the page, written in black ink in block-capital letters:

We have Carnegie, and he will pay for his rich-man sins.

More information to follow.

I handed it back to Holmes, who – with McCrae's permission – retained it, slipping it into his own coat pocket.

"You then notified the police?" Holmes asked the secretary.

McCreevy nodded. "It didn't say not to. I didn't know where else to seek help. This needs to be kept secret – knowledge that Mr. Carnegie has been taken could rock the financial world! We must get him back as soon as possible!"

"Mr. McCreevy arrived at the station early this morning. I myself happened to be there, and he spotted me as soon as he entered. I could see that something had happened. When I saw what the letter said, I notified my superintendent, who had arrived shortly. He recalled that you were here, Mr. Holmes, and sent us to enlist your aid, while he takes the matter discreetly to his superior."

"Have you made any investigation at the hotel where he was taken?"

"Not yet, other than to send my sergeant, Dufrain, to keep watch. I was uncertain as to the best way to begin without letting on through my questioning that Carnegie is missing."

Holmes nodded and then stood. He winced, and I knew that his shoulder was in pain. "Until we receive a further communication, examining the hotel may prove useful."

I held up a hand. "First, I must change Mr. Holmes's bandages. He received an injury yesterday."

McCrae raised an eyebrow. "I'm sorry. I had no idea. Perhaps you should instead stay here and recuperate – "

Holmes shook his head impatiently. "This matter intrigues me, and there are certain points of interest about it. We will be ready soon." And he turned and walked into his bedroom. I retrieved my medical bag and followed.

When the door was shut, he took off his coat, partially unbuttoned his shirt, and pulled it back to reveal his bandaged shoulder. I was relieved to see that the wound was already starting to heal, and there were no signs of infection, drainage, or blood poisoning.

"Did you notice the ransom letter?" he asked in a low voice.

I nodded. "The ink?"

"Exactly. You've learned a great deal during our association."

I finished re-fixing the bandage. "What do you hope to find at the hotel?"

"I'm uncertain, although the next ransom note should prove to be quite interesting – and of course there will be one. It's rather fortunate that we happened to be Dunfermline."

"Hmmph," I grunted. "I suppose so – although I'd rather hoped to be on our way home soon."

"I suspect that our delay will be rather short," Holmes countered. "In the meantime, let's see how this affair plays out." He shrugged back into his shirt, rebuttoned it, and then got back into his coat, which I held for him. "Ready?"

We joined the inspector and the secretary, who were standing near the door, ready to depart. Holmes and I donned our coats and hats, because the September Scottish mornings were already cool. Then we went downstairs, where Holmes had a quick word with the landlord to inform him that we might not be leaving that day after all, and to hold our rooms just in case. Then we went outside and climbed into a four-wheeler.

It turned out that we didn't have far to travel. Our own temporary lodgings were in Canmore Street, and we traveled south and then east for ten minutes or so. At one point, McCreevy pointed vaguely west and said that Carnegie's birthplace was not far in that direction, and that he'd chosen the inn where they were staying because it was near that old neighborhood. That seemed reasonable, until we arrived at The Whiteclaw Inn – a most unlikely place for one of the world's richest men to tarry, even if he were traveling *incognito*.

In fact, the lodgings where Holmes and I had spent the night, quite modest, were much nicer than the establishment which we now entered. It was an old building, with foundational cracks and moss-covered spots masking areas of damp and decay on the old stone walls. It was only two stories, and the slate of the low roof over the first floor was in terrible shape. In fact, there were several small trees growing up there in soil that had accumulated in valleys between the different peaks and gables. It exuded a certain shabby charm, which could also be said for the owner who met us as we stepped inside.

Mr. Ryan O'Connor introduced himself with a strong Irish accent. He was about forty with red hair and nose – the hair extending to his thick beard high on his cheeks, and even a few stray bristles growing from his bulbous nose. His thick brows lay across very blue eyes, bracketed by deeply grooved laugh lines which were now compressed with a wary expression. He recognized McCreevy and McCrae, as his wife, a short plump woman who joined her husband, asking, "What would the police be doing here, Inspector McCrae? The sergeant won't tell us a thing – he said you'd explain."

It was then that another man came down the creaking stairs and joined us. As there had been no noise prior to his appearance, he must have been sitting on the stairs just out of sight.

"This is Sergeant Dufrain," explained McCrae. "I sent him here after we were notified of the . . . incident."

"Incident?" asked O'Connor with surprise.

Holmes stepped forward. "It appears that Mr. *Smith* – " He glanced at McCrae to confirm that Carnegie had been known by that name here too. The inspector nodded. "It appears that he didn't sleep here last night."

"He's missing?" asked the women.

Holmes nodded, asking, "When was the last time that you saw him?"

The both started to speak at once, and then O'Connor gestured for his wife to continue. "It was last night, when I went up to retrieve their dishes after dinner," she said. "Mr. McCreevy's were in his room, as he'd already gone into Mr. Smith's sitting room. I went there next to gather those."

"That's right," agreed McCreevy. "I remember you coming in."

"And I last saw the two of them when they came back for the day," added the innkeeper. "About six, I expect."

The inspector nodded. "That's when the sergeant and I dropped the two of them off after their day of sightseeing."

"Who else is employed here?" asked Holmes.

"No one," responded O'Connor. "Not as employees – rather, it's family-run. My wife and me, and our daughter Emily, and Amos, my orphaned nephew. He's fifteen, and totes things, makes up the fires, and so on. Emily acts as a maid and helps with the cooking."

"Do you have any idea how Mr. Smith might have left the inn?"

The couple looked at each other and then back at Holmes, both shaking their heads. "We do not. The doors – front and back – are locked each night, and that's how I found them this morning. We have the keys for the main doors – we don't provide them to our guests. If someone is going to be out late and wants the door left on the latch, we refuse and tell them to ring the bell. We'll get up to let them in. And no such request was made last night."

"Would your daughter and nephew have honored such a request without telling you?"

"Of course not. Emily!" he bellowed. "Amos!"

He needn't have yelled. Both had been listening just beyond a nearly closed door, and they entered when called. They were about the same age, he being a big handsome lad and she quite petite and pretty. I noted that as they entered the room, their hands seemed to be falling away from one another, as if they'd been holding them while surreptitiously listening. I deduced from that, and the way they stood close together, unconsciously touching shoulders, that these two cousins might someday be asking for permission to wed. I wondered if the O'Connors were already aware, or if the two young people weren't as discreet as they may have believed.

Holmes repeated his questions about whether or not anyone could have arrived or left by the front and back doors, and they confirmed that there had been no such activity during the night to their knowledge. The family slept in apartments at the back of the ground floor, and there were currently no other guests.

Holmes thanked them, and then asked if we could see "Smith's" room upstairs. The sergeant turned and led us into the darkened stairwell. It wasn't a great distance to the next level, as the ground floor had those low ceiling so common in old buildings.

The upper hallway was lit by a window that looked out over the front of the building. There was enough light to see that there were four rooms, two with open doors on the left – apparently those currently vacant – and two closed on the right. McCreevy stepped past the sergeant to the nearer door, pulling a key from his pocket. "Mr. Carnegie's," he explained unnecessarily as he unlocked it. Then, without stepping aside to allow us past him, he entered first before stopping with a startled noise, blocking the way.

The sergeant, next in line, moved forward and nudged the secretary out of the way. The rest of us followed. It was a modest sitting room, much like the one that we had left at our own inn not long before. This one was older though, with exposed beams running along the plastered ceiling, and much darker and heavier furniture anchoring the old rug which nearly covered the wooden floor. There was a double window on one side, which I soon learned looked out onto one of the sloping roofs at the side of the building, and a door which led into a darkened bedroom. This chamber had no window, as it appeared to be an interior room aligned in the same direction as the other closed door we'd seen in the hallway – where it was assumed that the secretary had slept.

At first, I saw no reason for McCreevy's reaction upon entering. Then my focus narrowed to a round table near the center of the room, upon which a folded sheet of paper lay.

Everyone started in that direction, but at a sharp exclamation from Holmes, we stopped while he examined the rug, making his way carefully to the table. Only after he had looked at the paper from several angles did he reach and pick it up.

He examined it front and back, and his mouth pulled tighter on one side for just an instant. Then, he said, "Allow me to read this – the latest ransom note:

> *'If you want to see Carnegie alive again, gather £50,000 by noon. Instructions will follow.*
>
> *We are not afraid to kill him.'"*

The inspector glanced at the sergeant, both with scowls of irritation. I took the note from Holmes and saw that it matched the previous message – same type of paper and ink, and the exact block-capital handwriting. As I handed it back, McCreevy wrung his hands.

"We must hurry!" he said. "They've barely left us any time at all. Inspector – which way is the nearest telegraph office? I must wire Pittsburg immediately to arrange a transfer of cash."

"Wait a moment," responded the inspector. "Wouldn't it be best if we waited for Mr. Holmes to have a chance to complete his investigations? After all, there must be some clue as to how Mr. Carnegie was taken – and how this second note was left here in a locked room while the sergeant guarded the stairs."

"I favor taking O'Connor and the lot of them to the station and finding out what they know," interjected Sergeant Dufrain, his voice a low and intimidating rumble. "If there's a story to be told, he'd be the one to tell it."

Holmes shook his head. "No, Sergeant. Mr. McCreevy may be right – he needs to try to raise the money. There's no telling how long it might take to get to the bottom of this affair based on what clues there are here at the inn. In the meantime, these kidnappers seem to mean business. And I suspect that should word get out, as threatened, that Mr. Carnegie's life is in danger, financial markets on both sides of the Atlantic will be shaken."

The secretary nodded. "That's correct. Fortunes might be made and lost during the buying and selling that would occur if this news were to spread. Better that we pay them, get Mr. Carnegie back, and then see about catching and punishing them. Inspector, the nearest telegraph office?"

"I can have Dufrain take you."

Holmes raised a hand. "I need the sergeant for a different chore. Mr. McCreevy can go alone."

McCrae was clearly nonplussed, but he nodded and gave McCreevy directions to an office several blocks away. Then, looking at each of us quickly, the thin man departed. We heard him noisily and hurriedly descend the stairs, and then came the sound of the front door opening and closing.

Holmes turned to the sergeant. "About that chore – "

"Yes, Mr. Holmes?"

"Leave by the back door and take a different route to the telegraph office. Take care not to be seen. Does the building have a rear entrance? Do you know the employees there?"

"Yes to both questions."

"Good. Slip in the back and confirm whether McCreevy actually sends a wire. If he does, it will be immediately. No need to wait around too long one way or another. Return here when you're satisfied."

The sergeant glanced at the inspector, the beginnings of a knowing smile forming on his face. Then he slipped out of the room and was gone.

"You suspect McCreevy then?" asked McCrae. "Can't say as I'm surprised. He's an odd one, and that's a fact."

"I do. Watson, explain the ink while I look through his and Carnegie's rooms." Then he turned and began the type of examination to which I'd become accustomed – crawling along the rug, taking measurements and looking all around from different angles, all the while making a series of mutters and clicks and other odd noises to himself. This was clearly a distraction to the inspector, as he kept turning his head to glance at my friend while I told him about the ink on the letters.

"Holmes has indoctrinated me with his methods, and although I'm not nearly as good as he, I can see a thing or two. The ink on the first letter was clearly written some time ago – and not recently. One would expect that it would be written much closer to when it was needed, at the time of the kidnapping. Likewise, the letter we just found on the table here was of the same age – quite dry, and possibly written weeks ago."

"And the stationery," added Holmes, returning to the sitting room from the darkened bedroom.

"What about it?" I asked. "I didn't notice anything about that."

"It wasn't new – rather there are minute age marks and discolorations in the paper where the acids from the initial manufacture have begun to break down. This in and of itself is meaningless, but the dimensions of the sheets are trimmed according to American size and custom, not British. This leads me to assume that the paper was purchased some time ago in the United States and brought here." He looked toward the door. "One moment . . . ." Then he walked out into the hall and in the direction of the secretary's room. McCrae and I looked at one another and then followed him.

The other room at the back of the building was entered by way of a narrow hall that ran from the door and into the actual bedchamber. This hall must have run along the back of the inner bedroom used by Carnegie, as accessed from the adjacent sitting room. It had apparently been constructed this way to allow the smaller room its own window on the back corner of the building. This bed had clearly been used the night before, with the sheets rumpled and the covers thrown back. A small trunk was sitting on a stand near the window, and Holmes was already searching through it by the time we joined him. Heedless of the fact that his efforts would be obvious when McCreevy returned, he tossed clothing aside as he delved deeper.

Eventually he gave a small cry of satisfaction and leaned back, pulling a leather folder from the depths. Opening it, he held it flat and turned so that we might see: It contained stationery of the same size and type as that upon which the two notes had been written.

He flipped through the papers with his fingers until he found an example. Then he pulled one loose that had a name and address inscribed at the top: *Albert McCreevy, Arbor Street, New York, NY, USA*. "There are also blank sheets, as we saw earlier – the ransom notes. Those are for additional pages, should they be needed in addition to the cover sheets."

He handed the leather folder to us. "You'll notice that the stains match those on the ransom letters." While the inspector and I examined the papers within the folder, Holmes continued looking through the trunk.

The Dunfermline Tarriance by David Marcum

"At least then we can safely assume that this fellow really is Albert McCreevy from America, I suppose," said McCrae, folding one of the blank sheets and putting it into a pocket. "But what's his game with kidnapping Carnegie?"

Holmes looked up and shook his head. "Inspector, surely you don't think that man is actually Andrew Carnegie?"

McCrae frowned. "No, I suppose not. But he seemed legitimate enough yesterday – you can't fake a Scottish accent enough to fool a real Scotsman. And he looked enough like Mr. Carnegie from when he visited in '81. I didn't have any dealings with him then, but based on what I saw yesterday, I willingly accepted him. What makes you think that he's a fraud?"

Holmes looked at the piles of untrunked clothing and then seemed to decide that replacing them wasn't worth the effort. "Come with me," he said, leading us back to the larger rooms next door. Once there, he went into the bedroom and we followed. "Look at Carnegie's clothing."

There were a couple of suits hanging in the closet above a pair of worn shoes. Holmes picked up one of the shoes and began to examine it while McCrae extracted a suit, carrying it closer to the gaslight on the wall to examine it. He then looked at Holmes and was about to shrug when he thought to take a second look. Whatever he saw interested him greatly.

"Would you care to see as well, Watson?" asked Holmes.

"The inspector can enlighten me."

McCrae looked up and gestured with the suit. "It's well-worn – not the suit of a wealthy man. And it has London labels – it was manufactured on this side of the Atlantic, and not in America."

"While it's possible that Carnegie bought some London suits when he was last over here, and while it's also possible that he's a frugal man who doesn't dress to fit his station in life, the odds are more certain that these items belong to a much poorer man – one who is

The Dunfermline Tarriance by David Marcum

originally from Scotland, and who looks enough like Andrew Carnegie that making this attempt was worth the effort."

"But what attempt?" I asked. "If this isn't Carnegie, then a wire to America asking for ransom will be worthless, as they'll know Carnegie is there – or somewhere else. Anywhere but here in Dunfermline."

"But what if Carnegie really is over here right now," offered the inspector, "touring about in much the same way that McCreevy described, and these two got wind of it and concocted this plan to get the Americans to pay?" Then he shook his head. "But they would be in communication with the real Carnegie, and could quickly verify that he hadn't been kidnapped at all."

Holmes smiled and rehung the suit. "If the sergeant's report goes the way I suspect, then we'll soon know the next part of what Mr. McCreevy intends. In the meantime, let me see if I can determine just how our *faux* Carnegie left last night while the front and back doors were locked – since, in spite of the sergeant's suspicions, I'm not inclined to think that the O'Connor clan is involved."

With that, he moved to the sitting room window, overlooking the sloped roof across a portion of the first floor. He examined the window frame, and then unlatched it. "Notice," he said, "this window has been recently opened."

"The O'Connors might have done that," said the inspector.

"True," responded Holmes, "but it's unlikely that they needed to go outside." The latch had turned easily enough, and without hesitation, Holmes then climbed out onto the gently sloping slates, moving immediately to one side and with great care, as they were mossy and slick from the recent rains.

"Look," he said. "There are smudges and portions of footprints leading from the window down to the edge." He crept lower and looked over. "It's just a five- or six-foot drop here – and there are marks in the mud below where someone has jumped off."

Then he jumped off too.

The Dunfermline Tarriance by David Marcum

McCrae and I looked at one another, and then I shut the window and we returned to the center of the room. In just a moment, we heard the front door open. There was muted conversation below, and then the sounds came of more than one person climbing the stairs.

Holmes entered, followed by Sergeant Dufrain. "The prints in the mud are the same size and width as the shoes in 'Carnegie's' closet," explained the former. Then he turned to the policeman. "Your report, Sergeant?"

"As expected, the secretary started in the direction of the telegraph office, but then went into a pub. Still there, I suppose. Should I have had someone stay with him?"

"Not necessary," said Holmes. "So far this is all meaningless – the ransom notes, the mysterious disappearance." He explained his theory about the false Carnegie. "McCreevy has to come back here to add the final piece."

"And what's that?" asked McCrae.

We heard the sound of the front door open and close. Then there were quick steps upon the stairs.

"Thus begins the last act," murmured Holmes softly and cryptically.

McCreevy entered through the sitting room's open door, flustered and obviously quite upset. It took him a moment to catch his breath, and he held up a hand indicating that he would respond soon to our implied questions. Then, with a deep final deep inhalation, he straightened, adjusted his coat, flattened his hair which had become rather untidy, and said, "They can't do it! The American bank! Not that quickly!"

Holmes stepped forward, his voice oozing worry and concern. "Can't do what? Pay the ransom?"

McCreevy shook his head, and there were tears starting to form along his lower lids. "That's right. They can send us the money by wire, but it will take time to arrange for such a notable sum.

Verifications must be established on both sides. Before that can be done, the time limit will have passed! They'll kill him!"

"But surely," Holmes responded, "the kidnappers will understand. Perhaps if we leave them a note – "

"How? They've left no way for us to respond back to them. The communication have all been one way – notes left here on the table."

"An advertisement, then," said Holmes, energy in his voice. "We can place one in the newspaper, saying that we need more time. Will a day suffice, do you think?"

McCreevy shook his head, almost angrily. "We can't put anything in the newspaper that might give any hint that Mr. Carnegie has been kidnapped. The financial markets of several countries couldn't take the uncertainty that would cause."

"But if we phrase it so only the kidnappers understand?"

"No! Even if we could get it published *now*, what if they don't see it? What if they don't understand it? What if they simply don't believe it and kill Mr. Carnegie? No – we have to come up with the money *now* – Quickly! – and wait for their instructions on how to deliver it."

He fell into deep thought, pulling his lip and rocking a bit in place, casting his glance toward one of us and then the other. I was quite impressed with his performance, and would have believed that he was truly dreading the possible outcome of this terrible situation if Holmes hadn't alerted our suspicions. As yet, there was nothing illegal about this, other than wasting the policemen's time. I knew that the man's move must come soon. Finally he was ready and, with a seemingly genuine expression of beaming enlightenment, he looked at the inspector.

"Perhaps . . . perhaps some of the community leaders – the wealthy men of Dunfermline – can gather the ransom. Temporarily, so that it may be paid now, and then reimbursed tomorrow when the funds are transferred from America. If you can introduce me to them,

Inspector, we may be in time to avert this tragedy before the next note arrives with the delivery instructions."

McCrae frowned and started to speak, but Holmes stepped forward first. "But Mr. McCreevy, the delivery instructions are already here," he said. "They were put into our hands while you were away, sending your wire to the United States."

It was fascinating to watch how quickly the man's appearance changed. When he was worked up with concern regarding the unavailability of the ransom money, and then suddenly enthused at his idea of raising the funds from the Dunfermline elite, there had been two spots of color the size of pennies on each of his otherwise pale cheeks. Now, he was suddenly and completely white, and his skin had taken on a sudden oily sheen.

Holmes withdrew from his coat pocket a sheet exactly matching the stationery from McCreevy's room. Unfolding it, he said, "We found this in your room this time. Clearly the kidnappers were free to come and go wherever they liked. Would you like to hear what it says?

> *Take the money to Pittencrieff House and leave it on the fairy statue at two o'clock today.*
>
> *No excuses or Mr. Carnegie will be mailed, a piece at a time, to every post office in Scotland.*

"Pittencrieff House?" Holmes asked, looking up.

Sergeant Dufrain nodded. "There's a fairy statue in one of the gardens on the south side."

Holmes looked back at McCreevy. "Is that where your confederate was to gather the loot once it was deposited there?" No response. Sergeant Dufrain had quietly moved between McCreevy and the door.

"You should know that your partner has already peached on you," Holmes prevaricated with absolute sincerity. "He was seen dropping off the roof last night while effecting his mysterious disappearance. The constable was suspicious and followed and arrested him. It didn't take long to get the truth out of him. Then we simply had to wait and see if you also took enough rope to tangle yourself."

This blatant fiction wouldn't have stood up to a rigorous examination, but McCreevy was in no position to make one. One could almost hear the roar of blood in his ears as his mind raced to catch up, while considering his best path forward. Finally, determining that surrender was the only option, he gave a weak smile and took a couple of steps to the table, where he sank into a chair.

"You have me then, that's for sure. But – " he added, looking cannily at the inspector, " – what's the charge?"

McCrae started to answer, then looked from the sergeant to Holmes to me, and then clapped his mouth shut. He rubbed his jaw. Holmes smiled and shook his head.

"The best you can do is escort them both out of town, Inspector. Other than wasting your time, no crime has been committed."

"But if you had let him carry through with his plan – with leaving that next ransom letter telling us where to deliver the money – we could have brought charges."

"I don't think so – for after all, the plot, as flimsy as it was, would never have progressed to the point where the locals actually put up the funds."

McCrae nodded. "I suppose that's correct."

"Isn't it better to have pinched this off early, and avoid the pesterment of arrest and a trial and even incarceration – all at the public cost and the peripheral embarrassment of Mr. Carnegie – for something so ridiculous?"

The Dunfermline Tarriance by David Marcum

McCreevy seemed to bristle at hearing his plan so denigrated, but he didn't argue the point.

"Your compatriot," asked Holmes. "Do you know how to find him, or do we have to go through the rigmarole of making up a package and leaving it Pittencrieff House for him to recover?"

"But . . . but you said that you'd arrested him . . . ."

"I lied."

The thin American shook his head and explained in clipped tones that his partner, one Colin Dean, could be found at another inn not a dozen streets away.

And so he was – still asleep with a mostly empty bottle of whisky on the table beside him. It took quite a while for him to come to his senses and realize who we were, and I wondered if he would have been able to rouse himself and collect the ransom money, had the plan been a success. When he spotted McCreevy in our company, he initially thought that he'd been betrayed, and he awkwardly rose and lunged at his partner, but fell heavily when his feet became tangled in the bedclothes.

Holmes glanced at McCreevy. "You played a bold game with very poor cards," he said. "But choosing this thin limb to carry so much weight was a mistake."

"I know," said the false secretary, looking at his struggling associate with disgust. "I know."

Later, McCreevy explained to us, almost conversationally, that he (from Scranton, Pennsylvania, where he was aware of Andrew Carnegie from nearby Pittsburgh) and Colin Dean (of Glasgow), had met a couple of years before in France and had fallen in with one another. It wasn't confirmed (but implied) that they had worked together to fleece the gullible wealthy whenever they had the chance, through a variety of ventures. A month earlier, they had seen in the paper an article where the Dunfermline library, as funded by Carnegie, was set to open. McCreevy had noted Dean's rather remarkable resemblance to the wealthy benefactor, and the plan was born.

They had arrived unannounced, except for a vague wire to the police, with their story of visiting the new library and seeing the sites of some of Carnegie's boyhood memories without attracting any attention. They had boldly decided to notify the police for assistance, believing that officers in the smaller town wouldn't be sharp enough to see through their scheme, and that if they could rush the events forward quickly enough, there wouldn't be time to stop them. McCreevy had presented himself to the police that morning with the ransom note and his frantic worry, and it had meant nothing to him when the inspector suggested that they consult someone named Sherlock Holmes who happened to be in town just then.

Curiously, Holmes admired McCreevy's boldness, if not his execution, and nearly a decade later, the American confidence man was a useful recruit in one of the campaigns that Holmes contrived as part of his assault on Professor Moriarty's criminal web.

Some years later, we happened to be passing through Dunfermline once again and took the opportunity to visit with McCrae, now a retired chief inspector. We had stayed in touch over the years, seeing him occasionally, and he seemed glad to see us. He let us know that a year or so before, Andrew Carnegie had purchased Pittencrieff House, where the ransom was to have been deposited, and donated it to the city. Then, changing the subject, he said that he had something of a surprise for me, and made sure that we had time to accompany him.

Not knowing what to expect, we joined him in his automobile, whereupon he drove us through the city. As we neared Pittencrieff House, I expected that we would stop there, with our errand having something to do with Carnegie. Instead, we continued west, eventually arriving at a worn little cottage. With a smile, McCrae led us to the door while telling me, "I learned through a mutual acquaintance, that you have family here, Doctor. I thought you might enjoy visiting with your Great-aunt Grace."

Then the door opened, and I found myself face-to-face with the same terrible gargoyle of my long-ago youth. Despite her wizened condition and shrunken stature, she was still the shrew that I'd met so long ago, even as she now approached her century-mark.

And she remembered me, proudly recounting all the faults she recalled from our first and only meeting, and how it was obvious that none of them had been repaired or remediated in the decades since.

It was a terribly unpleasant hour, although Holmes and the inspector seemed to enjoy it. In fact, they appeared to find her quite pleasant company.

I have never cared for Dunfermline.

October 1883

The Adventure of the Wispy Widow

By Derrick Belanger

John Watson - *FAILURE*. That is what I thought should hang around my neck on a sign, in place of an albatross. It was a chilly October afternoon in 1883. The winds had been particularly strong, and I clutched at my jacket, hugging it against my sides as I made my way home. The weather matched my dreary mood. For the past two weeks, I had been unable to make any gains as a locum. The doctors I had assisted had no need for my services, and the few patients that I had gained on my own were either in good health or had passed from this Earth.

I was ashamed at how poorly I was doing in my medical practice and had each day lied to Holmes and Mrs. Hudson, telling them that I was going to work. In fact, I was spending my days in the library, hidden away in a quiet nook, working on writing a script. Since I was failing as a doctor, I thought I might make some headway as an author. I had spent the last two weeks going through a stack of foolscap, making some headway, but then, in the end tearing up my efforts.

The Adventure of the Wispy Widow by Derrick Belanger

My plan was to turn the story of Jefferson Hope into a piece for the theatre. I tried starting the story in Utah, then I tried placing it in London. I even tried putting it in San Francisco with myself as the lead. That version was absolutely terrible, even with my desperate attempts to inject humor into the piece. All my characters were caricatures. They had no depth to them at all. I knew Holmes wouldn't approve of the work, so I did my best to keep him out of the story. At one point I did have a detective named Sherrinford, but the name sounded ridiculous to my ears, too close to Holmes's Christian name so anyone familiar with the case would know to whom the character referred.

The other adventure I contemplated dramatizing was the case of Helen Stoner and her brutal step-father, Dr. Grimesby Roylott. I wasn't sure what to name the story, and was debating between *The Manor House Curse* and *The Doctor of Death.* Neither name captured the horrors Holmes and I witnessed at Stoke Moran, the former being too bland and the latter too sensational, but I couldn't conceive of a title that would encapsulate the terrifying episode and not give away the ending of the case. Any mention of a snake would ruin the surprise of seeing the weapon used by the evil doctor to attack his stepdaughters. Even if I had a title, I couldn't figure out how to make the story work for the stage, the case being too short for a full play.

As I treaded into Baker Street, I thought of possibly making the Stoner case part of a three-act play. I could always pair the story with other cases such as *The Robbery at the First Street Bakery* and *The Odious Organ Grinder and his Despicable Monkey.* So lost in my head was I that when I arrived at my home, I did not notice the landau parked at the curb. My brain kept jumping between possible plots for my writing, and questioning how I was going to tell Holmes that I would be short on my portion of the month's rent.

I slowly made my way up the stairs to 221B, trying to decide if I should admit to Holmes my poor fortune, or if I should hold out with the hope that I might get some work before the end of the month.

The Adventure of the Wispy Widow by Derrick Belanger

When I entered our rooms, Holmes was sitting in his chair, warming himself by the fire. Seated across from him on the sofa was a woman who can only be described as spectral. Her face was gaunt and ghastly pale. Thick black circles surrounded her sunken eyes which enhanced her skeletal features. Had she a hood over her head, she may have looked like the Grim Reaper himself. Despite her ghostly appearance, the woman wore a fashionable crimson-coloured dress. Her fair hair was up in a bun which held an ornate comb adorned with sparkling diamonds. Before I had a chance to say anything, my friend sprang from his seat, and invited me to sit in the chair beside him. "Ah, Watson, your timing is perfect. Please take your seat. May I introduce Mrs. Anne Cassini, widow of the late Mr. Roberto Cassini."

A client, I thought to myself. This meant that once again Holmes would be bringing in money while my coffers remained empty. I kept these thoughts to myself and politely bowed toward the woman. "It is a pleasure to meet you, Madame."

The pale faced woman smiled at me, and I could see that at one time she must have been a beauty. "I am glad you are here, Doctor, for I have come on a medical matter."

"Medical?" I asked.

"Yes, she is suffering from severe weight loss and believes someone may be poisoning her," Holmes answered.

"Not just someone," Mrs. Cassini lamented, "my betrothed." She took out a handkerchief and dabbed at her watery eyes.

"My word," I said and took my seat next to Holmes, across from the woman.

"Please, my dear," Holmes said, interlocking his fingers and stretching out his arms before resting his hands upon his knees. "Let us hear your story from the beginning. What makes you suspect your fiancé?"

"It is the tea, Mr. Holmes. I'm sure I saw him put something in it. That would explain my malady," Mrs. Cassini stammered.

The Adventure of the Wispy Widow by Derrick Belanger

"Perhaps it would," Holmes agreed, "but I have no context. Please tell us about your fiancé."

Holmes's gentle voice helped focus the woman. She sat up and while her hands still clutched at the handkerchief, she found the strength to explain her case.

"I met Bartholomew about five years ago. I had been a widow for a decade at that point. You see, I married Roberto when I was just seventeen years old.

"My father is a major shareholder in the Lougham and Fiske Mill. About twenty years ago, Mr. Cassini, Roberto's father, bought into the company. Since he was an Italian businessman and didn't want to leave his homeland, he sent his eldest son to watch over the mill."

"And that was your late husband?" I asked.

"Yes," Mrs. Cassini beamed at the memory. "He was a handsome man. Ten years my senior. When I saw his dashing face and olive skin, I fell in love with him. He did the same with me. It was just a few months later that we were married.

"Those were joyous days. We lived outside of Sherwood. We had a beautiful country home and soon I was with child. Our son, Antonio, was born that July, and all was marital bliss until the day it all came to an end. We were traveling to visit Roberto's family in La Spezia. When the train was traveling through a mountain pass, there was a rumble, and we looked out the window and saw a terrible wave of rocks barreling towards us. The train was thrown off its tracks and buried in the rubble. I lost my husband and my son that day. I was one of the few survivors."

"How tragic," I commented.

"It was, Doctor, and for many years I felt as I now look, like a ghost, wandering through life in a fog. I sold the house in the country, severed all ties with the logging industry, and moved back to London. I've resided in a small house in Notting Hill ever since. I pulled myself away from society, away from life. I didn't want to associate with

The Adventure of the Wispy Widow by Derrick Belanger

anyone. I left only a few times a month to shop. I always dressed in black and kept my face veiled. Much like our Queen, in a state of constant mourning.

"The years passed on and I still kept myself locked away in my house. It was like a tomb containing my sorrows. Then, I met Bartholomew. It was on a chilly October day, not unlike today. I was in my carriage and feeling particularly cold. I spied a fur store from my window and told my driver to stop. Perhaps it was the fates taking pity on me or God himself bringing comfort to a devoted servant. When I walked into that store, I was greeted by the owner, a young and rather gawky fellow who was already balding at the top. He was jolly and always smiling. He got me talking and after a while, my icy exterior began to melt, but not by too much," she added at the end, like a schoolgirl sharing a secret about an admirer.

"I began to find reasons to go to Bartholomew's fur shop. Sometimes I'd want a hat, or scarf, or muffs, and every time Bartholomew would talk with me, and he'd get me to smile, even to laugh. I hadn't been able to do that in so long. After a year, I asked him, yes I made the first move, to go out for a stroll. We started doing that regularly and over time, we became best friends. Two years ago, he asked me to marry him."

Mrs. Cassini held up her left hand to show she was wearing a gold ring with a cluster of diamonds in the shape of a heart at its center.

"Two years?" Holmes asked, raising an arched brow.

Mrs. Cassini nodded her head. "Yes, Bartholomew is a proud man. When I told him the full extent of my wealth, he almost broke off the engagement. He saw himself as beneath me, as outside of my class. Men are quite silly about such things. I told him that it didn't matter to me, but he said it mattered to him. Since then, he's been working long hours, increasing his sales figures. He still will not set a date until he reaches some goal of his. At times, I think I should just give my fortune away." Mrs. Cassini let out a long sigh. "That brings me to the reason that I've come to see you today.

The Adventure of the Wispy Widow by Derrick Belanger

"About six months ago, I started feeling ill. I would have an upset stomach after I ate almost every meal. The pain became intolerable, so I went to visit my doctor. He prescribed some medicine, some pills to take with my breakfast and dinner. It didn't stop the pain, though. So, I tried going to a few other doctors. They all gave me slightly different remedies from chamomile tea to ginger root to chewing mint leaves, but none of them seemed to work."

"Those are typical remedies for upset stomachs," I noted. "Did your doctors check for any physical cause of the pain like an inflamed appendix or an ulcer?"

"Yes, they did, Doctor. They were all thorough, but they found nothing of concern. Then, things took a turn for the worse."

"Ah, is that when your weight loss started?" Holmes enquired.

"That's correct, Mr. Holmes. For some reason, I started losing weight. Though I was still getting stomach aches after each meal, I didn't lose my appetite. I still ate plenty of food, but for some reason, I was rapidly shedding pounds. As you can see, I still am." She held up her arm which was as thin as a sapling's branch.

"This brings me to Bartholomew. Two weeks ago, Bartholomew started insisting on coming to my house after work and bringing me my dinner and tea. He was concerned about my weight loss, and he wanted to make sure that I was eating properly. I told him that he was fussing over me for no good reason, and that I had my own doctor to tend to my needs.

"He called my current physician and the others I had seen before quacks who did not know what they were doing. I could see the anguish in my betrothed and his concern for me, so I acquiesced. But I noticed that evening that my tea tasted a touch odd. I couldn't place what exactly was different and asked him. He said he'd check with Mr. Garrett, my chef, to see if he had used a different blend. He denied making any changes to his recipe.

"Then two days ago, I decided to spy a little in the kitchen. I crept down the stairs and saw Bartholomew standing at the table that held the tea tray. I saw him look around quickly, and then I saw him remove a small bottle from his breast pocket and pour some liquid into the tea cup. I don't know why, but I didn't confront him then. Instead, I returned upstairs and waited for him to serve me. After taking a sip, I asked him what he had been adding to my tea.

"'Whatever do you mean,' he asked, rather defensively.

"'I mean, my dear, this tea has a much creamier taste to it. You've been adding something. I'd like to know what it is.'

"'Err,' he stumbled. 'Just some honey, my dear. I thought an extra dollop or two added to your chamomile might help you gain weight. I hope you don't mind.'

"'Not at all,' I replied. I knew he was lying, but I wasn't sure why.

"I spent the last two days contemplating what to do. While Bartholomew wasn't looking, I've been dumping out the tea into some potted plants I keep in the dining room. I can't say it has made a difference with my weight, but it has only been two days. I considered going to the police, but quickly tossed away the idea. If I were wrong about my fiancé, it could lead to him becoming angry. He already feels inferior to me. If he knew that I suspected him of harming me, and I was wrong, why, he could break off our engagement for good.

"Then I remembered you, Mr. Holmes, and the work you did recovering Mrs. Harrington's necklace. Not only did you find out her daughter was the thief, but you did it in such a way as to keep their names out of the papers. I thought you could do the same for me, help me solve this problem, discreetly."

Holmes sat quietly for a moment, ever the stoic, his body as rigid as Michelangelo's David. Then I noted that the corners of his lips curled slightly upward into a soft smile.

"I shall help you in this matter, Mrs. Cassini. I do need some information from you, though. First, please tell me who in your household would have access to your food and drink."

The Adventure of the Wispy Widow by Derrick Belanger

"Well, Mr. Garrett, as I mentioned before, is my chef. Then, there's Mr. Kendrick. He is my butler and until recently served me all of my meals. He continues to do so except for dinner. Agnes, the scullery maid, would have access to food, I suppose. The only other member of my house is Mrs. Laurence, my lady's maid. I can't see how she'd have access to my meals."

"How is your relationship with your servants? Is your household a happy one?" Holmes inquired.

"It is, Mr. Holmes," Mrs. Cassini responded with a frown. I could tell she was a touch indignant at the question. "Mr. Kendrick has been my butler for many years. Since I am a household of one, he takes on extra duties such as that of driver and footman, yet he is well-compensated for his extra work. He helped care for me for all those years when I was ill, as did my lady's maid. They have treated me better than members of my own family, and I can assure you they'd do nothing to harm me. Mr. Garrett is the newest member of the household. I see no reason why he should want to hurt me. He has become good friends with Mr. Kendrick, who is an excellent judge of character. Agnes, the scullery maid, was also hired by Mr. Kendrick. She has been a faithful servant for more than three years now. Mrs. Laurence has told me that Agnes may be leaving the household soon. She has a beau and I wouldn't be surprised if I find out that she is engaged and leaving to be a wife. I see no reason why she'd poison me"

"How about your relations?"

"There are my parents, my brother and his family as well. They all live in Sherwood and work at the mill."

"And your late husband? What of his family?"

"After the accident, Antonio's father sold his stake in the mill. Since then, I haven't been in touch with his family. It was too painful for them. I assume they still reside in Italy, but I do not know that for a fact."

"I see," said Holmes. He looked to the ceiling for a moment and then said, "I will need the names and addresses of the doctors you visited as well as those of your family and your late husband's family."

"I can have them for you later today."

"Excellent," said Holmes with a clap of his hands.

"Oh, thank you, Mr. Holmes for taking my case."

Holmes looked puzzled and said, "Oh, I said I would help you. I never said that I would take your case."

"But... I don't understand."

"My dear, I am currently working two cases for Scotland Yard and one on a private matter. I cannot give my full attention to another case, particularly one such as yours which would require spending a good amount of time at your residence."

Mrs. Cassini's face fell at my friend's explanation.

"There's no need to fret, my dear. You will still be in capable hands." Holmes gave a broad grin. "My good friend and associate, Dr. Watson, will take your case."

"I will?" I said, quite taken aback. Mrs. Cassini stared at me, then at Holmes, then back at me. She didn't know what to say. Holmes decided to speak for her.

"I can personally vouch for the good doctor's credentials. He has assisted me on a number of cases over the last few years and has been instrumental in helping me solve them. Think about it, dear lady. When you came to me with your problem, you specifically said it was a medical matter. Who better than a doctor to help solve your problem?"

Mrs. Cassini started to speak, but Holmes continued before she could get a word out. "I will, of course, help investigate the issue of the poisoning. Having a medical man, such as Dr. Watson, staying at your home, interviewing the staff, and reporting back to me will be of the utmost importance. He will also act as protector should anyone in your household prove to be not as upstanding as you believe. He may

The Adventure of the Wispy Widow by Derrick Belanger

also be able to get to the root of the other problems you brought to us, the problems of your weight loss and stomach malady.

"What say you, Mrs. Cassini, do you have a spare bedroom?"

"I have several," the client responded quietly. I could see the gears turning in her mind as she thought through this unexpected outcome of having a doctor rooming at her abode.

"Ah, there you are," Holmes responded splendidly. "You will go home and tell your staff that Dr. Watson shall be arriving this evening and shall be staying on for a few days to determine the cause of your malady."

Mrs. Cassini chewed the idea around for a moment longer but then said, "Very well, Mr. Holmes. I shall do as you say." She turned to me. "I look forward to having you stay, Doctor. I do hope you can shed some light on my case."

"Splendid," Holmes said as he stood, indicating that it was time for our client to leave. I did the same, giving a slight bow to Mrs. Cassini. She thanked us.

As she opened the door to depart, Holmes offered one more condition. "Oh, and as it shall be Dr. Watson taking charge of your case, it will be the doctor who will collect the fee for his services."

"Very well, Mr. Holmes. A good day to you gentlemen." With that she left our rooms.

My gaze lingered at the door as I tried to make sense of the predicament Holmes had put me in. "Holmes," I started, "Why ever did you do that?"

He had already returned to his seat and was lighting his briar pipe. Once he got a few good puffs in, he responded. "I already explained it to Mrs. Cassini. This is a medical matter, and besides with her house and the cast of characters on staff, why, it may be just what you need to solve the problem you are having with your play."

"You know about that!" I was aghast.

The Adventure of the Wispy Widow by Derrick Belanger

"Watson, it does not take strong reasoning skills to see you pacing about the rooms in the morning, muttering about acts, and scenes, and troubles with your characters to know what you are up to."

I slumped into my chair beside Holmes and muttered, "I suppose you know about my work troubles as well."

"Yes," Holmes said, sympathetically. "You've been trudging up those stairs for the last week looking rather dejected. You wince anytime money is mentioned, and if I ask about your day, you grumble, give some vague detail, and then become mum."

"I suppose it doesn't take a soothsayer to see the predicament I'm in," I looked toward the floor, too embarrassed to make eye contact with my friend.

"There's no need to be glum," Holmes assured me. "You now have a client and a patient. This will provide you sufficient funds to make it through the month, and I'm sure as the weather continues to turn dark and rainy, many patients will need your assistance. I believe this investigation may also stimulate your mind and help you work out the problem of your drama."

"You really think I'm up for the task?" I asked quietly.

"Yes, I do. Just take sufficient notes and report back to me…not tomorrow, but the day after, in the afternoon, once Mrs. Cassini has finished her luncheon. That should give you sufficient time to visit me and then return before her dinner. Once you tell me what you've observed, I'm sure I can bring the case to a swift conclusion."

"You don't expect me to solve the case?" I asked, again surprised.

"Perhaps you shall," Holmes assured me. "If not, no harm in getting assistance from me. About half the Yarders do."

* * *

The Adventure of the Wispy Widow by Derrick Belanger

I did as Holmes suggested, and after spending a day and a half at the Cassini residence, I returned to Baker Street to report on my findings. When I entered our abode, I found Holmes at his desk, his face firmly attached to his microscope studying some powdered substance.

"Is that for one of your cases?" I asked my friend as I hung my coat on the rack by the door.

"Actually, it is for your case," Holmes corrected me. He looked up from the eyeglass viewer and said, "This powder is the contents of the pill from the first doctor Mrs. Cassini visited. The matter is harmless, just some peppermint and ginger."

"Well, I guess you won't need this," I took out from my pants pocket a small bottle. "I brought samples of the remaining pills and remedies prescribed by her doctors. They all seem to be typical treatments for stomach ailments." I put the bottle down next to Holmes's microscope.

I sat in my chair and cut a cigar while Holmes removed the slide he had under his device. "Did you visit the doctors?" I asked. "I was under the impression that you weren't going to leave your rooms for this case."

"I did not leave the room," Holmes assured me. He sat down in his chair beside me. I thought he'd reach for his pipe, but this time he took a cigar I offered him.

"Mrs. Hudson visited the doctors on my behalf."

"You got our dear landlady to assist you," I snickered. "How did you manage that?"

"Simple," he explained. "I told her that a poor widow needed our services and that I needed a female patient to see the doctors."

"And she agreed?"

"I also gave her an additional five pounds for her effort."

I laughed out loud at that. "But why not go yourself?"

"You should know, Watson, that doctors treat men and women quite differently. Don't get defensive, it is a fact. If I went to visit the doctors and claimed to have the same medical issues, I could leave with a very different treatment plan. That's why I hired our landlady for this task.

"Mrs. Hudson visited all of Mrs. Cassini's doctors yesterday and complained of the same maladies. She was very convincing. By the way, Watson, perhaps you can cast her in your play."

"Really, Holmes, enough about that. Was she able to get the same prescriptions?"

"It appears that she was," Holmes said and glanced at the bottle of medicines I brought from Mrs. Cassini. Then he turned back to me. "Now, tell me all you have learned from your time in the Cassini house."

I placed my cigar in the ashtray and then began, "Mrs. Cassini has a very nice corner row house in Elgin Crescent. When I arrived, her butler, Mr. Kendrick, greeted me at the door. I was surprised when I met him, for he is a jovial man, unlike many of the dour men I've met in the servile role. He keeps his mustache curled like that of a vaudevillian magician, and he has a friendly face, the type where the eyes crinkle a bit when he gives a warm smile. If Mr. Kendrick were to walk into a tavern, I'm sure he'd be friends with everyone in the establishment within an hour's time.

"'You must be Dr. Watson,' he said to me even before I rapped on the door. He had been standing out front smoking a cigarette. Mrs. Cassini forbids smoking in her home which ended up being quite auspicious for me."

"It allowed you to get to know the staff rather quickly, I presume," Holmes answered.

"That's correct. Not only the staff, but Mr. Bartholomew Cox. Once I was settled in my room, I gave Mrs. Cassini a thorough examination. All of her vitals seemed fine. Since she had undergone all of the usual treatments for stomach pain, I asked her about her diet. She eats beef at almost every meal, though she has fish and poultry on occasion. She detests pork. She also always has a full glass of milk with every meal and enjoys a good amount of cheese. I wanted her to eat more vegetables, particularly leafy greens to help with her digestion. I also thought removing beef from her diet might help. As you know, it can be difficult to digest beef, particularly that which is on the rarer side."

"How did Mrs. Cassini take your suggestion?" Holmes asked me.

"Oh, she wasn't with it, but she wanted to get better, so she agreed. Mr. Garrett, the chef, was the one who complained about it. He's a stubborn man who has quite a fiery temper. Bald with a curly beard, when he raged about the changes, his face became so red that I thought I'd see little horns sprout out from the sides of his head.

"Seeing his reaction made me suspect the man. However, when I asked Mr. Kendrick about Garrett, he explained that it was the inconvenience of having to change the supper menu so close to dining time which was the cause of his consternation. When I smoked with him later that evening, I learned as much. He apologized to me and assured me that he was also concerned about Mrs. Cassini. I got the impression that he wanted to say more to me, I'm not sure why, but I shall keep pressing him to see if he does know something about his mistress's poor health."

Holmes thought about this information for a moment. I could see the great thinking machine of his brain at work. Then he took a final puff from his cigar and asked, "What of Bartholomew Cox?"

I smirked, recalling my first encounter with our client's fiancé. "He didn't like me at first. He reminded me of a pelican. Thin and clunky with his body, yet with beady eyes and a rather large mouth. When I met him, I was alerted by the sound of a quarrel. I came into the parlor to see Mr. Cox with his hands all a-flutter complaining. 'Why is a doctor living in your house?'

"'I've already explained, Bartholomew. I am a sick woman. I need to be cared for so that I may get better,' I heard Mrs. Cassini sharply reply.

The Adventure of the Wispy Widow by Derrick Belanger

"'I don't like a strange man living in your domicile,' he snapped.

"'I can assure you, Mr. Cox, that I am a reputable man who only wants to heal your fiancée,' I said as I entered the room and faced the sniveling man.

"He eyed me over, and I saw at once the fear and nervousness that come from jealousy.

"'*That's* your doctor!' he sputtered and kept pointing at me with deranged jerking motions. 'Why *him?*'

"Mrs. Cassini put her hands on her hips and shook her head. I could see she was filled with rage. 'Because he comes highly recommended. At least Dr. Watson wants me to get better! Unlike *you!* I should think you'd want me to get better so that we can finally be married, or is that ever going to happen?' she spat at him, bobbing her head with each harsh word like a hen attacking a worm.

"'Please, both of you, calm yourselves. Control your tempers. There is no need for a lover's spat,' I assured them. I turned to Mr. Cox, 'I swear to you that you have nothing to fear, my good man. If my fiancée is perfectly fine with me staying at Mrs. Cassini's house then you should be as well."

"'You're engaged?' he asked me in a weak, deflated voice.

"'I am,' I lied. I said this in as commanding a voice as I could muster. 'If you don't trust me. I'm sure that Mr. Kendrick will keep an eye on me on your behalf.'

"'Yes, well,' he started in a meek voice. He looked to his feet as he shifted uncomfortably. 'Well, I suppose that's all right, then.'

"I then told Mrs. Cassini that she should watch her temper in her state of infirmary. There really was no concern with her heart. I just wanted to make sure any embers that were still flaring from their argument were fully extinguished.

"I stayed by Mr. Cox's side that evening as he served Mrs. Cassini her tea and her meal. I could tell that the man was perturbed by having me watch him. After they dined, he asked me to have a

The Adventure of the Wispy Widow by Derrick Belanger

smoke with him outside. He shared with me his concern for Mrs. Cassini as well as his love for her. I asked why he'd kept her waiting so long to be wed again.

"'I need to be worthy of her, Doctor,' he implored me to understand. 'It has taken me two years, but I believe I have finally come to the point where I can marry her.'

"'That is good news,' I said. 'What's changed?'

"'I have been making safe investments these last two years. After taking my investments and continuously reinvesting my profits, I have finally found myself on the cusp of having enough money to rightfully earn Anne's hand in marriage. I've invested heavily in a company which manufactures artificial limbs. I've just heard word that they are being purchased by an American conglomerate. Once the deal is sealed, my return will be enough to set our wedding date.'

"'Why that's excellent news, chap,' I congratulated him," I explained to Holmes. I then told him I hadn't learned anything about the liquid Mrs. Cassini said she'd seen Cox put into her tea. "She did tell me that her tea was back to tasting normal," I concluded. "I don't want to directly ask Cox about the liquid, for I'm sure he'd just deny it. When I get a chance, I'll ask the chef or the scullery maid. I still haven't had a chance to speak with her."

"I see," he said with a few quick nods. "Have you spoken to the lady's maid?" Holmes asked.

"Yes, she is a stern woman, a perfect counter to Mr. Kendrick. In fact, the two dote on Mrs. Cassini as though she were their own flesh and blood. Though I did not detect any romance between the butler and the maid, it is clear that they care deeply for one another. I'm sure, being with Mrs. Cassini during her time of solitude brought them closer together. They are both quite concerned with Mrs. Cassini's health, and they are both fond of Mr. Cox and look forward to the day when the two are married."

"Very good, Watson. Anything else at the moment?"

The Adventure of the Wispy Widow by Derrick Belanger

"Just that Miss Agnes, the scullery maid, has spent the last few days away, visiting her parents. Everyone in the household is convinced that when she returns tomorrow, she will announce her own engagement. Everyone appears happy with the way things are turning out. Romance is in the air at the Cassini household."

"Sounds like great material for a play," Holmes chuckled.

My eyes widened. "Perhaps you're right, my friend. Perhaps, you're right."

* * *

It was three days later when I returned to Baker Street with more news about the investigation.

"I see that you are in high spirits," Holmes said. I had practically burst through the door so excited was I with the information I had to share with my friend.

"Holmes, I believe I've solved the case and proven Cox innocent of any harm," I blurted.

"Well, this is good news," the detective said with a wide grin. He patted the cushion of my chair. "Please, come join me and tell me everything that has occurred."

"Thank you," I said and planted myself down in my seat, eager to talk.

"Yesterday afternoon," I started, "I was heading down to the kitchen to speak with Miss Agnes. She had returned from her time with her parents, and as the staff predicted, she returned with an engagement ring upon her finger. Everyone congratulated her, and there was much celebration in the house. I had also given her my kindest regards, but I still wanted to speak with her to see if she had any insights into the cause of Mrs. Cassini's ailment.

"When I opened the door to head to the lower level, I heard Mr. Cox arguing with another man. I crept a bit down the stairs, and I could make out that the other person he was arguing with was Mr.

Garrett. The chef's fiery temper was clear as he kept responding in a raised voice, 'I will not have it, sir. No!'

"'But you must do as I tell you,' demanded Mr. Cox. 'I shall be your master soon. You must obey my commands.'

"'You aren't my master now, and you may never be!' Garrett roared. 'I wouldn't be surprised if she throws you out on the street for this! Who knows what you'd have me put in her food!'

"'I've already told you, it's harmless medicine to help her. Just pour some of this on her roasted chicken this evening.'

"'I shall do no such thing and that is final!'

"'Gentlemen," I said, interrupting them. I was beginning to make a habit of interrupting fights in the Cassini residence. 'What's all this shouting about?'

"Mr. Garrett lit up at seeing me. 'Ah, Dr. Watson, I am glad you are here.' He then turned and pointed at Cox, putting his finger right in the meek man's face. 'This repulsive wretch wants me to taint Mrs. Cassini's dinner with some medical liquid.'

"'Medical liquid?' I asked.

"'Yes, he claims it will help Mrs. Cassini, but I wonder if he is the reason that she has taken ill.'

"'Well, Mr. Cox, what do you have to say for yourself?'

"Cox looked terrified, and once again he averted his eyes to the ground before responding. 'I…er…umm…well, I was trying to…er…that is…'

"'Come, come, man,' I snapped in frustration. He really is a sniveling mouse. 'Out with it.'

"He let out a long sigh. 'I went to my doctor and told him of Anne's ailment. He gave me this,' he removed a bottle from his coat pocket, a bottle which contained a milky white liquid. 'He told me if I added it to her tea, it would help her gain weight. I knew Anne would be angry with me for asking my doctor about her health and for getting him to prescribe medicine for her, so instead of letting her know about the liquid, I started sneaking it into her tea.'

"'Why didn't you tell me this earlier?' I asked sternly.

"'I was afraid you'd also be angry with me. After all, you are her doctor, and I know doctors don't like it when other doctors work with their patients.'

"As much as I detest the man, he did have a valid point about doctors. I made him give me the bottle, and I have it right here," I took it out of my pants pocket and showed it to Holmes. He took the bottle in his hand, pulled out the cork, and poured a little in the palm of his left hand. He sniffed at it. Then licked it. He winced at the flavor.

"I'll use my lab to analyze it. I believe it is nothing more than whey."

"Of course," I said and shook my head. "Why didn't I think of that? Socrates himself used it to improve his health if I recall from my schooling. I know some doctors prescribe it for weight gain, I just had forgotten about it, but it makes perfect sense, and confirms my belief that Mr. Cox is innocent. I'm almost certain everyone is innocent."

"That's quite a statement, Watson. Could you explain?"

This is where I was most proud. "Holmes, remember how I told you I had Mrs. Cassini remove beef from her diet," I beamed.

"Of course, old chap; and did it work?"

"No, it didn't, so I tried having her remove milk and cheese from her diet. The result has been astounding."

"She's cured?" Holmes asked me.

"Not fully, but she feels much better. It appears that she is allergic to dairy products. She had milk with every meal, plenty of cheese, and I'm sure the whey added to her tea also hurt her. I believe in a few days she will be back to her normal self and that she will gain back the weight that she has lost."

"Splendid, Watson. Bravo!" Holmes cheered. "You've done excellent work, my boy. Shall you be back at home this evening?"

"Not just yet," I explained to my friend. "Mrs. Cassini would like me to stay through the end of the week, just in case her symptoms return or she doesn't fully recover. I tried to tell her that she could just

The Adventure of the Wispy Widow by Derrick Belanger

send for me if that was the case, but she insisted I stay. With her filling my coffers, I acquiesced to her demands. I'd prefer to be back at Baker Street."

"No need to explain, doctor. It is probably best to put our client, or I should say, *your* client's mind at rest."

* * *

I spent the next few days at the Cassini residence. Mrs. Cassini's appetite returned, and I assumed that she'd begin to regain her weight, but despite my best efforts she still had aches in her stomach and she did not seem to be adding any pounds to her body.

I spent my time scribbling notes for writing ideas and completing research, trying to determine what could be the root of her illness.

Despite my efforts reading in books, it was Mrs. Cassini's lady's maid who provided the clue I needed to solve the case. She was folding laundry when I encountered her and she asked about Mrs. Cassini. I said that I was doing my best to support her.

"Poor dear," the lady's maid bemoaned. "She eats as much as a woman with child, yet she is still nothing but bones."

I jumped at this. "Did I say something wrong?" the maid asked me.

"No, miss, you said something quite right. Quite right, indeed."

* * *

Several hours later, I returned to Baker Street, exhausted. Holmes saw my condition and fixed me a brandy. "It is over, Holmes," I started, still visibly shaken from my ordeal. "If it weren't for her lady's maid, we probably would have lost Mrs. Cassini."

The Adventure of the Wispy Widow by Derrick Belanger

Holmes looked serious when I proclaimed this. He asked me to explain everything.

"Once the lady's maid said that," I told Holmes after catching him up, "I had Kendrick prepare Mrs. Cassini's carriage, and though she at first resisted, I had her sent straight away to the hospital. There, my worst fears were realized. One of her stool samples was inspected and found to contain eggs."

"Eggs?" Holmes asked, his brows arched.

I leaned in, eyes wide as I explained. "Worm eggs, Holmes. Mrs. Cassini had a giant tapeworm living in her intestines. She was fortunate that Dr. Starling had a history of working with such infections. He tried getting her to expunge it by having Mrs. Cassini ingest wormwood, but it didn't work. Then, he used a device to lure the worm out of her, at least he got its head out before using a rod to wrap the beast around until it fully came out of her body. It was sickening, Holmes.

"Fortune has shined on the woman, though. She'll be monitored for the next few months to make sure no eggs or larva have taken root. Dr. Starling said that she was lucky as sometimes worms enter the heart or brain, killing the host."

Holmes silently pondered what I explained to him. Then, quietly, he said, "This was a grave matter, Watson. You have done well. If not for you, Mrs. Cassini would probably have been deceased in a few months' time." Then Holmes admitted, "Much better than I had expected."

"Thank you, Holmes. I'm just glad Mrs. Cassini is all right. I'm not sure how the creature entered her, unless it was from some undercooked food. In the end, I suppose there wasn't much of a case."

Holmes got a curious look on his face, a look of speculation. He jumped up, went to his desk and pulled out the medicine samples I'd brought from Mrs. Cassini. He held up one of the blue colored pills from her first doctor. "I wonder," Holmes said, and looked at the interior of the pill under the microscope. I could see his face turn from a look of alarm to one that was grim.

* * *

It ended up that Mrs. Cassini's first doctor had a side business where he sold "diet pills" to women guaranteed to help them lose weight. The pills contained the head of a tapeworm which then came to life in the patient's intestines. As horrific as this sounds, it is an accepted practice and not enough to have a doctor's license revoked; however, the young doctor had made a grave error. He had meant to prescribe Mrs. Cassini his pills for stomach ailments and not his weight-loss pill containing the tapeworm. Because of this error on his part, the medical council did revoke his license. Unfortunately, that is not enough to stop a medical man from practice, and I'm sure to this day, he is probably hawking his pills on the streets of London or some other city.

The former Mrs. Cassini did become Mrs. Cox. The betrothed were wed a few months after the incident, and I was invited to attend as a guest of the bride. We have stayed in touch over the years. Though she was an older woman, Mrs. Cassini found herself pregnant a few months after the marriage and gave birth to twins. I was surprised to learn that Mrs. Laurence and Mr. Kendrick also wed. While I could see that they were close, I did not note any true love between them.

With so much romance in the Cassini household, I tried to turn this story into a play. With Holmes merely having a consulting role, I was able to make myself the detective in the story. I even coined the term *medical detective*. Still, when I put ink to page, I found the characters I created to be caricatures of the real players in this drama. After working on the piece for nearly a year, I gave up on it. I decided writing just wasn't for me.

As you know, years later, I returned to the page and tried my hand at storytelling. It is in the form of the short story that I made my

The Adventure of the Wispy Widow by Derrick Belanger

mark in the literary world, and Sherlock Holmes became a household name.

November 1888

The Spice of Life

By Gustavo Bondoni

"It's not a question of espionage for the sake of espionage, Watson," Holmes said. "The Prussians know that their German Empire must, unavoidably, clash with the British Empire at some point. There is no room for further expansion without conflict now that France is defeated."

He discarded the edition of *The Illustrated Police News* I'd brought for his perusal with a disdainful flick of the wrist. It landed face up on the table beside his leather chair. The front page of the periodical was adorned by the visage of a sinister-looking figure with a monocle and a handlebar mustache.

"It says the police are afraid that there might be a large ring of spies attempting to infiltrate the Yarlow Steel Works. It says that, even if they haven't been successful yet, they will continue in their attempts at gaining the plans for the new generation of boilers," I said.

Holmes tsked. "Of course they will. Prussians, Frenchmen, Russians. It wouldn't surprise me if the Americans and Italians had spies in the capital as well. The mere existence of advanced-valve

The Spice of Life by Gustavo Bondoni

technology that could allow much greater efficiency in steam engines all but guarantees that every major player would take an interest in order to keep the playing field level. Surely you don't need a lurid rag such as this to deduce that?"

"Of course not," I said. "I just thought it might be interesting to you."

Holmes picked up a glass of Port, savoring it, before placing it back on the table and staring into the fire for a few moments. "I'm much more interested in learning who it might be that has decided to visit us at this late hour, and why she would hesitate at the door for so long. Surely she must be aware that the fire inside makes this room much warmer than the exterior."

I looked around our large sitting room and wondered, not for the first time, to what Holmes was referring. Even last year I would have expressed my disbelief that any such visitor might be approaching, but I'd learned my lesson several times over. Instead of challenging him, I merely looked over to our door. "Should I open it?" I asked.

"I think it might be better to wait. I don't want to frighten her away."

"How do you know there's a woman out there?"

Holmes paused to light his pipe. "A hansom stopped outside the house. I heard someone close the door, but then the cab didn't start again for some moments. The only reason to keep warm horses immobile on a night like this is to wait for the person to enter the house. And if that person were a man, a cabbie would not bother."

"Maybe the fare asked the cabbie to wait."

Holmes smiled faintly. "The cabbie left after two minutes without anyone mounting again."

I nodded glumly and awaited the inevitable. A tentative knock sounded below and I prepared to descend to receive our visitor.

A tall woman in black, of about fifty years of age, stood before the door. The bitter wind that blew around her reminded me that the relatively mild November we'd been enjoying was over. Winter would soon be among us.

"Madam," I said. "Please come in."

"I... I'm not certain I should," she replied. "I may have made a mistake."

"At the very least come in and warm yourself by the fire. If you decide you have made a mistake, I will be delighted to locate a hansom for your return."

She hesitated for another moment before entering our apartment. I closed the door behind her with a sigh of contentment. The fire would soon warm the room again.

I expected Holmes to know who the woman was, where she lived and why she was here, but once again, he surprised me. He stood, bowed to her formally and offered her the seat I'd occupied mere moments before. "I am Sherlock Holmes," he said. "You've already met Dr. John Watson. Is it I, or he, you wish to consult on such a cold night?"

"It's you, sir," she said.

Despite her dress, which was perfectly respectable, cut from good cloth and well-tailored, her speech was not quite the polished tones one would have expected from her attire.

She sat. Then realized she was still wearing her coat, so she stood and removed it. After several moments of silence, she launched into speech. "It's my husband. Or should I say it's the police saying my husband was involved in things he shouldn't have been, that he'd had it coming. If you knew Thomas Keynes, you'd know he would never let anyone get behind him that way. He was a merchant, but he was brought up right. Learned the docks before he made his money. That's why the police can't have it right."

Holmes steepled his fingers, but instead of the explosion of impatience I'd seen from him so often when someone came in with a silly outburst, he simply asked, in a steady voice: "Why don't you begin at the beginning. When was your husband killed?"

The Spice of Life by Gustavo Bondoni

"It'll be..." she counted on her fingers. "A week tomorrow. Last Thursday, it was."

"And the police believe your husband was murdered over a deal that went wrong about some cargo? They think he was involved with smugglers? Opium sellers?"

The woman nodded, as if that were exactly the case, and I wondered how Holmes had gotten that much sense out of the cataract of words she'd sent forth. "The coppers think all of us that have dealings with the East are in the opium trade."

"Are they correct?" Holmes asked, bluntly.

The woman seemed shocked, but I could have comforted her: I could tell Holmes was interested in her tale, and when he got that way, he could have forgot his manners in front of the Queen herself. After some more silence, she shrugged. "Fifteen years ago, I would have accepted the verdict. But as it is... no. He was done with that life."

Holmes nodded. "And where was he killed?"

"At the docks. They found him behind a pile of sacks being loaded onto a ship, like the body of a dog."

"Do you know why he went to the docks that day?"

She shrugged. "It could have been anything. We had a cargo in from the East, and he also needed to speak to the tax man. And to hire porters. He never went down unless he meant to spend the day there."

Holmes considered the information for some moments. "He could quite easily have been victim of a failed robbery. The docks can be dangerous."

"Not for Thomas," she said. "He knew the docks like he knew his own house. He could smell trouble coming before it reached him." She paused, as if uncertain how much more to say. "And there's one more thing. The day before he died, he wasn't quite himself. He didn't come right out and say it, but I know my husband. There was something preying on his mind."

Holmes looked up. "Was he with someone before you saw the change in him?"

"He was with many people. He was in conferences all day. He even had his food in his study, not coming down. But I can tell you, he was himself in the morning... and he wasn't in the evening."

"Would you happen to have a list of the people he met?"

"He kept a ledger. I can have one of the boys run it down to you tomorrow."

Holmes shook his head. "I believe it would be better if we paid you a visit."

She gave us the address, and even tried to pay us for our time, but Holmes was having none of it.

"It might be a simple street crime," he told her. "In which case apprehending the perpetrator will not avail you of much, other than to give you the satisfaction of knowing your husband's murderer will hang... but I suspect you might be right in your suspicion. There may be more to this." He turned to me. "Watson, would you be so kind as to secure a cab for Mrs. Keynes?"

I braved the chilly night to locate the conveyance, but didn't begrudge it. If Holmes were interested enough to visit the woman's house, then this incident could have the effect of relieving the monotony of the past few days.

* * *

Our appointment at the Keynes' house was for noon the following day. I agreed to meet Holmes there, and after visiting a cousin near Regent Park, I took the Underground at Portland Road to the new station in Aldgate, which I'd never visited before.

Being early, I decided to walk the final stretch instead of taking a cab. My progress was immediately arrested by a bookseller overflowing with penny dreadfuls. Alongside the usual fare such as Black Bess and the weeklies like *The Illustrated Police News*, I spotted

The Spice of Life by Gustavo Bondoni

a slim book with a blue-and-orange cover and the title: *The Krakatoa Explosion Was Man-Made.*

Having stopped in my tracks to ogle this specimen, I was accosted by the proprietor.

"That's a good one," he said. "Sold ten already this morning. Everyone wants to know more."

"I've been fascinated by the eruption since news began to arrive of it in August," I told him, "and I went to Archibald Geikie's lecture on the subject in September. Nothing I've heard made me suspect the explosion was anything but natural."

"Ah. You're a learned gentleman, surely. Perhaps you should read the introduction."

I opened the book to the first page of text and saw exactly what I expected to see: a list of sources, including eyewitnesses, that I had never heard of and which I didn't believe existed. Still, I gave the man my penny, as I felt the volume would have value as a curio the next time I saw anyone related to the Royal Society.

When I reached the address in Limehouse, Holmes was nowhere to be seen. A team of workmen were laying cobbles some paces further up the street; two urchins were watching them. To my left, a stooped old woman sold apples from a cart.

It was still five minutes until twelve, so to kill time while I waited, I observed the house.

The ground floor of the building was occupied by a storefront with large glazed windows, which I considered daring for a shop in this particular neighborhood. But perhaps practical if one were able to afford a night custodian.

The sign above the awnings identified the store as Keynes' and Sons Spice Merchants, and the smell emanating from the door whenever it was opened confirmed the words. Exotic odors I couldn't quite identify wafted over the street. Was that cinnamon? I thought it might be.

The Spice of Life by Gustavo Bondoni

I looked around for Holmes, and found him standing beside me, a mischievous grin on his face.

Spurred by a sudden flash of inspiration, I looked over to the cart. It was still there, chained to a lamp post but there was no sign of the old woman.

"Did you spot anything interesting while you observed?" I asked him.

If he were disappointed that I'd recognized his ruse, he gave no sign. "Very little. The store is quite busy, and the death of its proprietor doesn't seem to have done much to slow the rate of deliveries or client visits. At least one of the people who entered was a marine captain."

"Nothing that could help us then?"

"Not unless some of the men who walked past were here to spy. It's possible, particularly as a number of them spent quite some time looking into the window. But nothing conclusive."

We approached the door and a man of about thirty years greeted us. "Hello to you," he said. "Buying or selling?"

"Neither. Mrs. Keynes is expecting us."

The man turned back towards the interior and shouted. "Mother, some men to see you." He turned back to us. "Go on up the stairs. The door to my father's study should be open."

He let us through and continued to look out the door, staring anxiously up the street every few seconds.

The study was small, perhaps four yards by four, and dimly lit. A desk and a table occupied most of the space, with chairs of dark wood scattered haphazardly between the larger pieces. The table was covered with papers, ink bottles and pens, while the walls were lined with shelves. Ledger books of different shapes and sizes filled the bookcases. The space gave the impression of being dedicated exclusively to work.

Our visitor of the prior evening sat behind the desk. She was attired in a different dress, also black, and nodded at our entry. "I thank you for coming," she said. "Would you like coffee? It is a particularly choice blend from Ceylon. You will not easily find its match in the city."

Holmes and I pulled chairs to the desk and sat before her. He accepted a cup of the dark liquid. I demurred.

"You mentioned a ledger," Holmes said.

"Yes. It lists the visits he had that day, and the time each took." She unearthed a large leather-bound volume from under the pile of papers on the desk. She handed it to Holmes. "This is the day before he was killed," she said.

"Seven meetings in a day. Is that normal, or is it a lot for one day?" I asked, scanning the writing in the book.

She shrugged. "I'd say that was a slow day more than a busy one."

I was shocked. I considered a day with five patients to be extremely busy. The men and women in the spice business must work truly long hours.

Holmes appeared to be absorbed in the contents of the book. Almost absently, without lifting his eyes from the page, he said: "Your son, the one at the door, seems to be preoccupied today."

She snorted. "You know how young ones are," she replied. "We're waiting for a shipment of spices that was delayed. He thinks the world will end and our business will come crashing down upon us if the goods don't arrive within the next hour."

"Would it be such a hardship?" Holmes asked.

"Not in the least," Mrs. Keynes replied. "We have plenty of stock, enough to weather long delays or the loss of a ship or two. The ships aren't ours, you see, we just reach an accommodation with the owners."

"I see two ship captains on this list. Browning, of the *Coral Sea* and Fenshawe of the *Invictus*. Are they owners of their own vessels?"

The Spice of Life by Gustavo Bondoni

"Browning is. The *Coral Sea* plies the Far East routes. The *Invictus* is owned by a cooperative, but Captain Fenshawe is the operator, and they generally work Brazil, although sometimes they travel to Africa or the Caribbean."

"What can you tell me about the other men who came that day?" Holmes asked.

"Well, Jones, McGuire, Saleh and Riordan are four of our usual clients. They run shops in London. The police were particularly interested to see that McGuire and Riordan had been here, since they are both known to sell to the houses on the docks."

"Opium houses?" Holmes asked.

Mrs. Keynes nodded. "They worked with Thomas back when he was getting started."

"And do you sell opium here?"

"Never," she replied. Then she seemed to think better of it. "Not anymore, anyway. It was too much work to keep that going. Police always around to see that we were selling only to licensed pharmacists, and then all the problems with our other clients…"

"I see," Holmes said. "This note says that Mr. Riordan did not arrive."

"The police were keen on that, too. They say it's probably an important fact," she replied.

"We shall see," Holmes said. "And this man? Mr. Daughterly?"

"I doubt he is involved," the woman replied. "He is a long-time client who buys for the Household of the Duke of Cleveland."

"Is he an independent agent here in the city, or employed directly by the Duke?"

"He is employed by the Duke. I understand he does most of the household buying."

Holmes nodded. "That is most helpful, and we have a lot to work with. Did you notice anything unusual about any of the interviews, or any unexpected happenings during the day?"

285

The Spice of Life by Gustavo Bondoni

"None. I saw Thomas in the morning, when he was in the highest of spirits, then, in the evening, he seemed to be weighted down by something."

Holmes stood. "Thank you. I will look into this."

"I truly appreciate your assistance. Any help to solve what has been a terrible blow to us."

"I understand," Holmes replied, and we emerged from the house, passing the still-vigilant son on our way.

* * *

"What do you think?" Holmes asked.

"I think that is a remarkable woman," I replied. "She has suffered a terrible tragedy, but is hard at work ensuring the future of her family. You can hardly tell she must be overcome, except by her actions in engaging you."

That earned me a long look. "You, my dear Watson, are one of the few people who always manages to surprise me," he said. "And while I admire your concern for the human element, what I meant was to ask whom do you think might have committed the crime? Are our friends at Great Scotland Yard correct in assuming Mr. Keynes was murdered by the operators of an opium Hell, or is Mrs. Keynes on the right path in suspecting one of his visitors?"

"I suspect the Duke's man. Daughterly," I replied, without stopping to think about it.

"Interesting," Holmes replied as he removed a pipe from a pocket and went about the business of lighting it. "And on what evidence would you say that?"

"He doesn't seem to belong," I replied. "The rest of them, the store owners and boat captains are exactly the kind of people I'd expect a Limehouse merchant to deal with on a daily basis. The factotum of a Duke? I'd expect him to buy his spices at Harrod's. But his opium... that would have to come from an unexpected place. In secret."

Holmes smiled. "But have you considered the fiscal aspect of the thing? Any duke who wishes to keep up with the times must purchase even legitimate spices in large quantities, and his representative would be expected to get the best price possible, something that not even a duke could manage at Harrod's." He puffed twice. "In fact, the very reason dukes have men like Daughterly is so they can avoid any direct dealings with the likes of the Keynes family."

"They aren't what I expected," I said.

"In what way?" Holmes asked, a twinkle in his eye.

"They are well-dressed and well-spoken. I only caught a hint of the streets in Mrs. Keynes' accent and none at all in that of the son we saw. The house was also furnished in good taste. Or at least what I saw of it."

Holmes nodded. "And you didn't expect that from working people."

I shook my head. "I remember the soldiers in my care when I was in India. You could tell where they came from, in the city our outside of it, to within a few streets, just by listening. And whenever they came into money—as the Keynes quite evidently have—it was usual for them to spend it on the gaudiest trinkets and furnishings they could find. That instinct seems to be absent in the Keynes." I thought about why that surprised me so much. "Perhaps my question comes from the location. I thought that any merchant in Limehouse would have to be completely awful."

"The city is expanding," Holmes noted. "And what Limehouse used to be isn't what it is today. You shouldn't be surprised to find pockets of civilization."

I looked around. "Perhaps. But you must grant that it is still quite savage."

He nodded. "You make a good point."

The Spice of Life by Gustavo Bondoni

"What about your cart?" I asked. I looked back to see where it had been tied to the post.

"It will not be there. I made arrangements to have it returned to its owner while we were in conference with Mrs. Keynes."

I hoped he was right. If not, some entrepreneur had made off with it. "What are you going to do now?" I asked.

"I need to return to Baker Street to create a disguise. Do you have time to perform some inquiries?"

"I would be delighted," I replied. It was true. If Holmes thought an incident were worth looking into, it was certain to be something I wouldn't want to miss.

"Good. If you'd be so kind, I'd like you to pay a visit to Inspector Lestrade. I would like to verify which of the opium dens Mr. Keynes' visitors were linked to."

My enthusiasm vanished. Did Holmes think the answer was as prosaic as violence caused by a difference of opinion among opium smugglers? That would be a disappointing outcome. Still, I had my marching orders, and we went our separate ways.

* * *

That evening, ten o'clock found me pacing to and fro before the fire. Holmes was conspicuous by his absence, so I waited, smoking, for him to make an appearance.

Half an hour later, I heard his key in the lock and after ascending the stairs, he entered, shrugging off his coat and removing gloves. "Ah, Watson. I suppose you have news from Lestrade."

"I do, but where the blazes have you been?" I retorted. "You don't appear to have been in disguise."

"Today's inquiries did not necessitate a disguise," he replied. "That will be a task for tomorrow. But over the past few hours, I have walked the waterfront as an interested gentleman. I am relatively certain that the criminal element—and even those other characters who, without necessarily breaking the law are nearby when it is broken—believe that I was there in some official capacity."

"I imagine they refused to tell you anything of consequence, then."

Holmes smiled enigmatically. "Often, what is said by omission is more important than what people might actually tell you. I have discovered a number of interesting facts."

Now it was my turn to chuckle. "Which you are going to share?"

"I said they were interesting. It will take a little more investigation to understand which are important. But don't be discouraged. I can relate quite a bit of my day."

I brightened.

"I spent my day at the Isle of Dogs, mostly at the new docks at Millwall and the old East India docks. I got a good look at both the *Invictus* and the *Coral Sea*. Quite apart from this I got a good notion of where opium is consumed."

"They were open about that?"

"Apparently, locating opium dens is the only accepted reason a well-dressed man might be asking questions by the waterside," he replied. "Once it was established that opium was my interest, sullen faces became welcoming, and closed mouths spilled information. Several men wished to guide me personally, probably looking for a tip." He held my gaze. "This is the reason I returned so late. The businesses involved open to the public with the fall of the sun, and I wanted to be certain that I knew the location and character of the more important ones. I believe I am reasonably expert now."

"Well, you were in the right place, at least. Lestrade says both our suspects have interests in the Isle of Dogs. McGuire's place is called the Lotus, while Riordan—the man Lestrade is convinced is behind this—is actually the proprietor of a pharmacy on Cuba Street that has a small den in a back room and upstairs."

"After tomorrow night, I will know of both."

The Spice of Life by Gustavo Bondoni

I sniffed the air, but there was no scent of anything but tobacco on his clothes. I knew Holmes was unafraid to experiment in the name of knowledge.

He smiled. "Good. I like to see your powers of observation tested. In response to your unasked query, I feel little need to partake of the opium dream in our current situation. I've found it to dull the senses and generate cravings which wouldn't help me concentrate on the matter at hand." He walked towards his room. "I beg your leave to retire. I have an early start tomorrow."

He disappeared, leaving me, as always, with more questions than answers.

* * *

The following day I woke early to find Holmes already gone and a note on the mantelpiece.

Please meet me at noon at the dock in front of the Coral Sea. *You will find it moored at Millwall.*

S

I sighed. Holmes enjoyed his little games, and I knew—even before leaving—how this one would play out.

Holmes would be nowhere to be seen, and I would wander the docks searching for him, only to be accosted by a seven-foot-tall oriental, or a wizened cleaning lady... who would turn out to be the very man I was searching for.

Still, I was excited to think that I was finally getting closer to the center of the mystery, even if—except for some inklings about opium dens—I had little idea what that center might actually consist of.

The Spice of Life by Gustavo Bondoni

I spent the morning in consultations. My patients were uninteresting, and I had to force myself to concentrate on the particulars of each complaint. The effort involved meant that, by the time I started towards my rendezvous with Holmes, I sported a splitting headache and was in a foul humor. I didn't play around with trains or peruse booksellers. Instead, I just took a cab straight to the indicated dock and decided that if anyone gave me trouble, I would show them how the Army had taught me to deal with ruffians.

To my surprise, the *Coral Sea* was a steamship. For some reason, I imagined the vessels plying the Eastern trade to be an East Indiamen of the traditional type: sailing ships with masts aplenty. This, on the other hand, was a beautifully painted white boat that looked to be brand new. It was easy to spot, since it was smaller than the rest of the sailing ships, with a single smokestack and also because it was the only vessel I could see that wasn't obscured by a flock of cranes and wagons.

I approached a man lounging on a pile of bags. "Is that the *Coral Sea*?" I asked, pretending not to have seen the name written on the stern as I approached.

"Yes Guv'nor," he replied languidly. "In from Singapore some days ago. Caused quite a stir."

I observed the dead calm around the ship. No one approached, and there was no gangplank lowered. "It seems quite peaceful to me."

"It might now. But you should have seen when it got in. No one was expectin' her. This isn't her usual dock, but her own down the river was taken. Then they unloaded with wagons teams no one had ever seen before, and had to pay off the regular workers." He grinned. "I'm waiting to see if they try to unload anything else. They only paid for one day, so if they try it…"

"It doesn't look like they're doing much," I observed.

His grin widened, grew more feral. "Merchant ships can't stay in port too long, and it isn't good business to sail without cargo. So they'll be loading, mark my word. And when they do, they'll have to pay the boys and me for not loading them ourselves."

He was obviously a ruffian, but his good cheer—even as he practiced whatever form of extortion he was involved in—was contagious. I felt my foul mood lifting in the face of such brazen disdain for the niceties of civilized society. "I wish you good luck, then," I told him.

"My thanks, Guv'nor."

I walked along the side of the ship, searching for Holmes. He could be any of the men passing by, loaded under sacks. Perhaps that large, well-dressed gentleman with the porters, face obscured by a copious beard. Perhaps the woman selling eels. A disreputable character leaning in the shadow of a tattered awning, cap pulled down over his head seemed a good bet, so I began my approach.

Along the way, a worker in a rough brown coat bumped me.

He touched his cap and said: "Roe's Pub, back table. I'll be there in ten minutes."

And with that, Holmes melted back into the crowd.

The pub was a short walk away, on a street that ran parallel to the river. Three tables stood empty far from the entrance, so I chose the one in the darkest corner and carried two ales there.

Holmes arrived, still dressed as a dock worker, sat, drank and grimaced. "Do these publicans brew their own with water from the canals?" he asked.

"I would hope not," I replied. "I'm not certain even the alcohol in the beer could disinfect it in that case." I leaned close enough to smell the genuine dock-worker's reek emanating from his coat. "What have you found?"

"I have discovered how to enter the opium dens this evening. I have passwords for both. And I have also studied the two vessels whose captains visited our victim. I assume you've already observed the *Coral Sea*?"

"Yes. Quite a smart ship, I thought."

The Spice of Life by Gustavo Bondoni

"Good. If you'd be so kind, continue up the docks a ways until you come to the *Invictus*, and look at her, too. I would like to hear your opinion as a military man tomorrow. Do not wait up for me tonight, I shall be late." He drained the beer.

"But blast it, man," I said. "Are you not going to tell me what you've discovered?"

"Yes," he replied. "I'm absolutely convinced that Mr. Keynes was not killed by a random act of street crime. The murderer needed Keynes—and a single unfortunate drunken dock watchman that no one seems to have missed, but who was also killed—dead for their own nefarious reasons."

"And can you tell me who it was?"

"Not yet. I will likely have confirmation this evening. Now please go observe the *Invictus*."

"Don't you want me to look into the opium dens as well?" I asked, irked.

He gave me an earnest look. "You are too upright a man for your opinion on places such as those to be of much use. All you would see, in either place, is confirmation of your prejudices." He stood and left me wondering whether I had just been complimented or insulted.

I forgot about it immediately. Holmes was never one to worry about overly sensitive reactions in others, so speaking to him on the topic would only let him point out that he was factually correct.

More to the point, however, I was eager to start on my commission.

The docks farther east on the Thames were slightly more run-down than those I'd already visited, but they also bustled with activity. The *Invictus* was no exception: swarms of workers and blaspheming sailors struggled with cargo nets as a harried-looking man in a grey suit, clutching a sheaf of papers hurried after them shouting instructions which no one appeared to hear.

The Spice of Life by Gustavo Bondoni

After the neat, trim Coral Sea, the *Invictus* was a shock. The paint was scuffed, the metal streaked with rust, and the general upkeep of the vessel tatty.

I studied it, getting all the details. Holmes would berate me if I missed anything, as this was the kind of thing he preached endlessly: Observe it all.

And this ship was worth observing. This one looked utterly disreputable. It also seemed larger than the *Coral Sea*. Though it was difficult to get a measure, I estimated it was at least half again as long as the other vessel.

What could I conclude from these observations? The first thing that occurred to me was that it would be much easier to hide contraband in a larger vessel than in a smaller one. Everything in this particular case indicated that the item to be smuggled would be opium.

The general condition of the ship was another black mark against it. A crew of ruffians would allow their ship to deteriorate on the relatively short trip to the Americas, while the more conscientious crew of the *Coral Sea* had kept their vessel looking shipshape despite the fact that, to arrive from Singapore in late October, they would have left in August.

I returned to Baker Street smugly certain that, for once, I would know the solution before Holmes told it to me.

* * *

The following day, Holmes woke an hour before noon. I hadn't heard him arrive, but I assumed he must have been out until the early morning.

"Good morning, Holmes," I said. "Was your night fruitful?"

"Decidedly so," he replied. "All that remains is to receive a single confirmation from the Customs men, and I'll have everything I need to declare the case closed. That must be the messenger now."

The Spice of Life by Gustavo Bondoni

Someone was knocking on the door to our rooms. I opened to reveal a young runner in a black suit. "For Mr. Holmes, Sir."

"Thank you."

The messenger then clattered down the stairs and ran off, but I spotted a small boy coming in behind him, whom I recognized as Jimmy, one of our regular—or perhaps irregular was a better term—assistants. He ran up the stairs and past me and handed a page to Holmes.

When our visitors were gone, I asked him: "What was that all about?"

"It's from the editor of *The Standard*," he told me. "These are the main stories for this evening's edition."

I looked them over. An earl's wedding had been announced, and the supposed spies had struck—successfully this time—against the ministry of war, stealing plans for an experimental warship with the latest boiler, and the rumblings of another war in Burma. I handed the page back to him.

"And the other papers?"

Holmes smiled. "Quite observant. These are shipping records. The *Coral Sea* left Singapore on August 25th, and the *Invictus* set out from Caracas on September 30th, and stopped for some days in the Canaries."

I waved to the collected papers in his hand. "Does any of this help us at all?"

"It sheds light on the urgency of our situation. I believe we need to move tonight."

"Move?" I asked. "Where do we need to go?"

"To the docks," he replied.

"What are you talking about, Holmes?"

"You'll have to forgive me, for I have little time to explain, and I have to ask you for several favors."

"Of course," I said. "Count on my help." Holmes loved his little theatricalities, but I knew him well enough that I didn't question the need to hurry. If he decided to move in a hurry, it was likely there would be no way to do things otherwise.

"Thank you, Watson." I need you to take a letter—which I still have to write—to Lestrade?"

He sat down with a pen and ink, wrote a letter and sealed it with wax. I fumed, thinking that he could have read it aloud to me so that I'd have all the information. When he handed it to me, he admonished: "Tell Lestrade it is of utmost importance that he give this its due consideration. If you must, hint that his career will be much enhanced if he heeds my words." He paused. "It is a pity that we should have to resort to that kind of inducement, but the world isn't the one we'd wish for."

As I finished putting my coat on, he spoke again. "I would like you to meet me at the entrance to Mr. Riordan's pharmacy at ten o'clock tonight."

"Are we going to visit an opium den?"

"Only if necessary," he replied. "Please bring your revolver."

* * *

A cold mist, thin but wet, blew from the river as I walked the final few steps. Though he hadn't said anything specifically, I was certain Holmes preferred I didn't arrive by cab.

The streets in this part of the docks were not quite deserted. Lone men walked, shoulders hunched against the cold, keeping to the center of the streets where they could watch for anyone lurking in the alleys or the shadows of the houses. Street lights were widely spaced. The mist seemed to muffle all sounds. My own footsteps sounded distant, dreamlike.

Occasionally, a group of men would pass, and in those moments, the weight of the Beaumont-Adams gun in my pocket was a comforting presence. There were very few things in the London night that couldn't be faced down by a determined man with an Army revolver.

The pharmacy had a streetlight only a few paces away, and as I watched a single man, hunched and furtive, was granted entry.

I stopped. Movement flickered from the shadows of the neighboring buildings and, even without being able to see anyone, I got the impression that the darkness held several men.

I was about to retreat when a figure separated itself from the darkness. Holmes; I would recognize his figure anywhere. He held a shuttered lantern.

The distance separating us seemed endless as I closed quietly on his position. "There are people watching us," I said.

"Yes. Lestrade's men," he replied.

"Are we going to raid the opium den?"

"No. We only met here because that is the conclusion anyone watching us would invariably arrive at. We're heading towards the docks. Walk with me."

We strode in the direction of the river. I heard scuffling behind us. "How many men did he bring?"

"Twenty."

"To catch a single murderer? We could have taken him ourselves. I doubt he would be so bold two-against-one and one of us armed with a gun," I said.

"You would be correct, except that this is no ordinary murder. In fact, the man who did the deed is likely the least important of the men we're following. Those will be on the ship."

"Ship? The *Invictus*? Are we going to try to catch them before they sail with the tide? Yesterday, they were loading up. Are they smugglers?"

I couldn't see his expression in the dim light, but I imagined the smile in his voice. "The *Coral Sea*. Come, tonight will be illuminating."

At first sight the ship appeared as quiet as it had been when I observed it earlier. We concealed ourselves behind the corner of a brick warehouse and watched it. Lestrade's men arrayed themselves in other places of concealment, and the inspector himself came up to us.

"Holmes," he said, "that ship looks like it's buttoned up tighter than the Bank of England. Are you certain about this?"

"Absolutely."

Lestrade peered at the ship. "I see no way to board."

"That's why we need to wait. No one has come onto that ship in the past day. I've had runners watching it. They have to come now if they want to escape with the tide."

"Who?" I asked.

"Here they come," Holmes hissed. "Quiet, now."

Two men emerged from the shadows. These didn't seem like dock workers or the kind of night creatures I'd been spotting all evening. These were well-dressed in dark suits and perfectly respectable hats. They could have been bankers.

Holmes turned to Lestrade. "Tell your men to be ready. But wait for my signal."

The men approached the ship and called up to the deck. I couldn't catch the words, but they sounded harsh in the stillness of the night.

The ship didn't respond, but the bow gangplank began to drop.

"Quickly, now," Holmes told me. "When we reach them, fire at the man on the gangplank winch. You don't need to hit him, just make certain he abandons his post."

We broke cover and ran towards the men waiting for the ramp to allow them onto the ship. They saw us coming and bolted, but were immediately tackled to the ground by several of Lestrade's men.

"Now, Watson!" Holmes shouted.

I took aim in the general direction of the man at the winch and fired.

The shot tore through the night like thunder. To my satisfaction, the bullet shattered a window near my target, and he bolted like a rat.

Holmes and the policemen unshuttered their lanterns and poured past us onto the *Coral Sea*. Soon, the ship was under their control, and a well-uniformed crew of seven sat under the watchful eye of the constabulary.

Lestrade came up to Holmes and shook his hand. "This is a coup beyond what I imagined," the inspector effused. "And to catch them in the act…"

"You will be well-rewarded," Holmes observed.

Lestrade cocked his head at him. "That's not what this is about, Holmes," he said, as if explaining something to a particularly vexing child. "This is bigger than one humble policeman. Now get out of here before I have to explain you to the chief superintendent."

We walked away, and Holmes remarked: "That is a truly good man. I'm glad he will reap the benefits of this."

* * *

I managed to contain my curiosity until we arrived at Baker Street, but once we sat by the fire, I could hold back no longer.

"Those were the German spies, weren't they?" I said.

"You came to that conclusion because you heard them speaking?"

"No. Because the ones that were waiting to climb the gangplank were carrying a document case. I concluded that all of this was about that case. The only thing that could cause such excitement and be carried in a case like that were the stolen plans."

"Very well done, Watson!" Holmes exulted, putting tobacco in his pipe. "You are to be commended."

The Spice of Life by Gustavo Bondoni

"Not at all. I was merely present at the close and understand what kind of activity would bring twenty men from Scotland Yard. But how did you spot them?"

"It began with Keynes. His wife was right to say that someone who'd visited him was responsible for his death. But the man who killed him wasn't on the list she showed us."

"I thought it was the Captain of the *Coral Sea*," I said.

"It was the Captain of the ship we raided. In that you're correct. but *that ship is not the* Coral Sea."

"I don't follow."

"You observed the two ships in this case. What did you think of them?"

"The *Invictus* was a slovenly heap. The *Coral Sea* was a respectable vessel."

Holmes smiled. "Once a soldier, always a soldier," he said. "You think in military terms. The army and the navy always have men available for drudgework such as keeping a steamer in pristine condition. A real merchant ship, though not necessarily as dirty as the *Invictus*, will always show some signs of deferred maintenance. The *Coral Sea* was suspiciously clean."

"And you acted on that evidence," I asked.

"That was merely the first clue," he said. "Confirmation came when I saw that the ship sailed from Singapore two days before the eruption of Krakatoa, on a path that would, necessarily have put it in harm's way at the moment of explosion. I'm sad to say that the real *Coral Sea* is most likely at the bottom of the ocean. Somehow, the Prussians learned of its fate and saw an opportunity to bring home the smugglers. But one man knew the truth."

"Keynes."

"Exactly. The captain must have gone to the meeting, and attempted to explain that the man Keynes knew and trusted was indisposed. Seeing that he wasn't quite believed, the Germans took measures to ensure his silence."

The Spice of Life by Gustavo Bondoni

"What a sad coincidence," I said.

"Most unfortunate. And, though I hate to pile on a man's misfortunes, we will have to inform the younger Mister Keynes that his shipment of spices will not be forthcoming."

I shook my head in admiration and we sat for some time, thinking by just what slim threads national interests sometimes hung.

December 1883

The Adventure of the Mummy's Menace

By George Jacobs

The weather of the last two weeks had been that of a typical London winter: grey, wet, and bitingly cold. There was little to tempt one out into the streets; therefore, I had largely confined myself to the rooms in Baker Street which I shared with my friend, Sherlock Holmes, finding what diversion I could in literature and the company of my pet bull pup.

Holmes had likewise little left our apartments, though for an entirely different reason. "What a sorry lot the London criminal class is," he had exclaimed after four days of inactivity. "A little inclement weather and it seems all their machinations cease! Not one client has knocked on our door these several days."

"Surely that is a good thing," I replied, "for it means that our fellow Londoners may sleep a little sounder in their beds, while the rain lasts."

He smiled at me. "Very true, my noble Watson, very true. But it is not a good thing for me! I grow bored, very bored. My mind revolts at inactivity."

The Adventure of the Mummy's Menace by George Jacobs

A week had passed since then, and Holmes's boredom had only worsened. He alternated between restless pacing with pipe in hand, and sprawling languorously over his chair with a gloomy expression clouding his gaunt features. I had, several times, attempted to engage him in conversation, hoping to distract his precocious brain, but he had given no appearance of having heard me.

The morning of the 14th found me sitting upon my well-stuffed chair, reading a novel by a certain Amelia Edwards. The book in question was a rather good romance, featuring a great deal of drama and excitement, with an undercurrent of the supernatural. I was finding it greatly diverting, but just then Holmes returned from a long walk, thoroughly soaked through.

"Any callers?" he asked, without much hope.

"None."

He nodded and tossed his coat into a heap upon the floor, leaving it to soak into the carpet. "What's that you're reading?" he asked with a raised eyebrow.

I held up my book for him to see and he tutted. "My dear Watson, why do you dally with such trifles? On our shelves there are a great many volumes of knowledge and wisdom, yet rather than filling that great warehouse of your mind with something useful, you amuse yourself with such foolishness as ghosts and spirits."

My companion's attitude did not surprise me, for his sharp mind was every inch the reasoning machine. "Do you hold the entirety of fiction in contempt, Holmes, or merely suggest that all talk of the supernatural is foolish?" I asked, putting down my book.

He sniffled. "Foolish or not, it is certainly beyond the realm of the practical, to which you know well that I confine my efforts."

He slumped into his chair and seemed about to enter one of his moods, when there was a knock at the door. "Come in," called Holmes, a trace of life re-entering his expression.

Mrs. Hudson opened the door. "There's a man downstairs," she said. "Asking to come up."

The Adventure of the Mummy's Menace by George Jacobs

"Did he say what for?" asked Holmes, now sitting upright.

"He said it was confidential."

"Then do send him up, please, Mrs. Hudson."

As our landlady departed, Holmes turned to me with a smile. "Well, well Watson, this is indeed promising."

A moment later the door opened again, and a tall, well-dressed man came into our sitting-room, holding his left arm stiffly. He had a tanned face with darkened eyes and moved with an air of hesitation. His gaze roved about the room, taking in Holmes and myself, but never pausing longer than a moment.

Holmes rose to greet the man. "Welcome, Captain," he said. "I see it has been a few weeks since your return from Egypt."

The man started at Holmes's words and took a step back towards the door. "D-do you know me?" he stammered.

"I have never seen you before," replied Holmes. "But you must admit, the signs are obvious. When I see a youthful man, still tanned by the desert sun, his left arm suffering from a rifle wound, who moves, despite his evident nervousness, with a certain upright and commanding force, and whose regulation moustache is neatly trimmed, I would have to be particularly unobservant not to identify you at once. And that is of course, without the subtler marks which I need not mention."

I smiled, for it was ever a pleasure of mine to see my friend's acute powers of reasoning at work, and I was privately glad that a new case seemed about to rouse him from the dumps.

"I suppose, I suppose," said the man. "You are right, of course, and I have heard word of your abilities as a detective, though it is quite a shock to witness them first-hand." He shook hands with both of us. "I am Henry Norfolk, captain of the Royal Sussex. Though, with my arm as it is, I am now invalided out. Pleased to me you both."

We each shook hands.

The Adventure of the Mummy's Menace by George Jacobs

"Now," said Holmes, "please take a seat and tell us what is it that brings you to see me. I am sure even my friend Watson can see by your agitated manner that something troubles you."

The man took the proffered seat and put his head in his hands, giving the very picture of a man at wit's end. He cleared his throat, then said, "I am worried I am going mad. Perhaps I even hope it, for the alternative seems worse by far."

A look of disappointment flickered across Holmes's face. "Madness? I am afraid that falls more within the realm of good Watson, over there."

"Yes," said the man, bobbing his head. "In fact, it was Doctor Watson I intended to seek out initially, owing to his position as an army physician."

"Former army doctor," I corrected.

"Yes, well never mind that. I believe I have a desperate need of advice of a psychiatric nature, but I cannot go to the family physician. I need someone who can... be relied upon for discretion. And someone who has encountered the stranger things in life. And, while I admit it was through your own growing reputation, Mr. Holmes, that I heard of you both, I had hoped that Dr Watson, as a brother soldier who has also helped you in your many and varied cases, would do me the great service of assisting me in my hour of need."

"Watson is certainly an admirable fellow," said Holmes. He took out his tobacco from the slipper in which he kept it and lit his pipe, the faintest signs of boredom returning to his face.

"Though of course, I had hoped you would also be willing to listen to my story, though I fear it may be beyond the bounds of your own specialities, for I know that many times you have had insight into a problem which at first appeared opaque and peculiar."

"Yes, of course," muttered Holmes. He sat back upon his chair and began to puff away on his pipe. "Pray begin, if Watson is willing."

The Adventure of the Mummy's Menace by George Jacobs

"I am, surely," I said, feeling much intrigued that someone should feel in need of my medical aid, in addition to the wondrous investigative skills of my friend. "Please, tell us what aid you require."

"Well, to begin at the beginning," said Norfolk, his voice growing stronger as he drifted into memories, "as you have alluded to, I have recently returned from service in Egypt. I had, along with the rest of my regiment, joined the expeditionary force sent to put a stop to the revolt against the Khedive, led by that rebel colonel, Arabi Pasha. I am sure you are aware of the general campaign."

"Indeed," I said, for in truth I had followed news of it closely, the exploits of the British army still eliciting great interest in me.

"It was going well for us, my men and me, and we received praise from Field Marshal Wolseley himself for our conduct at Kafr El Dawwar. However, at Tell El Kebir, while my unit was undertaking a flanking manoeuvre, we were caught in a great sandstorm. Separated from our comrades and lost in the desert, we soon came under fire from the enemy, an enemy who knew the lie of the land much better than we did. It was pure luck that we stumbled upon some ruins, half buried in the sand. With no better prospects, and despite the protestations of our local guide, we broke into the tomb and barricaded ourselves within."

"Why did the local protest your entering the ruin?" I asked, and Holmes favoured me with a smile and a nod.

"Because," said Norfolk, "he claimed that the tombs of his ancient ancestors were protected by powerful curses. At the time I dismissed it as superstition, and besides, the very real bullets that cracked through the air presented a much more apparent threat to my men."

"Indeed," said Holmes, and his eyes drifted to my closed novel.

"Anyway, needless to say, I survived, along with most of my men, having succeeded in holding off the enemy for several days until the storm cleared and a relieving force came to our rescue. It was during the battle of the tomb that I sustained the wound which has left my arm limp and feeble.

"Judged unfit for further combat, and with the short war already clearly decided in favour of our forces and those of the Khedive, I was then shipped home, only to arrive to find things in a state of some confusion, for my unit's apparent disappearance for several days had caused rumours to make their way back to Britain that we had been killed in action."

At this my friend looked up. "What was the precise nature of this confusion? A matter of inheritance?"

"Exactly that."

"On account of your presumed death?"

"Just as you say," replied Norfolk, now looking at Holmes with even greater awe. "Shortly before I departed for Egypt, my aged father passed away, and I, his only surviving child, inherited the family estate and fortune. There were those amongst my relatives who urged me to resign my commission and take up my familial duties, but I felt I had already sworn an oath to God and the Queen, and it would do me no honour to shirk this oath on the eve of a campaign; besides, my father's man, Hewins, was more than capable of managing affairs while I was away. I am sure you, Watson, can well understand my feeling."

"Indeed, I can," I replied, "and find it quite an admirable attitude."

"To whom would the estate pass, in the event of your death?" put in Holmes, now leaning forward in his chair. "I see by the lack of a ring that you are not a married man."

"To my uncle, Godfrey." Norfolk's face clouded. "He is not a bad old chap, but I must tell you, confidentially, that in his youth he was quite the decadent. I am told he overindulged in the smoking of opium and other substances, and it has left him quite vacuous of mind. He's not feeble enough to warrant sending to a sanatorium, but he would hardly be a fit person to run the estate."

"And where does this Godfrey live?" asked Holmes.

"He lives in the manor, with me now as he did before with my father. As I said, he's not really fit to manage by himself, and so the old bachelor has a few rooms to call his own in our old pile."

"But, despite his inadequacies, he had started to take possession of the estate prior to your return?"

"Well, there were only rumours of my death, nothing official. But yes, I am given to understand that the lawyers had begun making little noises towards him, in the eventuality my death proved real, and he was prepared to take the mantle, as it were, at least as far as he understood it."

"My, my," said Holmes, rubbing his hands together. "This is proving rather more interesting than I feared. But, please, continue with your narrative."

"As I said, there was some confusion, but, as I was manifestly alive, it did not take a great deal of effort on my part to sort everything out, and, wounded as I was, and judging myself to have done my duty to the army, I took to the task of familiarising myself with the running of the family estate. It was then that my troubles really began, and the reason I have come today to seek both of your advice.

"At first, it was just the glimpse of a strange figure in the dark, while I took an evening stroll through my grounds. There was something unusual about that figure, bulky and hunched. But it was always too far away to see clearly, and when I tried to approach, it disappeared into the gloom. I thought perhaps a vagrant had taken up residence on the grounds, or a poacher had come in, and so asked that the gardeners to be careful and keep an eye out. But they could find no one. Then I saw the figure a second time, this time from my bedroom window, I had the gardeners patrol about with cudgels, but again they could discover no intruder. The only trace that they did find were the marks of some footprints in the mud, which in truth may have been made by anyone.

"It was after I had been home a week, that the first true attack happened. I had been asleep in the master bedroom which I had now

The Adventure of the Mummy's Menace by George Jacobs

taken as my own, when I was rudely shaken awake. Upon opening my eyes, I beheld a terrible sight. For over me, illuminated by my sole candle, there stood that ghastly, hunched figure, who, now that it was close, I could see was horribly bound head to foot in mouldering bandages. I recognised it at once as one of those spectres which is called a mummy, and whose forms are said to haunt the strange necropolises of Egypt.

"I tried to move, but found myself unable to, as if paralysed by some night terror. The spirit grasped me by the shoulders, shook me violently, and cried, in rasping tones, 'You who disturbed my rest, a curse is now upon you. Doom is now your bedfellow! Renounce your life and all its trinkets, lest death take you as it did me!'

"With that, the mummy hurled me against the bed, extinguished the candle with a sweep of its hand, and clattered away into the darkness. I lay there trembling for God knows how long, until, eventually, I regained the use of my limbs and fled from my room. I scarcely need say that I slept no more than night."

Norfolk now paused and sank back into his chair. His face had once more taken on that haunted look and his eyes stared out blankly. Thinking on his strange experience evidently still had the power to greatly disturb him.

"I can see now why you are so troubled," I said to the trembling man.

"Very much so," agreed Holmes, to my surprise, for I had expected him to dismiss the whole affair. "I take it, that this was but the first of several experiences with this mummy?"

"Yes," said Norfolk, taking out a cigarette and lighting it. "Since that day, at least once a week, I have been so molested by this terrible spirit. Sometimes it returns to my room in the dark of night, and always I am unable to move when it shakes me and prophesies my doom. But at other times, I see it in the garden, staring up at my bedroom window. I have, as you can imagine, ceased taking walks at night.

The Adventure of the Mummy's Menace by George Jacobs

"And the worst part is, no one else in the house has seen or heard anything. Of course, I have had to be casual in my manner of asking, but it truly seems I am alone in my experiences. Apart from those footprints in the gardens, there seems no evidence of the existence of the mummy. My first fear was that I was going mad! It had happened to a great aunt of mine, at least so was obliquely hinted at by my father, and they do say it runs in families. And I think the servants are starting to suspect something. They look at me queerly. One time, when I saw the thing out in the gardens; in a great terror, I fired upon it with my service revolver, shattering the glass of my window and making a dreadful noise. But the bullet seemed to pass right through it, and it came again the next night to my room! It was a tricky business to explain to the butler, Headley, what I had been doing, but I must confess my wits are feeling so strained I scarcely care but that they should know what ails me.

"And yet, for all this fear of mine for my mental state, the experiences feel so real... The hands gripping me, the voice in my ears. And of course, there was the fact that I had been into an Egyptian tomb, and the superstitious natives had warned me, hadn't they? And, there had been those footprints in the gardens which the gardeners had also seen..." He ran a hand through prematurely thinning hair. "You don't... you don't think I really could be cursed, do you? I must admit, I have been half tempted to heed the mummy's terrible words and give up my estate, if it will only bring me respite from this torment!"

I looked over at Holmes and saw that he was frowning in deep concentration.

"Well," I said, filling the silence, "I think the realm of the supernatural is rather outside my expertise, and in my life as both medical man and soldier, I have never seen evidence of it. But I must say, equally, I have certainly never encountered anything like the experiences you recount. Holmes?"

"No," he replied curtly. "No curse. And, if Watson agrees, for in that area I will defer to him, I do not think you mad either. No, something quite different is afoot, if I have any inkling." He put his hands together and his sharp face took on a far-away look.

"I certainly do not find you mad," I said to Norfolk. "Though of course, certain queer delusions may manifest in otherwise perfectly normal individuals."

Norfolk gave a weak smile and lit another cigarette. "It is certainly a relief to hear these statements from you both, however tentative they may be. But I must confess, if you think I am neither mad nor cursed, what source of all this do you propose?"

"It is too soon to say," said Holmes. "But there is the start of a theory forming in my mind. I think Watson and I may need to pay a visit to your estate, if you are willing?"

"By all means. If you feel anything may help rid me of this terror, then I am willing to do whatever you deem necessary."

"Good. However, first, your interesting narrative does suggest several questions to me. You have already stated that your uncle would inherit, should you perish or, presumably, renounce the estate?"

"Yes. But, if I follow that vast mind of yours at all, and I am not certain I do, then I assure you, he is incapable of conducting such an elaborate plot as this, for his mental faculties are very ravaged."

"As you say. Then, have there been any other changes to your estate which occurred between when you left on campaign and when you returned?"

The young man put his fist to his brow and pursed his lips. "The only thing that comes to mind is that there were a few changes to the servants employed. I am still not quite sure what happened, but it appears that there was an issue with my father's man, Hewins, and he was let go, replaced by a new butler named Headley, hired on the recommendation of one of my cousins. And I believe there were a few others, a valet, perhaps a cook and a liveryman, who departed with Hewins, and Headley brought in their replacements. But, while I must admit I have had little contact with them, I have seen all the letters of recommendations, and Headley seems a thorough enough chap. And besides, I am not sure what a servant could hope to gain through driving me mad or convincing me to abandon the estate?"

Holmes's face was still, held in a mask of concentration. "I thank you for bringing this to my attention," he said at last. "Watson and I will certainly look into it for you, though as Watson hinted at, I am afraid a case of madness cannot be ruled out until we have more data. But I will say that I foresee that outcome as a doubtful. There are a few things I wish to check over here, but if you will leave us your address, Watson and I will be around in the morning. That is, if my friend is willing to brave the weather, of course?"

"Gladly," I laughed, with a rueful glance out the window.

"Then there remains just one thing before you may be on your way," said Holmes to Norfolk. "I would ask that you do not make it known to your household the purpose of our visit. I do not wish anything disturbed by the knowledge that I am investigating."

"We could say I was an old friend from the army," I suggested.

"Perfect, my good Watson, a capital suggestion. And, as part of this, I request that we not mention any of your case in front of anyone save the three of us."

"I shall do as you ask then," replied Norfolk, "and gladly, for I have no desire for what ails me to be common knowledge among my people. And now I suppose I will bid you farewell till tomorrow."

We saw him out, back into the rain, and then Holmes and I returned to our sitting-room, where Holmes took down several volumes from his shelf and began to puff away on his pipe while scanning through them. I could see that the young officer's strange tale had sparked some great interest in my friend, and I was happy for it, for Holmes is always at his best when his remarkable mind has some problem to turn on. However, I must admit that at the time, I was quite unsure of why Holmes had entertained such a fanciful story, for it was his usual practice to dismiss any case presented to him which seemed to smack of the so called paranormal.

The Adventure of the Mummy's Menace by George Jacobs

I shrugged to myself, for it was by no means an unusual occurrence for me to be unable to fathom the thinking of Holmes and, realising that I would get little company from my friend this evening, I picked my novel back up and began to read, as the rain beat down upon the city outside.

The next morning found Holmes and I sitting in a first-class train carriage, eating a simple meal of biscuits, on our way into the Hampshire countryside. The sprawl of London was soon left behind, and the fields and woods of old England whipped past our carriage window. Accompanying us was my bull dog, Wellington, which Holmes had asked me to bring along, though he had not chosen to furnish me with an explanation for this.

"I apologise for keeping my own counsel last night," said Holmes. "But you see, I had rather a lot of thoughts all working away in my mind, and I wished to pursue them while the iron was hot!"

"There is nothing to apologise for," I replied. "I have got quite used to the intensity of your investigations over the last year, and the wide-ranging trains of thought which take hold of you."

"That is well. So then, tell me, what do you make of this case, as presented to us by Captain Norfolk?"

"Well, I must admit I was a little surprised it interested you so, for, given its nature, I had expected you to dismiss it as a hoax or some madness, as I have seen you do before when presented with tales of hauntings and the like. Was there something about this one that made you suspect it may be a true instance of the supernatural and so worth investigating?"

"Quite the contrary, my dear Watson! I am convinced it is a case confined to the happenings of this world, and I am fairly convinced that Norfolk is as sane as you or I. There were a number of statements from Norfolk that reminded me of a case from '63 that occurred in Bremen, and still another earlier in Pontevedra. As I have had cause to remark before, there is little in the world of crime that is new, and the more unusual the crime the simpler the explanation, more often than not."

"Then you believe a crime has occurred, or is in the process of occurring?"

"Indeed, I do. There are a number of little theories I am currently entertaining within my skull, but it is dangerous to theorise too much without sufficient data."

"I must confess I find myself unable to align some of Norfolk's experiences with a rational explanation. How, for example, would you explain his strange paralysis when he is visited by the creature, or how he shot it to no effect?"

"There are ways of accomplishing both of those things by purely natural means," replied Holmes. "But, as I said, I need more data before I allow myself to come to any firm conclusions. But I see now we are pulling into the station. Fetch down your valise, Watson, and remember, you are an old friend of Norfolk's today!"

We took a carriage from the state to Woodhollow Hall, the estate belonging to Norfolk. The weather here was fairer than it had been in London, and every inch Blake's "green and pleasant land." Holmes was quiet, having lapsed back into thought, but my bull dog seemed to be enjoying his trip outside the capital, yapping at every passing bird.

Woodhollow Hall was a suitably impressive building, an imposing structure in Georgian red brick, set amidst spacious grounds with a large, ornamental garden dotted with bushes and trees that provided both many open spaces and secluded spots.

The carriage deposited us outside the large entrance, and a footman came out to greet us. We were informed that we were expected, and Norfolk would meet us in the drawing-room. The inside of the manor was quite as impressive as the outside and, thinking on Holmes's suspicions of crime, I began to feel that someone might indeed go through a great deal of rigmarole in order to secure such a fortune as must provide for all this.

The Adventure of the Mummy's Menace by George Jacobs

Norfolk was waiting for us and smiled as we entered the drawing-room. He still bore the ghastly, haunted look, but I was impressed by the strength of character he displayed in how well he was bearing up in front of everyone.

"Watson, old friend," he said and strode forth to shake my hand.

"It is very good to see you again," I replied. "And this is my good friend, Underhill," I said, gesturing to Holmes, the false name being his idea, for, after our adventure which I had attempted to chronicle in *A Study in Scarlet*, Holmes's name had become more widely known, and though I judged it unlikely that the type of London criminal familiar with Holmes's skills dwelt out here in this idyllic place, I readily acquiesced to his request.

"Very good to meet you," said Holmes. "I hope you don't mind, but I was forced to bring my bull pup, Wellington, with me." He indicated the snuffling animal whose lead he held. "He's quite a rascally chap, but I'll do my best to see he doesn't damage your furniture."

Norfolk had cigars and some brandy brought in, and a saucer of milk for my dog, and we spent a pleasant half hour chatting on this and that, giving the appearance of friendly comradeship to any who may have been within earshot.

Casually, Holmes asked how Norfolk's evening had been the previous day.

"Oh," said Norfolk, his eyes darting around and alighting on the footman who stood by the door. "It was quite fine, thank you. I had an appointment in the city that ran late, so I ate a quick meal in my club before returning here and going straight to bed."

Holmes nodded and puffed thoughtfully upon his cigar as if some vital piece of knowledge had just been imparted. But he said nothing further, and conversation returned to more general matters.

I heard a shuffling behind me, and turned to see an old man wander into the room. His face bore a confused air, and his aged skin hung limply upon his spindly frame. He made his way over to us, constantly playing with the fingers of his left hand and mumbling under his breath.

Norfolk rose. "Gentlemen, may I present my uncle, Godfrey."

Holmes and I rose, shook hands, and introduced ourselves.

"Watson is an old army friend," said Norfolk. "I mentioned he would be visiting."

The old man bobbed his head and wetted his lips. "Oh, I suppose you did, yes. Nice to meet you, gentlemen, I'm sure. I just thought I would pop in, but I am on my way to the kitchen. A powerful hunger, don't you know." He smiled vacantly at his hands and wandered across and out of the drawing-room by the far door.

"As I said, his mind is rather gone," said Norfolk, "but he is a nice enough old coot. Anyway, is there anything in particular you gentlemen may wish to see or do, while you are here as my guests?" He looked at Holmes meaningfully.

"Why not give us the tour?" I said.

"Yes," said Holmes. "I would particularly like to see the master bedroom, if you please," he added quietly.

Norfolk led us upstairs, making a show of pointing out particular paintings and indicating the library, before showing us into his bed chamber. It was a large room, wood-paneled and neatly furnished. Norfolk shut the door behind us, and at once Holmes leapt into action. He handed the dog-lead to me and began by patrolling around the bed, looking under it, and then examining the walls. He tapped upon the wood with his knuckles, producing a dull thud. He frowned, his eyes scanning the room. Then, with a cry of "Ahah!" he knelt beside the wardrobe and plucked something off the wall. He turned it over in his hands, smiling, then tapped upon the wood. The sound was subtly different.

He stood and held out his find to me. It appeared to be a few white threads. "So, one of my theories proves correct," he said.

The Adventure of the Mummy's Menace by George Jacobs

But before I could ask him to explain himself, there was a rap upon the door and an upright, elderly man with immaculate clothing entered the room. "Sorry to interrupt you, sir," he said, addressing himself to Norfolk, "I had not realised you already had company. However, luncheon is ready to be served."

"That's quite all right, Headley," replied Norfolk. "I am quite famished." Again, he projected an air of good cheer to his man, yet his smile was tight and his gaze wavering. My own eyes found the large bedroom window and I noticed the panel at the bottom left which was slightly different from its fellows. The one Norfolk had shattered with his pistol shot.

Lunch was a pleasant enough affair. The food was well-prepared, fish featuring heavily, which Norfolk explained was the result of the cook advising him that the oil of fish was restorative in nature and did wanders for the brain.

Norfolk's Uncle Godfrey ate with us, though he only picked at his food. I supposed he had eaten his fill earlier, when we had seen him depart for the kitchen. Again, he had the air of not truly being present in the room, continually gazing about and stroking his fingers.

The only event of note was that, while Norfolk was recounting the story of his unit's involvement in the battle of Kafr El Dawwar and all eyes were on him, I saw Holmes surreptitiously pluck several items of food from Norfolk's plate and drop them under the table, which my pup happily ate up. I raised an eyebrow at this, for, Bohemian as he was, it was not in Holmes's habits to act in such an uncouth manner towards his host, but I did not comment upon it.

After the meal, we decided to take a walk in the large gardens of Woodhollow, accompanied by Norfolk's valet. It was very pleasant, wrapped up in our great coats, and Norfolk rather lit up as he showed us the winter flowers and several ancient fir trees. My bull pup also seemed to be enjoying himself, and I was surprised that Holmes had offered to walk him, maintaining the obscure fiction that the animal

The Adventure of the Mummy's Menace by George Jacobs

was his. What was equally obscure to me was the question of what all this was in aid of, regarding the case at hand.

"Where was it that you saw that intruder?" asked Holmes, casually.

Norfolk started, then composed himself and nodded towards a murky clearing in which stood a small fountain, and which was surrounded by high, bushy evergreens. "It was over here that I first saw the... poacher."

"And where the gardeners saw the foot prints?"

"Indeed."

We headed in that direction and Holmes made a show of admiring the foliage and the marble fountain. This area seemed to be a favourite of the avian inhabitants of the gardens, their winter songs filling the air.

Holmes was making his way back towards us, when he unaccountably slipped and fell face first upon the grass. His lost his grip on the dog-lead and, now free, my bull dog gave a bark of joy and plunged headlong into the bushes in search of the birds and squirrels.

Getting to his feet, Holmes tried to brush the dirt from his clothes and smiled weakly at us. "Must have tripped on a root," he said, by way of explanation. "But let's not stand about, we have a dog to catch! Norfolk, you know the lie of the land, take Watson and make your way around the back of this copse. I'll take the more direct route." And, so saying, he ran into the bushes in the direction my dog had taken.

I must confess that Holmes's behaviour today had struck me as very odd, but at the time I had attributed it to his long period of boredom and the excitement he was taking in the opportunity to put his mind to work on this strange case.

Despite his rousing words, it took the three of us, assisted by Norfolk's valet and the gardener on duty, well over an hour of running about the grounds to capture my bull dog and calm him, and we all trooped back to the manor thoroughly exercised. Yet, I noticed that

The Adventure of the Mummy's Menace by George Jacobs

Holmes wore a mysterious smile upon his face, and when he caught my eye he winked conspiratorially.

Norfolk's expression displayed plainly the same bafflement at Holmes's behaviour that I felt, and I could tell that he wished to ask Holmes to explain himself. However, we three were never alone, for always there was a footman or maid or Headley within earshot. Back in the manor, we cleaned up with the assistance of Headley, and Norfolk leant Holmes a change of trousers and jacket that had belonged to his father, for Holmes was much taller than Norfolk himself.

By now the hour was quite late and we made our way downstairs to be told that dinner was ready. Again, the food was well-prepared and the meal enjoyable, being well flavoured with spices, though again fish was widely in evidence. This time, however, Uncle Godfrey did not join us, and Headley reported that he was not in his room. This was not unusual, so Norfolk said, for Godfrey often took to wandering in the evenings, taking the air when the brightness of the sun had diminished.

During the meal I kept a careful eye on my friend and, with a sleight-of-hand I would not have credited him with, once again I saw Holmes scoop up a forkful of Norfolk's meal and feed it to my dog under the table. I was the only person who saw, thankfully, and to my slight horror Holmes repeated this with the next course too, all the while keeping up his end of the conversation as if he had done nothing.

Dessert was brought out, and I heard a strange, bestial groan. Looking down, I saw that my bull pup had slumped forward and was quivering, his legs twitching ineffectually. Worry filled me and I made to reach for the poor creature, of whom I was very fond, but Holmes put a preventative hand upon my arm.

"Don't fear, my friend," he hissed into my ear. "Trust me. He'll be fine." Then, sitting up straight, he said in a louder voice, "Don't worry, here's your spoon, Watson." And so saying, he lay my spoon, which I would swear had been in its proper place only a moment ago, upon the table. And, true to Holmes's word, before dessert was done, my Wellington had sat up and resumed his quiet snuffling as if nothing had happened.

After we had finished, Holmes declared that the dinner had been one of the best he had ever eaten, and asked Norfolk if he might be permitted to go down to the kitchen to pay his compliments in person.

"That's very kind of you to say," said Norfolk. "I'll have Headley bring her up here."

"Oh, don't be silly," replied Holmes. "There's no need to trouble either of them, I know how hard servants work in a house as large as this. I will just pop briefly into the kitchens, if a spare footman may show me the way."

Norfolk of course acquiesced to Holmes's wishes, and Holmes disappeared off to the kitchens in the company of a young footman.

"Quite a character, your friend," remarked Norfolk.

"He is that," I agreed. "I have known him for not even three years, yet have had adventures and tribulations with him that would almost equal those I saw in Afghanistan."

Holmes returned with a curious look of satisfaction upon his face and when he caught my gaze his eyes fairly sparkled. Returning to sit beside me, he yawned theatrically.

I looked out at the darkness beyond the dining-room windows. "It is getting rather late," I remarked.

"Yes," said Holmes. "And I recall you saying earlier that you had business to attend to in the early morning, did you not?"

"I did? Oh, yes, of course, how silly of me to forget."

"So," continued Holmes, turning to Norfolk, "I am afraid we must bid you adieu. I thank you again for your warm hospitality and excellent food; it has been a pleasure to meet you."

"What?" asked Norfolk. Then, composing himself, he continued, "I had expected you to stay the night."

The Adventure of the Mummy's Menace by George Jacobs

"I am afraid that is quite impossible," said Holmes in a clear voice, "for I have business of my own in London tomorrow. But I do hope you will pay us a visit when you are next in the city."

"We would be honoured, however, if you would see us into our carriage," I put in, for in truth I was as confused by developments as Norfolk evidently was, and I hoped that once out of the manor, Holmes might find an opportunity to explain himself briefly to our distressed client.

The evening was cold, and I shivered as I got into the carriage. Norfolk walked so close to Holmes that he almost kicked his heels, and I heard him whisper something to Holmes. My friend put his mouth to Norfolk's ear and gave him some reply, which I could not catch. It evidently heartened the poor man, however, and his face assumed a more determined set. He bid us farewell, and we parted.

As we trundled along in the dark towards the train station, I leaned over to Holmes. "What are we doing returning to London?" I asked, keeping my voice low. "I pray you will let me into the workings of your mind somewhat, for I confess I am totally in the dark about what has occurred today and have found your behaviour most odd, yet I seem to perceive you have met with success in whatever strange objectives you set yourself. And what was all that business with my dog?"

Holmes gave me a friendly pat on the shoulder. "I am sorry, I often forget your mind does not run in sequence with mine. You are right in your suspicion, of course. In fact, I am almost certain of what has been occurring to our friend Norfolk, and who is responsible and why they are doing it. And, if we act now, and have a little luck on our side, we might well catch them in the act tonight!"

Before I could follow up this statement with any of the many questions it prompted, Holmes rose and knocked on the wood beside the driver's seat. Leaning out, he said, "My apologies good driver, but I have just realised I left my valise at the manor. No, please don't trouble yourself, it is not a far walk and we could do with stretching our legs. You best turn in for the night, as I fear by the time I have retrieved my luggage, we shall have missed the last train."

Holmes then hopped out of the carriage and I followed him in some bewilderment, carrying my bull pup. Holmes set back off in the direction of Woodhollow, his long limbs lending him considerable speed, and I struggled to keep pace with him.

"So we are not leaving?" I asked.

"Of course not," replied Holmes. "That was just a little theatre for the benefit of our quarry. Surely you must see that they would have hardly attempted to menace Norfolk had strangers been sleeping down the hall. No, that would introduce too many variables."

"So it is someone at the house who has been causing Norfolk to believe he is haunted?"

"Yes, yes. Do please keep up!" He paused in his stride and turned to face me. "Sorry, please forgive my forcefulness. But, you see, I am all caught up in the case and the possible eventualities that may unfold when we get back to the manor, and it is very difficult to slow my mind down and explain the process by which I have placed all the pieces of the puzzle together. I know that it may be asking a lot, but I would ask you to put your trust in my abilities, as you did in the Jefferson Hope case, and I promise I will explain everything to your total satisfaction at a later time."

"Very well, my friend," I replied, somewhat touched, if also a little piqued, by his words. "Let us go and see what awaits us."

We entered the grounds of Woodhollow stealthily, aided by the lack of a moon. Holmes led the way, his sense of direction unerring, and soon we found ourselves in view of Norfolk's bed chamber window. The faint light of a candle shone there, and a fire was visible in the servants' quarters at the far, lower end of the manor, but all the other windows were in darkness.

"Good," said Holmes. "Norfolk has done his part." He pointed at one of the ground floor windows beneath Norfolk's bedroom. "He has left that window open, that we may gain entry. I must say, it is

The Adventure of the Mummy's Menace by George Jacobs

very satisfying to deal with a client who puts such total faith in my, and your, abilities. But we must not be too hasty, else we are likely to be noticed once inside by some servant or other. Keep an eye on Norfolk's room, and the moment one of us sees movement, we must rush in and make it to his bedchamber with all speed."

"Very well," I said. "I will just tie my bull pup to this tree, for I fear he would not help our mission of stealth." And, for good measure, I took out some of his favourite treats from my coat pocket, hoping to buy my animal's silence.

Holmes and I waited in the darkness for what felt like an hour, but now on reflection I am sure it can only have been a matter of ten minutes. And then, together, we saw a shadow move across Norfolk's window.

"Now!" hissed Holmes.

We ran across to the open window, climbed inside as quietly as we could, passed out of that room into the darkened hall, and took the stairs two at a time. I could hear a voice coming from Norfolk's room as we raced along the landing. Holmes did not bother reaching for the handle, but rather crashed through the door shoulder first, I on his heels.

The scene before us was just as Norfolk had described to us in Baker Street. He lay in bed, his muscles quivering uselessly, while over him raved the figure of a mummy.

The mummy turned with a start as we burst into the room and made to run to the left, and I was conscious that there was now an open space in the wall beside the wardrobe where earlier there had been none. But Holmes was having none of it, and with surprising agility, he leapt across the room and tackled the mummy to the floor, wrapping his long arms about the struggling figure.

"Quick, Watson," he cried. "Help me bind her."

I seized a belt from the dresser and helped Holmes bind the mummy's arms. All the while the creature was writhing and grumbling, cursing us in many inventive ways.

The Adventure of the Mummy's Menace by George Jacobs

Holmes took hold of the bandages about its head and began to unwrap them. To my shock, the face that was revealed was that of a handsome young lady.

"I'll keep her secure here," said Holmes. "Go and fetch up Headley and have him summon the police, then attend to Norfolk. I'm sure he will revive shortly, and will be very pleased to find his torment is at an end, even though," and here he nodded at his prisoner, "he must now replace his rather excellent cook."

* * *

It was the next morning, after we had returned to Baker Street and enjoyed a large breakfast that I finally asked Holmes to make good on his promise and explain all that had occurred the day before.

"I am still at a total loss as to how you knew what was going on at Woodhollow," I said. "And how, if I take your earlier statement as still holding true, you knew that the cook was behind it?"

Holmes smiled indulgently and fetched out his tobacco from the Persian slipper, then lit his pipe. "My first suspicion was when Norfolk mentioned an inheritance. I am sure you don't need me to tell you that whenever there is a good deal of money involved, there are likely to be nefarious schemes. This suspicion was compounded when Norfolk mentioned that, owing to confused information making it back to England, he had briefly been thought dead. Surely, anyone who had been interested in the question of the inheritance, and especially of the passing of it from Norfolk to his uncle, would have been rather put out by Norfolk's unexpected return.

"And consider too the words of the mummy: 'Renounce your possessions.' It was clear to me, on the assumption of the creature being in truth someone of flesh and blood, that the aim of that person must be related to Norfolk's inheriting of the estate."

"I can follow this line of reasoning," I replied. "But to me, it still seems that only Godfrey would have benefited from Norfolk's death or renouncement, and yet he was not the mummy, nor did he seem capable of originating such a scheme. Rather, it was the lowly cook who so menaced our client, and she would seem not to benefit at all."

"That would be true," smiled Holmes, "save for one important event. For, taking advantage of his foolish and simple nature, the cook, on learning, or believing that she had learnt, that Uncle Godfrey was about to inherit, induced him to secretly marry her. I am sure you did not fail to notice how he kept playing with his fingers. What you may have failed to truly observe, however, is that it was his left ring finger that was the focus of his attentions, and that there was a small discolouration of the skin there. But I did observe it, and correctly deduced that Godfrey was in the habit of wearing a wedding band there in private. This was further confirmed when I visited the kitchen, and saw him there attempting to embrace the young cook in a rather passionate manner, to which she was responding with a poor mask of pleasure, at least until they observed my approach."

"Well," I said, and let out a long breath. "When you lay it out in that manner, it does begin to make some kind of sense. But then, what was the business with my poor dog?"

"As I mentioned yesterday, the case as presented by Norfolk reminded me of several historical crimes that I had come across previously in the reading of my annals, for this is not the first time that a hoax of a supernatural kind has been used for various criminal ends. And one thing Norfolk mentioned in particular, his paralysis, was an almost perfect match for the Bremen case, where a kind of poison extracted from a peculiar pufferfish had been used to render the victim helpless during the haunting. This separately led me to suspect involvement of the cook, for who else is better placed to administer poison than the one who prepares your food? And of course, there was also Norfolk's comment, when we arrived, that he had had an untroubled sleep the previous night, and he had also not eaten at Woodhollow but in his London club.

The Adventure of the Mummy's Menace by George Jacobs

"Therefore, I thought I might try a little experiment. By feeding your animal a bite of Norfolk's food, I hoped to independently confirm my theory. The luncheon meal proved untainted, but dinner was a different matter. By the temporary paralysis of your bull pup, I had proof that Norfolk was being poisoned, though of course with his much larger body, Norfolk took some hours to digest and experience the affects.

"It was then that I persuaded Norfolk to let me visit the kitchen, where not only did I observe Godfrey and the cook, but also saw the strange little eggs of the poisonous fish, unnoticed by everyone else amidst all the other fish which she had persuaded Norfolk it was beneficial to consume."

"You are a wonder, my friend," I exclaimed.

"Hardly," he replied, but his flush of pleasure was quite evident. "It was all quite elementary. And I feel I ought to mention two further points, which allowed me full confidence in my theory and led us to our capture of the cook. The first was when we visited Norfolk's bed chamber. You will remember I showed you my discovery, though I don't think you understood its importance."

"The threads?"

"The threads. They were threads of a bleached linen, of the kind which is commonly used to make bandages. And they had been trapped between two of the wooden walls panels. It is a fact, dear Watson, that many old houses have secret, or at least forgotten passages. Some were built to hide priests during the Reformation, others simply to allow for the ready supply of food or care to the resident of the room without needing to pass along the public halls. By this discovery I knew that we were not dealing with an apparition, but a real person, slipping in and out of the room at will."

"And the second point?" I asked, eager to hear the rest of Holmes' account.

"There your wonderful pet again came into his own. I had a great desire to explore the gardens without company, and my

The Adventure of the Mummy's Menace by George Jacobs

accidental fall and releasing of your animal afforded me that opportunity. While you, Norfolk and the servants were hunting for your bull pup, I searched out the unusual foot prints. And I found them, Watson! Small foot prints, unlikely to be male. And they led me to a dilapidated and locked shed, hidden in an overgrown corner of the gardens, which I am fairly sure the gardeners have forgotten exists. On picking the lock and venturing inside, I beheld a scarecrow, wrapped up in bandages, hidden beneath a large canvas sheet. And thus was answered the riddle of how Norfolk had been menaced by a figure standing in the garden, and how he had shot the creature without apparent result."

"By Jove!" I exclaimed. "Really Holmes, you have wrapped this up very neatly. Truly, I am in awe of your faculty for reasoning."

"You are too kind my friend. And now, let us go for a walk, for the night's work has left me still quite famished, and I feel that with the cheque Norfolk made out to us, I may be able to sate our appetite in some welcome luxury."

Bonus Story:

April 1883

The Fairy Tale Mystery

By Geri Schear

Once upon a time, a much put-upon former military surgeon shared a flat in Baker Street with an extraordinary detective named Sherlock Holmes. They faced a number of trials together and solved many mysteries, but none stranger than "The Fairy Tale Mystery," as the doctor called it.

One sparkling morning in mid-April 1883, Holmes held aloft a letter in his long, pale fingers. "We are expecting a client, Watson," said he. "A peer of the realm, no less."

Taking the letter, the doctor, that is, I, read the brief contents.

"My dear Mr. Holmes," it began, *"I am faced with a most peculiar situation involving my daughter and the filthy state of her feet every morning.*

"I cannot possibly explain these peculiar circumstances in a letter. By your leave, I shall call upon you at half-past eleven.

Sincerely,
John, Earl of Flodden

PS: I was referred by Inspector Lestrade of Scotland Yard.

"This is what I have been reduced to, Watson," Holmes said. "The matter of a child's dirty feet. I was hoping for a case, but this…" He gestured with a disdainful hand towards the letter.

"Sounds like that fairy tale, you know the one about the dancing princesses?"

"Dancing princesses?" he asked as he lit his pipe.

"It's an old folk tale. There's a Scottish version my mother used to tell me, about a girl found with dirty feet every morning."

He fixed me with a look of annoyance. "I am unfamiliar with the genre," he said, "nor do I see it being of much use in this situation."

"Your parents never read fairy stories to you when you were a child?" I asked. "Beauty and the Beast? Cinderella? Jack and the Beanstalk?"

"Really, Watson, this is just tomfoolery."

"What stories did your parents read to you?"

"Homer, Herodotus, various philosophical works."

I shook my head sadly. I have nothing against Homer, but he seemed a poor substitute for a decent fairy tale. Changing the subject, I said, "What do we know of the Earl?"

"An upstanding young man, I gather. He inherited the title some ten years ago when his father died following a long-standing illness. Since then, he has acquitted himself well in the diplomatic corps. Other than that, I'm afraid the Who's Who was less than forthcoming."

We heard a knock on the door below. "Ah, our client, I believe," Holmes said.

I rose to leave, but Sherlock Holmes entreated me to stay.

"Your insights and wisdom more than make up for your lack of observational skills," he commented. "Besides, who else possesses your vast repertoire of fairy tales?"

By this time, I knew enough not to take offense at his comment, nor to question his sincerity. I was, besides, intrigued by the Earl's letter. I agreed to stay.

Our guest entered our room a moment later with the air of a man used to being in charge. A tall, distinguished looking fellow in his early forties, with thick black hair threaded with silver, a mouth made for laughter despite his melancholy demeanour, and sharp, intelligent eyes.

I felt there was something broken in him. I could not pinpoint what it was. A bleak expression in his eyes, and the downward slope of his shoulders suggested an unbearable sorrow. This was a man who had been forced to endure beyond his limits.

"Please have a seat, My Lord," Holmes said. "I am Sherlock Holmes. This is my friend and colleague, Dr. Watson. How are you adjusting to being back in England after your long time in the Orient?"

"You know me, then?" the man said, startled.

"No, indeed, but your tan is deep and suggests a long term spent in a warmer clime. Further, your jade cufflinks are engraved with the Chinese symbol for peace, and your very elegant tiepin depicts the 'fu,' the bat. The most potent symbol of good fortune in the Chinese culture. How can we help you?"

"You are perfectly correct, Mr. Holmes. I am rather embarrassed about the letter I sent you yesterday; I should have presented the facts more intelligently, but this whole affair has so agitated me that I hardly recognise myself."

The Fairy Tale Mystery by Geri Schear

"Pray tell us what it is that has so disturbed you, and how we may help."

"Thank you, you are very kind. I must say I found Scotland Yard exceedingly unhelpful, but Inspector Lestrade said you specialise in the strange and obscure." He drew out a gold cigarette case and said, "Do you mind if I smoke?"

"Please," Holmes said, and set an ashtray before him. The earl's hands trembled as he lit the cigarette. He inhaled the smoke deeply before saying, "I beg your indulgence, gentlemen. The tale I must tell you is complex, but it is essential you understand.

"A mere six months ago, I was as happy and contented a man as you could find. I was happily married, with six-year-old twins, a boy and a girl, and had inherited a considerable estate from my father after his long illness.

"Perhaps I was no more doting than any other father, but I confess I adored my children. My son, Jack, and my daughter Juliet, were the light of my eye."

"What changed?" Holmes asked, his voice unusually gentle.

"My son, my boy... Jack disappeared one night and has not been seen since. I was in China on a diplomatic mission at the time, but my secretary, Mr. Waltham, immediately took the matter in hand. He called in the local constable, arranged for the area to be searched, and so forth, but they found no sign of him. I should explain that I live in my ancestral home, Wanstead Lodge, in Wanstead Park, with my wife, mother, the children and the servants. Gwendolyn, my wife, informed me of the news via cable. I was distraught, as you can imagine, but the Chinese matter was at a critical juncture, and I could not return home. I knew Waltham would handle matters, and I tried to have faith that the boy would be returned."

"Did your wife receive a ransom demand?" Holmes asked.

"No, nothing of the sort. We would happily have paid any ransom...

"I returned home two days ago and spent all of yesterday reviewing the steps that had been taken to find Jack, searching the area for myself, and meeting with my tenants. Although I was satisfied that every reasonable action had been taken, I decided to come to town today to see if Scotland Yard would look into it. I must admit, my expectations fell after meeting with their inspector. Since so much time had passed, he thought it would be a waste of their time and resources to handle the case, though they would do so if I insisted. Frankly, I thought they would prove a hindrance rather than a help.

"As I was about to leave, the inspector suggested that I come to see you. 'Mr. Holmes is something of a miracle worker in the most difficult cases,' he said. Though, ah, I was not supposed to tell you that."

"It will be our secret," Holmes said, amused. "My Lord, can you tell us about the area where the boy went missing?"

"Wanstead Lodge is as charming a home as one might wish, though it is vast. We are surrounded by countryside. Rills and streams, long fields, ancient trees – apple, oak, and maple – all flourish there, as do the bluebells when they are in season."

"It sounds idyllic," I said.

"It is. No man could ask for more. Unfortunately, given the size of the estate, it took a very long time to search. The tenants helped, as did all the servants, but… nothing."

"And what of your daughter?" I asked.

"Her mother questioned her carefully, as did the local constable, but Juliet could say nothing. That is no mere hyperbole, gentlemen. My sweet little girl who sang and chatted all day long has been mute ever since her brother disappeared."

"How dreadful," I said.

"The search for Jack continued, has continued until I returned, but he was gone. Gone. In addition, his poor sister is in deep distress for the absence of her brother. Now we find ourselves with a new mystery.

"Mr. Holmes, every morning we find Juliet in her bed with her feet and slippers covered with mud. I realise how trivial a matter this must seem, but... I cannot bear to lose her, too. I think my poor wife would go quite mad."

"I dare call nothing trivial," Holmes said. His brow furrowed in thought and I could read the concern on his aquiline features. "I assume there is no obvious means of egress?" he said.

"None. There were already bars on the nursery window for as long as I can remember, as well as on the windows of the children's bedrooms. In addition, I have had staff taking turns sitting at the door each night. They insist my girl never leaves her room, and yet each morning, there she is with muddy feet. For the love of God, Mr. Holmes, help us! Please, help us!"

The poor fellow tried to contain tears, but they streamed down his cheeks unchecked. I poured a glass of brandy and handed it to him, though it was not yet noon.

"It is a mystery, to be sure," Holmes said. His relaxed pose belied the concern on his face. Like me, he was deeply moved by the earl's story. "I assume all the outer doors in the house are locked?"

"Yes, and the windows. I have even taken to locking Juliet in her room, though I wait until after she has gone asleep, so I do not frighten her."

"And the staff you have assigned to sit outside, you trust them?"

"Without question. They are loyal retainers and have been with my family for many years."

"Have you observed any other untoward behaviour in your daughter since your return?"

"She hasn't been herself since... since that night. She is six years old and a bright child, but she seems frightened. Uneasy. We have all remarked on it."

"We should like to come to Wanstead Park. When would be convenient?"

"We are entirely at your disposal, Mr. Holmes. I have one or two business calls to make in town, but I can return at around two o'clock and we can travel to Wanstead together in my carriage. We can make you very comfortable for as long as you need to stay."

"That would be excellent. Very well, My Lord. We shall see you at two o'clock."

After the unfortunate fellow left, I observed Holmes sitting in that silent pose he liked to adopt. He stirred moments later and said, "A peculiar tale, eh, Watson?" What do you make of it?"

"Very odd, indeed. Do you think it's related to the boy's disappearance?"

"Perhaps, but it is an error to theorise in advance of the facts."

"Despite the apparent silliness, it is very odd that the little girl manages to get herself so muddy if she is not able to leave her room. Unless, like Rapunzel, she makes a rope of her hair and climbs out that way."

For a moment Holmes looked bewildered then, in a tired voice, he said, "Another fairy tale?"

At precisely two o'clock, we climbed into the earl's comfortable carriage and began our long journey to Wanstead Park. His capable driver ensured our journey was as smooth and easy as possible. The day remained bright and dry, and the prospect of spending a little time in the countryside filled me with delight. Or rather it would have done, if only the case before us were not so steeped in tragedy.

When we arrived at last, I beheld an extraordinary building of Regency architecture. The cream and white façade glowed in the light of the late-afternoon sun. It stood three stories high and stretched wide, with ten tall windows on the ground floor alone. The elegant doorway sat in the exact middle, between these windows, with a tier of steps leading up from the long driveway. The building faced a small lake which boasted ducks and swans and, no doubt, offered some excellent fishing. The entire estate lay in the heart of some of the most exquisite scenery I have ever seen.

As the earl led the way into the building, I found the interior every bit as elegant as the exterior, with high ceilings, splendid works of art, marble flooring, and so forth. I cannot recall ever being in a house of its equal.

The butler showed us to our rooms. We learned that Holmes's bedchamber sat next to the nursery, on the other side of which was the bedroom where young Miss Juliet slept. My room was next to Holmes's. Our rooms matched the rest of the house being both spacious and charming. To my delight, I discovered that my window overlooked the lake and the surrounding countryside.

"After you have freshened up," the butler said, "you are invited to join Lord John and Lady Gwendolyn in the drawing room for afternoon tea."

*　*　*

Lady Gwendolyn greeted us with all the grace of a queen. Tall and beautiful, with rich auburn hair and green eyes, she wore a pearl necklace and a simple gown of grey silk. I felt quite breathless at the sight of her. For all her elegance and beauty, however, she seemed bowed by grief and loss. Her attempts to appear genial seemed a strain.

"Our daughter is with nanny in the nursery," Lady Gwendolyn said. "You shall meet her after tea."

"And I'm afraid my mother is lying down with a headache," Lord John added. "I hope she will be able to join us for supper."

Lady Gwendolyn and her husband made genial hosts, and they took pains to engage us in conversation and to make sure we were perfectly comfortable. It did not take long for Holmes to come to the point of our visit.

"I realise this is a painful subject," he began, "but it would help me considerably to know the circumstances of your son's disappearance."

"It happened almost six months ago, on the 25th of November," Lady Gwendolyn replied. "The children were exceptionally boisterous that day, possibly because their nanny was unwell, and their grandmother and I were kept too busy to do more than check in on them from time to time. I sent them to the kitchen. They love cook, and she's very good at giving them little tasks to keep them entertained.

"We had a small dinner party that evening," the lady said. "Eight guests, although one sent his apologies, Major Oldham. He's getting on a bit, and his memory isn't what it was. I suspect he simply forgot until the last moment.

"The children came in to say goodnight before they went to bed. Our guests made quite a fuss of them." Lady Gwendolyn smiled with pride at the memory. "They are precocious children and remarkable conversationalists for their age... Were, I should say.

"One of the maids got them ready for bed, young Maggie." Lady Gwendolyn continued, "She said they were giggling and laughing, but didn't give her any trouble. Our guests left quite late, after midnight, I believe. I spoke to the staff for a few minutes and then went to kiss the children..."

At this, her voice broke, and I could see that her grief quite overcame her. Lord John squeezed her hand and spoke gently to her.

"Your son was not in his room?" Holmes said, gently keeping them on topic.

"No, Mr. Holmes, they were both missing. Their beds had been slept in, and their clothes still hung neatly in the wardrobe. We assumed they had gone down to the kitchen for a snack. However, we could not find them. A thorough search revealed that they were not in the house.

"Mr. Waltham sent one of the lads to fetch the local constable and organised a search. Two hours later, young Michael — he's one of the footmen — found Juliet in the wood, crying. He brought her home. The doctor examined her but found no injury. She was, however, extremely distressed. No matter what we said, she would not, or could not, reply. She merely kept shaking her head and pointing."

"At what?"

"Towards the wooded area where she had been found," Lady Gwendolyn said. "Michael brought Mr. Waltham, the constable, and several others to the area where he had found Juliet, but though everyone searched all around for several days, we found no sign of him. After a week, we most reluctantly dragged the lake. We found nothing, however."

Lord John added, "Over the following months the search continued thanks to the efforts of Waltham and the local constabulary. Our servants and tenants also helped. Waltham put up notices in the nearby towns and offered rewards for information, but... nothing."

"And now whatever fiend stole our boy is coming for our girl," Lady Gwendolyn cried, her voice rising.

"Hush, my love, hush. Mr. Holmes won't let that happen, will you, Sir?"

"Indeed not, Lord John. Perhaps now would be a good time for us to meet your staff?"

* * *

Holmes took pains to speak to everyone and was frustrated to find none could add to the events as described by Lady Gwendolyn. Mr. Waltham, a thirtyish man with calm eyes and a deliberate manner, seemed particularly distressed by the events of that evening. There was no doubting his honesty or his commitment to finding young Jack. The servants, too, were united in distress, none more so than cook and the housemaid, Maggie. Holmes took some time talking to cook alone, while I tried to calm the young servant. Maggie seemed to believe she had been negligent in her duties in some way, and my assurances did little to calm her.

* * *

With the meetings with the servants complete, we were ready to meet young Juliet. Lord John himself led us to the nursery. Nanny was reading a story of some sort to the child. The girl stood up as soon as we came into the room. She gave a little curtsey to us and to her father. Lord John kissed her forehead and asked how she felt.

In answer, the little girl smiled widely at him, her dimples showing. She was a pretty little girl, six years old, with dark red hair similar to her mother's and eyes an unusual shade of turquoise.

"Juliet, this is Mr. Sherlock Holmes and Dr. Watson. They're here to help us."

I was about to speak, suspecting that Holmes was uncomfortable around children. However, very much to my surprise, he sat on the floor, cross-legged, and said, "Good afternoon, Miss Juliet. I am very pleased to meet you." He offered her his hand.

After the briefest of pauses, the girl accepted and shook hands very solemnly. She then shook mine.

"I think perhaps we might do better on our own with the young lady," Holmes said. "If you do not mind, Juliet?"

She nodded and smiled. Lord John said he would be in his library if we needed anything, and then withdrew.

Holmes asked the child if she liked games. They played draughts and then some other board games.

Nanny sat in the corner sewing, and I sat on the window seat, watching. Neither of us spoke.

After a little while, Holmes stretched his back and said, "I'm a bit stiff. I've been sitting for too long. I say, would you like to show me around?"

She seemed eager to do so.

She started in her own bedroom. It was large, bright and airy. As Sir John had told us, there were bars on the windows, and we could see the lock on the door was new. A fireplace, currently unlit, sat to the right of the bed, with a tall bookcase to its left and a doll's house on the table to the right. There were more toys than I had ever seen in one place at a time. The little girl, who had not made a sound since our arrival, showed us her dolls, her games and books. Holmes seemed fascinated by everything.

"You like to paint," he said, observing the pictures that were strewn all over a table. "May I see your pictures?"

She seemed happy to oblige him. They sat side by side and he examined each drawing with the close attention one would devote to a grand master.

"Is this the wood near the lodge?" Holmes said, as he held up one picture. "It looks very frightening."

The child nodded in that serious manner one sees only in the very young and politicians.

"What is this?" Holmes said, pointing to an image in another picture.

The girl made a gesture that suggested someone evil. "A monster?" I guessed.

Her response was difficult to interpret. She shrugged and shook her head.

"A wizard?" I tried again.

She pointed to her dress.

"Ah, a witch!"

She nodded vigorously.

"Juliet," Holmes said softly, "Was this the person who took your brother?"

She bit her lip and seemed frightened.

"She can't hurt you," I said. "You know, Mr. Holmes has magic far greater than any witch. Holmes, why don't you cast a protection spell on Juliet so the evil witch cannot hurt her?"

Holmes sucked in his cheeks in an effort not to say something scathing. However, he chanted a few lines of ancient Greek which I vaguely recognised as Athena speaking to Ulysses. Something about her being famous among the gods for wisdom and cunning wiles. I managed to suppress a smile, but the sight of Holmes waving his arms around the child and doing a little dance made this almost impossible.

"There now," he said. "You have the most powerful protection against evil. You need worry about nothing."

To my surprise and to Holmes's astonishment, the child flung her arms around his neck.

"Juliet," he said, "May I keep this picture?" It was the one of the 'witch'.

The child nodded and solemnly handed it to him.

"Thank you, I shall treasure it. Would you show Dr. Watson to my room and leave the picture on my desk? I want to do a protection spell over your room so no one wicked can enter."

This seemed to make perfect sense to the child, and she happily led the way to Holmes's chamber. I talked to her about various games and books, in order to give Holmes time to search her room.

He joined us again a few minutes later and smiled at the girl. At his behest, she showed us around the house. Though evening was drawing in, the sky remained light enough for us to wander about outside. We went to the lake and around the neatly trimmed garden. Beyond the western end of the house lay the woods and these seemed to glower like a hostile force as the sun set behind them.

We returned to the house and changed for dinner. Lady Agatha Flodden, the earl's mother, joined us. She was feeling much better, she said.

Holmes seemed unusually interested in the history of the house and the environment. The older woman seemed delighted with the topic and regaled us with stories about her family and the various curious characters who lived in the area.

"One was Mr. Buttons. Oh, that wasn't his real name, but he was fascinated by those things. His pockets were always full of them, and he would show them off to anyone who paid the slightest interest. My dear mama, may she rest in peace, made a point of saving any buttons she could so she would always give them to him. It was good luck, she said."

"Country people tend to be superstitious," Lord John said, smiling indulgently at his mother.

"Perhaps," she said, "But it does not make them wrong."

"I suppose there are ghost stories," I said. I confess, I have always enjoyed a good ghost story.

"Oh, certainly," Lady Agatha replied. "The house is supposed to have a white lady who is seen in the grounds sometimes. And there's supposed to be a witch who lives in the woods."

"A witch?" Holmes said.

"Just a legend," the Earl said. "I must say, Mother, I have never seen either of these things."

"Well, you don't have the gift, dear."

I was charmed by the affection I saw in this small family. The dignity with which they bore their sorrow, and the respect in which everyone was treated.

"Of course," Holmes said, "many of these myths and legends are built upon true events."

"That's true," Lord John said. "There is an ancient story of a witch, probably just a healer of some sort, who lived in these parts many years ago. As a result, any poor old woman who isn't part of society is deemed a witch and held in suspicion."

"Is there anyone currently who fits that bill?" Holmes asked.

"Mother Ellis," Lady Agatha replied. "I don't know her real name; she's been called Mother Ellis for as long as I can remember.

She's an old woman who lives in a hut in the woods. She's... odd, but quite harmless."

After supper, the ladies excused themselves, and Lord John returned to the subject that, I'm sure, was never far from his thoughts.

"Tell me, Mr. Holmes, do you make any progress?"

"Oh yes, a considerable amount. Indeed, my Lord, if you will join the doctor and me this evening, I believe I can demonstrate the truth to you."

"I am at your disposal. What do you need me to do?"

"Meet Watson and me in the kitchen hallway. Wear your hunting attire."

"Do I need to bring my rifle?"

"No, not at all."

* * *

At nine o'clock we met in the hallway adjacent to the kitchen.

"We must keep to the shadows," Holmes said. "And no matter what happens, I implore you to remain silent and do not react. It is of the utmost importance."

Our wait seemed interminable, particularly as we did not know what we were waiting for. Holmes and Lord John remained as alert and silent as ever. The earl, I thought, would have made a fine soldier.

A few minutes after the clock struck ten, we heard a strange clanking noise. The earl and I exchanged bewildered looks, but it seemed this was what Holmes was expecting. Moments later, a small door on the side of the wall opened, and Juliet climbed out. She was wearing a coat over her dress and a pair of slippers.

Very quietly she reached the back door, took the key off its hook, opened the door and stepped quietly into the night.

With his finger on his lips, Holmes waited a full minute before he led us after her. She was some distance ahead of us; it was impossible to judge the distance in the dusk. Softly, softly, we followed, keeping her in sight as she headed for the woods.

Although none of us spoke, I thought it was a brave little girl who would leave the comfort and safety of her home to venture into the woods at night. No wonder she had been so grateful to Holmes for his "protection" spell.

She led the way along some path only she could see. She paused once or twice when the sound of various animals came near, but otherwise remained resolute.

"Do you know where she's heading?" Holmes asked the Earl.

"I believe we're not far from the big oak where Michael found her."

Even as he spoke, Juliet fell and lay still. Before Holmes could stop him, Lord John ran through the trees and picked his daughter up in his arms. Holmes sighed.

"Well, I suppose this was inevitable," he said. "Lord John, would you be kind enough to take your daughter home."

"You are not coming?"

"Dr. Watson and I still have a task to complete."

The earl nodded and returned to the house, still carrying Juliet.

"Where are we going, Holmes?" I asked when we were alone.

"To find a witch."

I must confess, being in the woods late at night was not at all my activity of choice. While I have no superstitious fear of witches, the word sent an icy shiver down my spine. On top of that, I was not confident that we would be able to find our way back to the lodge.

Before I could remonstrate and suggest we leave our task till morning, I realised that Holmes was studying the ground and leading us deeper into the forest. Within a few minutes, we had reached a tall and ancient oak tree. Holmes turned to me with a satisfied smile and said, softly, "We are on the right track. We must be very quiet. I do not wish to alert our prey to our presence."

The Fairy Tale Mystery by Geri Schear

Pushing aside the dozens of questions that came to mind, I merely nodded and continued to follow him.

How many times over the next half hour did I stop myself from protesting and begging that we return? I cannot even say what drove me on except I knew in my heart that Holmes needed me, and our cause was a just one.

I carried on doggedly and was startled when we suddenly stopped. Holmes indicated a pale light that glowed from inside a small cottage. Not cottage, shack.

We squatted on the muddy grass and listened. I heard a low sound. It took me a moment to realise it was a woman humming.

With great stealth, Holmes led the way to the old building. Then, without preamble, he suddenly pushed the door open.

There came a shriek of outrage, and I beheld a wild old woman with hands as gnarled as tree roots, and hair that could have been knitted by spiders. In the dim lamplight, she seemed as terrifying as any storybook witch.

"Hush," Holmes said, his voice both authoritative and gentle. "We have not come to harm you. We just want the boy."

At that moment, I spotted the lad hiding behind a battered old armchair.

"Hello, Jack," Holmes said. "It's time to go home."

It felt that as if we all froze, reduced to a tableau. Only Holmes seemed himself.

"You are Mother Ellis," he continued to the woman.

She nodded.

"I am Sherlock Holmes. This is my friend, Dr. Watson. We mean you no harm. We just want to bring the boy home to his family. They miss him. I'm sure you miss them too, don't you, Jack?"

The boy looked uncertainly at the woman. To my surprise, she smiled affectionately at the boy and nodded. "Aye, 'tis time," she said.

"Can you tell us how he came to be here?" Holmes said. "He and his sister sometimes came to spy on you, yes?"

"Aye. They meant no harm, but... sometimes they threw stones at my roof and frightened the cat, but they are only children." A sleek black cat glared at us from beneath a battered table.

"What happened that night?" Holmes persisted. "Jack had an accident?"

"And they say *I'm* the witch!" she said, chuckling. "Aye. He tried to climb up the tree out yonder so he could see in my window. But the branch broke, and he fell. Knocked him out, it did.

"The little girl went crazy, screaming that he was dead."

"And you were frightened that you'd be blamed."

"An old woman living alone is an object of derision," she said, "if not fear and hate. They don't understand so they put wicked names on me. I don't care, but they won't bother about the truth, only what it looks like."

"You should have returned the boy straight away," I said. "The girl would have supported your story."

"It's not a story if it's true," she snapped.

"My friend just means it became more difficult with every day that passed."

"It did that, aye."

"When the girl was screaming you were afraid. You had to silence her."

The old woman nodded. Holmes continued, "What did you do? Did you tell her you'd put a curse on her if she spoke another word?"

Her eyes burned into his. "I didn't say I'd put a curse on her... I said her brother would die if she made another sound. I meant no harm. I just wanted her to be quiet."

"The child has not spoken in six months."

"I didn't mean that to happen." She sat heavily in the tattered old armchair by the fire. "I didn't mean for any of this to happen."

"I can help you," Holmes said, squatting down and holding her gaze. "Jack will help us, won't you, Jack?"

He nodded vigorously. "Of course."

The Fairy Tale Mystery by Geri Schear

"What will you do?" she asked.

"Jack will say he was taken by some rough man he didn't know. His sister managed to get away, but she was so frightened by what happened that she lost all power of speech. You found the man and managed to get Jack away from him. In the struggle, the fellow dropped Jack and the boy was injured; you nursed him back to health. The rest of the story is true: You were afraid you'd be accused of stealing him yourself and punished. Jack didn't want you hurt and so he stayed here voluntarily, until I came to bring him home. You were already planning on doing so, in any case."

"What about the girl?" I said. "What do we say about her climbing out every night?"

"That she was coming to see her brother — that's true, isn't it, Jack? — and Mother Ellis was trying to heal her voice. Is there perhaps some talisman you can give me that I can give the girl and tell her it is the last step in her recovering her voice?"

She thought for a moment and said to the boy, "Esmerelda."

He found an old rag doll and handed it to her. The old woman tied a ribbon around the neck of the doll and handed it to Holmes.

"Tell her when she removes the ribbon she may speak again."

"I will."

Suddenly, the woman reached out and took Holmes's hand in hers. As she studied it, she said, "You have a fine mind, but an even finer heart. Though you do not seek them, you will find true friends everywhere. Even if you should leave them for a long time and find yourself alone in cold and hostile places, your friends will await your return."

"Thank you," Holmes said. Then, discreetly, handed her several banknotes, "for taking care of the boy."

* * *

Holmes wrapped the lad up in his coat and we stepped out into the woods for the long walk back. It was around midnight, I thought, and I was glad Holmes seemed to know where he was going. Almost an hour later, the lodge looked up ahead of us. I was surprised to see many of the ground floor rooms lit up.

As we came out of the woods, I heard someone cry, "They're back! My Lord, they're back! They have the boy!"

The man came running towards us and I recognised him as Waltham, the earl's secretary.

By the time we reached the kitchen door we were surrounded. The earl stared in amazed joy as his son climbed out of Holmes's arms.

"I'm here, father," Jack said. "I'm all right."

"My boy! My son!" Weeping, he took the child in his arms and carried him into the drawing room where his mother and grandmother waited.

"Gentlemen, how can I thank you?" the earl said, as his wife clutched her child to her breast and wept over him.

"I am happy that we have been able to restore you son to you," Holmes said, somewhat embarrassed at the exuberance of delight that surrounded him.

"But... how? I was sure he was lost to us forever. How did you find him, Mr. Holmes?"

"I deduced that the boy had been kidnapped by a ruffian. In his attempt to escape, he fell and was knocked unconscious. One of your neighbours found him and nursed him back to health."

"She took ever such good care of me, mummy," the boy said. "It took such a long time for me to get better."

"She? Do you mean that dreadful woman who lives in the woods?" Lady Gwendolyn asked.

"She's not dreadful, mummy. She saved me," Jack's voice was insistent.

"But why didn't she bring him back?" Lady Agatha asked.

"She was afraid of being accused of taking the boy. In fact, she was planning on returning him in a day or two but was trying to muster up her courage. She has been helping Juliet, too."

Jack was now hugging his sister, and I saw him whispering in her ear.

"Mother Ellis has been trying to help you get your voice back, hasn't she?" Holmes said.

"That's right," Jack piped up. "That's why she's been coming to see Mother Ellis in the evening."

"I am to tell you that there is only one last thing for you to do and then you can speak again," Holmes said as he handed the bedraggled doll to the child. "You must remove the ribbon from around its neck."

Very solemnly the little girl did as Holmes said, but she remained silent, perhaps afraid of what might happen if she spoke. However, Jack was not about to leave her that way. He tickled her and she laughed then cried, "Stop it, Jack!"

Her parents gasped in delight at the sound of her voice.

"I am still puzzled about one thing," Lord John said. "How did you know that Juliet was using the dumb-waiter to get out?"

"It is directly behind the dolls' house. There are faint scuff marks on the floor where Juliet moved the table in order to access the dumb-waiter. Your cook told me that this old dumb waiter had been replaced by a newer one that connects the kitchen and the upstairs drawing room. The old one ended in the hallway adjacent to the kitchen. Once she got downstairs, it was easy for your daughter to take the key and let herself out. When you checked that the doors were locked, you were thinking of intruders, not of someone letting themselves out."

"You might want to seal that dumb-waiter up," I said. "The children are lucky they never came to harm on it."

"First thing in the morning," the earl said. "You may count on it."

The Fairy Tale Mystery by Geri Schear

"Now, my precious babies, it is time for bed," their mother said.

"Thank you, Mr. Holmes," young Jack said, and shook Holmes's hand in a quite adult manner.

Young Juliet curled her finger, indicating she wanted Holmes to bend down. This he did and, to his astonishment, she kissed him on the cheek. "Thank you for bringing my brother home," she said.

* * *

The following morning after breakfast, Sir John ordered his driver to take us back to the city.

"I shall never forget your kindness nor your genius, Mr. Holmes," he said. "I know nothing can repay it, but I hope this will go some small way in expressing my appreciation."

He handed an envelope to Holmes. My friend opened it and stared amazed at the cheque.

"That is exceedingly generous, my Lord," he said. "May I ask one other small favour?"

"Anything, Mr. Holmes."

"Look after that old woman. She is odd, I know, but she has a good heart, and she is very fond of your children. She deserves better than that hovel in which she lives."

"I will take care of it, and her, Mr. Holmes. You have my word."

The horse clopped down the driveway and soon we were on the road back to London.

"You are unusually silent, Watson," Holmes said. "What is on your mind?"

"I'm thinking about how much that poor family has suffered. If they had only brought you in back then when Jack went missing, you could have spared everyone so much agony."

The Fairy Tale Mystery by Geri Schear

He said nothing and I turned to face him, surprised to see a rare look of pleasure on his features. "Thank you, Watson," he said, his voice husky with emotion. "I will attempt no false modesty and attempt to deny it. I believe I could have had a significant impact on all their lives had I been consulted earlier."

"I have no doubt Sir John and his family will sing your praises far and wide. No doubt you will see a significant increase in your number of cases."

"I am more interested in quality than quantity," he said. Then, as he lit his cigarette added, "But I confess, it would be most gratifying to have a choice."

* * *

At Holmes's request, I did not write this story until many years later when I could be sure no one might be hurt by the telling.

The family never forgets to send us Christmas cards. Though he has never said so, I know Holmes has kept all of them as well as Juliet's drawing in a safe place. In a letter that the earl sent us a couple of months after Holmes restored Jack to his family, we learned that Mother Ellis refused a new home, but was happy to accept the extensive repairs the estate's workmen made on her old cottage.

The children are all grown up now. Juliet is married, and Jack has followed his illustrious father into the diplomatic corps. They are a credit to their devoted family. And, I'm sure, as all the best storybooks say, they will live happily ever after.

BELANGER BOOKS

BELANGERBOOKS.COM

The Adventure Begins!

Belanger Books presents

Sherlock Holmes:
A Year of Mystery
1881

edited by
Richard T. Ryan

foreword by Robert S. Katz, BSI, ASH, MD

The Adventure Continues!

Belanger Books presents
Sherlock Holmes:
A Year of Mystery
1882

edited by
Richard T. Ryan

foreword by Jeffrey Hatcher, BSI
screenwriter, Mr. Holmes

The Adventure Continues!

Belanger Books presents
Sherlock Holmes: A Year of Mystery 1884

edited by
Richard T. Ryan

foreword by Tracy Clark,
author of the Cass Raines Chicago Mystery series

Printed in Great Britain
by Amazon